Time's Fool

Time's Fool

A Mystery of Shakespeare

LEONARD TOURNEY

A Tom Doherty Associates Book
New York

TIME'S FOOL: A MYSTERY OF SHAKESPEARE

A Forge Book
Published by Tom Doherty Associates, LLC
175 Fifth Avenue
New York, NY 10010

www.tor.com

Forge® is a registered trademark of Tom Doherty Associates, LLC.

ISBN 0-765-30304-3

EAN 978-0765-30304-2

First Edition: June 2004

Printed in the United States of America

0   9   8   7   6   5   4   3   2   1

To
Judith
for whom love is not
Time's fool

Acknowledgments

We know too little of Shakespeare's life, and even less of his personality and character—all the better for the novelist, whose imagination needs time unaccounted for and a certain expanse of blank canvas. Therefore, with the details of Shakespeare's life during the years in which the story takes place I have taken those little liberties—call it poetic license if you will—that have become conventional in novels whose grist is names, dates, and works of actual persons. In so doing, I point to the worthy example of Shakespeare himself, who presented not a few historical characters on his stage, filled their mouths with words they never uttered, and invested those characters with personalities that may have been quite different from those they actually possessed. To readers offended by such practices I offer this poor palliative: History, too, is a work of the imagination.

For helping bring this book about, in ways large and small, my thanks to the following:

To the Davidson Library of the University of California at Santa Barbara and its staff for a ready supply of books, articles, and documents on England's greatest playwright and his time.

To my agent, Elizabeth Winick at McIntosh and Otis, Inc., for her faith and extraordinary diligence.

To my quick-eyed copyeditor, India Cooper, who saved me from a multitude of literary sins of commission and omission.

To my daughter, Anne Tourney, for invaluable technical help in preparation of the manuscript.

To my editor, Bob Gleason, who after viewing an earlier version of this book first suggested that Will Shakespeare be permitted to speak for himself.

Finally, to my wife, Judith Olauson, actress and director, whose production of *Measure for Measure* inspired certain elements of the novel's plot and whose patience and encouragement are pearls beyond price.

Time's Fool

To Whoever Finds
This Book

LOVE IS BITTER and love is sweet, but more bitter than sweet, and a nearer cousin to grief than to pleasure.

These are my very words. I wrote them once, years ago, in a play never performed, never even finished. I should have carved them on my heart.

Sour grapes, think you?

Truth, rather, friend. The voice of experience, which does speak more loudly than Seneca or Socrates or whatever other cobwebbed philosopher please you. Ask the man and not the mantle. By Mary's blessed son, he'll tell you the same.

But I write not of generals, rather of particulars. Which brings me to this book, a book I write as much for penance's sake as for monument to her whom I once loved and whose death I caused. Not because I murdered her, but because I bred—without intention—madness and treachery and, yes, murder, too.

A conundrum, you say? A mystery?

So it was, a mystery to me as well as to others. My penance is this memoir, nothing extenuating, nothing concealed, every jot and tittle of the broken law laid bare before your eyes that you may judge how I did acquit myself, for what reasons and in what peril to myself and to my friends.

Therefore, friend, when you find these yellowed papers in time to come, secreted behind plastered wall or buried deep in well or cave, pray do not cast them off or use these mortal pages to feed some ravenous fire. I promise you they will not warm but chill the blood with something novel, something strange. My repentance will not serve me unless I confess at least to one other soul. Talk not to me of confessor or of priest. I've had my fill of them; that's not my church that dispenses grace for mere recitals of a rosary or a farthing for the poor box. Give me, rather, one honest reader, practiced in the art, alert to follow plot and read between these lines the agony of a troubled heart.

Let it be you, friend. Let it be you.

Now, NEAR A dozen years later than the events I will relate, I am well-to-do in Stratford. Do you know the town? Built upon sweet flowing Avon, with Holy Trinity's gorged churchyard to mind me of mortality?

On sunny days I reign in my garden, a companion to my long-neglected and much-abused wife. A veritable picture of domestic tranquillity. Imagine me so. There I hold court to friends who seek me out and drink my health, ask about my London years, and talk of friends hid in death's dateless night. I am well fed, and the great feather bed in the upper chamber would let me sleep soft as silk did not my conscience, like an unruly guest, keep me awake at nights banging upon the walls of my heart.

As for making of plays, with that I'm done. Dame Prudence has pocketed my money and sent me scrambling home again, and I am content that my Muse, the shadows upon the stage, the forest of words, shall be no more substantial than an old man's dream. In years to come both they and I will lie in rich obscurity, unread and unremembered. Not even echoes of their poor selves.

But this book I would have saved for my posterity. It is not about kings or princes but about myself, about deception, murder, treachery, and vengeance. About the shadows of my past, real and imagined, that stalk me still.

Of these things I promise to speak plainly, without fustian or thrasonical digression, and to set down naught but sordid truth.

I am William Shakespeare of Stratford, *Johannes Factotum,* once of London and well allowed as not a bad actor and as a maker of plays of no mean distinction. Yet in truth, friend, as much Time's fool as any other wight.

This is my book.

Read it if it please you. Believe it, whether it please you or not.

One

HERE BEGINNETH THE lesson.

So say our learned divines when they would preach, yet I'm only a crafter of plays—or was. I'll not sermonize. The lesson was mine, not yours. But I will begin, although where I will end, God knows.

So, imagine then a bleak December, cold, wet, foggy; roofs dusted with a fine snow, and the air a stew of smoke and dirt. It is the Year of Grace 1603—the year the new king came in and the plague made itself free with the city, the two events belched from the maw of Fortune so importunately as to cause one of philosophical bent to suppose them somehow connected. In that dreadful summer before, heat made the pestilence worse. The plague bill was longer than Methuselah's beard, and the death carts made the rounds harvesting the dead the way an earnest farmer plucks up radishes. The great public ceremony of James's crowning, postponed. Theaters closed, along with the bear pits, all of the churches, most of the brothels. Those who remained in the city locked doors or, if abroad in the streets, smoked tobacco, chewed orange peels, or paid through the nose for rosemary. All these trifles were supposedly effectual to ward off the pestilence.

I cover my face to conceal the laughter. Lot of good any of it did. Many a friend I did not see again, and poor Ben Jonson's young son was snatched, too. God's judgment, cried our learned divines, but I couldn't see that the righteous were spared any more than the sinner, the rich man any more than the poor. Death had held a great feast and, being a fellow of infinite generosity, he admitted one and all.

So we actors fled London, hit the road for the provinces with the plague dogs in hot pursuit. Spent the summer that way, wagoning from one town to the next, as restless as colts. Innyards, great houses, street corners. An actor acts where he can, plays to whoever comes; mugs, sings, dances, juggles, soliloquizes for his supper.

Come autumn, the plague fell off. We turned toward London again, lay a while in Mortlake, then came to Wiltshire in November and performed for the first time before the king, who'd taken up residence at Wilton House. What did we play there? *As You Like It?* I think; something light and frothy, I remember.

From that notable visit we had applause and a generous thirty pounds from the king, the friendship of the noble earl of Pembroke, whose house it was, and an order to perform at the kings' command, for we were now the King's Men, a distinction we had long coveted, and at our royal master's beck and call.

In preparation therefore, I returned to London and my lodgings at the house of Christopher Mountjoy, a Frenchman and tire-maker. You know, fine ladies' headgear, and not just hats to keep the ears from turning blue in foul weather, but bonnets of the ornamental sort, decked out with silk and ribbon and bejeweled with gold and silver—baubles all trumpeting the wearer's husband's money.

But I promised to be plain in my telling.

Mountjoy's house was a substantial tenement, with twin gables and beetle-browed eaves, a handsome sign lettered in red and gold, and a bay window of glass crouched beneath a jetting second story. My upstairs chamber was comfortably furnished with a goose-down bed, a fine writing table, and sturdy shelves for books and manuscripts and was well heated for the season, for I was—

and remain—a lover of warm fires, cozy nooks, and intimate spaces.

When I wanted company, I had it in rich supply. There were my fellow actors, as genial and talented a band as ever strode the boards or took applause. I loved all as brethren in a common cause. My friends the Fields lived nearby on Wood Street, and that great house of the Nevels, built of stone and timber, occupied the corner opposite. All the silversmiths who were anybody had divers fair houses in the neighborhood.

All this I mention not to boast but to inform. To understand my story, you must understand how it was with me then. I assure you all's material to what happened later and why.

Onward, then. The theaters of Bankside? All were still closed by order of the Council. Yet I lived in a fool's paradise of conviction that it would spare me, not just the plague but any disaster. I was thirty-nine or forty years and, having inherited my late father's properties and made investments that earned handsomely, I did not want for money. I had more than enough for myself, nor did I leave my wife and children in Stratford unprovided.

Thus, I was fortunate in my friends, in my king's patronage, and in my domestic arrangements, wherein I lived a London bachelor and Stratford husband, intermittently faithless to both callings.

Yet despite all, I was not content. Something gnawed upon me, a niggling dread like whispers in the cellarage. It misshaped my dreams and disturbed my waking life. It was as if my own tormented shadow meant me ill, dogging my steps. My only son, Hamnet, had died years before, and yet the wound bled still. Then, after, my father. I thought perhaps that long-nurtured grief was my melancholy's cause, for while as a young man I had been sanguine, not teary or morose, in my middle years, I'd changed. My handwriting was less legible, my grip less firm, and my eyes strained from too much reading. My bald pate shone in lamplight, crow's feet etched my eyes, and my paunch bore witness to soft living and too many sweets.

Then came this portentous letter, soft and subtle like a snake into the precincts of my garden.

Delivered by a messenger who did not wait for reply.

Writ on very fine parchment, this unholy missive. You could feel the quality of it. Perfumed, too, with a scent I recognized. No signature closed the text, but I knew the hand that wrote it. A man so besotted with love as I was then remembers such small things—a scent at the beloved's throat, the curve of letters upon parchment, a stirring of the loins at the sight of a woman's wrist or the swelling of an alabaster breast or the soft whisper of a promised meeting.

In substance brief, it implored me to visit and gave directions to where she lived, a shop in St. Savior's parish, in the environs of the Rose and the Bear Garden. Within hailing distance of the big church of St. Mary Ovary. A stone's throw from the Globe.

I read it twice over, wondering what it meant. Years had passed without one word of *her*. Our passion was like an episode in a half-remembered play. And now this. What could she want of me but for some devilish reason to stir up the dead embers of an old fire? Or to rip open old wounds and make them bleed afresh?

Such perversions, which had once intrigued my worst self, would not have been beneath her. Then or, I presumed, now. The leopard will not change his spots. If men or women then be bad in youth, they are worse in age. If they be good in youth, yet will they hardly improve with age, since temptations increase as will wastes. True repentance is a chimera, a sop for dreamers, a cruel imposition of our self-righteous clergy, whose own hope of heaven, without grace, would be naught but smoke.

I thought about ignoring her summons, making my silence a statement. Years before, we had parted company on the worst of terms, with mutual accusation, disparagement, and, on my part at least, shame and self-loathing. Yet within an hour of having opened the letter, I'd resolved to go. Why? Was it mere curiosity to see how the years had treated her? Or some stirring of long-ungratified lust?

Whatever it was, God knows I went, yet determined to keep my visit as private as my purse, thinking that Rumor had flapped her thousand tongues often enough to my disgrace, linking me with ever so many women and some men, as though my perfervid pen were not demanding mistress enough.

I told no one about the letter, not even friends, some of whom had been close enough to my bosom in those days to be singed by the fiery passion that had consumed me.

As to the intervening years, I knew little of what she did or with whom. I had heard that she made her living now as a seller of thread, trinkets, and other junk—a duplicitous cover for plain harlotry—that her doltish husband had died, and that she had been abandoned by erstwhile friends, among whom was the high-born lover who had been my rival for her affection. True, I had sometimes wondered about her, taken a little satisfaction in her fall from grace, more's the pity. But my wiser self recognized that I was well rid of her. An expense of spirit in a waste of shame, as I think I once wrote in a delirious, self-disparaging sonnet.

Her name, you ask? I won't tell it. It would do no harm now, but no good either. She sleeps, she dreams. Let God judge her as He will presently judge me.

Of that, no more.

Two

THE SHOP, WHEN I came upon it, was dreary and on a poor narrow street with half its cobbles missing and filth everywhere I looked. A center gutter ran with a dark noxious liquid, and I pressed my handkerchief to my face for the unpleasantness of it. I regretted now I'd come, but it seemed foolish to go back without seeing her.

I entered and found less than I expected. As a shop it looked unattended, its master or mistress long gone. There were a few tables and shelves empty of goods. The walls were without adornment. The room was cold and dusty from apparent disuse. In the far corner of the room were stairs. I called out her name, once, twice. I waited.

Then she appeared.

It was late in the afternoon, already growing dark. She held in her hand a stub of a candle—a small economy in her straitened circumstances, I wondered, or a strategy of seduction? She greeted me by name as she descended, and it was the voice more than her outward shape that affirmed it was she and not some other. That sonorous organ had not changed but was as I remembered. It was slightly accented with her native tongue, with vowels that were not quite English and inflections full of erratic rises and falls. Yet she was in general appearance much altered. Where she once dressed carefully and well, she now wore a drab, shapeless gown with a high collar that would not have offended a nun. Her face was covered by a white lace veil, so that she could see me but I could not discern anything of the high cheeks, full lips, and dusky complexion I remembered. Her hands emerging from the ends of full-blown sleeves were pale and trembling. I could see by her tremor and the unsteadiness of her walk that she was sick, and it passed through my mind that it was unto death. I imagined that she had died already, that this was her corpse and her winding sheet.

"So you've come," she said. "I feared you wouldn't."

The greeting of a ghost is not quickly answered, and a silence fell upon us like that in a dead man's chamber where the body lies undiscovered and alone. Then she asked me to follow her. We climbed the stairs to the floor above, where there was a narrow landing and two doors. She opened one, standing aside to let me enter first.

The chamber within was meanly furnished, which did not surprise me given what I'd seen of the house so far. There was a small table, a narrow, unkempt bed, the scampering of mice as we entered. You know the kind of place I write of, where a man can barely stand upright, where there's hardly air to breathe. The woman shut the door behind us and set her candle on a little table by the narrow bed.

It had indeed been a long time since our last meeting, and to say she had changed much in the meanwhile was to say too little, yet following her now, up into some bedchamber, did bring back memories not all of which were unpleasant. There was a time when I was so besotted by her exotic beauty that I would have traded my hope of heaven to mount after her.

More still to mount her. Such was my obsession with her body. I'm ashamed to write of it.

She turned toward me. We were both standing. She spoke slowly, her voice weak and raspy. "You see I'm not well. It's the pox. What we used to laugh about. You see I'm not laughing now. Each day may be my last, each breath."

She said this without pity for herself or her condition, as though she were remarking on the weather or speaking of a stranger's grief.

I admired her resignation—it was dignified, stoical—but was not surprised at her fate. I knew her tastes and the intensity of her passion, the number of her lovers, the variety of her affections. In love she was insatiable, in lovers indiscriminate and violent. She loved novelty, danger, risk. A bright flame, as she was, does not burn long.

As for the dreaded pox, in faith, here was no matter for gibe or jest. Had I not seen the symptoms many times in this Sodom on the Thames? The plague would have almost been more merciful, snatching her up within the compass of a day or less. Her present condition was a wasting disease, begotten in pleasures of the flesh and unyielding to the appeal of a devout repentance, attacking the organs of generation, then the flesh without, finally assaulting and rotting the throne of reason until the poor miserable wretch paid the full measure of his fornication.

Or hers.

I tell you true, I prayed she would not lift the veil. It would be too much a testimony to the mortal worm that gnawed finally upon us all. Better to laugh. Better to drink. Better to romp in the meadows than to think about the poor forked stick that was man.

At her breast, I now saw, hung a crucifix. I thought: She has gotten religion, turned Papist. The grossest sinner is nearer to the saint than the man of modest vices. Perhaps her penitence was real, now that she was within arm's reach of her deathbed.

"You see I've not long, Will, and how love has served me at last." She said this with great dignity and sat herself upon the narrow bed.

It crossed my mind that she intended I join her there, that we should embrace and couple as before in a fury of twisting arms and legs. But she only pointed to the single chair and told me to sit. She wanted to talk, she said. To see me one last time. I was not unmoved by this.

"I'm grieved," I said. "Grieved that you are sick."

"It can't be helped. The physician has tried all his skill. The herbalist and apothecaries. I've had a dozen treatments, all useless. Don't worry. I'll not show you my face. Better you remember me as I was."

For her tragedy I could offer no consolation I would not myself have despised for its hypocrisy and sham, although none in England had a greater skill with words. In her prime she had been a blunt, practical woman, as whole-brained as she was wholly woman in her most feminine endowments and in her amorous attainments. I would not now insult her intelligence with facile hopes of a cure, or of redemption in the world to come. I knew how she had lived and therefore what hope she had of heaven. If she believed otherwise because of some priest's soothing sophistry, then more power to her.

Of a sudden I wondered if she had invited me to her shop to accuse me of murdering her by infecting her. Of that I was innocent, I knew, for never had the burning ignited in my groin. Her infector had not been I, and if she supposed it was then I would give her the lie to her face, her condition notwithstanding. But, alas, all self-defense is vanity. I was a fool, a fool before her and before God who witnessed the scene.

But then I thought perhaps it had been my noble rival for her affections. I didn't know; I was not sure I cared.

"Did you invite me here to tell me that? You might have spared your pains of seeing me again, put all in your letter. It would have cost you another line, maybe two. No more."

"I need a favor, Will."

"A favor?"

"I pray you, Will, be kind."

I gestured to her to speak.

"Our lives have turned out quite differently," she said.

"It's true," I said, wondering where she went with this.

"You're famous, Will. The king's servant. You have a place, respect, money."

"Granted," I said.

"Everyone knows your name. Speaks to your credit."

"I have my detractors." She ignored this.

"They flock to see your plays and quote you as if you were Holy Writ. You see, while you may have not been mindful of me, I've followed your career, watched you sail across the heavens and blaze in glory like a comet."

I nodded to acknowledge her words, all this flattery. Her bow was bent. I waited for her to make from the shaft. I leaned forward, wishing now that I might see her face, her eyes, where I might find something more akin to truth.

"You're a tall tree, the tallest in the forest. I'm a shrub, lowly. I want your shade, your mercy. In a word, Will, your money."

So it was thus. I might have known. "How much do you need?" I said, reaching for my purse, imagining myself putting a few crowns in her palm. A token for old time's sake, a sop to a guilty conscience, before I took my leave and life and left her forever in the darkness.

But she laughed, low and mockingly. "What I need, I doubt you'll have in your purse. It's a considerable sum, I grant you, but my expenses have been great—the physicians, the medicines. You see how I live here."

She paused to glance around the dreary, dusty room with its meager furnishings. "Surely you can afford it, what with your fine house in Stratford, your share of the company. What's your percentage these days?"

I had no intention of telling her the minutia of my business, much less of paying her more than I'd offered, but I was curious as to what sum she had in mind.

She named it, and I was astonished at her boldness. It was the cost of a coach and six, more than I had paid for my house in Stratford. More than the Globe's income for six months.

"You jest," I said. It was my turn to laugh, but I couldn't.

"Not at all."

"I can help you with modest expenses, but not—"

"Curse you, Will Shakespeare," she said, suddenly furious.

"You see my case, how it's altered—and I see yours. You owe me this."

"What you want is unreasonable—if not impossible. I'm not a wealthy man."

"Wealthy enough," she said.

"Not *that* wealthy, I—"

"Liar! I do know your worth, down to pounds and shillings."

I again denied her. Silence again, this time full of enmity. Then she said in a low, threatening voice, "It would be unfortunate should your newfound respectability be—how shall I say it?—besmirched by nasty stories of your past. It would be a shame if your wife and daughters were to learn of me. If the king were to learn what manner of man Will Shakespeare is. Long and eloquently could I speak of your amorous tricks, your duplicitous stratagems, your outrageous violations of the marriage bed."

"Therein you'd expose yourself," I said, not very confidently.

"Would I care? What have I to lose? No, Will, that's my sole advantage. I've nothing to lose. But you do."

Now I understood her game. She might have been on her deathbed, given her wretched condition, but it was never too late for a little extortion. As I've said, leopards are leopards still. I had loved her once beyond reason, more than my wife, more than God, but never loved her for her virtue.

"Tell whom you please," I said. "Broadcast it from the rooftops. My wife knows about you. I confessed all in my sonnets. She's read them. It's an old breach, long healed."

"Long healed, is it?" she said.

"Like a schoolboy's skinned knee ten years later."

"Skinned knee? Clever, Will, but not apt. Tell that to one of your learned friends at the Mermaid. Not to me. I'm a woman. I know how wives think."

"You know nothing of my wife," I said.

"More than you suppose," she said. "Is she not a woman?"

"She is."

"Then I know her, for I am one. You thrust upon your stage my sex, but you don't know whereof you speak, for I have yet to see one I believed was more than some pimply boy gowned and wigged for the nonce."

I did not respond to this casual slander of my boy actors, but again affirmed that I had revealed all to my wife and she had forgiven me.

My former mistress fell quiet for a moment. I imagined her studying my face behind her veil, searching for the truth behind my words, which was that I had told my wife nothing about my intrigue with my dark mistress and to my knowledge Anne had never yet read a single line of my poetry.

"Women have long memories, Will. New revelations would uncover your perfidy. It would be like pulling off a scab. Besides, there's still the king—and all the fine ladies and gentlemen that fawn upon you. And what of your townsmen? Surely they would be dismayed, shocked. It would give you something else to inscribe on that coat of arms you think so much of."

"The king lives in this world, not the next," I said. "He has indiscretions of his own. I doubt mine would compete. As for my townsmen, they love gossip. Were my life in London as unstained as the pope's alb, yet I would be whispered about. Truth, fiction, it makes little difference, save that a naughty fiction is always preferred before dull truth."

Then she grew silent again, so silent I wondered if she had fallen asleep. I wondered, too, how long charity required me to stay. I was on the point of going when she reached out a hand and clasped my own in a grip of surprising strength.

Do you know, friend, what it is to be touched by one who's dying and knows it? No matter that the bone is covered still with smooth white flesh, yet it's bone you feel, the bone you will become. Let the flesh be warm or cold, yet it is the bone.

"Before you leave," she said, "do me one other favor."

"What favor?" I said, my heart beating rapidly as though her request, mildly uttered, had been the most baleful of threats.

"A poem, Will. A pretty sonnet. Recite my favorite."

I pretended not to know whereof she spoke.

"The sonnet you wrote to love—how time passed but not love."

"Forget the sonnet," I said. "It means nothing now."

"Oh, for pity's sake, Will, do but recite the sonnet as you did once when we loved hotly, when our love was fresh and you were as passionate as a stallion."

I laughed, but mirthlessly, astonished that she could first extort, then plead for a sonnet. Yet she had ever been thus. Changeable, tempestuous. I had once been fool enough to find it charming. She repeated her request, this time her voice rising, becoming urgent.

"Oh, the sonnet, Will. I can't remember all the words, though in the nights I try."

"I'm not sure I remember it myself."

"Please, for God's sake."

I sighed heavily, resolved to do what she willed and then be gone forever. *"My Mistress's eyes are nothing like the sun,"* I said, drawing the words out slowly, letting my mouth curve around the syllables, as though I were coming upon each by accident.

"Not that one, Will."

"Which, then? I know not which you want."

"The one about impediments, about love and time."

I knew which one, but I could not bring myself to recite it. It did not suit the time or the place; it did not suit me, nor *us*. Indeed, I was not aware she even knew it, for I had never made her privy to the whole of my verse. How could I? Some of the sonnets did not flatter, and she would have taken them ill.

"Will, I beg you—for old time's sake."

"Very well," I said.

And so I began.

Let me not to the marriage of true minds
Admit impediments; love is not love
Which alters when it alteration finds,
Or bends with the remover to remove.

Here I paused and looked at her, thinking perhaps the first quatrain would satisfy her sudden and most surprising thirst for my poetry. But she signaled for me to proceed, and I supposed that it was better to recite the rest and have done than continue to debate with her. I had suddenly grown very tired, as though it were late in the day when it was hardly dusk.

O, no, it is an ever-fixed mark
That looks on tempests and is never shaken;
It is the star to every wand'ring bark,
Whose worth's unknown, although his height be taken.

"Comes now the part that likes me best," she said as I finished the second quatrain.

The interruption vexed me. I resolved to give my words no more feeling than what was required to speak them. I read flatly, like the stolid merchant who is asked to read the text on Sunday from which the minister is to preach and can barely construe the letters.

Love's not Time's fool, though rosy lips and cheeks
Within his bending sickle's compass come;
Love alters not with his brief hours and weeks,
But bears it out even to the edge of doom.

I could recite no more. I couldn't bear to remember what she had been to me then. The contrast of my memory of her and the pathetic and disgusting figure before me was too agonizing. Despite her blatant extortion and the malice beneath it, I felt hot tears fill my eyes, my own words cutting me to the quick. Through my tears I could see her reaching out toward me. Then suddenly she withdrew her hand and finished the poem for me. Her voice was low, melodious, sensitive of meaning as though she had writ the words herself.

If this be error and upon me proved,
I never writ, nor no man ever loved.

So it was finished. I made to leave, standing and looking toward the door, but had no sooner done so than from below I heard glass breaking and then thunder. But not thunder, an explosion rather. It shook the house.

"My God, what's *that?*" she said.

My nostrils pricked from the closeness of the room, the stench of gunpowder and smoke.

She pulled aside her veil, revealing for one instant her face. It was not wasted as I had feared, but older, her swarthy complexion unnaturally pale and drawn, her black eyes resting upon dark half-moons, as though she had long gone without sleep. It was the vision of an instant before she replaced the veil.

"Fire!" she cried. "The house is afire."

I ran to the door and looked down the stairs. The shop was no longer dark; bright licks of flame spread ravenously across the floor in a terrifying suddenness. I remembered in the same moment the shattering of glass I had heard before but made no sense of. The window. The odor of gunpowder. This was not hap; rather, some incendiary device, some petar, some instrument of war, contrived and deliberate.

She lurched forward, ready to descend, to fight the flames, but I pulled her back. Already it was too late—either for her house or for our own escape. The flames fed greedily on the few furnishings. There was much smoke now. "Come away," I said, spitting the words, my eyes burning. "No passage for us there. The smoke will kill us, if the flames don't. All's lost. We must get out."

She turned from the conflagration and glared at me wide-eyed, almost angrily, as though I were to blame. As though I had somehow brought the flames with me. For a brief instant I felt the shame of her unspoken accusation. Had I given her the pox? Had I somehow caused the fire?

Slamming the door behind us, I ran to the casement and tried to wrest it open but failed. For a moment I struggled with it again, then she took my hand and drew me into the back of the room to a small door I had not before noticed. It was secured with a wooden bar and seemed only large enough for a person to squeeze through. She struggled to draw the bar aside, failed, then urged me to try, all the time crying that we were going to die, that we would be burned alive.

No soldier ordered to battle ever threw himself against the foe with the passion with which I attacked that bar and forced it back. I flung open the door, saw where it led out to the roof. From below, alarms, cries, curses. For a moment I imagined the terrified neighbors, running to the inferno with buckets of filthy gutter water, more afraid for the safety of their own homes than for the imperiled life within.

I wedged myself through the door, pulling her after me, but terror had made her strong. Once through the aperture, she clambered over me as though I were nothing, and with wondrous agility, given her sickness, she scrambled down the incline to where the roof ended and disappeared in the smoke. Behind us the whole house was aflame.

I ran to where I'd seen her disappear. A narrow alley separated the burning house from its neighbor. With a leap I landed upon the adjoining roof, where I found a ladder had been put up by some well-meaning neighbors.

I don't remember climbing down. I don't remember my hands on the rungs, nor running from the flames and smoke, but I do remember finding where her body lay.

SHE SPRAWLED FACEDOWN like a cast-off puppet. I started to kneel beside her but was pulled to my feet by passersby who expressed concern for my own injuries. They dragged me from her, despite my protests, across to the other side of the street and into a glover's shop where the smell of leather—how familiar from my father's trade!—mixed with that of the smoke from the fire.

"Your mistress is dead, sir. She broke her neck."

The voice was kindly. Who spoke? I couldn't see.

"Not my mistress," I said, half delirious. "She was no mistress of mine."

Then what was she now, now that she was dead, and why was I

so moved? When I was with her, before the fire, I wanted nothing more than to be gone. Her disease repelled me; her feeble attempt to extort disgusted me. The exaggerated idealism of my sonnet made me despise my verse and wish to be an honest carpenter or bricklayer. Now here I stood in the squalid, smoking street mourning my dead.

It crossed my mind this was a dream, or perhaps a scene from a play. The closure of tragedy, wherein my dark mistress would only seem to be dead. At play's end she would rise alive and, beaming, bow at the crowd's applause. Afterward, she—he— would go to supper with his fellows, the other players. They would tell jokes, drink immoderately, get lucky with women, or men.

"She's dead, sir, dead as a nail," the same voice said over my shoulder. "Broke her neck falling. She shouldn't have jumped, sir. She should have come down the ladder. Like you did, sir."

I turned to look at the man, only half comprehending his words. He was a hunchback, hideous, covered with ash, grinning stupidly.

"She was terrified," I said, stricken with guilt without knowing why. What had I done, then or now, to bring about this end? And why was I trying to justify her act, this woman to whom I owed nothing and who had caused me nothing but shame and regret?

"Better leave her be, sir," the man said. "The whole street's lost, by my reckoning. It'll be a miracle if all the Bankside doesn't go up in smoke."

I heard a chorus of shouts and then a crash. It was her house. It was all gone but smoke and cinders and rubble.

I held my head in my hands, my eyes burning, my cloak smoldering and reeking with bitter smoke, my brain reeling. My dark lady was dead, and I had escaped the same fate by the skin of my teeth.

Three

THE DAY AFTER my old mistress died, I could not write or blot a line. I stayed indoors, a quaking wretch. Sent word to friends that I was sick, which was as good as truth, so sick at heart I was. I spoke sharply to my landlord and his wife when they asked how I did.

They called me Master Stoneface, which I suppose I was. For I thought much on death and cold decay, suffocated in regret, and despaired of heaven. The fire, my old lover's death, my near escape—like a notary's seal, these events had confirmed my fears and dropped me into a void of confusion and despair.

The terrible night before now seemed the worst of nightmares, in which I envisioned my quondam mistress all aflame and tumbling, her bootless agony like shrill bird calls, though in the real event her agony had been silent and, if anything therefore, the more horrible. In the light of a bleak day it was hard for me to believe she was dead. It was only when I looked at my green satin doublet singed and filthy and stinking with ash—my good cloak had been consumed in the flames—that I knew it had been no dream.

Her death had quickened pity in me where before was all hate and scorn. Her poor abused body—who would see to it? I didn't want her to rest in a pauper's grave.

And so on the third day, still so benighted by melancholy that I thought I might die thereof, I made another journey to her street. Charred and smoking still, the most of it. Yet I wanted to know what they had done with her body.

Next to where her house had stood, I found a man searching through the rubble. He said he was a baker. This was the blackened remains of his shop, he said with almost defiant pride as though to challenge me to claim otherwise. On his wife's orders he was searching for a brooch she had lost in the destruction. He was a big man with a heavy brow, a lantern jaw, a drifting right eye, and a booming churchman's voice to call sinners to repentance. He would have made a powerful figure in the pulpit or on the stage.

"All told, three died that dwelt therein," the baker said, regarding me curiously. "The woman that fell from the roof, an old man, and my apprentice. The old man died of stark fear, I think."

"And your apprentice?"

"Edward Goode? Marry, sir, his body's not to be found, but I think he's dead. He's not been seen these three days. Maybe his blackened bones rest here somewhere."

The baker pointed to the mound of charred debris. "He was a troublesome boy," he said, as though the statement should be his apprentice's epitaph.

I said, "The dead woman—what's happened to her corpse?"

"She? Carried off, I suppose, sir. Before it rot and spread greater pestilence."

"No one claimed it?"

"She lived alone, said she was a widow, but with her kind who could know? My good wife says she was hardly better than a whore. Marry, sir, where be her lovers now, now that she's dead? The fire started in her shop, you know."

The baker stopped his probing in the ashes and stood full tall. He gave me a cold eye. "And who are you, sir, to ask such questions?"

"She was my sister, my mother's daughter."

I credit myself as an honest man, yet now I lied freely, not

wanting to give the baker any satisfaction in labeling me afterward as one of the dead woman's lovers, though such I had been.
The lie seemed to create a greater regard in the baker.

"Gone," he said. "Carried off in the dead cart."

"Dead cart," I said.

"The cart that comes round to pick up them dead of the
plague lest the pestilence increase. Since no one else came forward
to pay for such other exequies and obsequies, nothing else could
be done. They weren't my dead. I fear your sister is quicklimed by
now, sir. Yet her soul may go to heaven still."

The baker spoke more feelingly than before; he removed his
hat and stood with it dangling, as a gesture of sympathy, or perhaps only as a hint that I should give him money. I reached in my
purse, gave him a shilling. "Here, baker, for the rebuilding of
your shop."

The baker smiled, showing his crooked teeth, made a little
bow, asked God to bless me.

"By the way," I said in such a manner as to make him think I
cared not how he should answer. "This fire—what think you
caused it?"

"Well, sir, it did begin in her shop. That's where we first saw
the flames. There was a man that was with her on the roof, and we
supposed him one of her—"

The baker hesitated, remembering perhaps that I was after all
the dead woman's brother and would not take kindly to the insinuation that she was more whore than shopkeeper.

"One of her custom," the baker continued, his contempt showing like a petticoat beneath a skirt. "He got himself down a ladder. Walked away unscathed, or so they say. I was too busy
pouring water on my own walls to have seen him. Little use it did
after all. Yet it's a blessing and a miracle, too, that all Bankside is
not ash and thousands dead where there were but three."

I thanked the baker again and turned to go, but he reached out
and touched me on the shoulder.

"Your tongue, sir," he said.

"What's wrong with my tongue?" I said, misunderstanding him.
"You don't sound like your sister. She talked differently. Where
were you born, sir?"

"Warwickshire," I said, conscious of the Warwickshire burr in
my speech that for all my years in London I'd never lost. My dead
lover had been a mixture of nations—part Spanish, part Moor,
part Sephardic Jew, part I know not what. Her speech, husky and
full of vowels, had always pleased me and mystified me, too.

My answer seemed to satisfy him, though I don't know why it
should. Maybe he'd never heard of Warwickshire, or thought it
was in Portugal or Spain. What did I care? I wouldn't be seeing
the baker again, or he me. What difference what he believed or
didn't?

I DID NOT often go to the Globe, not in those melancholy days.
As I have said, all theaters in the city and suburbs had been ordered
closed for the pestilence. So, too, the bear gardens, some of the
taverns, most of the brothels. For Londoners the plague was bad;
the deprivation of their pleasures was almost worse. The King's
Men rehearsed in the city, in the back rooms of taverns, sometimes at Blackfriars. Though citizens might be deprived of the joy
of the player's art, the new king would not be. He had the courage
of his pleasures, though some detractors called him a drooling fool
and pederast, a piss-poor substitute for Great Elizabeth.

That wasn't my opinion, you understand. I owed the king
much gratitude. He had not been ten days in England before
instructing Sir Robert Cecil, Keeper of the Privy Seal, to issue a
patent raising me and my fellow actors to the new dignity of
grooms of the chamber. No mean achievement for a country boy,
come to London not above fifteen or sixteen years before with
hardly more in my purse than dreams. And words, yes, always
words—for this was the coin of Will Shakespeare's realm.

I approached a side door, unlocked it, and entered—the main
entrance being barred with a heavy cross beam—and came into

the yard to survey my domain. The open sky above the great O was pale and wan, curdled like milk; beneath my foot crunched a multitude of discarded nutshells. The sight of the empty stage at a time of the afternoon when actors might have strutted deepened my desolation. Here, more than in the solemn precincts of a church or in a king's gaudy court, I might have found peace, or it found me, but it was not so. The emptiness of my little kingdom made my condition worse.

Then I remember wishing I had someone to unburden myself to, someone gifted not with ready tongue but with compassion—a ready ear without a mouth to trumpet its owner's wit. Say Robert Armin. Good Robin, aye, there was a good pair of ears, but of too sanguine a temper to give credence to my fear. He would do no more than drag me to the nearest tavern and ply me with strong ale. Drink. It offends me not, yet I'm no man to view the world from the bottom of a glass. The world's twisted enough viewed cold sober.

John Heminge and Henry Condell I likewise discounted. They were too timorous, while stout Dick Burbage was cursed with so logical a brain that he should demand mountains of proof before he would grant me an iota of sympathy.

I could imagine the scorn Burbage would heap upon my inference that the fire had been aimed at me. Why, what pride is this, good Will, Burbage would say, that every blaze is seen as aimed at your particular self and not an accident of nature or the negligence of the householder who piles the faggots too high or stands too close to the fire and burns his bum?

In London, fires are as common as fleas.

Most true. Yet I knew Burbage would be wrong. I remembered the tinkle of broken glass and the explosion that heralded the smoke and flames. That had been no fugitive cinder casually engendering a fiery progeny, but a missile hurled, deliberate, and most murderous. The flames had spread too quickly, had been too intense—fueled, I suspected, by more than the milliner's paltry stuff.

Peering into the furnace, I had sniffed gunpowder. No, dear

Burbage, prince of logic and most excellent of tragedians, not nature's work but human mischief had set that fire. The work of someone who knew I was closeted there. Knew, too, that the house was small with but a single escape from the upper floor so that I should be consumed along with the worldly vanities of the shop. An obscure end that might be deemed nothing more than a strange disappearance, since none knew I was there.

Ignominy as well as death. Limed over in an obscure grave.

I who had so rarely wanted counsel—oh, how it fed my pride to stand alone, untottering—now tottered on the brink. Wanted rescue who before was rescuer, a practical man quick to provide common sense to hysterical friends.

Some hulking bodyguards would not do. I needed no such hedge against the devil. I took my lover's death as a prophecy of ill to come. Therefore knowledge was what I wanted. Knowledge of my enemy and his design. Knowledge of how to destroy before being destroyed. I needed someone cunning, yet honest; someone tempered himself in the crucible of experience with such as used violence and deviousness and other subtle Machiavellian arts.

I climbed onto the boards and sat down on the apron of the stage, legs dangling. *Who?*

My answer came hard upon the question. If I needed such a special friend, should it not be more than a colleague with infirmities of judgment and dearth of experience to match my own? Should it not, rather, be someone with power of such magnitude that he no sooner gave a command but it was done, and with knowledge of stratagems and malicious devices of such profundity that a plot against Will Shakespeare would not be discounted as a peculiar madness, but deemed possible, even plausible?

Even certain?

Who qualified for such a role but the king's little beagle, the great Robert Cecil himself?

I had spoken more than once to Cecil but knew him better by reputation. For Cecil plots were his mother tongue. He had been privy to more confessions of deception, murder, and treason than a score of hangmen. If I was prince of players, then Cecil was prince of politicians.

And in sum, if Cecil would not take my old lover's death as a murder, deliberate and cruel, and me as an equal target of an unknown enemy, who would?

Besides, I thought, Cecil would have a vested interest in my case. It was his business to keep the king happy. He had once said to me the very words. How then could the king be happy if his prince of players were not so?

PAST NOON I got me to Whitehall, where I found Master Secretary's antechambers besieged with suitors, crowding with their petitions and bills and jealous of their place in line. Being one of so many—most titled gentlemen or lordly churchmen—I, a lowly player, was ready to cut cable and run, then heard my name.

A tall, overfed young man of ruddy complexion and spade-cut beard, dressed well in somber colors and ruff collar, approached. It was a style I detested, but no less popular at court for that. His name I remembered, Thomas Stanleigh—not as one of Cecil's men, but the young earl of Pembroke's, at whose house in Wilton I stayed some weeks before.

I wasn't sure why Stanleigh was there, and did not ask him, for to do so would have been impolitic to say the least. Great men must communicate with other great men, their secretaries and flunkies likewise. So Stanleigh.

I liked Stanleigh's master, the earl of Pembroke; the nephew of Sir Philip Sidney, he shared his illustrious uncle's love of literature. Cecil I did not love—he was not a lovable man—but I feared and respected him.

I was glad to see Stanleigh. I was in need of a familiar face, and perhaps of someone who could get me in to see Cecil.

"Master Shakespeare," Stanleigh said. "We're well met."

"Are we?" I said.

"Indeed, Lord Cecil and I were speaking of you just this hour."

"I'm honored to be the subject of his lordship's contemplations," I said, adopting the fatuous language of the court. "I was hoping to see him. It's a matter of some urgency."

Stanleigh looked at me questioningly with his cherubic face, and I thought he must have been a beautiful boy, although age was now doting on him and he had a little of the dissolute look of James's courtiers. When I was not forthcoming as to my purpose, he looked disappointed but persevered.

"The king keeps his lordship very busy these days, as you may imagine, Master Shakespeare. Yet I am sure he will see you at his earliest. He is a great admirer, you know, believing you to be the greatest playwright of them all. Indeed, greater than the ancients, Sophocles, Aristophanes, or even Seneca. I pray you use me, sir."

"I thought you were my lord of Pembroke's secretary?"

"So I was," Stanleigh said. "Now I am in the service of Lord Cecil. I've advanced, you see, to more important business."

I did not inquire as to what this business might be. It was not my concern, who have no love for politics or court intrigue. I thanked Stanleigh for his offer, received his promise to tell Cecil of my need, and left emboldened by his assurances of his master's high opinion and Stanleigh's own readiness to serve me, even though his fulsome praise I thought bordering on the absurd. A great man's patronage is almost useless unless one has found a go-between. Stanleigh offered himself. So be it.

A DREARY WEEK passed before I heard from Stanleigh, who came to Mountjoy's house to say Cecil at last had time for me. "Sir Robert prays you will not feel neglected, Master Shakespeare, for he professes his love for you and your art."

"When?" I said, my hopes revived.

"This very afternoon," Stanleigh said.

Four

DURING THAT WEEK I played hermit as before, a wonder to my friends who looked for my companionship and made inquiries at mine host's door to be assured I was not dead. I worked upon a new play, that was my excuse; was lost in thought and could not abide interruption. The truth was that I neither wrote nor read, but often stared into space, thought nothing of my plays or of my troupe, of wife or daughters in Stratford. I could hardly get myself dressed of mornings, but lay in bed until the light suffused my chamber and noise without in house and street made me ashamed to be so dissolute.

My lame excuses friends took on credit, so left me alone to the fears ever nurtured by solitude.

In those days, Cecil had chambers at Whitehall, at his house on the Strand, and at the vainglorious pile he maintained at Theobalds that was of such splendor I heard the king determined to have it for himself. As it turned out I was to see Cecil at his house on the Strand. Stanleigh was waiting when I arrived and was my usher to Cecil's private rooms. There he left us alone, but not without first accepting my thanks in the form of half a crown, which he pocketed with such speed you might have thought my coins hot coals.

I was shocked by Cecil's appearance. I knew Master Secretary to be of about my own years, but he seemed to have aged even in the short time since I had last seen him. His face, hard lined, was gaunt; his complexion, too much of indoors. And yet he was very merry with me.

"Ah, Master Shakespeare," Cecil said. "What a relief. I thought it was the Dutch ambassador come to call. But a player is directly opposite an ambassador. Can you sniff the riddle?"

I made a show of pondering, my mind preoccupied and yet clear with respect to my own purpose. I liked not riddles, clownish stuff, but in such a circumstance I feigned delight and answered: "Because, Your Honor, players lie by trade, but ambassadors trade in lies, and so are opposites though both smile and bow and will make themselves liars and fools for applause."

At this he guffawed and appeared not so wan as before. "You are too quick for me, Master Shakespeare. I was about to reply in the same general vein, but you are the more eloquent. Sit you down. Are you hungry?"

He motioned toward a little French table in the corner on which sat a tray with silver goblets and a silver plate arranged with sweetmeats and other dainties, a sumptuous banquet, though to feed my belly was farthest from my mind.

I declined with thanks and, upon his entreaty, took the chair opposite the great table he used for a desk. It was spread with books and papers, but not matter for my taste. I preferred English poetry and Italian novellas, translations of Ovid and Herodotus, and histories of England and other lands, all for me a rich store of imitation and plagiary. Cecil's library was more dismal stuff— documents of state, letters, codes, and treatises on government and law, a great Bible, and some religious tracts I warrant he consumed looking for treason against the state rather than to enrich his soul. The chamber smelled of mildew and of the lamp and was cold despite a fire in the grate and a small fortune's worth of wall hangings.

"I trust your visit has something to do with your players. The king thinks more than highly of you and your company. Name your wish and trust it will be granted."

"My business has nothing to do with players," I answered, unsure of just how to launch my tale. Now, facing the great man, I felt unsure about the wisdom of seeking him out. Taking a deep breath, I said, "It's a personal matter."

Cecil lifted an eye, a flicker of disapproval, but hung fire. He signaled me to proceed.

I wondered if he thought I needed money—was just another tedious supplicant, more eloquent than most but just as abject and obsequious. Wasn't it money that players were supposed always to have in short supply? Or perhaps he supposed I had got with child some gentlewoman of the court. An easy theory that, rife with plausibility.

"For the past months—since the queen died, I have had a presentiment—"

"Presentiment?" Cecil said, when I lingered upon the word.

"Presentiment," I repeated, feeling foolish indeed and wishing now a ready escape from the man and from the great house. It was not a word I favored, being as it was too long and French.

"If you require evidence—"

"Evidence?" Cecil interrupted. "You speak of law, then? I pray you're not in trouble of that sort, Master Shakespeare. As good fall into Satan's grip as a lawyer's. You'll find the devil more gracious and merciful."

"No, Your Honor. Nothing of the kind," I hastened to answer. "Someone wants me dead."

"Someone?" Cecil said with a dry laugh. "Undoubtedly this somebody you mention is more than one if you're an average man. My enemies are legion. I have learned to live with them. If only to enjoy their disappointment at my successes."

Cecil laughed again when he said this, but I could tell by his heavy brow that he took his own enemies very seriously. The question in my mind now was whether this lord would regard the enemies of a mere player worth his trouble, given his great charge in the kingdom.

"This is a particular enemy," I said. "He's not content that his malice should take the ordinary forms of calumny and spite. He's made attempts on my life. Whether he be some disgruntled actor, a rival playwright, or some other—I know not."

At this Cecil's expression darkened. I could not read it. Was it outrage at the thought someone wished me ill or impatience at my long, inconclusive tale?

"Tell me of these attempts, as you call them," Cecil said. "Begin at the beginning."

It was hard for me to begin there, there at that first event, which had not seemed an instance of anything at all until later when I construed it differently. The fire in Bankside was the least ambiguous. Yet I started at the beginning as I understood it, telling the story slowly, wondering as I did whether I was spinning a foolish tale or furnishing the evidence Cecil would require to take action, what action I didn't know.

Cecil nodded, listened, a good audience now. "And there were other like instances?"

"Yes, Your Honor."

"Tell me those, too. Everything, no matter how improbable it may seem."

Two more times I told of, nothing withholding, then about the Bankside fire. But of my dead mistress, how I came to know her and write about her most fulsomely and gravely in my pretty sonnets, I didn't speak, rather described her merely as a woman I called upon for old time's sake. Which of course was true, too. I told of the broken glass, the explosion, the odor of gunpowder, and the suspicious rapacity of the fire.

Suddenly Stanleigh came in. He apologized for the interruption and leaned down to whisper into Cecil's ear.

I watched as Cecil's expression changed. "Tell His Majesty that I'll come at once."

Stanleigh sped to the door, glancing once at me in passing.

"I'm most sorry, Master Shakespeare, but a good pack horse must do its master's bidding. At the moment my royal master bids me bear some new burden of state. As to your matter—"

"Nothing compared to your duties," I said, leaping to my feet so I would not be sitting when he arose.

"On the contrary," Cecil said. "What you tell me concerns me. And deeply. These untoward encounters you spoke of give cause to worry. However, as to your interpretation. It is sometimes possible—"

He paused, like an actor who'd forgotten his lines.

"It is possible for a man to be so undone by fear that he imagines in the odd incident a perverse design. You take fires. Even fires of dubious cause are regrettably commonplace."

At his temporizing, my heart failed. So I was not to be regarded as really threatened, or merely mad, but somewhere in betwixt? Now I sorely regretted having bared my heart. How foolish must I look in this great man's eyes, pitiful, bereft of the dignity I enjoyed upon entering his chamber. The great English playwright become the great English blubberer.

Cecil rose and steered me toward the door and seemed on the point of ending our meeting when he said, "I know someone who can help you, Master Shakespeare. A clever man, whose cleverness and skill are well allowed."

"Your Honor," I said. "I'm most grateful. But give me his name and I'll—"

He raised a hand to silence me.

"Master Shakespeare, even had I the hours to spend, which I have not, I could not do as much to make you safe, discover the origin of these strange events, and bring the perpetrator to justice."

I waited for the name of this paragon.

"He of whom I speak," Cecil said, leading me into the long corridor, "is none other than yourself."

"Myself?" I said, amazed.

"Who in England has such knowledge of evil? Look at your plays, Master Shakespeare. What's your subject but the works of devious men? Look at your bloody Andronicus. Look at your most circumspect and ingenious Prince Hamlet. Is that not a murder mystery for you?"

"Yes, Your Honor, but I—"

Cecil ignored my protest. He went on, "Not to mention your excellent histories of our English kings, princes, dukes—all veritable manuals of statecraft. Why, Machiavelli cannot hold a candle to you. Even your comedies reflect an understanding of malice, treachery, subtlety, conspiracy, vain ambition, labyrinthine plottings, and unnatural acts."

On another occasion so elegant a compliment would have pleased. Now Cecil's praise was ash in my mouth. I could hardly speak. I bowed awkwardly and mumbled my thanks like an inarticulate idiot, feeling myself a figure of ridicule and gross absurdity.

"Go now, Master Shakespeare," Cecil said, turning to me. "Have courage in the face of this unusual adversity. You've told me your story. I have listened and advised. We shall not, however, tell His Majesty, who is so undone by fears of conspiracy and murder himself that should he hear talk of fires and murders he would not set foot in his own palace, much less a theater. I should be as sorry as anyone for that."

Again I took my leave. Stanleigh appeared to escort me the final paces to the door. He smiled, "Your meeting was fruitful, sir?"

"Yes, fruitful."

For form's sake I said this. Young Stanleigh had done me a service, but what fruit I spoke of I had no thought. I offered to give him something for his pains; this time he refused me flatly, saying that he had too much respect for my art to do me any good except for love of me.

I TOOK LEAVE of Cecil unsure whether I had been helped or mocked. As I've said, I admired the king's minister and feared him, as what Englishman in his right mind did not, but Cecil was more fox than beagle. To be told to help myself was not the counsel I sought. I had desired his wisdom, and maybe the muscle of his servants. Stanleigh had been helpful, but he was a minor functionary, adept at compliment, greasing wheels as he went. But myself? What could I do that I had not already done, except clasp my own hand in the darkness?

Holding a true mirror to myself, I saw I was not a hard man

but a soft; as often foolish in my waywardness as prudent, readier to run than to stand, sooner to beg off than to contest. I might be clever, even ingenious, as Cecil had said, but all my wordsmithery was but dressing old ideas new. What had experience taught me about devious men? What did I know about statecraft and treachery and conspiracy but what I had read in books? I had been told I knew hearts. The truth was otherwise. I wrote only the voices I heard, letting the language spin itself like a busy spider until the intricate web that was the tragedy or comedy resonated with something akin to truth.

After that I didn't go home but went to a tavern I knew in Cheapside, got very drunk there, and went upstairs with a girl with pale eyes and golden down upon her slender arms.

Or maybe that was another dream. If it was, at least it gave me pleasure rather than torment.

At dawn I woke on a mussed pallet that was crawling with vermin and rank with sweat and lust. The pale-eyed girl was gone. So was my purse, a fine-tooled Spanish leather belt with silver buckle, and a gold ring I wore upon my third finger.

At least Madam Charity left me my shoes and stockings.

Feeling wretched, I got myself up, dressed, doused my face with water and went home.

In the brutal light of day I came to terms with my condition. Cecil had spoken true. If there was indeed no help but myself then my way was clear, despite the magnitude of my timidity and self-doubt. I did not want to die and be limed and buried in an unknown grave or left to rot in some reeking ditch. I wanted to live. And if not live, at least know my enemy's name, face, and heart before I died, so that at the very least I could accuse him before heaven, if by God's grace I should come there.

Five

FRIEND, IF MY history thus far has pricked you on, I hope my seeming cowardice has not pricked you off again. Trust me, there is more befell than I've told here. For I have set down naught yet of those dreams and strange occurrences that, even before my old lover's death, put me in cold sweat. Swallowing pride, I revealed these things to Cecil, Master High and Mighty. But the truth is this. I couldn't bring myself to record upon these pages such seeming silly fantasies of an idle and timorous brain before I gave account of my fatal interview with my dead mistress. You'd read no further. You'd think yourself in the company of a whining wretch that starts at dreams and imagines stalkers at every street corner.

And so, like a skilled advocate at the bar who would persuade the court of his client's innocence, I gave best evidence first to create a good impression—not of madness but of circumspection. Given the manner of her death, who could deny my life was in danger, or could believe, given that fateful event, what happened before is not part of the same sinister plot?

I now freely tell the rest of my story.

FIRST, THEN, A fortnight before her death, I dreamed a wicked dream. I had not drunk that night. Nor eaten overmuch. Nor had the day been fraught with trouble. A common ordinary day it was, with no more business than on any other day. I should have slept the sleep of the just, but instead a vision of torments came my way. Judge for yourself.

In my dream I walked freely on the Strand, that great thoroughfare that bisects the city like the swift stroke of a sword. Imagine now it filled with sundry folk, coming and going, and I bound for somewhere I knew not. Turning of a sudden from the main way, I found myself in a stinking smoky lane with houses timber-warped and leaning as though, like drunken men, they would topple onto the vomity cobbles.

I wasn't alone. By me walked a barrel-shaped man, looming and hooded like an executioner and as silent as a monk. He carried no sword or ax, bore no hangman's noose, made no threats against me with tongue or icy stare. I said nothing, nor did he speak to me, but I believed that wherever we were going with such purposeful strides, our destination was the same, and I was afraid.

Then behind me of a sudden I heard the clatter of hooves and the rattle of wheels. I looked over my shoulder and saw at the street's bottom a wagon pulled by two wild-eyed and sweating stallions. The wagon was heavily laden with cordwood. Despite its burden it advanced with frightening speed.

As suddenly, I was aware that my grim companion had disappeared, although I knew, too, that he had brought me here, had left me alone to suffer whatever was to come, and for this he had been appointed. By whom?

The street had narrowed. By stretching I could touch the houses that formed on either side a solid, doorless wall. Fearing for my life, I turned to hail the driver, as it was clear there could be no passage for man, beasts, and wagon in so narrow a space, but the driver, whom I could distinguish now with a sudden sickness within as the inamorata of my sonnetry, whipped the beasts to greater effort. Her black glossy locks splayed about her head and black eyes flashing, she shouted that the cursed beasts were beyond her control and that she could do nothing with them but save herself.

I saw her leap from the wagon, which came rumbling toward me.

You say such dreams are common? A trick and wink of the mind's eye? Let me tell you, then, how I could smell the sweating horses; how I could feel the vibrations of their beating hooves and hear the grinding crunch as wheel rims chafed the walls. By Christ's tears, how I ran. Behind me the wagon kept on, despite the narrowness of the street that seemed to stretch to a distant, converging point from which I could see no escape.

I woke myself. You know the way you do and can when the nightmare is too much, when nothing's worse.

I sat up to such Cimmerian darkness that I thought myself blinded, wondering if my screams—for they echoed still—had awakened the whole house, or if Monsieur Mountjoy would call out the watch, as the tire-maker was wont at any random uproar in the street.

That I should dream of executioners was no great thing. I had written lines for enough of them. Their handiwork was spiked upon London Bridge for the edification of the populace. I had met one once, an executioner. We had shared a bottle, elbow to elbow, mouth to ear. I listened to his stories of blood and gore and courage most marvelous as malefactors faced eternity with steely indifference or bold contempt. The man had regarded his work as does a carpenter or miller—as that to be done, no great fuss to be made about it. He looked like any other big hardy fellow who works with his hands, save he wore a hood and sleeveless shirt to show his muscles' bulge.

Was it my death I feared? I think not, although death is fearsome enough, even to gospelers who have their salvation by patent, as I do not. Rather, it was her appearance that gave me pause. Why should I think of *her,* her whose memory I thought erased? Can nothing be erased forever but secretes itself in the folds of the brain and heart? Is there no oblivion that's not a curse but devoutly to be wished?

Yet there *she* was, wild-eyed and vengeful, her expression cold and stony like Medusa's mask. And as I huddled there upon my bed, my bedclothes pulled round my chin for comfort's sake, my body cold yet dripping, my heart full to bursting, I knew my greatest fear had been *she,* not the executioner, not the wild-eyed horses. He, perhaps, brought death; but she, a nameless and therefore more terrifying torment.

FOUR DAYS LATER, this dream was added upon. First came a violent encounter that otherwise I thought little of, a consequence of living in a crowded city, a cost of doing business, nothing more.

Friend, I write no more of dreams or visions but of cold fact. Near collisions between wagons and pedestrians are not uncommon in this crowded city with streets that had been set down before such heavy traffic was conceived, when London was a mere village by the river in old Roman times.

This, then, as I've said, was no dream but happened in my waking world. There walk I on the street and comes the driver— a portly bearded groom now—whipping his horses up while more than a few who walked within the street curse him for the danger, call out warning. Where did he think he was—in open range? Did he not care that he trampled the king's subjects under foot?

The wagon in its wild career clipped my heel, sending me sprawling. The driver did not stop, but later when I inquired of several shopkeepers as to whether the man and wagon had been observed before in the neighborhood, they all insisted that it had not. Never seen before. Neither wagon nor driver.

What of that, you say? London is full of strangers and their wagons and horses. Why should strangers be more careful in their driving than those who live within that neighborhood?

But my suspicion had grounds more relevant than this. For on that very day, by exchange of messages I had arranged to meet a certain actor who owed me money. The meeting was to take place where the actor, a man named Woodbury, lodged with a carpenter whom he occasionally helped with his labors, for actors, you must know, are not so well rewarded for their talents they can afford to do nothing else. Yet when I later sought him out, the actor denied ever sending such a message,

Passing strange, isn't it? Woodbury said he could not pay me just now and begged to have the debt renewed, there being no decent work for most actors at the moment, and no carpentry but the building of coffins, which he disdained. Besides, Woodbury insisted, he did not lodge in that particular neighborhood at all. He said he lived with his sister and her husband in Bishopsgate near Hog Lane. All who knew him could affirm it.

Finally, when I inquired of his companions who had brought the message, I was told that a boy did, a strange boy no one had ever seen before or since. And so my coming into that unfamiliar neighborhood, at that certain hour, and for that very reason, made my scrape with death all the more suspicious.

The last—and with Cecil I made much of this—happened one evening when I was on my way home from a long night of drinking with the company and with Ben Jonson and friends at the Mermaid. The two men came out of the night bearing no torch or lamp, forcing me against the wall. One brushed against me roughly, demanding in a voice dripping with contempt that I should take care where I walked and asking me if I were blind or besotted that I could not see to put one foot before another.

"Not so much that I cannot steer a straight course upon a broad street," I said.

I'd been tipsy. I don't deny it. That evening the wine had flowed more freely than the talk; good company had made my companions generous, even lavish, treating the table time after time. Cold sober, I would have had sense not to provoke the pair, big men who wore the shabby garments of laborers, their eyes alive with mischief. Stinking of fish, both of them. Cod, eel, herring. Fishmongers, these big men in shabby clothes.

"Oh, you have a sharp tongue, sirrah, seeing that you are alone here in the street. My friend and I are two against your one."

This was said by the taller and broader, who glared at me, as though to give me leave to confirm the implications of his arithmetic. He added:

"Two 'gainst one be uneven, and yet we'll make no objection to it. Isn't that so, Clarence?"

This Clarence gave his fellow a baleful look, told him with good round curse to shut his trap and keep it so, then gave me a stinging blow upon my cheek with his hirsute hand.

I didn't see it coming, the blow. I reeled and, at once, felt cold steel against my throat.

"Take my purse. There's silver," I blurted, my eyes awash with tears of pain and humiliation.

"Clarence, take his silver, too," the other man said, "then this meeting shall be truly worth our while."

"By God's blessed son, we be no thieves or robbers," Clarence said, "but honest men and true. As for you, player, you'll shake no more scenes in this town. You—"

The threat, each word of which I recall now as though written upon my brow, was severed. Out of the corner of my eye I could see light at the end of the street. Distant voices, laughter, my friends, advancing upon me. Thank God, I thought.

"Clarence. It's the watch!" hissed the man who had not been named.

"Christ!" exploded Clarence, with no reverence in it.

"Now take you his purse, Clarence."

I felt the knife withdrawn. My purse was cut from my belt.

The two men fled.

Sick with fear and rage, I slid down the wall until I sat on the hard, damp cobbles, as limp as an eel, moaning like a puling child.

A robbed man loses pride as well as purse. That loss is worse, for money he may have again—it's but trash—but let him think upon the theft, the injury returns, the wound raw and open.

So was I found in such indignity by a half dozen revelers who returning to their own houses in the dark believed they had come upon another robbery of a poor gentleman unwisely traveling London streets alone.

———

NEXT NIGHT AT the Mermaid with my good friends I shared the tale of my disgrace. I first received much sympathy. Like stories of robbers came from Condell and Heminge both of whom swore they had lost purses, chains, hats, knives in nocturnal encounters with desperate men. "The city is full of thieves and ruffians," Condell said. "Those that are such by trade, and a hundred times that number who are dishonest by opportunity."

"Or need," another said, I don't remember who.

"That's virtually the entire city," Ben Jonson said with a very dry wit. The others laughed grimly.

I said, "True that the city has no dearth of the dishonest, yet these two weren't robbers."

"How so?" Ben said. "Did they not take your purse? Did they not threaten your life? Pray, what's a robber but he that takes by force or fear? You say the one called Clarence held a knife at your throat? You say neither carried torch nor lamp? Wherefore would they stalk the streets at night in such a fashion did they not intend to steal?"

"But that wasn't their intent, at least at first." I said. Ben mocked me. It was his damnable humor. I hated it. I said, "The unnamed man said it to Clarence. He let the name slip. Clarence protested he was no robber."

Ben said, "What was he, then—a constable with a grudge against nightwalkers? A preacher with a new method of engaging his flock during a dry sermon?"

More smiles and laughter then from the others, but not from me. This night, chastened by the last, I had drunk nothing but one cup of wine with a little sugar, just enough to wash down supper. I was sober as a judge. I knew I would be taunted by my friends. I knew I should take it in good grace or they would detect my seriousness and then torment me mercilessly, crying, "Robber, Will, robber," at the most unlikely moment to mock me. These were the games we played, we brethren of the theater. But I was in no mood for raillery, good-humored as it might be.

"You say you saw this robber before," Ben said. "Well and good, but how many scurvy faces have you looked upon since coming to town these dozen years? Faces in audiences who might have caught your eye and then away again, would-be actors at your heels like begging puppy dogs for some scrap, not to mention a hundred thousand nameless faces one might pass in the street, fix upon for a moment?"

What craggy-faced Ben said was true. And yet for all his logic, the more I thought, the more I was persuaded that robbery was not the cause. Clarence had been clear: He was no robber. He was a fishmonger, he and his companion. Their stench betrayed them. Now, the London fishmonger is a particular breed and not above a little larceny, but look to him to inflate the price of pickled herring, not to cut your throat. This finny tribe does not go in for random violence.

Besides the which, I could tell the picking of my purse had been an afterthought, perhaps to convince my rescuers they had interrupted nothing more than a midnight mugging. I knew it was something more and wondered if these felonious fishmongers were imposters after all, their stink as much disguise as their half-hidden faces.

Of this I was certain. Clarence knew who I was, not just an easy mark, but Will Shakespeare. He'd called me player, made the tired pun upon my most punnable name. Shakescene. Would Clarence have slit my throat if the carousing gentlemen had not cut his proceedings short, or was Clarence's intent merely to frighten me? But why?

Hirelings, then. Both making a little ready money by a display of muscle.

Ignoring Ben, whose massive shaggy head had turned elsewhere to explain a Latin phrase, I gave my reasoning to Burbage, who listened, then shrugged, regarding me with sad, doglike eyes.

"You make too much of this event, friend Will," Burbage said. "Your imagination doth overwhelm you, like a raging sea does the pebbled shore. Because you're well known in the city you think it must be your person for which you are assaulted and not your purse—as though you were above the rest of us, whose value is in our purse alone. Beware of pride, Will. It's worse than thieves in the night. It will steal your immortal soul."

I protested that I wasn't proud, insisted that I had grounds relevant. I told him of my dream. Told him how I was near run down, betrayed by a false message. He nodded sagely, stroking his beard in that thoughtful way he had. Then he worked through all the evidence again, with a lawyer's logic, a lawyer's love of the thicket of language.

Burbage wouldn't be persuaded. He offered to walk me home. "Remember, Will, how much wine you consumed. 'Tis wonder you made it home, crapulous as you were when you left our honored Maid. Are you sure this untoward incident happened at all? That it wasn't some drunkard's dream?" He laughed and poked me on the shoulder, roughhousing. "Perhaps you merely lost the purse in the gutter."

I protested that I had not been that drunk. Besides the which, I downed a deal of beef to temper the effect.

Burbage scoffed, then feigned belief and winked.

More laughter at this. Our conversation had not gone unheard.

Another of my companions said I was like an old woman who, hearing her cat come home for supper, thinks it an invading army and will not be persuaded otherwise, or like a child finding a man as tall as a horse and thinking he's a giant and not merely long in the shank.

Burbage reached forward and clapped me by the shoulders. "William, you furious scenemaster, you bilious bard, let it be. Don't torment a wart until it bleed. For all's well that end's so, as I think some one of this illustrious company has said. True, you're out a few pieces of silver. But consider your good fortune."

"What good fortune?" I said wearily.

"Why, the good fortune that you were robbed after your debauch and not before. Had you not drunk up the bulk of your money and lavished the rest on your friends, these dastardly fishmongers would have left the scene even richer. As is, they incurred danger of capture, and for what? I answer, hardly enough to keep them in ale and herring for a week. Your good fortune, too, that you're alive. Here in the Mermaid and not six feet under. There's always that to be grateful for."

I dug deep for a civil answer, then thanked Burbage for his companionship. Good faithful Burbage, how I loved the man, but he could wrench me where it hurt. I didn't want to walk the way home alone that night, though I didn't admit this to Burbage.

THERE'S ALWAYS A price to pay for honesty; a wise man assesses the cost before he speaks. But drunk or sober, I'm not always wise. I had become a figure of ridicule among them, and though the raillery was good-hearted it caused me to seethe beneath the outward civility I wore like a mask. I am, when all is said, a tolerable actor and can make faces for all seasons.

My misadventure was now ycleped "Master Shake-in-His-Boots's great robbery"—as the villainously witty Ben was referring to it a week later, taking a rare opportunity to make me who had so often made fun of others the butt of jokes. Tit for tat it was to be. Turn about. Fair play.

With Jovian laughter breaking his pocky face into a maze of wrinkles, Ben had proposed to make the incident a subject of comedy. "I shall set it in ancient Rome, like unto your own comedies, Will Shakesbard. Ipso facto the first hint to the general public that I have forged my plot out of honest history and not the plagiary of old books, as I think some authors of renown are given to. I forbear to mention names so as not to offend any of the present company."

Ben had made a mock bow, looking in every direction at the table except where I sat. Thunderous laughter all round. I laughed at the joke at my expense to save some little face. Ben, obviously delighted by having seized the center stage, raised his voice and continued in the same vein, his expression a satirical leer.

"Then, for antagonist, there shall be diabolical fishmongers of the town, and principally two, more evil than their stinking brethren. For protagonist I choose a poet of small skill who would be a playwright of less." He stopped to lick his thick, winy lips. "Lacking advancement in his art, he then concocts the most improbable tale to glorify himself and come to the attention of the law and the court, to earn the undeserved sympathy of his friends, and doubtless, too, to win the sympathetic hearts of the women of his life, of whom I hear there are not a few."

There was more laughter at this, and nods toward me; two or three removed their hats out of respect for my vaunted prickman-ship, a dubious celebrity I did not deserve.

Ben's voice droned on, full of himself. "Not to mention to advance himself among his fellows as one who has provoked the enigmatic malice of the fishmongers of the city. A brainless race if there ever was one."

Ben's stepfather had laid bricks. I said this to them. Who was he to judge so harshly men who worked with their hands? But it was Ben who had the stage, not I. I was the target of his raillery, not the object of attention.

"And yours sold cheap gloves and went bankrupt," Ben returned sharply, reminding all of my own origins and the family disgrace. So I'd struck a vein. He continued. "Granted, these are a step or twain above fishmonger, whom by your improbable tale you evidently despise. But I cry you mercy, that you yourself do not shake your spear against those below you in station—you who have a new house in the country, with ten fireplaces and two gar-dens and two barns, and, if rumor doesn't lie, have a coat of arms, whereupon, I trow, two fishmongers rampant will dodge a hail of spears."

It would be a month before the mention of fishmongers and robbers was replaced by another risible theme and Ben's mordant wit found another victim. I decided I would not run that gamut of ridicule again. I made no more mention of the robbery, excluded my old friends from my confidence, and found myself quite alone in my melancholy.

Now paul's big-throated bells sang in the cold night. From somewhere near, a watchman's hoarse cry confirmed the hour. All's well, said the voice. Cold, bleak, December morning.

I knew I would sleep no more. I couldn't rid myself of thoughts of my conversation with Cecil. I supplied myself with a hundred different lines, ways I might have convinced. Had I only put my case this way rather than that. Oh, the foolishness of trying to change what *was,* when what *is* lies before us as the only guarantor of what will be.

Thought was fruitless. I supposed Cecil supposed me a madman, as conflicted and addled as my Prince Hamlet, and perhaps as dangerous to the state. I was convinced Cecil wanted to be rid of me, and now I feared for my position at court as well as for my life.

I found an old refuge, tried and true. Scorning sleeplessness and dragging my blanket with me for a shawl, I lighted a candle, sat at my writing table, and spread before me the oft-palmed sheets on which *Measure for Measure* had been drafted. I baptized my best goose quill in good black ink. After a few moments to find my bookmark, I read.

I replaced one word with another, struck out a line here, amended a phrase there. That's what writing is, devoid of its *mysterium*—a mechanical operation, a multitude of decisions.

My pen scratched. Silence else. My eyes strained in the flickering light. My work, my life, my passion. I saw myself as another might see me who, passing by, looked in the window to glimpse this paunchy, balding middle-aged clerk at his labor. Solitary, preoccupied—a figure provoking as much pity and scorn as admiration for his dubious art.

I stopped thinking about my interview with Cecil. Stopped thinking about the evil angel of my sonnets. Stopped thinking about myself. The play was the thing. There was nothing else.

Six

THE PLAY'S THE thing whereby my moody Danish prince proved his wicked uncle's perfidy.

For me *Measure* was no *Hamlet,* but yet serviceable as a distraction, or the hope thereof. Daily I tinkered with the playbook, adding and subtracting. The mundane mathematics of authorship. Its very title took on new meaning to me. *Measure for Measure.* A title not brilliant but good enough. Meaning not tit for tat, as before my old lover's death, but line upon line, precept upon precept. Thus the stolid pace of my education in my own troubles. I was like a desperate ship captain who, his vessel fixed upon a rock, orders his crew to the pumps, when it's only time he buys and not salvation, an illusion, a pathetic dream.

At night it was not so easy to forget.

Then Cecil summoned me again—to the imposing house on the Strand, but to a different chamber, a small, intimate room as bare as a monk's cell. Cecil looked even older and more beaten than before, as though the burden of the state were crushing him. Outside a dismal rain pelted the desolate gardens.

He said, "I've considered your case, Master Shakespeare. Considered the issue as both academical and practical."

He studied my response to this distinction, which I could make nothing of. I forced a smile. Cecil continued, "*Academical*

because we must draw a fine line between the vagaries of melancholy and real menace. Having suffered black melancholy myself,
I well understand how its baleful influence could reshape the look
of things. *Practical* because if it is menace and not melancholy,
what shall be done to protect you?"

He went on in this way in a kind of wandering search for a
point, pacing the room, his hands behind his back, his eyes down
on the Turkey carpet as though the answer to all were there in its
intricate weave. I tried to be attentive, but it was difficult. He
had conversed with the king, he said. Had told him of my fears
after all.

"And the king was—?"

"Disposed to take your warnings seriously," Cecil said. "His
Majesty is nothing if not judicious. As for your prophetic dreams
and these most strange coincidences, well, His Majesty's predilec-
tion for the supernatural is well known."

For my part I had mixed feelings about the king, which I here
reveal in full trust that by the time these words are read several
successors at least will have worn the crown and old criticism will
not seem treason.

On the one hand I was grateful. My star had risen under his
reign. The King's Men were now preeminent as players in the city.
We were well funded, protected, sought after, envied. The Globe
was the best theater in England, perhaps the best in the whole
world.

On the other hand, I thought the little Scot a most unseemly
monarch. In appearance he was most unkingly—corpulent yet
spindly-legged as though at any moment he would topple over.
Upon his chin were a half dozen gray whiskers aspiring to be a
beard. His hair was unruly and shaggy, nothing masculine in it.
His tongue appeared too large for his mouth, protruded, made
him look a fool. In sum, His Royal Majesty looked about as regal
as an ape in a satin doublet.

Not that Cecil himself, prematurely gray and hunchbacked,
delighted the eye. Yet Cecil was well read in science and in art,

good at conversation, a pleasant companion over drinks, or so I'd heard, for he had never drunk with me. The king was a pedantic bore with a stupid wife and a penchant for theological controversy that sat oddly with the crassness of his humor and his delight in the hunt. I'd heard he took joy in plunging his hands into the bloody entrails of a stag he'd killed.

Then there was his perverse fondness for handsome young men, idle gossip I assumed was true.

"It was the king who first brought you in," Cecil said, forcing me to pay attention again.

"Brought me in?"

"To the conversation. It was in his bedchamber. Your name was practically the first thing out of his mouth."

What the king had said, Cecil did not deliver right away. First, the king's secretary must recount the circumstances of his interview, drawing me a picture, painting a scene as though the whole thing were to be staged at the Globe sometime soon, furnished with characters. I listened and imagined:

It is nine o'clock of the morning. The king lounges in his silk sleeping garments, his hair a crow's nest, doubtless, for he's no neat man by nature. Saliva trickles from the corner of his mouth, and he's hungover from the previous night's banquet, where he had presided at a feast more like a tavern debauch than a state dinner.

So Cecil describes it. He pauses for effect, and I understand he wants to know if I appreciate the enormity of this. He continues:

The bed curtains are unparted. Five well-appointed, sober-faced servants attend: One bears the king's breakfast upon a silver platter; one stands ready to wipe the monarchical bum, should it need that service, and remove the reeking chamber pot. Two other straight-faced servants are prepared to help the king of England and Scotland truss up should he deign to dignify the day by getting out of bed before ten o'clock.

The fifth man is a supernumerary in the attendance business. He is a young Scot with a clear eye, a razored chin, and a finely molded chest, firm-thighed and calved. Hardly more than a boy, this person is to bear messages should there be any to bear; to walk the king's hounds, who sprawl, doze, and scratch by turns upon the velvet bedcovers, as idle as their master; to laugh at the king's jokes, and perhaps delight His Majesty's eyes should they turn in his direction.

Cecil knows they will.

All this he describes. I record it as I heard it.

So then, imagine Master Secretary seated in a rigid, high-backed chair designed to discomfit its occupant—by royal invitation, for the king is often informal in such matters. His royal predecessor might have kept the principal secretary kneeling at bedside on an imperious whim—within arm's reach of the royal bed, a four-poster of such heroic dimensions that Henry the eighth of that name could have reveled there with all of his wives at the same time.

"And we shall have Master Shagsbear's play?" says the king.

"We shall, sire. I've spoken to the man not three days ago. He affirms the players to be ready and willing."

"When next you see the man Shagsbear, tell him we are pleased. Tell him we hope to be entertained," the king says.

James's Scots brogue is thick as glue. Cecil sometimes feigns a bad ear so as not to offend his master when the king speaks quickly and Cecil cannot follow, cocking his head as he remembered his father, the great Lord Burghley, had done when in his sixties and his hearing had truly failed.

The king hates to repeat himself. This I surmise myself, not from Cecil's report, for what monarch has the patience to feel otherwise? The king seems at times to have equal difficulty understanding his English courtiers and servants. James had already offered Cecil a remedy to clear his ears. Cecil had politicly lied and sworn he had used it, but although he was a loyal servant he was not about to stick goat's dung in his ears to gratify a king's belief that he possessed all wisdom.

"Tell Shagsbear, too, that we hope there is naught that might give offense in it, this play. Although the people delight in sword-flashing and thunderings, they need models of virtue, not spurs to rebellion."

"The play is in the works, Majesty," says Cecil, who is aware James is fearful of the multitude and always alert for rebellion. "Master Shakespeare promises to finish it by the new year."

Cecil doesn't say so, yet I trust he's told the king my plot. How the play is politicly set in Vienna, not in England, where danger always lurks. Vienna. What Englishman cares what happens there? It's the story of a duke of that land who must journey unto Poland, a land even more remote from England's interest. The duke leaves a zealous deputy in his place, who proceeds to enact strict laws against the immoralities of the town.

Cecil says, "I told the king some players take liberties. They think it nothing to show an anointed king deposed or to have him disgraced by some scurrilous conduct unbecoming a king. Not Master Shakespeare. I said he should find nothing to displease. Only satisfaction and delight. Moral instruction. Language pure and undefiled."

I smiled despite myself at this flattery. "How did the king take these assurances?" I asked.

"Well," said Cecil. "He took them well. I said the play will show a mighty prince, such as himself, naturally aloof from the multitude, exacting justice with sternness and mercy."

"Will it?" the king said, drooling, I suppose, but looking pleased with himself and doubtless with me. "I would be just and merciful, too."

I remembered it did not appear so when, coming first to England, James condemned at Newark-on-Trent a snatchpurse out of hand, seeing him hanged there and then, but spared all those in prison, save those guilty of murder, treason, or papistry. Where was the king's justice then? A man hanged without a trial? Did the new king think he could so readily ignore the sanctities of England's law? If a man can be hanged before he is tried, why can he not be tried before he hath offended?

The witty Sir John Harington—he that was the old queen's godson—had said that. Ben Jonson heard him say it.

"The king would have you come to court, Master Shakespeare. Perform the play there. That and others," Cecil said.

"I would be honored. My whole company would be so," I said.

"I hope before, however, that this personal matter you spoke of will be resolved. I would not have your fears taint the performance."

"No, Your Honor," I said promptly with feigned resolve, for like my Prince Hamlet I knew what I must do, yet I was hesitant and uncertain. I looked at Cecil. The king's secretary seemed worried, although whether it was for me and my strange case or for his own position as endorser of my virtues it was hard to tell. I knew then that while alone in my peculiar fear, I was not alone more generally. All men feared. This great little man before me, the second most powerful man in England; the king himself, preoccupied with court intrigue and plots, haunted by demons. Then myself. The question was not if a man feared; that he did was as certain as life or thought. *What* he feared was the thing.

"The king would speak to you about the play. Since it deals with a prince who would enact strict laws, he wants to make a few points."

"Points?" I said.

"In regard to the virtuous model of kings. Surely you would not mind some counsel with another author."

"I would be most honored," I said, dreading the event.

The king was, in very truth, an author. He'd written a book about witchcraft. I hadn't read it, didn't intend to, but Ben Jonson had perused it and granted it wasn't bad, given the kind of thing it was, slapdash scholarship and blatant self-congratulation. Those were Ben's words, not mine.

Cecil said, "Then let it be tomorrow, unless this damnable rain should stop. If it is sunny, I shall go hunt instead."

I thanked him for his good words with the king, prayed secretly for sun, and at his signal rose to take my leave. He brushed my elbow, only for a moment, looking up at me, since I was the taller, with his fine, clear gaze.

"Take care, Master Shakespeare. Since the king believes your fears, I can do no less. Still, I offer you the same counsel as before.

Save yourself. God gave you such a wit that were you to write a thousand plays there would be wit left over. Use your wit, sir, your wit."

IT WAS NIGHT when I was done with Cecil—or he with me. I thought about what he'd said as I walked homeward, steeling myself against the cold and rain.

Cecil had flattered me to have me gone, and yet there was truth in what he'd said. If there was a common theme to my plays it was intrigue, deception, false seeming, the counterfeit smile, the feigned good wish. Even where there was no murder there was deceit. It mattered not whether the play was comedy or tragedy, historical or pastoral. What you will, there was mischief in it. Was not this then familiar ground to me? Was not I a forester in this thicket?

I knew I must replace vacillating Hamlet with doughty Fortinbras and off to the wars with grim resolve. Besides, the play was done; the actors ready. I could no longer escape in my writing.

What remained was to avert my own tragedy.

Seven

I WOKE NEXT day to the end of cold and teasing rain, wherein my resolve to confront my enemy should bear an unseasonable fruit. The sun shone; a warm wind advanced against London, conveying the city's smoke and rancid breath toward France. Good riddance. Cecil would keep the king company at hunt after all. No audience for me, then, with His Majesty. I was greatly relieved.

Madame Mountjoy, the kind of woman who measures health by appetite and would cure the world with a steaming, aromatic chowder, was glad to see me give her generous breakfast its due. I ate ravenously, was pleasant in my talk, smiled much, and flirted with their daughter Mary, a pretty young wench soon to be married. The verdict of these happy householders was that I was recovered, although none said from what. My gloomy seclusion had not gone unmarked.

Yet my resolve had to find a means. I wanted to be free from danger, liberated from a perilous ignorance, but how? I had not seen my fellow actors for a week or more, and since the king's command was news I decided to assemble the company, who had in my absence whiled away their time as they pleased.

A willing boy lingering about my house conveyed my summons to the company while I waited an hour or more in my chamber above meditating my former lover's death. Then to the Globe, still meditating as I walked, for I am a man who can sometimes think better on his feet than on his bum. Looking back, it's strange that I feared no danger from assault, despite my dreams of being run down by carts and their maniacal drivers, despite my waking encounter with the dubious fishmongers. Lost in thought, I walked without interruption except to acknowledge an occasional greeting, for although I was not so well known in the city as to have my comings and goings generally remarked upon by the citizenry, occasionally an actor out of work, a novice playwright, or a woman of my acquaintance would wish me good morning or good day or, in the case of the actors, look for work or beg me to lend them money. Which sometimes I did in a fit of Christian charity, but not often.

That morning the whole world seemed to recognize me and honor me with their attentions. Perhaps it was the weather that had put the city in a better frame of mind. Or the spreading rumor that the plague had subsided. Or heaven's blessing. For with such a cloud of witnesses how could I be victim of my enemy's assault?

One—a noxious lawyer named Fanshawe with whom I had had some unhappy dealings—stopped to rail at me about his long suit for payment, which I had ignored deliberately for his incompetence's sake. I endured this fellow's insolent protestations and threats for a minute or so before I told him where he might stuff his briefs and quiddities, but during this rancorous exchange looked behind whence I had come.

There, out of the corner of my eye, I saw a figure dart. It happened in a wink, as fairies are glimpsed by foolish maids when they fall asleep and wake and think they see something staring between the leaves, though it be nothing at all.

But this was not that, no vision. He was there. It was as though this person followed me and feared I'd detect his presence. He darted, as I said, but so much that I did not mark him for one I knew, not well, surely, but certainly. It was the very boy I'd paid to summon my actors.

It crossed my mind that he followed so I might pay him more. I had given him a penny or two, a generous enough offering, but somehow I knew that was not his reason.

I proceeded on my way, crossed the bridge into Southwark, and then deliberately took a different route than my customary, winding up and down narrow streets, glancing back upon a mere whim, and noticing that he followed still, stealthily.

I turned into a fetid alley and waited in the shadows of St. Savior's Church, hard by the boneyard. Presently this same boy came and as he turned out I seized him by the collar and pulled him toward me so we were face to face, although he was the shorter of us.

He looked at first amazed and then afraid, trembling and sickly pale. I demanded to know why he followed me, and then before he could get word out I denounced him as a thief and cutpurse, threatened him with arrest, and offered him the gloomy prospect of a public hanging for his intended crime.

He looked around him desperately as though to call for help, but then his shoulders slumped, he sighed woefully, and tears filled eyes that were large and almond-green. Again I demanded that he tell me why he followed.

I felt him trembling in my hands and started to pity him. He was not above twelve or thirteen, I judged, thin as a stick, with tousled yellow hair beneath his filthy cap, and complexion fair as any girl's.

"What's your name, boy?" I said.

"Edward Goode," he answered.

Now it was my turn to be amazed. Unless there were two boys of that name, before me stood the baker's apprentice whose master said he perished in the flames.

"If you're Edward Goode, then you're dead," I said.

A puzzled expression crossed his face, then he said, "So thinks my master. When the fire started and consumed the house, I watched, then ran away. I hoped he'd reckon I'd died, for my master's cruel. Besides, I wanted another life."

"What's that to do with me?" I said.

"I want to be an actor," he said, looking up at me hopefully.

I laughed despite myself. So that was it. This wretched under-fed lad in dirty smock was no robber or agent of my enemy but just another would-be player, enchanted by the stage and of its cost as ignorant as a sheep.

"I must go," I said. "I'm late—for a rehearsal. I have no time for this."

"I beseech you, Master Shakespeare—"

"Be off!" I said.

He didn't move. So I did. I stalked out of the alley and back into the street, as though our brief encounter had never happened. I hadn't walked a hundred paces but I heard him scrambling up behind me. Then a voice not his. A woman's voice, soft and sweet in its pleadings, and the words familiar to me, for who but I had written them? I stopped and turned. He completed the speech. Ophelia. Her pathetic account to her father, old Polonius. Act two, scene two. I forget the line numbers, but this wretched boy had the speech most competently.

"How came you by *that*?" I asked.

"At the theater, sir."

"You have a most prodigious memory."

"I know many parts by heart, Master Shakespeare. You can put me to the test and see that it's so."

His voice dripped honey, the perfect timbre of womanhood, and I was half in love with him already for that voice, for it's more than youth and beardlessness that fits a boy to play a woman's part. Not every twittering pipe will sing; only such that is neither thin nor shrill, forced nor false, but mellifluous, expansive, and pliant as a tender branch.

Yet I was resolute. I snarled and grimaced, motioning him away, threatening.

But he would not be cowed. He plucked me by the sleeve and said in his own voice, "I saw the fire, Master Shakespeare. I saw him who set it."

"You saw what?"

"The fire, sir. I was there, a passerby. My master had sent me on an errand after dark, to bear some new loaves to a gentleman's house. I had no lamp, for I knew the street well enough, as well as a blind man. On my way home, I saw the man who came at the dead woman's door—she whom my master called the Whore of Babylon."

"It was I who was at her door. I who almost died with her."

"I know, sir, I watched. But it was not just you I saw, but he who made the fire. I saw him creep to the door as stealthily as one who filches sheets or chickens. He did not move for a long time. Then I saw the upstairs window alight. I waited longer, and he— this man, I mean to say—pulled something from beneath his cloak. There was a flash of flame and then he tossed whatever he had through the window so it broke. He fled when the house took fire, but it was he that caused it."

"How do you know it was a man?" I asked.

"I saw his face, sir."

"In so dark a night? You have an owl's eye as well as so sweet a voice."

"His face was all lighted—by the fire."

"Describe him."

"By your leave, sir, he was betwixt my years and yours."

"Marry, that's half the world or more. Had he a beard? Scars? A villainous look? A nose of unusual properties, or one good eye?"

"A beard, I think."

"What manner?"

"Neither long nor short."

"Dark, was it?"

"I can't remember."

I cursed, more out of frustration than anger.

"As for the rest of him, he seemed not taller than your average man, nor rounder. He had all his parts, but I would know him again if I saw him."

"Would you?" I said.

"I swear it, by God I do."

"Be careful what you swear and by what powers, for angels watch us," I said.

I looked him over again. Washed and better clothed, he'd make a pretty maid. Besides, I believed his words. He'd seen the man; his story had the ring of truth. The opinion of his former neighbors was that the fire had started by some accident. Edward Goode knew what only I had known before, that the fire was arson.

He renewed his plea. "Let me be one of your company, Master Shakespeare."

I looked him up and down again, as if I were considering his petition seriously for the first time, although the truth was that I had already decided what I was to do with him.

"Come," I said. "We'll clean you up, feed you, then test your mettle as an actor and as a witness. If your promise in either fails not, I'll find a part for you to play."

Eight

COME TO THE Globe, I found my companions assembled there and all in a merry mood to be together again, or so they claimed. Talking and laughing like schoolboys, some expressed amazement at my most strange absence and urged me to tell the cause. Dick Burbage appraised me like a tailor measuring me for a new suit and said my complexion looked pocky and wan, as though I were recovering from some pestilence. When he said that, others in the company regarded him sternly, and one, Robert Armin I think it was, chided him for uttering the thought, for some think the very word "plague" to contain within its dreadful monosyllable the cause of this distemper.

To this invasion of my privacy I mumbled vague answers to which my friends gave little note, much to my relief. I had no desire to heighten their curiosity or make myself further butt of their slurs and jests.

I then indulged in a brief contest of wit with Burbage, from which, God curse me if I lie, I came off winner. Vindicated on that score at least, I told them about the king's command performance of plays saying it would be round Christmastide or thereafter, upon which all applauded. There was more joking and laughing and exchanging of gossip. This went on for a good half of an hour or more before we settled down and went to work.

All this while Edward Goode kept to a corner, perhaps doubting our bargain. He did not understand how important it was to me that I find out who this arsonist was. He probably thought me still some whoremaster come to pay a call to his queen of the night. I had no reason to disabuse him of this—at least for now. But what better way to keep my chief and only witness within my grip than by making him one of my company? Besides, as I have already said, the boy had talent.

I beckoned him from his hiding place. He came all abashed, like a young maid called from her chimney corner to meet the man her parents would have her marry.

"Gentlemen, meet young Edward Goode, who would be an actor."

My friends responded amicably. Some shouted their approval; some snickered, while others cast lascivious looks as though they would strip the boy naked. It was how they always were with newcomers, and especially boys—half suspicious that the boy would supplant them, half pleased that someone wanted membership with us. For we were one of many companies of actors, yet none of us but knew we were the best.

"We'll put him to the test," I said. "Let him play Mariana, she who is betrothed to Angelo."

I passed Edward the playbook, pointed out a scene, and told him he had a half hour, no more, to learn two dozen lines. He didn't flinch but looked at me with such pathetic gratitude my heart did quite melt within me, and I remembered when I, like him, would have given an arm or leg to mount the trestled stage and grow to be the cynosure of every eye.

I left him to his study, he found a seat within the lower gallery, and I watched Burbage play Angelo to another boy actor's Isabella; listened, too, for I was ever alert for the missed word, the slurred syllable that ruined the meter. I hadn't penned my words that they should be clipped, slurred, or snubbed but that each should be given its full value and strength in the solemn march of the line.

The play, *Measure for Measure,* had an improbable plot I'd

filched from the Italian Cinthio and George Whetstone's silly play. From Whetstone I had the bawdy stuff that pleased the crowd. By stuff I mean the pimps, whores, and underbelly of the city. These I politicly shipped far from England, fashioning the play thereby into a better article, more abundant in mercy, more optimistic in its conclusion. *Prince Hamlet* it was not, nor *Caesar*. It offered no such mighty protagonists and was more comic than tragic. Yet it pleased my humor, and perhaps fed it. And as Cecil had discerned, a curious reader might have found its circumstances a flattery of the king. If so the king believed, it mattered not to me. I was the king's good servant now, a member of the royal household. He could believe what he wished.

Angelo's hypocritical pronouncements now grated in my ears. Yet who but I had made this whited sepulcher, writ his every word? And so it served me right. I watched the stage, the actors, not wanting them to think me inattentive to their labors, but my mind withdrew like a treacherous servant making off with the family silver. I thought of what Edward had witnessed, the face he'd seen, the face I was confident he would remember were he to see it again.

I sat overwhelmed, hearing nothing. I had gone deaf to words, words that only seemed to cushion me against some horrible and disguised truth. I was in a stupor of thought, overwhelmed with grief and the more angered at myself for weakening in my resolve.

Then I shook myself and thought: Must I be prisoner to these emotions? Could I not apply some logic to my case? Must I always play Hamlet and never decisive Fortinbras, who might have in some other life of mine been hero of my play?

I remembered the Stratford grammar school, where as a boy I learned my Latin and my Greek—such as it was—under Master John Cotton's tutelage and first delighted in the tales of Rome and Greece, saw in mind's eye Troy's mighty walls and Helen's beauty and heard Priam's sorry tale. There I learned not just to construct a phrase but to understand the rules of cool, dispassionate reason—how it built upon itself like a worthy mason laying brick. To my dilemma, could there not be an effectual antidote in reason's cold stare?

And so I set my feelings aside. I posed a premise: Someone wished me dead, burned alive along with her I had loved so long ago. I granted the same: Would there not be a motive for such a wish? Summon up, Will Shakespeare, the names of your enemies. Call that long roll of blackened hearts.

In all modesty I must declare the list was short. I was no courtier or politician who makes an enemy for every friend, a bully who in his cups must leave someone bloody on the floor. Rather, I was an actor, a maker of plays, and, in my salad days, no mean poet. But then and now I had rivals. Need I name them? Stolid Ben Jonson, George Chapman, poor Kit Marlowe who was dead. It was a noble company yelping at my heels. Nor could I forget the acting companies that might have earned the royal patronage had I and my men not snatched the honor first.

I thought of wretched actors whom I'd sent packing, depriving them of livelihood. I thought of citizens whom I had disappointed when they came to the theater to laugh and left in tears, their coins unreturned. I thought of constables and courtiers, lawyers and whores, captains and hypocritical priests; I had subjected a multitude to scorn and ridicule. Did not one among them harbor a grudge of such magnitude that murder was its only relief?

Weighty reasons to murder me, these petty offenses? Not in the eyes of heaven. Nor in my own feeble sight. And yet every day you heard the stories. A throat cut over a bar bill (think of poor Kit Marlowe again). Bullets exchanged between brothers. Fathers killing sons with stones, sons murdering fathers in their beds. What news here?

Good friend, ask not why there is murder in the world, but why there is not more, human nature being what it is. The crime may be unnatural. It is not unusual.

And so the rest of the morning I looked into my past—and into hers, thinking there might be convergence there that would answer the mystery *who* and lead to *why*.

OUR REHEARSING ENDED upon the hour I set. I watched young Edward do the scene I gave him, and he did wondrous well, as though he had pronounced the words a thousand times before and had so instilled into his breast poor Mariana's woes that he was *she* in truth. All the company applauded him, coming forth to shake his hand and slap his back in generous fellowship— even the other boys, whose admiration for his excellent voice trumped their fear that he might take their place.

Anon my company claimed pressing business, although do not ask what business pressed them save drinking and wenching, for we were a rowdy crew—even the wived among us: no sober clerics or diligent tradesmen to whom duty was the voice of God, but lovers of wit and words, purveyors of pleasure, and, if the truth be known, subtle subversives of the state. Some of us had good heads for business and kept our ship on even keel, but for the most we were vagabonds, still as suspect to the respectable as thieves and Gypsies.

I said farewell to them all, appointing first the next date we should meet. Then all left, except for Edward, whom I bade stay.

"Now I must fit you out in woman's weeds," I said.

Edward smiled and looked again at me with unbelieving gratitude.

"Come," I said. "I'll show you a part of our Globe you've never seen."

We mounted stairs and came to our storage, which was built above the upper stage and was repository for every prop and costume.

There I unlocked the door, taking the key from its hiding place beneath a plank. The door agape, there appeared a long room so filled with garments of every sort and quality, bucklers, swords, shields, and, in sum, stuff of such divers uses that it was only with some difficulty that both of us found place to stand.

I remember saying to the boy, "This is not half of our gear, lad. We players become heirs of dead lords and ladies of the kingdom who enjoy a lingering existence on our stage, wraiths of their former selves. Were it asked of me, I could, like God, cover the nakedness of the House of Lords, and yes, the Commons, too, with these proud costumes, and arm a company with sword and shield."

Great God, how the urge to brag comes upon a man, like a sudden need to void the bowels. It matters little where he is or with whom or about what he's thinking. He's made himself an ass and fool before he knows it.

So there I stood, before this wide-eyed lad, prattling on about our wealth of good cloth, not the shabby, moth-eaten dress players were sometimes accused of bearing upon their backs for their impoverished state, but fine wool and some silk, a wealth of color and texture, smelling somewhat of mold, it was true, but nonetheless an impressive store.

Upon the wall, shelves had been built, and thereupon were in wild profusion dozens of hats of various shapes and crowns of kings and dukes, all bejeweled and dazzling as though the stones were real, not paste. Yet another shelf offered a brave display of ladies' headdresses, and from the ceiling hung a brace of shields and weaponry burnished and ready for battle.

I pushed aside the heavy garments, making a path through doublet and cloak, Edward following like a faithful dog, expressing his wonder at the great store.

It was then I smelled something beneath the damp odor of wet wool and lingering sweat of many bodies. Something burnt, it was. Not a live fire but old, reduced to ash.

Like a desperate parent concerned for his child's safety, I forged ahead through the forest of clothes and found presently what I feared.

It was—or had been, for there was but a charred remnant left—one sable cloak among the lot. Like a penitent I knelt upon the wooden floor and picked through the remains. The fire was old, the ashes cold. The damage had been done before. When? Perhaps days earlier.

I knew the cloak.

It was the one the actors wore when they would go invisible, whereby our audience knew the wearer was not to be seen at all, a pure spirit of the air. I myself had worn it last in *Hamlet,* when as his poor father's ghost, in solemn, sepulchral tones, I bade my son avenge my foul and most unnatural murder.

The part of the cloth that covered the wearer's heart was singed black around a gaping hole, and I knew he who had ignited the fire had sacrificed the innocent cloth upon the altar of his hatred of him who wore it.

I cradled the violated garment in my arms as though it were my dead son, struggled to hold my tears, and then gave in to grief in great sobs. I wept not for the cloak, not even for my son—although what father has not an endless store of tears for such a loss—but for my pitiful, cowardly self, who could so easily be brought to confusion and helplessness by obscure enmity.

Behind me, Edward Goode said nothing but stood silent witness to my grief, which I am sure was quite beyond him, for the wardrobe still had cloaks aplenty. He did not know what cloak it was, how it was used, and what it might mean to me who wore it last and in that most particular part, a murdered father fated to have a murdered son.

After a while I dried my tears and explained to Edward how it stood with me, a father who had lost a son, an actor whose cloak of invisibility had been violated. He shed a tear, I thought, on my behalf. I placed the burned remnant where I found it.

I pondered how this desecration had been done. The door had been fast shut, and few in the company beside myself—Burbage, three or four others, all beyond suspicion—knew where the key was hid. The outer walls of the theater rose high and smooth. A fly could hardly mount them. Casements there were, but petty apertures for light and ventilation only, not for entrance or egress. How could the arsonist have entered? And why?

To prove he could?

To show nothing mine was safe?

To rub my son's death in my face and thereby forecast my own fiery fate?

I told Edward to say nothing of what we'd found; he so swore.

Among the plenty, I found a gown for him to wear, a pretty thing with flowing purple satin sleeves and a bodice cut deliciously to show the white of throat and breast. He put it on; a perfect fit. Padded and wigged, he looked so every inch a maid my heart was quite deceived.

I left the relic where I found it. I wanted whoever struck the match to think, should he be watching when I went out, that I never found the cloak at all, never contemplated the meaning of its despoilment. I wanted him to think the gesture had made no sense at all, had been a waste of time.

God knows the truth was otherwise.

Nine

Poor edward had not a farthing to his name. He had slept in the streets since escaping his master, living on rats' tails and ditch water and sometimes begging. I took him home with me, introduced him to Madame Mountjoy as the newest member of our troupe, and saw that he was given a place in the kitchen corner where it was warm and dry and where he almost swooned at the smell of my landlady's cuisine, though it was French rather than plain honest English fare.

Next day, I bade him keep me company as I strolled about the city looking for the denizens of my world, the actors and the playwrights. I visited a dozen taverns where I knew they were wont to gather. I had it in my mind that Edward might fix upon the face he remembered, but although he must have viewed a thousand, not one stirred his recollection.

I told no one beside Edward of my purpose in this sudden burst of socializing but acted as if we were boon companions, which caused many to suppose I intended him for my catamite, whereby I suffered more than one lascivious glance from those among the actors of that persuasion.

By late afternoon I was half drunk from enduring so many toasts to my health and happiness, and my young companion was footsore and weary. We returned home.

I had given thought to moving to new lodgings. After all, I had many friends in London who would put me up, feed me well, and let no one know where I was. But then I thought: What good would it do to move elsewhere? I would only be dogged to my new abode, wherever it might be. The devil who stalked me would find me out. Besides, I would miss the Mountjoys' happy household with its twitter of French—a language of which I knew but a modicum, yet the sound thereof delighted me—and boisterous laughter and the Mountjoys' pretty young daughter.

Still when it came time for sleep I made sure my chamber door was bolted, the windows fastened. I put my sword unsheathed beneath my pillow but felt its cold steel with little comfort.

That night I was about to undress for bed when a knock came at my door. I asked who it was and heard the tire-maker's familiar voice.

"My apologies for awakening you, Master Shakespierre," Mountjoy said, his English dripping with Gallic undertones. "But I forgot to give you a message. It arrived while you were gone."

Mountjoy was a round, smiling man of years a half dozen shy my own, with a shock of sable hair graying at the ears. He handed me a paper, folded several times over and sealed. Upon the front my name was scrawled. I recognized the hand but could not believe it true.

"I pray your news is good," Mountjoy said. "Maybe from your wife in Stratford."

Mountjoy liked to speak of my wife. It was his way, I think, of reminding me that his nubile daughter was not for me. I thought the tire-maker's faith in my conjugal bond too simple. I was too much man not to covet the wench, who was fair and sweet, yet I was happy enough to endorse the courtship of Stephen Belott, Mountjoy's former apprentice.

Mountjoy waited, curious. I gave his snooping no satisfaction but tucked the missive in my pocket, thanked him, and said good night with such finality he took my meaning well. He nodded, mumbling something beneath his breath. I shut the door.

When I could no longer hear his steps, I took the message to my bed, where I read by candlelight. I sweat with dread, for I recognized the handwriting—the handwriting of a woman whose lifeless body I had seen on the cobbles. The dark woman of my passion, my betrayal, and my lust.

I slit the seal of the folded parchment with my dagger and read.

Th' expense of spirit in a waste of shame
Is lust in action, and till action, lust
Is perjur'd, murderous, bloody, full of blame.
Savage, extreme, rude, cruel, not to trust.

There were but the first four lines writ. I supplied the rest. It was an indictment. But then there was more:

The sins of the fathers shall be visited upon the children.

I read the message again, my heart beating.

No ghost writ this, although I knew I was meant so to think by the skillful forger of the letter. It showed that he who stalked me had known her well, well enough to imitate her hand. He knew, too, where I lodged, knew my private griefs, what haunted my dreams, doubtless what I had breakfasted upon.

But then I felt a strange relief. For here at last was evidence, hard and beyond denial, of malice aimed at me. Something I could show to Cecil and dispel his doubts if he had them still and thought me mad.

Although it was now almost the middle of the night, I ran downstairs, hoping to find Mountjoy still awake. I was not disappointed. He sat by his fire and rose at once when I entered.

"This letter, Master Mountjoy—"

"Bad news, as I feared," Mountjoy said, his heavy face already assuming an expression of infinite sympathy.

I had decided to lie, for I owed my landlord no accounting. I said, "No bad news, good rather. But the letter isn't signed, and I would know who delivered it."

"A boy, sir."

"What manner of boy?"

Mountjoy snorted with laughter. "A boy as all boys are. Two-legged and saucy, even like this one you brought home."

"And his speech?" I said. "Was there anything about his speech?"

Mountjoy shrugged. "He said two or three words and not a syllable more. 'This is for Master Shakespierre,' he said. He spoke low, a whisper. I had to listen hard to understand him. 'Pray give it to him when he returns, the boy said.'"

"'When he returns,'" I said. "Then he knew I was not at home?"

"*Oui*," he said. "You give it to him when he returns. So he said. I have a very good memory, Master Shakespierre. There can be no mistake."

At that moment, Madame Mountjoy entered. She asked when her husband would come to bed.

"Peace," Mountjoy said curtly. "I'll come when I will and not before."

My landlord's wife received this rancorous reply in kind and railed in French, I know not what, but it was sufficient to make her husband bellow. Then they both exchanged more words in that same language, until my ears ached with the din of their combat.

This woman of whom I speak—this Madame Mountjoy—was a frowzy wench with a razor tongue and abrupt manner. She had a drooping eye, a rough complexion, and a swollen nether lip to make one want to cry for pity. Yet for all these deficiencies of nature, she had a lover, one Henry Wood, a mercer of the city. That Mountjoy knew of the affair and tolerated it was the juiciest gossip of the neighborhood and the source of much merriment in the local taverns and bawdy houses.

When I had their attention again, I repeated my question about this messenger to her.

"Yes, I saw the boy," she said, breathless from their spat. "Was he a thief, then? I supposed as much when I saw him enter the shop. What would a boy like that want of the fine hats my husband makes? thought I. Was it news of wealth?" she asked, speaking of my letter.

"No."

I was surprised she had not steamed the seal and examined the letter for herself. So much for privacy in this house.

"Of death or loss?" She asked.

"No. Advice, a Bible verse."

The woman made an expression as though to say she spat upon such stuff. "*Mon dieu,* it hardly warrants all this fuss," Madame Mountjoy declared with caustic disapproval. "Now, husband, come to bed, for as I live, if you do not you will take no pleasure of my body for a year or more. I am weary in my bones from this day's trouble and can find no rest with you roaming around the house getting into God knows what kind of mischief."

This woman's scorn now seemed to number me among her foes, as though I were to blame for all. Mountjoy, his anger spent, was now her ally. Calm, he nodded agreeably and took his lady by her plump arm as if to go to bed.

Weary of them both, I bid my landlord and his wife goodnight and mounted the stairs, clutching the letter in my hand like an ill-gotten gain, although it was fair gotten and no gain at all, save in that peculiar sense I've said: that now I had evidence of my stalker's enmity.

I slipped the letter between the pages of a book, used the chamber pot, and undressed, donning my long nightgown and nightcap, which I pulled down over my ears against the drafts that in the house were everywhere.

I blew the candle out and was embraced by a bitter darkness. I tried to sleep, but the more I tried, the more I stayed awake, the words of the letter searing my poor brain. What did it mean? Why the words of just that sonnet? And what meaning for me had the biblical mention of the fathers' sins? What sin had my father done beyond those sins that ordinary mortals do? True, he had been a winebibber, a generous feeder, a bankrupt, and somewhat of a scoundrel. He died in the old religion, I am told, his prayer book clutched in his hand. But evil? I think not. I pray not.

Finally I felt the subtle hand of sleep. Beneath my pillow, I sought the cold of Toledo steel, found it, and was disappointed in my hope that it would comfort me.

THE DAY AFTER, I again went to Cecil's house on the Strand and found neither him nor Stanleigh there. I had taken the letter with me, and also Edward, whom I was determined to keep leashed until such time as the mystery was resolved and I was secure again. I returned home and was having supper with Mountjoy and his family when Stanleigh came knocking. He said he had heard I'd called upon Master Secretary that day and thought he might be of assistance. "His lordship was with the king. Now he's home again. Let me be your guide."

I don't like to walk abroad at night in London. It's foolhardy in the best of weather, stark mad in dire winter. But Stanleigh had come with two armed men, and all had torches. Confident in this escort, I called to Edward where he sat at table in the kitchen but found him dead to the world in sleep, his arms sprawled upon the table and Mountjoy's cook watching over him like a guardian angel. I decided to leave the boy, although I would have welcomed his testimony to Cecil to bolster my case.

And so away.

IN HIS NIGHTGOWN, Cecil read my letter several times over, examined the quality of paper on which it was written by holding it up to the lamp, and felt its texture between his fingers.

"Well, there's piety in it," Cecil said. "Its author quotes Scripture."

"As the devil might," I said humorlessly.

"Indeed. This miscreant tantalizes you, Master Shakespeare. Has joy in your fear. There's a clue, too, in the sacred verse."

"About the sins of fathers?" I said.

"What do you make of that? Has it a meaning?"

"I had a son. Hamnet."

"Hamlet?"

"Nay, Hamnet. I named him after my good friend Hamnet Sadler. I have daughters, Judith and Susanna. Hamnet would have been twenty had he lived. He died nine years past. I was not in Stratford when it happened. A sudden fever. My wife said it came upon him before she was aware. She watched him die, helpless. He was my only son."

Cecil murmured in commiseration. I'd heard he had children, too.

"And your father?" he asked.

"Dead. Not two years since."

"I'm most sorry. This is hard for you."

For whom is it not? I thought, then gave in to my grief, not caring that Cecil should see me weep. The boy had been my only son—a strapping lad who looked like me and had, by his mother's account, my witty tongue. What father would not weep to see his line so early spent? I was to blame. For I had passed the boy's life in London, coming home once a year at best to be greeted by an ever-changing mirror of my young self. Every year different. Now there was nothing but failing memory the boy's grave could do nothing to refurbish; nor could Christian faith, weakened by constant diet of death and decay, console me with its prospect of some future reunion. All was void, a gaping hole into which I peered like a child peering into a well so deep there was no reflection there nor sound of dropping stone.

"My wife said once it was my fault, the boy's death," I said. "Although she spoke from depths of grief and begged me to forgive her words after, I took them to heart then and perhaps now, too."

"How your fault?"

"For my sins. My London sins. She knew—or imagined, or heard tell—how I lived here. She thought I had brought some pestilence home with me, infected him. Perhaps infected her and our daughters, too. The judgment of God, she said, for an immoral life. Her condemnation was all the madness of grief. It passed before it deepened into hatred. Of that I'm sure. But as I say, I think she may have been right."

"You had no more children?"

"None, Your Honor, not after the twins, for of such my Hamnet was one, my daughter Judith the other. They injured my wife's womb in their coming forth, and so my posterity was full."

"She does not blame you now?"

"I have seen no sign of it. She welcomes me when I return to Stratford, with just such hugs and kisses that ordinarily pass between a loving pair. Weeps and blesses me when I go away again. Is as pleased at the prospect of growing wealth as ever a wife was."

And yet, I thought, but did not say this to Cecil, she rarely speaks of Hamnet. Will not visit the grave with me. A woman's mind. What man could sound it, or her heart?

Then I told Cecil about Edward Goode, not about his acting but about what he'd witnessed.

"A witness?"

"Indeed, Your Honor."

"Worthy of trust?"

"I have no doubt of him. He knew too many details to fabricate. He's a decent lad who'll make a tolerable actor. You shall see, Your Honor. You shall see in the play."

It was now nearly midnight. I could see my visit had wearied Cecil. "Keep indoors, Master Shakespeare," he said. "I'll see you do not walk the streets unless you're accompanied. Tonight, you may lie here. Stanleigh, see to it."

THAT NIGHT I slept fitfully in a strange room and in a strange bed with sheets as soft as a young girl's thighs and a pillow smelling of sweet herbs. This was the gentle life I'd coveted, surrounded by luxury, waited upon by servants who at their master's word treated me like an earl or duke. Why was I not happy?

The next morning I returned to my lodgings on Silver Street, accompanied by the same brave fellows Stanleigh had brought with him the night before and who had since been ordered to follow me about. I had been told their names but could not remem-

ber them, and indeed they looked so alike in height, girth, and
beard that one might have played Rosencrantz to the other's
Guildenstern. They wore black leather the both of them and were
so severe in their expressions that I thought of them as a pair of
jackdaws.

I found Mountjoy and his wife in a great dither, for when I did
not return to my rooms they supposed I had been murdered in
the streets or, worse, arrested for some treason, which might have
implicated them as my landlords. Mountjoy, being a foreigner,
was particularly worried about such a fate. He and his family had
fled France with other Huguenots after the great massacre of St.
Bartholomew's Day, and although he made headwear for the
court as well as for other citizens and had good reason to think
himself welcome in the city, he lived in constant fear of govern-
ments and their power.

After assuring them that I was well enough off, I went upstairs
to the garret that Edward was sharing with one of Mountjoy's
apprentices, expecting to find him studying his lines as I had
directed him to do in any odd hour of freedom. He wasn't there.
I went downstairs again.

"Where's Edward?" I said, for my plan was to resume our tour
of the city on the chance he would see my enemy.

"He's gone," said Mountjoy, busy now in his shop.

"Gone where?" I asked.

"A message came for him. He said it was from you and that you
should come after him." Mountjoy didn't look up from his work.

I told him I'd sent no message, not a word.

"No message. Impossible," Mountjoy insisted. "He said it was
from you. The boy said so."

My blood, warmed from the exercise of the walk, now chilled
suddenly.

"When did Edward leave?"

"By seven," Mountjoy said. "The house had been awake since
dawn."

It was now something short of noon, and Edward had not
returned.

I left the house at once, my jackdaws following at a distance as I had instructed them. It began to rain again, a slow steady drizzle. The guards of my body were not happy about being taken out into the rain and, I suppose, had planned to stay indoors with me. Yet they obeyed without complaint, and quickly I made my way up the street, inquiring as I went of any passerby if they had seen that morning a boy of Edward's description passing there and if they could tell what direction he went.

I searched the neighborhood, my escorts lurking behind and fast losing interest, I could tell, in the enterprise. I had not told them of the reason for my frantic search.

Then I had some luck. A tavernkeeper standing by his door not far from the Great Hall of the Barber Surgeons said he had seen such a boy walking at great speed toward the river. This made sense. I could not now assume else but that my stalker had forged the message, and it seemed likely that he would place me at the theater.

I quickened my pace, lost my pair of jackdaws somewhere in the curve of the street, and hurried as if my own life depended on it and not that of a twelve-year-old boy I had met only a few days before.

London's streets are full of boys, and of men who are hardly more than boys, apprentices most, but also householders' children, going to and fro. The poor dress so alike that at a distance they seem almost in uniform, and when the weather's foul, as now, telling one from another is even more difficult. Yet I continued to search, more and more convinced Edward was in danger by this counterfeit summons.

I came to Westminster Stairs, found a waterman at the bank, and crossed to Southwark. Now the rain fell in sheets, and I was soaked to my skin but paid no mind. Set ashore, I ran for the theater, entered the usual way, and standing in the dripping yard roared Edward's name.

When no answer came, I called again, almost breathless from the run and shaking in the cold. This time, though, I was answered.

It was no more than a strangled, gurgling cry of terror or warning. It came from the tiring house beyond the stage.

I climbed upon the boards, calling Edward's name a third time. Behind the false front of an Italian city I found him.

This part is painful to me to relate, which may seem strange from one who spent his years writing plays rife with blood and gore. But they were figments of my imagining; this was real.

He was leaning with his back against a wall, his bony knees drawn up toward his chest. He was bound, hand and foot, with leather straps. A deal of blood stained his shirtfront, dying it crimson. He looked at me with round, amazed eyes, uttered a gasp, then his eyes rolled back in his white face, and his head fell to the side.

I had come in time to see him die.

I stood horrified, sucking in the air that stank of blood and excrement, for death had loosed his bowels even as it had freed his immortal soul. I tried to pray but could find no words, and for a few moments I imagined, given the place, that the boy was making his debut as an actor and that presently he would stand up, dripping with pig's blood, and receive the applause his final scene deserved.

His white throat, slashed from ear to ear, bloomed fresh with gore. The gag that had stuffed his mouth had been removed before my coming, but only just before, else I would have heard his warning. The cloth, a handkerchief, lay wadded beside the body.

I stared down at him, unable to pull my eyes away from the horror. While hot tears of grief and rage ran down my cheeks, I imagined Edward's soul drawn heavenward. Would he remember there Ophelia's words, or the new lines he had learned from *Measure for Measure*? Or did memory die with the body, dissolved into a nothingness of rotting flesh and bone?

I imagined, too, what had happened. The murderer had waited until I came, wanting me to find the boy while he was still alive, wanting me not only to suffer the death, but to suffer the dying.

Wanting me to come, but to come too late.

And I knew the murderer was still here.

Ten

THE THEATER IS a worthy hiding place for miscreant or knave. Its stage is by its very nature a palpable falsehood, its *frons scenae* and backparts the very womb of enormity, its galleries and Lords' Rooms a wanton wilderness.

This I thought while I stood pale and quaking, a witness to the sacrifice of innocence.

There was no chance Edward's murderer had slipped by me. I would have heard his footfalls, going down or up, felt his hot, rancid breath, or the insolent splash of his boots in the sodden yard as he fled for the street. At two score years, my eyes are not what they were, yet my hearing is like that of the hawk, who detects the mouse's whistle in the grass and drops upon him like a stone. I had heard nothing.

Yet I knew he was here. The corpse was too fresh for me to suppose otherwise.

I had heard men say who'd been in war that though fear is common, courage rises not from duty or conviction but from mindless rage. Then the grim-faced soldier forgets his life, his cause, his wife and child at home, even his beloved country. He thinks only of his enemy and how he hates him. The brain and heart narrow to a single point, and on that point sit Wrath, Revenge, and Despair.

And so stood I. I cared not a fig for safety. Had I done so I would have darted like a hare. My mind was on my boy, whose knowledge of the arsonist's face had been his death warrant. And was I not to blame? Had I not paraded him through the city in search of a face he remembered? Had I thought for a moment of what danger I put him in?

What had I been thinking?

It was not my custom to walk abroad an armed man, though I owned a sword, a dagger, and a poniard, which I kept close within my chamber. Even during the weeks since my old mistress's death I had not armed myself. Why not?

Perhaps it was because I didn't want to think I was in so great a danger.

Perhaps because I knew my skill with sword and dagger was no match for my adversary's, though I had wielded both with some aplomb upon the stage. Let's be honest: Two actors at fence is a different story than two men who wish each other dead.

There was a small arsenal in the wardrobe above the upper gallery, as I have said, but the distance between where I stood and where I would find sword and buckler might well have been a furlong. I looked about me and found a piece of board the length of my arm propped behind a stage post. This I made my club and turned stalker who was before a quaking wretch, beginning with the middle galleries, where I thought the murderer might have crouched to watch me make my gruesome discovery.

My disgust surpassed my rage. "Stand forth! Stand forth!" I cried, calling my unseen enemy those names I thought would flush him out—a monstrous litany of abuse drawn from every play I'd writ where words were goads. Let him come with razor sword or bloody knife, I cared not now, if he'd but come. I wanted to see his face, so that I could tell him: "This thing you did, and may you burn in hell forever for it." I ran from gallery to gallery, looking behind every row. My grief had turned me mad.

I might have screamed until my throat was raw. It did no good. If he was there, he would not come out, no matter what insults I flung at him, what dares, what taunts, what calumny. He had found safety and enjoyed the spectacle.

For I knew he was still there, watching.

Now I understood my state. Like an actor on a stage who sees his son slain before his eyes, I had performed for my adversary who had staged the scene. My shock, my grief, my guilt, my ranting and indignation—all were viewed from where he hid. I had played at once a dozen bereaved fathers my pen had made.

From the center of the yard I looked up to the galleries, to the Lords' Rooms above the tiring house, and farther still to the little cabin atop it all.

Nothing stirred. I saw no watching face, no shadowy form.

Up I went to the wardrobe. The idea that he might have taken refuge there had been in the back of my thoughts since finding Edward. After all, the murderer had been there before when he vented his rage on my cloak of invisibility. It was a country he knew, a place where like a dog he had hiked his leg. He might be there again, crouching within the wardrobe.

At the door I paused, breathless. I found the key where I had laid it and advanced toward the lock, only to find the hasp loose already. It crossed my mind to lock it again, supposing that my adversary was within, then changed my mind. What if he were there after all? Better to find out now, then search elsewhere.

I entered—and saw nothing but what was there before, no human presence save my own. No smoky stench this time, but only mildew, old sweat, leather, wet wool. I moved slowly amidst the stuff, pushing things aside, heading for my arsenal of sword and shield, cuirass and pike. No movement there, but the light from the few small windows not enough to give good view.

When I came upon my store of weaponry, I traded my club for Spanish steel, hefted it, and had no sooner done so than I heard what I had waited for, yet it came so quick I doubted my senses. A sudden motion, hurried steps. From the corner of my eye I caught the vision of a cloaked figure dash toward the door I'd entered, close it upon me with a crash. I heard the key turn in the lock.

Too late I reached the door. I threw my shoulder against it and then grimaced with pain. I waited until the pain was spent, then began to beat upon the door like a lunatic. This I did until, devoid of strength and voice, I felt hot tears run down my face.

In due course I found my manhood. I went to the window. It looked out on the thatched rooftop of the adjoining house. Even if it had been large enough so that I fit through it, it was too far to the ground for safety. The street, Maiden Lane, was empty.

And then I saw a solitary figure walking away from the theater. I shouted to him and waited for him to turn to see what madman it was who called out. But he didn't turn round. Oh, how I yearned to see that elusive face! I would have pawned my soul to do so. One man's back is too much like another's. I watched helplessly, seething with rage that a murderer should walk free. But so he did. I could do nothing.

Then I saw him fling something into the air, a small thing that I might not have distinguished even if we were much closer. Yet I knew what it was.

It was the key to the storage. It arced above him in the air, like a taunt, like an obscene gesture.

IT WAS AN hour, maybe two, before I heard voices without and knew my imprisonment was to have a shorter date than I had feared. I am good at voices. I rarely forget an accent or inflection, although I must admit that in the exigencies I had quite forgotten the owners of these.

It was my two guardians, my jackdaws. They had tracked me down at last, and in good time. I called to them, and presently they came beating upon the lock.

The door open, they looked in shamefaced, as though they already knew how the king's secretary would take this report of my imprisonment. I reassured them they were not to blame, said the fault was mine that I had outrun them, and praised them for knowing where I went and coming there in due time. Even as I said this I was full of self-contempt, for I flattered them ridiculously out of craven gratitude that I'd been saved.

We went below to where the body lay. It broke my heart again to see Edward Goode as he now was, pale and wide-eyed, full of amazement at his own abrupt sending off. I stood for a moment, dumbly staring at the gaping wound, at the heart-shaped face that had seen my assailant, once in the street, then again before he died. Did he know when he saw the arsonist again that he was now looking at his own murderer?

Behind me the jackdaws said nothing; I assumed that being men at arms they had seen many a slit throat, therefore saw no reason to comment upon this one. Then it occurred to me their stoniness might have another cause, that they might suppose me to be the boy's murderer. And why shouldn't they? There I stood, the lone person in the theater with a dead body soaked in its blood and no one else to blame it on.

"This is not my work," I said, turning to face them.

"No, sir," one of the men said.

"As God's my witness," I said. Both men received my protest with glum looks, almost as though I hadn't spoken, accustomed, I suppose, to holding their peace until they found out how things stood in such bloody matters, whose side to claim, how to exculpate themselves.

"I had no weapon," I said, and then remembered they found me with Toledo blade still clutched in my hand and had looked at me with some concern when they discovered me standing there, ready to strike.

I told them about the false message, my desperate search, my terrible discovery, my imprisonment. And then I repeated all again. "It was someone else. The man who imprisoned me where you found me. He did this."

The taller of the jackdaws nodded, but whether he meant to acknowledge the truth of what I said or only to signal that he'd heard it I couldn't tell.

"We should send for the constable of Southwark," I said,

despite my memory that the man was a fool on whom I had modeled more than one of my theatrical constables. Yet he represented the law. What else was I to do? The body could not remain here in the theater.

"We'll take care of it, Master Shakespeare," said the shorter of the two men, whom I had heard the taller call Marbury.

"But this is a murder," I protested.

Marbury placed his hand upon his heart, as though he were taking an oath. He said, "This is the king's business. Lord Cecil serves the king. We are under orders—to keep you safe. Therefore, the murder is the king's business, not the constable's."

I smelled a fault in his logic but was not prepared to debate, and I confess to my shame that I was somewhat relieved. I doubted the constable would believe my account of things. For the more I thought, the more guilty I saw myself appear. To wit: My message sent to Mountjoy that the boy should come to the theater, with only my word to deny I sent it. My jackdaws who could readily testify they found me alone in the theater with only the dead body for company. And where did they find me but in a room full of weapons and with a fine, lethal sword in my hand?

I imagined even further my return to my chamber, explaining to the Mountjoys what happened to Edward and framing a tale, for I could not tell them the truth. And in that lie I would be further condemned.

So I was relieved and wept for the dead boy, while the taller of the men pulled one of the hangings from the wall and wrapped the body in it.

I looked at the boards where Edward had lain; they were bloody. The mark would be there on the rough planks as long as the Globe stood, and I would know whose blood it was even though others seeing the stain would suppose it stage blood for such stuff we used commonly to make our actors bleed.

Now the tall man picked up the body as though it weighed nothing at all and carried it off the stage and across the dripping yard. Marbury and I trailed as mourners do at a funeral, which I suppose this was—that is, all the funeral Edward was to have.

I whispered to Marbury, "What's to be done with him?"

Marbury shrugged. "Spurgeon will know."

The tall man was Spurgeon, then. Now I knew both their names.

We left the theater, the four of us, three living men and one dead boy. Observers seeing us leave—if there were any in this dismal weather—would suppose us actors, removing old clothing or costumes, and would never think we compounded murder in our solemn retreat.

The theater was built on pilings on the Bankside, so it was no time at all before the cold brown water lapped at our feet.

I looked out over the watery expanse. At first, I saw no wherries, nor would I have expected to, for who would cross in such a drizzle? But then I saw one draw close, and Spurgeon, who had put his burden down, hailed the boatman and beckoned him ashore.

I waited in cold rain with Marbury while Spurgeon talked to the boatman, a person of so marred a face he was a very fright to look upon. Their conversation went on, with the boatman holding up his hands and turning as if to push off again, and Spurgeon seizing him by the shoulder to importune him to stay, making to strike him if he did not, and then speaking to him soft again, patting him upon the back. He said something that made the boatman laugh. I saw Spurgeon reach into his belt and extract his purse. I must suppose he paid the boatman what he wanted for a fare. The boatman gave his head a jerk, pushed his craft into the water, and jumped in.

Spurgeon motioned us aboard. He picked up his bundle and lifted it into the bow. I sat beside Marbury, midships facing aft. The rain fell harder, turned to snow. I couldn't see the bank opposite, much beyond the bridge, much upriver, much down.

I THOUGHT WE'D make a quick crossing and be at the stairs in no time; instead, we headed downriver, drifting in the stream like a leaf. We huddled in the boat, a solemn crew. We floated beneath

London's pride, the great bridge with its houses upon it like a little town unto itself. The Tower came into my view, where Essex died and Sir Walter Raleigh would the next year languish. The boatman steered us close to the southern bank where the reeds grew tall and thick and dead stumps sent roots into the swirling stream.

I heard a splash. When I looked behind me Spurgeon sat alone in the bow, and what was left of Edward Goode was gone.

Eleven

MONSIEUR MOUNTJOY WAS most amazed at my return, for I, transformed to a watery sprite, was dejected and sodden, not the trim and curried gentleman who had left his house just hours before. I had lost my hat somewhere on the river and caught my death in the cold and wet. I had lost Edward Goode somewhere in the same lethal flood. How different a man I was than he that rose that morning Mountjoy could not know, and even I was yet to understand.

"You did not find Edward, Master Shakespierre?" Mountjoy asked, looking up from his worktable, on which he was shaping an elegant chapeau. Said hat crowned a featureless plaster head.

Like a wayward husband caught betwixt sheets with the maid, I was ready with a lie.

"He's gone," I said. "Run away. Gone to ground."

The Frenchman smiled knowingly. He had had, I knew, apprentices who had broken articles and vanished, traitors to a generous master who neither beat nor starved. My lie dripped with plausibility. In truth, the grim lot of an apprentice was different from the actor's work. In the theater, a boy with a fair face, good memory, and voice as yet unformed by his sex was a prize, no miserable creature constantly underfoot to be misused and endured. No, the life of an actor was much too attractive, but I didn't expect Mountjoy to understand that.

The Frenchman's wife took one look at me, scolded me for bringing half the Thames indoors, and urged me to bed at once. I quickly agreed, both for fear she'd escort me to my bed and tuck me in like a child and also because I hungered to be by myself. Spurgeon and Marbury had left me at my door. Good riddance. I was beginning to wonder how I could free myself from them without offending Cecil.

I stripped, climbed into bed, and was asleep before I knew it. I didn't dream, though I feared I might, but slept as profoundly as though I floated in as deep a current as wretched Edward. But such sleep, I have learned, only invites the worst of dreams, and when I woke—it was not yet dawn—the image of Edward floated before my eyes, his savaged throat, his sightless yet comprehending eyes, his bloody shirt like a badge of honor, and the stage where his lifeblood had pooled.

The stage. I sat bolt upright. I remembered the great deal of blood that soaked the boards. What would my friends think when they came upon it?

I knew what I must do, return to the Globe, and at once. I had no reason to suppose any of my companions would be there, but I couldn't take the chance.

At first light I left the house while breakfast grace was being said. The morning sky was gray, the air cold, and the streets covered with a light snow. Spurgeon and Marbury, alert to my comings and goings, fell in behind me, keeping their distance but not so great a distance as before. Where had they spent the night? Surely not in the street, for their cloaks and hats were dry. It was as though they simply materialized, like spirits who existed only to guard me and when there was no need, they ceased to be.

I found a wherryman, not the ghastly death's head of the day before but a pleasant, ruddy-cheeked fellow. We crossed to the Bankside, I and my jackdaws. I tried not to think about the river and the dead boy, but it wasn't possible. The mind of man isn't given to that discipline, not when the eye is filled with the scene of the crime. Edward's would not be the only sodden corpse rotting there, down amidst the reeds and the mud and the unspeakable waste of the city; his not the only evidence of an offense to God and man.

And so, with such gruesome musings, we came to the closed theater—bereft of pomp or circumstance, a shell of itself, and now for me as welcoming as a tomb.

It came to me as I mounted to the tiring house that I might find no stain there but plain unsullied wood as pure as the sturdy English oak from whence it came. Then I might conclude I'd dreamed and Edward's vile murder been a vision of the night.

A vain wish. It was no dream. The bloody smear was there, more expansive and deep grained than I remembered. I found a bucket, water, a rag. I got down on my knees like a washerwoman and began to scrub, my jackdaws looking on. I thought to ask one of them to do it but was afraid. My birds were violent men, quick to anger, quick to hide a corpse, but slow to do a woman's work. If I commanded and they refused, what then? Report their insolence to Cecil? Complain to the king, or to God?

But my own labors did not serve to erase the evidence, though I scrubbed until my arms protested; my sciatic knees were as sore as an anchorite's. The damned spot would not yield; the water made it somehow deeper, more incriminating.

I was thinking then of covering it over with some assorted furniture, or pulling up the very boards, burning them entire, and with virgin wood disguising the event. But furniture could be moved, and I was no carpenter.

Then I heard loud voices in the yard. One voice hailed me by name and with certain authority.

I recognized him who spoke as Miles Cheetle, constable of Southwark and deep sworn enemy of me and mine—a meddlesome, officious fool, ever fond of plaguing actors with his judgments and false warrants. A big, swollen man like my Jack Falstaff but without his wit, Cheetle wore a leather doublet, a wide belt, and boots that came almost to his knees and of which he was proud as a cock. He had been a tavernkeeper before his elevation to his present office and, before, a petty thief. Since then he'd got a dose of religion and was as notorious a hypocrite as one might wish. With him he had three sturdy knaves he called his officers, but I would have called them his toads, for they hopped after slavishly.

I leapt to my feet, my joints aching. My jackdaws looked at Cheetle's men as though reckoning how they would come off if threatening looks came to blows.

"Rehearsing, Master Shakespeare?" Cheetle said.

"Yes," I said, relieved that he could not have seen from his vantage point what I was doing, and yet I had no sooner responded to his greeting but he advanced, leapt upon the stage—a wonder given his bulk—and within a wink advanced upon me, his arms outspread as though to embrace me. I drew back. Then he stopped, staring at me, my bucket, the wet floor. The stain. Taking all in in one swoop and, I feared, understanding what he saw.

"He's thrice dead who bled here," Cheetle said, winded from his exertion. He looked at me inquiringly but with more pleasant curiosity than horror or disapproval, even though I could tell he knew what he had interrupted.

I did not reply for want of words. Though I had them, yet they were futile. Any explanation would sound false as hell, even to one less disposed to be my enemy. Besides, Cheetle knew blood when he looked upon it.

"We found a dead man on the shore. A dead boy, about thirteen or fourteen years. About a mile downstream where the reeds grow," Cheetle said, fixing his eyes on me. "Some in the neighborhood have said they saw the boy with you. Some that they heard screams coming from this place. Yesterday about four o'clock. Screams like one dying, torn apart by bear, or his throat slit. What say you, Master Shakespeare?"

I was about to answer that a man or boy whose throat is cut is unlikely to do more than expel air, then thought this was no time to tutor Cheetle in gross anatomy. He lacked the brain for it, and teaching wasn't my calling.

Cheetle glanced beyond me for a moment at the back of the box as though there were someone there, frowned a little, then continued, "Of course, the body may be that of some other wretched boy. There are enough of 'em on the Bankside and not a few who come to God by the devil's help. Come see for yourself, Master Shakespeare. You may be able to say who 'tis, and if no, then a rotting corpse is always an instructive lesson in mortality. We have it in a cart, the body I mean. Just beyond your door. It will keep you no longer than a minute."

This was more command than invitation, and I had no reason to deny him. There was, I thought, some little chance that the new-found body was not Edward's, that the death had been wrought by some less bloody means. There was a chance, though I knew it so slim as to be no chance at all.

Cheetle led the way with his three men following us all. Out on Maiden Lane was yet another officer standing by a small, rickety cart with half the spokes of one wheel missing. We all went over to see what was there, but I saw at once that my hopes were vain. The body was wrapped in the ripped curtain the larger piece of which still hung in tatters behind the stage for all to see, proof irrefutable that the dead body had been carried from the Globe. Now I knew what Cheetle had been looking at just beyond my shoulder. The canvas curtain was adorned with painted flowers and nymphs. I had never seen another quite like. Evidently neither had Cheetle.

Cheetle pulled back the cloth and with no little satisfaction showed the bloated corpse.

I felt a searing pain at my heart. It was Edward. There was no blood now but a long bluish line of puckered flesh just below the pale-white chin and stretching ear to ear. His eyes were milky-white, and at his once rosy lips strands of tangled weed were wrapped as though placed there by some unfeeling hand that he might seem to kiss them.

I could no longer look.

" 'Tis the boy, isn't it?" Cheetle said, daring me to deny it. His eyes narrowed; his breath was strong.

I decided not to compound my guilt with yet another lie.

"His name's Edward Goode," I said. "He was a player, or wanted to be. New to our company this very month. The King's Men." I added this latter distinction unsure as to why. Perhaps it was some effort to bolster myself in Cheetle's regard, to show him that I was someone to be reckoned with, not a detestable actor whose very calling proclaimed him guilty of any number of loathsome vices, but a servant, no matter how low in the order of things, of the king of England.

"Ah, yes, Master Shakespeare. I quite forgot the honor the king did you. And pray tell, what did this Edward Goode do to so incur your wrath that you killed him? For as I entered, I watched before I spoke, and witnessed you on your knees, turned cleaning woman."

Cheetle smiled triumphantly, his bad teeth all displayed, and while I had long despised the man, I had not until now hated him. For I saw what was, that he did not give a fairy's fart for Edward Goode, but only that the corpse might be a lever whereby to dislodge me from my envied place and advance his own. So much for his so-called religion and moral purity, by which he disdained the practice of us players.

Now I confess I hated him with a hatred pure and undiluted by mercy—with a more pure hatred than what I felt for Edward's murderer. For while betwixt malice and hypocrisy, there may seem little to choose, if put to the test the hypocrite's the worse.

"I didn't kill him. He was killed by someone who broke into the theater, an intruder," I said.

"An intruder whose name you don't know," Cheetle said, as though I were a child whose every utterance needs to be parsed.

I said that was true. "A false summons lured him here."

"False summons? A writ of law?"

"A message. From me, he thought, but not so. I never sent any."

"So you say, Master Shakespeare." Cheetle looked hopefully to my jackdaws to see if they would confirm my words. But neither man spoke or seemed inclined; they looked on passively as though neither had aught to do with me, or with Edward Goode, or with anything beyond their own private business. Nor would they have anything to say. They didn't see the messenger, couldn't confirm my story about the false summons one way or another.

I was about to offer my French landlord as my witness and then remembered that he could confirm nothing but what Edward had told him. Only my own word stood between me and the conclusion that I had indeed lured Edward to the theater. Besides, I doubted so obdurate a patriot as Cheetle would take a Frenchman's word for anything.

There was, then, no hope in that direction.

"He's a goodly boy—or was, this Edward Goode," Cheetle said, relishing his poor pun and turning an appraising eye on the body, which remained uncovered to the glowering sky and was now drawing the attention of a growing crowd.

Cheetle spoke directly to my jackdaws, demanding to know their names and what they'd seen. But if these somber creatures had Christian names, they were no more prepared to reveal them to Cheetle than they had been to me. "We are servants of Lord Cecil," Marbury said, thrusting his chest out a little and making much of his superior height over Cheetle, who lacked even my inches.

"Did you see this murderer that Master Shakespeare speaks of?" Cheetle said.

Spurgeon said he hadn't. Marbury agreed.

"I have a witness that says you three were seen together, conveying the boy's body," Cheetle said.

"What witness?" I said, trying to act indignant but unable to keep the uncertainty from my voice.

"A certain boatman. He's over there," Cheetle said.

My eyes followed Cheetle's gaze. As if on signal, from behind a house nearby a fellow emerged and made his way toward us. I recognized him, no doubt of it. It was, alas, the pilot of our craft, our dour Charon. There could be no two visages quite so foul. Poor wretched *memento mori,* reminding me of all the nightmares of my recent days.

"Are these the three?" Cheetle asked the boatman unflinchingly, and I supposed that Cheetle knew the man and had become accustomed to his marred visage.

"They are," said the boatman, looking at me, Spurgeon, and Marbury in turn.

"And they paid you twofold for conveying the body?"

"What 'twas I knew not," the boatman said, eager to be blameless. "A bundle and large, 'twas. I thought it nothing more than the gentleman's furniture made fast 'gainst the weather, which was very bad. The threepence extra was to go downriver farther, not to dump bodies dead. I knew nothing about that, any murders, that is."

"So you helped Master Shakespeare get rid of this lad's corpse, which Mr. Shakespeare here says some intruder killed?"

Before receiving his response from the boatman, Cheetle turned to me. "Wherefore should you do that, Master Player? Has Southwark no law, that you throw bodies in the river? That's not the act of an honest man, Master Shakespeare. That's against the king's law. You actors think you're above the law. But not so. You wear its yoke as well as do I, and the sooner you and your kind learn that the better you shall be."

Sermon done, Cheetle turned to my jackdaws. "You say you're Lord Cecil's men, then why are you here? I see no players upon this stage, or crowds within. Or is Lord Cecil so abundantly served that he can afford to allow two such brave fellows as you to loiter here?"

"Our charge is Master Shakespeare's safety," Marbury said self-importantly.

Cheetle looked doubtful. "Pray tell what dumping bodies has to do with safety. Lord Cecil's command, I suppose it was?"

"Master Shakespeare's orders, sir," Spurgeon said, missing the irony. "We take our orders from him."

I looked at Spurgeon's hard face, a face I never liked. Now it pleased me even less.

Cheetle asked me if what Spurgeon said was true.

"I thought to send for you, Master Cheetle. But these men persuaded me otherwise. I didn't know where we were bound when we set out upon the river. When Master Spurgeon threw the body overboard, no one was more surprised than I."

"Surprised?" exclaimed Cheetle. "Then where did you think you were going downriver, to see the sights?"

I told the truth. I didn't know, I had been confused. I couldn't tell Cheetle how my heart had broken at Edward's murder, for which murder I blamed myself as much as his murderer. Cheetle would have distrusted such a profession and concluded what he would, the wrong thing. He had already intimated such. I couldn't stop lying; the more truth I told, the more guilty I seemed. I was also enraged at my treasonous jackdaws, who had so freely borne false witness against me. Yet I understood their treason. Seeing my ship sinking, Prudence found them a safe port. It was my word against theirs, and they were Lord Cecil's servants. There was no point in berating them. I decided to say nothing more, let Cheetle do what he would.

"I like not this, Master Shakespeare," Cheetle said. "Murder in my neighborhood. I don't like you players coming to Southwark with your lascivious shows, bringing your bawds and whoremasters with you. Polluting the town."

I said nothing in reply. The Puritans parroted this slander yet were quick enough to pocket the profits of the crowds that flocked to Southwark to see plays and the bears baited.

I thought surely he would be quoting Scripture next; instead, he said, "Well, I must take you before a judge, Master Shakespeare, and your men as well, for though they be servants of Lord Cecil, that does not put them any more above the law than it puts you, sir. So I say yield yourself to me and my officers and go peaceably."

"You make merry at my expense, Master Cheetle," I said.

"Nay, sir. I do not make merry but speak plainly, as God is my witness. I arrest you, Will Shakespeare, for the murder of Edward Goode. You say you're innocent. What evildoer does not say so? The evidence is strong against you. Let's see what the judge may say."

"We had naught to do with any murders," Spurgeon said, glowering. "We serve Sir Robert, not some petty constable of the town. You will not arrest us, upon pain of Lord Cecil's displeasure."

Marbury protested the same, and my two bodyguards assumed a warlike stance, their hands resting on the hilts of their swords.

"I care nothing for your lord's displeasure, if he indeed be your lord," Cheetle snorted, his nostrils flaring and his belly thrust forward like the prow of a ship. "I serve the king, sirs. I know my duty when I find it—a dead body, murdered, as any eye can tell by looking at the ripped throat of that boy, a witness who can swear he saw the body disposed of and by whom. And I myself who stood within this theater and saw Will Shakespeare on his knees, scrubbing up blood to conceal the crime. Pray, sir, given these facts, why should I believe Master Shakespeare's story of an intruder, whom no one has seen but himself and who I warrant you exists only in his fancy."

Threatened with arrest, my erstwhile bodyguards changed their tune and became more pliant. A crowd had gathered around us and the cart, drawn by the prospect of a fight and curious since discovering that a dead body lay in the cart and, for once, it had not died of the plague but from murder. Yet it was clear that although the multitude could hear little of what was said, they were with the constable against us. He was, although despised and feared by many, one of their own, while Spurgeon and Marbury—and even I—were from beyond the pale.

"To tell truth, Master Constable," Marbury said. "We doubted Master Shakespeare's story from the first. He had a sword and a lying look. We had his word. Naught else."

"And you took it?"

"We took it, sir. We'd never have removed the body but he ordered us in our master's name to do it. We are law-abiding men, true servants of our master, Master Secretary Cecil, and of the king."

"Just following orders, were you?" Cheetle said.

"As we hope to be saved," Marbury said in a sudden burst of piety.

My anger now at the mendacity of my jackdaws was at the full, and in my extremity I found my courage. I told Cheetle to do his worst, to take me away, under whatever color of law he chose. I denounced Spurgeon and Marbury as the liars they were and was amazed that neither man blanched to hear such an accusation, as though they were well accustomed to slanders upon their honor. I said I'd plead my innocence before a judge, any judge in England, and I said other things to offend those present and increase their ire against me that never would I have said had reason not been toppled by rage. But if I thought my boldness would turn Cheetle from his purposes I was much mistaken. Officious fool he was, and hypocrite, but even a fool can keep to his resolve, and a hypocrite can always find paint to color his actions.

Cheetle put up with my fulminating for a minute or two and commanded me to silence, with which I complied, having exhausted all my invective's store.

"If you're quite finished, Master Shakespeare."

"I'm done," I said.

"Are you sure, sir?"

"I'm done," I repeated.

"Then we shall proceed." The constable turned to look at Spurgeon and Marbury. "Gentlemen, surrender your weapons and your persons, for so the law demands."

Cheetle signaled to his men, who came forward to take swords from Spurgeon and Marbury. Both men gave them up without further protest. I was amazed to see these bold men so subdued. "Come, come." Cheetle said. "The less trouble, the better for you all. We'll see what the magistrate says."

"Your magistrate will find me guiltless of any crime," I declared as we were led from the theater. Yet even as I spoke I knew my protest was thin and wavering—like a child's voice in a gale.

Twelve

THE MAGISTRATE, I was told, dwelt in Southwark, not far from a house owned by my friend and fellow actor Thomas Pope. I knew the neighborhood well, and I knew Thomas knew the magistrate. I hoped, therefore, for a tolerant judge who would weigh the evidence against me and find it wanting. We proceeded on foot, on wet cobbles and then, later, in slush. In our wake was an ever-increasing crowd of the curious and hostile, a rabble of tradesmen, unruly apprentices, and street urchins. I heard voice raised in anger against us, charging us with murder, robbery, and assorted other crimes. Had this uproar not been occasioned by our arrest, it would probably have been suppressed as a riot.

My traitorous jackdaws, as irony would have it, received the brunt of the unruly crowd's suspicion and abuse, for I was dressed like a gentleman and, being in the immediate custody of Master Cheetle, was probably taken to be one of the constable's officers.

When we were come to the magistrate's house, I saw it was a fair and worthy one given the neighborhood, two stories of stone and timber, cross-braced most craftily, with a high pitched slate roof, not thatch. Before it was a garden ravaged by winter but adorned with statuary, nymphs, satyrs, and so forth. A wooden gate was our port, where several of the constable's officers stood guard to prevent the crowd from coming in, for their heat had grown and become ugly, their faces more menacing, the curses more violent.

Where before I was annoyed by the constable's accusations and my arrest, now I trembled and sweat, looked about me nervously, and felt the yoke of my guilt though I had none to bear.

Up a brick walk we went, to a door agape. We were admitted by two of the magistrate's liveried servants, who regarded us with great contempt, and came anon into the parlor of the house, very spacious, with furniture a nobleman might have envied, though I understood the magistrate was not even a knight but a merchant tailor who had done well enough to secure his commission as justice of the peace.

I remember a fire burning in the great square hearth and the odor of wet wool from all the gentlemen therein who, having been out in the weather were now indoors and dripping.

At the end of the room, a thin, white-bearded gentleman of sixty years or more sat behind a polished table in a high-backed chair. He wore a black robe and a red velvet cap that fell about his ears; both robe and cap seemed made for a more robust man. A chain of office dangled from his turkey neck. He looked at me under cold, hooded eyes.

"Good Justice Swallow," said Constable Cheetle, with a self-satisfied grin, directing me to stand in the center of the room, "this is William Shakespeare, player."

"I know Master Shakespeare," Justice Swallow said in a low, dry voice. "Tell me, then, what law has this man offended now?"

Single words are not without their weight, and the appendage of the modest temporal adverb "now" did its work in persuading me that I was indeed no innocent at the bar but a practiced malefactor whose present charges were only the latest installment in his life of crime. I surmised that here was a justice by the king's commission. Yet would he do it, justice—at least for a poor, abused player? I thought perhaps his friendship with Thomas Pope would make him favorably disposed to me.

How mistaken I was.

Now I must confess that I wear good clothes, keep mustache and beard trimmed and, practice moderation in all my courses. I am used to being well regarded in the city and above the common rout that runs afoul of law and order. And so to be in that place and to be so despised by the magistrate was mortification of my pride, and my face burned with unexpressed anger and frustration.

I glanced aside at my fellow arrestees, Cecil's men, Marbury and Spurgeon. They stood out from the others in this congregation in their black leather doublets, with their wide belts and the empty sheaths where swords, now taken, had formerly asserted their authority. They smiled complacently and seemed to take their arraignment as a lark—as though it were happening to men other than themselves. I thought this curious indeed, for the constable had said we were confederates all—an unholy trinity of murderous rogues in which I was chief. By order of logic, were I guilty as charged, they shared the blame.

But now the doughty constable was deep into his account of how Edward Goode's bloated body had washed ashore and been found by some boys playing thereby, who brought the news to Master Cheetle. Inquiring among the boatmen, he had been fortunate to find the very man who had conveyed the body downriver.

This fellow, whom Master Cheetle had in tow, now stepped forward, trembling as much as I. He held his cap in his hand and, half weeping, said he had done nothing wrong.

"Good boatman, what is your name?" Justice Swallow said firmly, interrupting the wretched man's protestations.

"Will, your worthiness," he said, and gave a little curtsy like a maid, whereupon there was a deal of laughter in the room that the magistrate silenced with a barking reproof. When all was silent again, the boatman proceeded.

Our boatman told the story of the three men who brought a burden aboard, then tipped the bundle over the side. He also related how he had picked them up at the Bankside, right by the Globe.

I did not speak at this. How could I? I was not about to give the boatman the lie. Though he might be a villain and as ugly as sin, yet I could not fault his account, save I expect he may have known more about the contents of the bundle than he confessed.

After that, I hardly listened as the constable went on. I was uncomfortable, needed to relieve my bowels, and was most anxious about my condition. I was beginning to see in what new peril I stood. Where before I looked to the law as my salvation from my enemy, I now saw that the law, too, was an enemy, and I wondered if somewhere in that unruly crowd that stood sentinel outside my tormentor maintained his vigil, delighting in my misery as the rude multitude takes pleasure in the mishap of the poor hapless dupe.

I was brought from these imaginings by the magistrate's stern address.

"How answer you these charges, Master Shakespeare? Did you not murder this boy?"

"As God is my witness, I did not, sir," I said, trying to control the trembling in my voice so that I sounded neither guilty nor uncertain.

I made a silent prayer that I would be believed and that my delivery from these present circumstances would soon come, but even in the midst of my appeal, I feared it would be otherwise. I was no fool. I was praying for a miracle, for an outcome contrary to nature and the order of reason. I saw how my removal of the body and my scrubbing of the stains might look to someone ignorant of the truth. Why should innocence work to suppress the murderous act? Why was I not the one to bring word to Constable Cheetle? That had been my duty, the duty of an innocent man. Even one less biased against me might have reached the conclusion that I was guilty as sin.

"The constable says you murdered the boy," Justice Swallow

said, obviously not content to take my plea of innocence at face value. "What say you to his body in the theater? Your removal of the corpse? Your effort to conceal the fact?"

I said, "The boy was newly taken into our company. We are King's Men by royal patent."

I had to mention that, the business about our patent, if only to see if it was worth more than a little allowance and a new suit of clothes at the king's coming in. But it seemed to do nothing for the magistrate, who showed no more reverence for my office than for my person. I continued:

"Edward Goode was drawn away from the house. It was a message from me. But not from me."

"From you and not from you, Master Shakespeare! Is this a player's paradox that mere mortals can comprehend?" said Justice Swallow.

"It bore my name, but I never sent it."

"So you say, but is it true?"

"I sent no message to Edward Goode. On my honor."

"It's your honor that's in question. And your truth. Do you have this so-called false message?"

"No, sir. It was not in writing, but delivered by mouth to him."

"That's most convenient, Master Shakespeare. Well, go on," said Swallow. He made a motion to his clerk that every word I spoke should be written down.

"The message summoned him to the Globe. I followed, found him in the arms of death. I could do nothing. He was dead, or dying."

"Then you ordered these men to bear the body off, to drown it in the river." It was no question but as certain as the Gospel. I grew desperate.

"No, sir. Next I searched the theater for him who'd done it, and found him in the wardrobe. Yet he escaped."

"Ah, another convenience," said Swallow. "What manner of man was this, this murderer?"

"I saw not his face," I answered.

"Was he tall, portly, crookbacked, bearded? Tell us."

"I could not see, Master Swallow," I said. "He appeared, stopped to mock me with a wave of his hand, and then was gone in an instant. Later I saw him from the window, but saw him only as a shape. His back was to me. He was moving away."

"And after this you returned to dispose of the dead body?"

I admitted it. I could hardly do otherwise.

"And the next day returned to clean up the bloody evidence of your crime," Swallow said.

"Not my crime," I said.

"Concealing evidence of a murder. Is that not a crime?" he asked. He looked around the chamber at his clerks and attendants, at the constable and his men, at the onlookers who had managed to fit into the parlor as the spectators of my disgrace. There was much nodding and murmuring in agreement and evil looks at me. Like an actor who holds forth on center stage, this elderly gentleman basked in the approval of his audience.

"I suppose it is," I said. "But it was not my intent to break the law."

"What was your intent?"

"I had advice. From men who convinced me they knew of such matters."

"What men?" Swallow asked.

"These men," I paused to point them out, noticing now that Spurgeon was no longer there, that only Marbury remained, his countenance composed and self-satisfied as before. "This man and his companion, Masters Spurgeon and Marbury, were appointed by Lord Cecil as my guardians."

"Guardians," said Swallow, with mockery in his close-set eyes. "You look old enough, sir, not to need 'em." He smiled, the first I'd seen, but such a smile that gave no joy to the beholder. Such a smile a hangman might use before he wields his ax and sends the condemned soul into eternity.

"My life had been threatened, and it was of value to Lord Cecil, and to the king."

"Your life threatened? The plot thickens, playmaker. It is very like one of your idle works, isn't it? Are you sure you have not confused your art with reality?"

Had I not been beside myself with fear, I would have put this smug gentleman in his place, but thought the better of it. I said, instead:

"I am not confused, sir. I presented my evidence before Lord Cecil. He believed it. Otherwise, he would not have appointed these gentlemen."

"Gentlemen," said the magistrate, looking over my shoulder. "I see only one. Do your scholarly attainments not extend to arithmetic? Or is the fault mine?"

"Not yours, sir. Spurgeon is gone, but he was here when I came in and for a while thereafter."

The man had somehow slipped his tether. How he had done so in this press of bodies so focused on the accused men I cannot imagine. I suspected some conspiracy among the officers. One had seemed to know Spurgeon, had taken him aside for private words. I had thought little of it at the time, preoccupied with my own accused state. But it made sense now. What might gold not work in this corrupt world? By corruption, Spurgeon had achieved what I had only prayed for. A speedy deliverance.

Thirteen

SPURGEON'S DISAPPEARANCE CAUSED a stir. The constable sent his remaining officers to search the grounds, but I knew the search would come to nothing. Spurgeon had escaped. How, I didn't know. The escape gave me a glimmering of hope. Perhaps Spurgeon would redeem himself by giving notice to Cecil of my predicament. In this delusion of hope, I half forgave the man for his perfidious testimony.

"There were two men," I said. "Master Marbury here and his companion."

The magistrate looked at Marbury. "You serve Lord Cecil?"

Marbury said he did.

The magistrate asked him if he had a companion named Spurgeon.

"I do, sir, a companion and friend of long standing," said Marbury. Marbury pled ignorance of his friend's whereabouts but acknowledged that he had been assigned as my guardian and said that he found me alone with the body and had only followed orders in helping me dispose of it.

"Whose orders, Master Marbury?"

"This man's, sir," Marbury said, pointing an accusing finger at me. "Our duties were to do his bidding. So we had been instructed by our master, and we could do no less."

There was more murmuring at this, and I saw that in the eyes of the onlookers, despite his companion's strange disappearance from the scene, Marbury had made himself appear a faithful servant whose only crime was following the orders of his superiors, among whom I was one.

I asked Justice Swallow if I might question the boatman, who after his testimony had been thrust into a corner, where he huddled during my exchange with the magistrate.

"Go on," said Swallow.

"Good fellow," I said in a way to assure the boatman I bore him no resentment for his testimony against me. "When you were engaged to make our journey downriver, did you ever speak to me?"

"No, sir," said the boatman. "'Twas the other gentleman. He who has fled."

"Spurgeon, you mean?" said the magistrate.

"If you say so, Master Swallow," said the boatman.

"And did I give you money for your pains?" I asked.

"No, sir. It was the one who was here but is gone. Master Spurgeon."

"And the body that was thrown over the side? Was it I who did it, or Master Spurgeon? He who isn't here."

The boatman paused for a moment, then said, "Truly, it was Master Spurgeon."

"So," I said, "did you suppose when we three were your passengers, that I had charge of all? Or was it Master Spurgeon who spoke to you, paid you, and threw the body overboard to my great amazement? Was it he who gave orders to the rest of us?"

The boatman hesitated, confused. He turned to face the magistrate, then looked back at me. "I thought it was Master Spurgeon."

"And so it was." I turned to Swallow. "It was not my intent to obscure the boy's death by such subtleties. Edward Goode was a gifted actor. He might well have given enough pleasure to you that you would change your opinion of the theater and its work—as well as to others in this city for whom the theater is a source of wisdom and delight, not sin and subversion. He witnessed an act of violence aimed against myself—the burning of a house. I was there; so was a friend, who died in leaping from the roof where we had taken refuge. All this he'd seen—along with the man who set the fire."

"When did this happen, Master Shakespeare?"

"Not a fortnight ago, Master Swallow."

"I remember it well," said the magistrate. "The fire caused much alarm. It was feared the whole Bankside would be consumed. You were there?"

"I was—at the house of an old friend, a woman. Someone I used to know when first I came to London. The fire started in a shop she kept. We escaped the house. She fell to her death, but a ladder was provided me."

"So you think this setter of fires, this arsonist, intended to kill you?"

"The both of us, sir."

Swallow screwed up his face in a thoughtful frown, and in that brief silence hope sprang up in my heart again that he would believe and I would be free and sent on my way. But, again, it was not to be.

"Oh, William Shakespeare," Swallow said. "You amuse yourself with these fantasies. Why would someone want you dead, who is so busy providing what you call wisdom for the multitude? What should we do without you and your breed, you players, who show us the world as it ought to be and not as it is, who seduce foolish women and lazy apprentices to abandon their duties to see your spectacles?"

To this bilious pronouncement I made no answer. What answer would have served? Swallow and his constable were of the same church, the holy pharisaical congregation of the self-satisfied and self-righteous. To them, we players were the warts and wens of the commonwealth. Criminals. Polluters. Enemies of the state.

I stood helpless, a man condemned by his vocation.

Then there was another commotion behind me. I thought it might be Spurgeon come again. I turned from my unreasoning interlocutor.

It was not Spurgeon. It was the baker. Edward Goode's old master. The man who had told me once that Edward had died in the fire—a prophetic utterance that had ironically come to pass, for Edward's murderer and my arsonist-stalker were almost certainly the same man.

Edward had called the baker a brute who worked his apprentices to death; to me he had seemed more angered by Edward's presumed death than grieved. For these solemnities he had put on a different face. He was a bereft parent of the poor murdered child. He had seen the body where it lay in the cart, exposed to public view. He wanted now to confront the murderer, who he had heard was indoors and for whom he had nothing but contempt and hatred.

I was chilled by this description of myself, and realized then that although Justice Swallow might not have decided yet whether I was not merely a detestable actor but a murderer, too, the baker, like the crowd outdoors, had already reached his verdict.

The baker said he wanted to give evidence, and looked at me when he said it.

"What evidence, baker?"

"This common fellow here," the baker said, pointing toward me with much disdain. "This fellow came to my shop three days after it burned and I thought my apprentice burned with it. He asked me questions. About the fire. About my apprentice. I was naturally suspicious."

"Suspicious, why suspicious? And why naturally so?"

"Of his interest in him, for Edward Goode was as goodly a boy as his name. Of very fair face and complexion. I don't doubt that it was this varlet," he said, again pointing an accusing finger at me, "who seduced him into running off, using the fire to excuse his treason. So that he could use the boy unnaturally."

I told the man he lied, and reminded him I had asked about the woman, not about his apprentice. It had been the baker from whom I first learned that Edward existed at all. As for his insinuations that the boy and I were lovers, I called this the damnable lie it was and declared that my only interest was in Edward's talent as an actor—and certain information he had about the fire.

The baker grunted contemptuously at my efforts to defend my innocence and said something under his breath about damned sodomites and the lies they told to cover up their atrocious sins.

Much angry murmuring followed this, and I could tell that had the present company been my jury I would have been condemned. The chamber had grown very hot within and rank because of the press of bodies. My shirt beneath my doublet was damp, and my forehead felt feverish. The baker's slander had completed the case for the magistrate, who wanted only a motive for my murder of Edward Goode. The baker had confirmed his most deeply held prejudices against actors. I saw that now, and my hopes for a quick resolution to my case began to vanish.

"So, William Shakespeare, what say you to these charges?"

"What charges, Master Swallow?" I said, enraged that this baker, who under other circumstances was of no account in the world save in his own estimation, should have become, by Swallow's grace, my prosecutor.

"This honest baker's charges. To wit, that you pursued the boy. That you induced him to break his articles. That he was your filthy catamite. And that, finally, you killed him over some lover's quarrel, after which you tried to dispose of his body and cover up the evidence of your crime."

I was aghast at this incriminating recital. Justice Swallow looked at me sternly. Finally I found my voice.

"Of none of this am I guilty. If I speak otherwise, then let me burn eternally in Hades, for not a word the baker says is true, but all false as hell. This baker never had love for Edward Goode. He abused and starved him. It was for that Edward ran off, not for any inducement of mine. Edward told me himself."

"A dirty falsehood, Master Swallow," the baker said, addressing the magistrate. "Edward Goode was like a son to me. Ask my neighbors. Ask my wife. She will not say differently."

The magistrate addressed me sternly. "It will do you no good,

Master Shakespeare, to impugn the honesty of this worthy baker, whose only purpose here is to mourn his apprentice and tell truth. I know an honest face when I see it. He has one. You have not."

I started to protest again my innocence of these calumnies, but Swallow cut me off, ordering I be seized by the officers, who previous to this had been content to stand by my side. They handled me roughly, as though I intended to escape their grip, and cursed me beneath their breath, calling me a base sodomite and child-killer.

"Master William Shakespeare," Swallow intoned, rising from his chair to his full height, so that I could see that, although old, he was still an imposing figure, nearly six feet tall. "You and your fellows may be made gentlemen by royal command, may boast a coat of arms and other appurtenances of gentility. You may own land in the city and in the suburbs, yet to me you are still a poor, penny-sparing player, a maker of dreams and foolish visions. Your theater, as you please to call it, is a very circus of corruption and sedition. Were I king, I would not countenance it longer than it took to set it all aflame. I would trample upon the ashes and sow nettles there. I would build a bonfire for your vanities, your plays and masques, your lascivious interludes and vain shows. As is, I am only a justice of the peace, yet I am not without power. I therefore order that you be bound over to the next assizes to stand trial for the wanton premeditated murder of Edward Goode."

Then he commanded an officer to bind me and convey me to prison.

A great roar of approval now came up from those in the parlor. Cruel manacles were fitted to my wrists, and my captors seemed to take pleasure in my disgrace. There was a din of noise as Constable Cheetle and one of his officers led me out.

In grim procession we passed from the house into the garden. The crowd was larger than before. It filled the entire street. All about me were faces twisted in anger, and some gleeful at observing my demotion from gentleman to disgraced felon. The common rout of men ever takes joy in witnessing a fall from grace.

THE RICKETY CART in which Edward Goode's body had been brought was now replaced by another and more capacious one, and this became the means whereby I was to be transported to my prison. The crowd, however, was not content that my punishment wait upon a trial. In the magistrate's parlor, I had found myself the target of much vile abuse. I was called a liar, an abuser of boyish innocence, a murderer and procurer of accomplices and vile whoremasterly rogue. Now I was the target of stones, garbage, and more insults. What little dignity the falseness of my indictment had left me had dwindled to nothing. The playhouse and bear gardens closed, such poor creatures as I remained the crowd's only entertainment.

What would my stalker do now? Would my imprisonment and disgrace quench his thirst for revenge? Was I, irony of ironies, finally free?

Fourteen

I HAD BEEN in London a dozen years or more at the time of the events I tell of, but never in prison. Ben Jonson had that honor, and Tom Nashe, too, for offending in their play, *Isle of Dogs*. Then, Ben again for killing some one of Lord Pembroke's company, although he protested it was self-defense. Which I wholly believe, for the dead man was a notorious rogue and roarer, a choleric man without a brain to boast of. So, yes, sometimes actors went to prison.

But not your humble servant. I was too respectable for that. From the time I first came to London I was careful, prudent, scrupulous in my compliance, eager to fit whatever square hole was presented to me, and no whiner. I fought no duels, avoided debt, and scorned to hold a grudge against my fellow man, though God knows, I oft had cause. If I pissed, I pissed in a pot, in no man's cap.

I speak crudely, but you get my point, sir?

Now what was happening to me seemed to be the life of some other man—a part I was playing in a tragedy by a malevolent spirit who blocked my moves though the words he left to me.

I'd been condemned to the Marshalsea, a wretched pile of gray brick. How can I describe to you—you who have had the good fortune to avoid such fate—the inhospitality of its clammy walls, its close, vaporous interiors, its stern-faced, truncheon-bearing wardens? Worst were the denizens there, not innocent wretches like myself, victims of false witness and fickle fortune, but the criminal class, the obdurate villains who preyed upon the populace and, in prison, preyed upon each other.

There I was thrown in with two dozen of these creatures, and only after I proclaimed myself a gentleman and identified myself by name was I, thanks be to God, taken notice of by the chief warden. He, as fortune would have it, was a frequenter of plays and besotted with my play *Hamlet,* which he claimed to have seen a dozen times. This he presently proved by quoting two soliloquies, my lines as the old king's ghost, and some bold bawdry I put in the mouth of the gravedigger. Indeed, his discourse with me was more audition than interrogation, and I would not have been surprised at its conclusion had he given over his office at the prison and offered to become an actor, for he was a brave man, tall, with handsome eyes and, but for a hairy wart on its tip, the nose of a Roman senator.

Be as it may, this worthy man, whose name I think was Peacock, or some likewise paradoxical appellation given his vocation and manly form, plucked me from my villainous companions and the stench of their cell and moved me to more habitable lodgings. These were reserved for gentlemen, most of whom were imprisoned for debt or for offense against the state, and unlike most of the noxious chambers of the place had the blessing of several windows that looked out into the street, decent beds, and food that didn't turn the stomach, purchased daily and brought into the prison. Thus I avoided the usual prison fare, which had I eaten it I would have been half myself upon my release, if alive at all.

I didn't tell my new companions the whys and wherefores of my imprisonment. I had discovered from my dalliance with the learned Justice Swallow that a wight who claims to be stalked by murderers is more likely to be scorned than pitied. Instead, I made up a little plot about a treacherous brother-in-law, a dispute over an inheritance, a jealous wife—the raw stuff of comedy, to be sure, but common enough, and credible. I did say—so that none would think I planned an indefinite sojourn in the Marshalsea—that I hoped for deliverance through the help of a well-positioned lord who had shown me many favors and would not likely let me languish.

This fiction was no sooner minted than I imagined how half the inmates of the place might make the same boast, and felt like a fool and braggart. No man wants to think himself without friends, for while God may disdain his acts, yet surely there is one other human soul who understands, who loves despite all. Yet my remark caused a flurry of interest in my new companions, one of whom was a lawyer named Pryce.

Pryce was a narrow, shifty-eyed gentleman, slovenly garbed for one of his profession in dirty collar, frayed doublet, and hose with holes the size of tennis balls. He readily confessed his internment for embezzlement and made jokes as though theft were a duty of his office. He wondered if I could use my influence with this unnamed lord to do him some good. He said he feared his trial and the remonstrance of his piteous victims, mostly widows and orphans whose estates he'd plundered.

Like the chief warden, Pryce was a lover of the theater and had seen several of my plays, the plots and characters of which he recalled in impressive detail, even going so far as to quote a soliloquy or witty exchange. I congratulated him on his memory, which he said he had put to school to make it more perfect, for he had found it useful in the courts. He said, "I have a thought, Master Shakespeare, if you will be so good as to consider it."

Then he prevailed upon me to give a performance, to turn the sad venue in which we found ourselves into a theater. This was a request in which he was quickly joined by my other cellmates, a butcher, a merchant tailor, and a scrivener, who all declared that the worst of prison was the tedium and that a play, even if it were a single scene or a few verses, would be just the thing to bring them relief.

They pressed me so earnestly with this desire, and it seemed to cost me so little, that I consented, and the first night of my incarceration I took as my stage a corner of our chamber and was, in succession, Julius Caesar, Prince Hamlet, Juliet and her Romeo, and a half dozen other persons whose lines I half remembered, though I swear I wrote every syllable. I danced, I sang, I told jokes and pulled pranks. I was clown and king, swain and shepherdess, and I never changed clothes, concealed my face or did more than modulate my voice and expression.

These performances gave my companions much delight and, I confess, helped me assuage my own misery, for I was often placed in the mind and heart of one of my own creations whose torment was much greater than my own.

Beside my performances—and there were more while I was resident there—I studied how to alert my friends to my imprisonment. The warden kindly provided me with paper and pen. I wrote letters to Burbage, Condell, and Heming letting them know where I was and for what reason, although I was spare in details. My life in recent days had become a tangled skein, and the most skilled of weavers could not disentangle it.

I also wrote a letter to Lord Cecil in hope that he would issue a warrant for my release, or grant me pardon, or create whatever instrument of law might work my freedom. I declared myself falsely accused and prayed for his good offices. My status as King's Man had done nothing to help me with Justice Swallow. It may have worked against me, for the inhabitants of Southwark have an inborn resentment of Londoners and come close to thinking themselves their own country.

But I knew Cecil would help me. If any man could see how I'd been undone by false insinuation it was Cecil, who was conversant with such stratagems and did not assume them to be figments of an addled brain.

I WROTE THESE missives at noon. The warden's son—a goodly lad, whose father assured me of his trustworthiness—was off with them an hour later, for which service I paid him the last few coins in my purse. By three of the clock, Burbage appeared at the prison, holding a basket with fresh bread, cold chicken, hazelnuts, and a pottle of ale. He also brought the good wishes and fervent prayers of my fellow actors, who, having been informed by Monsieur Mountjoy of my disappearance, were half convinced that I was dead.

"We're with you, Will," Burbage boomed, his great beard quivering with indignation. "These charges are malicious, trumped-up slanders by the puritanical imbeciles of Southwark. Nothing pleases them but to find some excuse to decry plays and parade their own hypocritical virtue. What was the name of this so-called magistrate that committed you?"

"Swallow. Samuel, I think—or some other prophet."

"Ah, a skinny bugger who looks like a corpse in a fur-faced gown?"

"The very man," I said, laughing beside myself.

"By heaven, I know him. Appeared before him once for some infraction. He has a heart of stone, is deaf to all entreaties and too stiff-necked for bribes. I came away with a heavy fine, but only in place of a day in the stocks. It's a wonder you escaped with imprisonment. The man has been known to turn malefactors over to the crowd for private justice."

My honor still bled from my public humiliation. My ears burned with the abuse of villains who did not know who I was or what I did and may have been guilty themselves of the most unseemly vices. The crowd dwindled as we got nearer the prison, but when I was brought to the portal my cloak was stained with foul matter from the mob, and I stank like a pig rooting in the middenheap.

Yet they railed and cursed and threw stones as if they had no sin. Oh, what a world, and what a creature is man—the worst of his vices is his presumed virtue, and the best of his virtues is the honest confession of his vices.

Burbage wanted to know what he could do to secure my release. I told him I had sent a message to Lord Cecil and expected my liberation at any time. "In faith, Dick," I said, "Cecil won't let me rot here."

I had never told Burbage about my stalker. I did not do so now, but I trusted him with a trust that may have been foolish yet was real and steadfast. I provided my friend with a pretty version of my sufferings. I confess that never in my life had I lied with such frequency about my affairs. Every time I turned round I was inventing another tale. But who can blame me?

"And your wife?" Burbage said. He regarded me beneath heavy brows, a fatherly expression (though he was younger than I), judgmental, censorious. I bridled.

"What of her?" I said.

"Does she know?"

"Know what?"

"Of your imprisonment, your arrest, these insane charges."

"She knows nothing."

"Great God, man, write the woman. She's your wife. She has a right to know."

"I won't write her," I said. "There's no need to worry her. All this will pass. By the time she gets word in Stratford, it will be over. It'll be matter for laughter."

It wasn't worrying Anne that bothered me. She might think prison was my comeuppance. It had been a while since I had been home to Stratford, and our last parting had been bitter, although my London labors had done much to elevate our station in the town and I hoped to be better loved thereby. Instead, we had quarreled the whole time I was home. Don't ask the cause. I can't remember it—or them. It was ever thus, as though there were some deeper grievance between us that neither could speak of. I thought it might yet be the death of our son, but when I asked her if that was it, she said nay and would not say what was. Cold stone she was when I went out the door, and when she called after me I did not answer but set my face toward London and the life I had made for myself here.

Burbage dined with me. We drank the ale, talked of business, reminisced and scorned the cruel teeth of time. Burbage was hardheaded but philosophical, too, and was ever a good companion for my sullen hours. But all the while I was uneasy. When we spoke of *Measure for Measure,* I thought of poor Edward Goode, how he would have played Mariana, how much he wanted to be an actor. And I also thought how ironic it was that this prison was the safest place I had been for days and the first place I had acted in months. I had not thought to make the Marshalsea my stage, but so it had come to pass, with my consent but not by my design.

What had I become but a puppet?

But who was the puppeteer?

Fifteen

THE NEXT THREE days, I lay in prison thinking of the sins of fathers and my dead boys, Hamnet and Edward. My enemy had introduced me to this solemn theme, and the more I contemplated these sad events, the more deserved my condemnation seemed. Both I'd watched die, helpless to save. And but for me, both might be yet alive. Truth was, I had been a better father to myself than to my children, who like stray dogs took scraps from my table. This was a bitter thought to me.

Meanwhile, Burbage and others came and went, so I did not want for company or for decent food. Yet I could not understand why Cecil did not descend upon my prison like Jove resolving a dispute among his wayward children, or send Thomas Stanleigh or another of his men. How difficult would it be for one so great in place and repute to work my release? A word from the king's chief minister would do it. No Southwark justice of the peace could withstand that.

Then I thought: What if Cecil were with the king somewhere outside of London, and Stanleigh with him? It might be a month or more before he returned. I had been given to understand that I would be tried at the Epiphany quarter session, less time than that away.

By the time Cecil discovered my plight I might be hanged and buried.

Then I thought the explanation might be simpler. Lord Cecil never received my message. It was never delivered. I remembered Cecil's household, the army of attendants, secretaries, undersecretaries, servants, grooms. How many hands would have passed his message along till it reached one who in a fit of indifference or negligence or simple malice decided that Will Shakespeare's legal trouble did not merit bothering the second most powerful man in England?

And then there was another explanation. My stalker.

I had concluded now that Cecil's theory had been correct, that at least for the time being my fears and misfortunes were providing the Southwark arsonist with too much perverse entertainment for him to kill me, although both Cecil and I suspected that might be his ultimate purpose. Perhaps he had somehow managed to intercept the message, for I suspected that his eyes followed me while I was taken to prison, just as he had lured me to the Globe so I could witness Edward Goode's murder.

During those three days I could hardly think of anything else. Then on the fourth morning my friend the warden came to where I was and said I had a visitor.

I thought it was Burbage or Condell come again, for my friends had been faithful in their attendance. But it was not; it was Thomas Stanleigh, Cecil's man. I looked into the rosy-cheeked countenance of the servant I had despised a little for his foppishness and almost wept for relief and gratitude.

STANLEIGH TALKED FAST, obviously more than a little uncomfortable in my grim surroundings. "Lord Cecil has been with the king. Moving around from one place to another this whole week."

"My letter—?"

"Received, but belatedly. It was only when we returned that

his eye fell upon it, along with dozens of other messages, letters, petitions."

"What did he say?"

"Conveys his sorrow. Asks you come to him as soon as your release can be arranged."

"How long will that take?" I asked.

Stanleigh smiled brightly. "No sooner said than done, Master Shakespeare. I've a writ for your release, signed by Lord Cecil himself. I've given it to the warden. You'll be free to leave with me."

"I am deep in your master's debt," I said, my thanks heartfelt. "And in yours, Master Stanleigh."

Stanleigh made a little wave with his hands. "It's my pleasure, Master Shakespeare, to do you service."

I marveled at how with a stroke of the pen a man of great public authority could work my release.

"In truth, Master Shakespeare, you are only being bailed."

"What?"

"I'm afraid you may still have to stand trial for your murder— I mean, the crime of which you are falsely accused. At least for the time being until the true murderer is found. For now, you are in my master's charge, who has given Justice Swallow security for your appearance."

As I was bidding my Marshalsea companions farewell, Pryce the lawyer pulled me aside.

"Master Shakespeare," he said in what I would have called a conspiratorial voice had he not always spoken in my presence thus, "if you would speak to Master Secretary Cecil on my behalf I would be much indebted to you."

Since I did not anticipate requiring the professional services of this larcenous lawyer, I gave him no encouragement, but he persisted. "I would make it worth your while."

"You'd bribe me?"

"Oh, say not bribe, Master Shakespeare. As you can see, money have I none," Pryce waved a hand at his filthy suit of clothes as evidence. "Knowledge, rather."

"What knowledge?"

"First, your oath."

"Even were I to give it, it might avail you nothing. Me less. Your offenses are rank."

"You could try," Pryce said, clutching my wrist like a drowning man. "That would be better than nothing."

Pryce's manner since my coming to the Marshalsea was ever prideful. Now I saw a different face, the banality and piteousness of his condition. A clerk at law, he was as much a thief as he who picks pockets on the Strand or filches chickens from the honest husbandman.

"You say you have knowledge. Of what?"

"Of one who is curious about your affairs."

"My affairs?"

"I beg you for your oath."

"I swear."

"That you will plead for me with Cecil."

"Yes. I swear it. You have my oath."

"I have a former friend," Pryce said after he had paused for a moment as though gasping for air. "We had a falling-out. For this month we have not spoken, nor are likely to. He is a lawyer, like myself, but if you think I am treacherous in my dealings—compared to him I am an angel."

"I care not for lawyers or for angels," I said.

"Patience, sir. You shall see. This lawyer, whose name is John Fanshawe—"

"I partly know the man," I said, my heart leaping with expectation. For this had been the very same wretch I had quarreled with in the street the day Edward Goode was murdered. "Say on."

"Fanshawe had a client; he didn't tell me his name. He—this client—wanted to know your business. What properties you owned. What investments you had made. What allowances had been granted from the king. Sales from the theater. Also with whom you kept company, whom you knew at court and whom you knew ten years ago."

"Ten years ago!" I said, astounded.

"I've a good memory, as I have said."

"This was Fanshawe's client, not yours. How came you to know of Fanshawe's business?" I said.

Pryce gave a derisive laugh. "Fanshawe doesn't know the meaning of discretion. He will have his drink, and when he drinks he talks. He was paid well, you see, and wanted me to know that his prospects had improved because of this client he had."

"Whose name he never said."

Pryce shook his head.

"Or described him?"

"No."

"But he wanted to know my history?"

"What you did and where you went in London—and in that town you came from."

"Stratford. Warwickshire."

"The very place. He wanted to know about your wife, your children. In what manner you lived there."

"But why?" I said. "Wherefore should he be so curious? This surpasses mere curiosity. This is obsession."

"Fanshawe never said. To him it didn't matter, the why of it, but only if there was money. Fanshawe was being paid. Generously, or so he claimed. Besides, he had held a grudge. For certain fees he claimed you owed him. That's enough for Fanshawe, who is one of those who may forget a friend but never an enemy."

"I didn't pay because he didn't provide," I said sternly, not wishing Pryce to think Fanshawe had good cause to hate me.

"I tell you this for what it's worth, Master Shakespeare. And pray you keep your oath."

"What oaths I give, I keep," I said.

Sixteen

STANLEIGH TOOK ME by coach to my lodgings, where I washed and changed—for my cloak still reeked of the refuse that had been heaped upon me at my arraignment, and to that had been added the noxious odors of the prison itself—then we set out. Along the way I complained of my guardians Spurgeon and Marbury, who had borne false witness, then treacherously abandoned me.

"Rogues and villains," Stanleigh said scornfully. "They've disappeared. I've looked everywhere."

I told him how Spurgeon and Marbury had assured me they would see to the disposal of the body, then later accused me of ordering them to do it.

"I never trusted either man, especially Spurgeon," Stanleigh said.

"Then why were they my guardians?" I asked, amazed at Stanleigh's casual acceptance of their untrustworthiness.

"My master misjudged the men," Stanleigh said. "He thought them otherwise than they were. But I promise you, if we find them, they'll have much to answer for."

AT CECIL HOUSE, Stanleigh escorted me to his master's private rooms. There I found Cecil in a long velvet dressing gown of exquisite workmanship. He was reading a book, a slender volume with a black leather cover and a gold-embossed title I couldn't quite make out. He looked surprised to see me even though Stanleigh had assured me I had been announced.

"Ah, Master Shakespeare," Cecil said, rising. He nodded to Stanleigh, who took his leave. "How now after your ordeal? I cannot believe prison can be endurable to one of your sensibilities."

I told him I was well enough now and thanked him again for working my release.

"Now tell me about this murder they say you did."

And so I spoke, surprising myself at my stumbling, for I would have thought, having practiced it in my own mind many times, that my narrative would be seamless, omitting nothing. Yet it was otherwise. I was relieved to be able to tell my distinguished patron everything, for with others I was always holding something back.

While I talked, Cecil listened with a judicious expression that invested his long, narrow face with a calm dignity. At times he stroked his beard and nodded, or made reassuring noises. I tried to read his eyes, looking for disbelief or derision. No clue. The man was the most inscrutable soul I had known. I could understand why life at court appealed to him. When he wished, he was stone. If he needed, he could weep at will.

He sat meditating after I had done. I waited for him to speak. The chamber was very warm. My collar was tight, and I was uncomfortably damp beneath my shirt.

Finally he said, "This is a most unusual story you tell, Master Shakespeare. This Edward Goode murdered by a person seen only by you. Thereafter, the constable finds you cleaning up the bloody evidence—and a dirty-minded constable who can think only of buggery as a motive. Such are the times we live in."

I did not speak at this, on tenterhooks to know his drift.

"Your accusers have a case, Master Shakespeare. Yes, it's all circumstance and inference, and yet I've seen many a man prance upon the gibbet with less proof against him."

"But I protest, Your Honor, I never—"

He reached forward and took my hand comfortingly. "Don't torment yourself, Master Shakespeare. Forgive me if I view your situation with reason too cold and dispassionate. So might a jury do, eager to simplify matters and hie home to supper. But I'm on your side. Nothing you've told me persuades me against my earliest view. You have a most devilish enemy. Having tried to kill you, he now plays you like a pipe, fingering your stops."

"But why?"

"To make you the more wretched. The proof of which malignity is in the bitterness of your recent misfortunes. Your adversary's motive is to drive you mad. The Marshalsea is a pit, but Bedlam is worse. Worse than death."

His words had their intended effect. I was astonished by this vision of horror. I, imprisoned with lunatics, acting not on the stage but in the dank cells where the idle and curious might pay their tuppence to gawk at me? It was a fate worse than death. The absolute end—what I would be remembered for, not my plays but the loss of my mind.

I wanted to ask, why such malice? What had I done so to offend—either gods or devils? But I knew that Cecil knew no more than I. At least not at present.

"I have a suggestion," Cecil said.

"Your Honor?" I said, eager to hear it.

"Leave London, go away for a while. Back to Stratford."

My heart sank, for this strong suggestion was farthest from my thoughts.

"You hesitate," Cecil said, "but give me leave to persuade you. Your adversary feeds upon your misery, which he enjoys only because he can behold the fruits of his labors. Now, say you're simply gone, vanished. Where will he find his pleasure? Perhaps he'll grow weary of the game, give over. At the very least, gone from this place you would purchase a little safety."

"I'm not so inclined, Your Honor."

"Maybe some other place, then. Scotland, Ireland? Even Italy? Have you been there?"

I said I had not, though I had written about these places

enough, mixing Boccaccio and Fiorentino with a heavy dose of imagination to create a half dozen Italian cities; none of which, I suppose, was like the real, but who cared? I was a writer of plays, not a learned geographer.

No, I wouldn't go to Italy. Nor dour Scotland nor, heaven forbid, boggy Ireland.

Then I thought about Stratford. Stratford by Avon's sweet flowing stream. Stratford where I had family and friends. Stratford, the town that once I couldn't wait to get out of, but that was now removed from the dangers of London. And I thought about my situation: my old mistress's neck broken, and Edward Goode slaughtered. This constant harping on the sins of the fathers. Of what grand and sinister design was this all a part?

But was Stratford a haven, or was it the stage for my adversary's next act?

I was seized by fear for my wife and daughters. Were they not in danger because of me? Had not the prying lawyer Fanshawe inquired about my Stratford business? What did that mean?

Suddenly I had a great desire to go to Stratford, yet how could I do so and be assured he would not follow me there and do harm to my family?

Then the answer came in no more time than it took me to take a single breath. In *Measure for Measure,* I'd created a noble duke who leaves the city in order to allow his deputy, stern Angelo, to enforce a strict morality. Then this same duke, well disguised, returns to his capital to observe his deputy's conduct without being recognized, finds him false and hypocritical, and brings all to justice.

So my answer was there. The play was the thing, after all.

I would get me to Stratford but appear to go elsewhere, say, to Scotland or Italy. The farther the better, lest he try to follow. By this I could both escape my adversary and protect my family.

I told Cecil my plan. He listened, stroked his beard, and studied me with his shrewd, dispassionate gaze.

"Let me understand you. You would only appear to leave England?"

"Yes, Your Honor."

More thought on his part. Then he said, "This pleases me well, Master Shakespeare. You're a master of disguise. When I saw you play Sejanus with your helmet on and flowing beard, I could not believe it. You seemed transformed, your look, your voice, your very carriage."

"I believe it would work," I said.

"Then get you to Stratford," Cecil said. "Tell no one—not your landlord, not your friends, not even your fellows at your theater. Stay a month—visit your wife, your children, but do so that only they know it's you."

"But how am I to do all this, create this conspicuous leave-taking?"

Cecil laughed, but not boisterously. Slyly, rather, as though he and I were accomplices in an elaborate joke. "Never fear. Do you think you're the only magician in London? That I can't create my own illusions?"

It was not a question I could afford to answer in the negative, so I said nothing.

"I'll have a dozen witnesses see you board a ship. A captain will swear upon a dozen Bibles you sailed with him. Italians of my acquaintance will write to London friends to say they met you in Bologna or Rome."

"And the reason for my sudden travel?" I said. "In faith, who would believe in the suddenness of my voyage—I who have never traveled abroad, save in books and poems?"

"Nothing easier," Cecil said, warming to his theme. "Charged with murder, you've fled England to avoid hanging. Trust me, Master Shakespeare. You're not the first man who assessed his chances with one of our English juries and decided his own case. Italy is full of Englishmen who dare not show their face in their own country. They have left all—family, friends, property—but saved their lives in doing it. As for your sudden urge to see Italy, nothing is more probable than that you should take advantage of your temporary freedom and extend it indefinitely."

He was right. I wondered that I had not seen it. My adversary, in making me a murderer, had given me a perfect cover for my flight.

I gave Cecil my thanks many times over, and then remembered my promise to Robert Pryce.

"While I was in Marshalsea I meet another prisoner. A lawyer named Pryce."

"Robert Pryce," said Cecil quickly, as though he had been thinking about the imprisoned lawyer all this time. "The legal fraternity is a small circle, mostly of villains who love dark corners and obscurity as other men pray for light. Trust me, his abuse of office is well known and much condemned."

"He was my pew-fellow," I said, "or one of them. He told me about a man he knew in the legal trade. Fanshawe, a lawyer with whom I had myself some rancorous dealings—a botched lawsuit, a disputed fee. Fanshawe had a client, most secret to him, who hired Fanshawe to pry into my affairs—"

"Affairs?"

"My private business—friends and associates, my properties, everything about me—here and in Stratford, and for years back."

"Most strange," Cecil said.

"Indeed!"

"You think this Fanshawe or his mysterious client may be your adversary?"

I didn't know what I thought. If Fanshawe's prying and my adversary's menace were coincidences it defied all reason, but I was not prepared to explain the connection. Not yet.

Cecil had no such reservation. He spoke bluntly. "Pursue this man, this duplicitous pettifogger. He pried into your history for money. Judas-like, he may betray his client's name for money, and you become the wiser thereby."

"For this intelligence from Pryce," I said, "he asked a price."

"A price from Pryce? Why am I not surprised?" Cecil said, amused. "What was it?"

"Intercession," I said.

"Are we talking religion now?"

"More practical."

"Intercession then for whom?" Cecil asked.

"For himself, Your Honor."

"And you vowed I'd intercede on his behalf—with the judge?"

I laughed a little at this. "No, Your Lordship. That was beyond my power. I told him only I'd ask. He knew the risk. The risk of your refusal, even perhaps of your inability."

"Then you've asked and I'll answer, Master Shakespeare. Leave Pryce to heaven. I understand the man's a Papist. If not, he's at least a wolf in sheep's clothing. That's worse than his religion, if he has one. He can rot in the Marshalsea for all I care. I'll not lift a finger to help such a one."

I couldn't dispute this. Pryce had been most forthcoming. For that, he had my thanks and my oath, but his crimes were crass and unforgivable. If he languished in the Marshalsea until the end of time, he might have my oath, which I had now faithfully executed, but not my tears.

Cecil took my elbow and steered me toward the door. Thomas Stanleigh appeared to guide me to the street, for a great house is easy neither to enter nor to leave. Cecil said, "Be ruled by me, Master Shakespeare. Go to the snooping Fanshawe. Find out what he knows. Then be ready early tomorrow for your journey. Travel lightly. All else will be provided you."

"What of my indictment? The charge of murder?"

"Think not of it. I'll carry all."

"And my reputation?" I asked.

"Ah, reputation, a most exaggerated and suspect commodity. The charge is murder, not pimping or pickpursing. A murderer may mingle with gentlemen in England without shame, for half the so-called nobility have so sinned, truth be known. Not all sins are equal. Some are—how shall I say?—of a higher order, more dignified, even fashionable. So murder is. Besides the which, you'll be in Italy."

"But I'll be in Stratford," I said. "Not Italy."

"All's one for now. Your patience will be rewarded. Justice is a good strong mastiff, and every dog must have its day."

I wasn't sure what justice had to do with dogs, but I surmised that I must be hopeful that all would work out in the end. Yet it didn't seem possible to me now. Rather, all seemed dark and despairing, like a sea without bottom, like a winter without end.

Seventeen

By late afternoon I was home again, no hulking guards for me. Better to fend for myself than be so encumbered, and I told my mighty patron so. Cecil looked concerned but seemed to take no offense at my refusal. He cursed both my jackdaws, called them traitors, villains, vile complotters, and much worse, then, of a sudden, laughed most heartily and said he hoped my courage was not foolhardiness. He insisted, however, I would next morning have an escort to my ship—and of sufficient number to make a great show of my departure should I be observed by my stalker.

Monsieur Mountjoy wanted to make a feast for my homecoming and was in the midst of directing his wife to prepare it when I told him my plans for foreign travel.

"Leave England, Master Shakespierre!" he exclaimed, his eyes wide with amazement. "You are going to France I pray not."

"Italy," I said.

"Italia!" He spurted some Italian phrase, laughed merrily, and said it was a perfect place for a fleeing felon since all Italians were criminally inclined and I might not be so conspicuous there.

My Frenchman began relating his own escape from France, which he told with Gallic flourish. I had heard the story before, and it was always different. Each version was adorned with new persons and incidents, the only common thread being Mountjoy's

ingenuity and cunning. Fearful that he would keep me half the
night, I begged his pardon, explaining that while I purposed to
take ship in the morning, there was one thing I needed to do
before, and that was find a certain lawyer who owed me money I
would need for my journey. This was a politic lie, for I had
decided, given the inquisitiveness of my stalker, the less anyone
knew of my affairs and purposes—even among my proven
friends—the better.

My landlord's good wife pressed upon me a slice of her newly
made cheese and a cup of ale. Such was my supper, I having
refused to be feasted. I bolted my food like a famished hound, bid
farewell to the Mountjoys, and by dark had set out to the lawyer's
house.

A YEAR HAD passed since my falling-out with Fanshawe, but
before that I had been twice to his house in a narrow lane near
Paul's, where he dwelt with his wife in circumstances no grander
than my own, though he told me that he did much business in the
city, had at all times half a dozen suits at law and much influence
amongst judges and other officers. Even then, I surmised this was
so much talk. His residence was a newly built tenement, divided
into four habitations. He and his wife lived in the upstairs. I
remembered that they had small children there, one I think a boy
of eight or ten, with a loud incessant voice with no music in it and
an insolent manner of which I greatly disapproved, being myself
a stern disciplinarian as a father, at least when I was home to be
so. Fanshawe's wife was a shrewish fishfag who railed at her husband in the presence of his clients to avenge herself upon him.

Even before I came to the door I could hear the woman's
querulous tongue. I had hoped this was a sign that her husband
was at home. Instead she was denouncing the son of whom I
spoke for some infraction of his duty.

Seeing me, she did not look pleased, even though I recall that
at the time I was her husband's client she spoke with pride of having so notable a playwright grace her humble home. She had never

seen a play, but she had heard my name bruited about among people she knew, and that was enough for her.

"Marry, what would you?" she snapped. "My husband's not here."

She was a big, loud woman with a raw complexion and a belly of impressive magnitude. She was taller than I and looked down from her Amazonian height with contempt.

Her anger, I now saw, was directed not entirely at her unruly son, who was sitting in the corner whimpering after his chastisement, but at me. I wondered if her husband had told her that I owed him money and had refused to pay.

"It's most important that I see him," I said. "I sail tomorrow for Italy. It would please me to settle my debt with him before."

I had planned what I would say to her in her husband's absence before leaving the Mountjoys, and the lie about my willingness to pay for services poorly rendered had the very effect I intended.

"Well, sir, if you are here to settle a debt, you may give your money to me, for a wife and husband be one flesh. Their purse be one likewise. So you will spare yourself from searching him out in the stews and fleshpots of the city, where I have no doubt he wallows even as we speak."

I understood from this speech the bitter well from which Mistress Fanshawe's anger had been drawn, and remembered that my cellmate Pryce had mentioned Fanshawe's drinking, which I took to be in excess of that modest tippling or infrequent drunkenness that most men are guilty of, but I was not ready to pay and go my way. I had no interest in throwing good money after bad.

"We have not settled on the exact sum," I said. "Besides, he and I may have more business when I return to London."

"You're leaving London?" she said, looking at me suspiciously as though the debt I had offered to repay I was now prepared to ignore.

"I'm going to Italy," I said, glad to have the chance to relate this to her. The more people who knew my false purpose, the safer I would be in Stratford.

"And turn Papist?" she said and screwed up her face as though she intended to spit at me.

"Religion has nothing to do with it," I said.

She ignored this and commenced to make disparaging comments about the Italians, their religion, their poisonings, their licentiousness, although it wasn't clear to me she knew any of that nation or had ever been in Italy herself. I waited until her tirade was done. My endurance of her learned lecture paid me well: She seemed a woman who was not used to being listened to, for all her railing, and finding me respectful of her opinions she grew calm and even friendly, who before had been a bawling, brawling harridan of the first water.

Again I asked her where I might find her husband.

"I'll tell you, sir, if you must know. God knows, it's more home to him than here. It's a bawdy-house in St. John's, Clerkenwell. He's with his slattern, a woman named Delia. A filthy, insolent drab as infamous for her foul tongue as for the multitude of her lovers."

I knew the establishment to which she referred. Its proprietor was one Lucy Negro, who once had been one of the queen's gentlewomen but had since fallen from that grace and opened up a whorehouse sans pareil. She was well known as the Black Nun of Clerkenwell, an appellation that pleased her.

"You know his whore and abide her?" I asked, hardly able to believe it.

"She feeds his dreams," she hissed. "He calls out her name whilst asleep. He moans, groans, twists and turns, flings covers to and fro, and makes my bedchamber his bawdy house. I told him I would prick his needle if he so much as mentioned her name again, or saw her. He said that I might cut off what I could, he had a sharp knife, too, and if I depricked him he knew some brave parts of me he would make mincemeat. We have made peace on that ground."

"Peace!" I exclaimed incredulously.

"He goes his way with his whore, and I have found a man who does not disdain my charms. Yet I keep my knife sharp, sir."

Mistress Fanshawe paused, thrust out her chest, and glanced down menacingly at my groin, which gaze caused me much fear for my manhood. My wife and I had quarreled oft, but the Fanshawe marriage surpassed anything I'd seen in violence and acrimony.

I took my leave of the woman with much relief and set out to find her husband.

I FORBEAR TO speak more of Lucy Negro's establishment for fear you will think I advertise its dubious charms. Besides, what dissolute place does not look like this?—a cluster of trestle tables and benches under a ceiling low enough to put a tall man in peril of being brained, much talk and boisterous laughter all about, drawers and waiters whose only school is to be rude, tapsters whose duty 'tis to water drinks and pick pockets, entertainers of sorts—puppeteers, singers, magicians, dancers. Add to these the clientele: idle tradesmen, profligate younger sons, random drunks, lascivious gropers, old soldiers and sailors, and painted-faced strumpets and their punks all mixed together in an unsavory stew of corrupt humanity. Oh, it's a merry mad world, my masters, and never so much as in a London whorehouse.

Already, like Jove, I'd changed my shape, for while I went openly to Fanshawe's house, my journey to Clerkenwell took me into the maw of danger, and I was not eager to be known. A Dutchman's hat concealed my bald forehead, my cloak wrapped around me like a second skin, and I wore a false beard I had amongst some other properties I kept at home in a chest. The hat and beard quite hid my face and—I suppose, for I had no glass to see by—surely added twenty years to my back. I adopted an old man's gait and tremor and went boldly in, drawing some impudent stares as though to ask what such a fatherly figure as I should want in this fleshpot of youthful concupiscence.

Inside was as I have described, but very warm so that I sweat beneath my cloak. I could not find a place at table and stood for a quarter hour or more looking from face to face for Fanshawe. I saw a half dozen men I knew. One was a scurvy fellow we had used to gather admissions at the Globe and sent packing when we found he pocketed every second penny he took in. I don't think he penetrated my disguise.

Now came a pasty-faced waiter, who looked me up and down with fine contempt—whether for my beard or cloak or perverse curiosity—and asked what I would. I ordered, not wishing to be conspicuous in my abstinence. Anon came the drink, by which time I needed it sorely because of the heat, the closeness of the room, and the rude joggling customers at my elbow, pushing and shoving for a little ground.

Then, a loud cry at my ear—a warning shout. Meant for me, who knew? I swiveled, caught the flash of blade and spurt of blood, a groan of agony, the vision of a man's throat ripped ear to ear, the man's eyes filled with terror and his body sinking into a sanguine sea.

Oh, sweet celerity of death, you show no kindness to us mortals that you dally not. In the next moments all was confusion of cries and oaths about me, and in my mind I thought: It's Fanshawe that's dead, slain before my eyes. Fanshaw taking his secret with him.

Fanshawe it was not. The dead man—for his soul had slipped the veil—was nothing like the man I sought. Above the slain man, the killer now revealed himself, his back against the wall, his chest heaving, and he the master of an eight-inch blade to ward off any who would seize him. He babbled Dutch, German, Frankish— something like, but speak he did, his eyes glassy with rage, terror, and suspicion.

All stared at the carnage, averting their eyes from the man who'd wrought it, as though to look there upon his face were to earn the same reward as the man freshly dead. Who wanted that? I had heard no quarrel, no exchange of threats, no warning— only the sweeping motion. Like a gust of wind, as sudden as it was deadly. It had taken everyone by surprise, as death so often did. My heart beat with such violence that I clutched my chest to calm it.

A silence fell upon the place that a minute before had been all merriment and delight.

The spell broke; panic followed. From every corner, Lucy's custom broke for the door, pushing and shoving, kicking, screaming as though the house were afire, and I thought of that night in Southwark when I stared down into the flames and felt the wreaths of smoke choke me. Now the sullen murderer, standing where he had done the deed, himself turned toward the same portal, still brandishing his bloody knife. People stumbled over each other to get out of his way.

I continued to watch as though I were watching actors, directing their motions. Then I saw at the top of the stairs, amidst other men who had come forth from the chambers above to see what had happened and were steadfast like marble monuments, John Fanshawe himself. Beside him was a hard-faced slattern with the painted face and scarlet gown the Puritans delighted in condemning to hell. This I assumed was his doxy, Delia, so much despised by his wife. The prospect that the murder would presently bring officers had turned to my advantage, for disguised as I was, I doubted I would be admitted upstairs, being thought to be in my feigned decrepitude beyond the years of venery.

The murderer fled into the night; no one dared to stop him. The tavernkeeper and some of the waiters and drawers were taking the dead man out. His arms hung limply at his sides. The man had bled generously on the floor; a waiter was cleaning up. Meanwhile Lucy's custom were drifting back into the room as though nothing had happened. I heard loud voices, laughter, but all seemed forced to me now. It was not as before in the room. Death had invaded the precincts that liquor, lust, and jollity had striven to keep out. The body could be taken, the blood cleaned off, but death could not be excluded from this company.

I saw now that Fanshawe and Delia were no longer to be seen, and I supposed they had returned to their former pleasures. But the man who had sat as watchman of the stairs had gone to help carry forth the dead body.

My opportunity had come and would soon go, when things would return to the way they were, for men soon forget these terrors, else their lives would be unbearable. I went to the stairs and climbed up with no one questioning or ridiculing, a grandfatherly figure, his privates shrunken and impotent, aspiring to the lusts of youth.

On the landing, I beheld a long corridor of doors, all shut. As I proceeded I could hear within laughter or cries, grunts or murmurings—of passion, state secrets, gossip, sometimes tearful confession. Do you think men patronize such a place only for lust's sake? Only for a feel or a quick rush of pleasure? Not so, friend. But how could I tell into which room Fanshawe had gone with Delia?

Interrupting a man in his guilty pleasures puts in peril both him who interrupts and the interrupted, for neither will readily forgive the offense. I had just seen a man's body and soul severed in an instant. Had there been in his slayer's incomprehensible gibberish the justification for the act—umbrage at an insult, revenge for an old grievance, the hatred of one nation for another? Or was it merely an act without reason or passion?

I walked slowly, listening, hoping that no one would emerge until I had found the place I sought.

Timidly I knocked on the door when I thought I heard Fanshawe's voice, but when it opened a dull-eyed, flat-chested slattern appeared, not Delia.

"Well, Father Time, you're in the wrong place," she said, with little reverence for the years she ascribed to me.

Within, her lover could be seen where he sprawled in brazen nakedness. Asleep or drunk, who could tell?

I begged her pardon. The doxy slammed the door in my face.

I continued my search, ready to give over the enterprise.

Then I heard Fanshawe.

Eighteen

THIS TIME THERE was no mistake. His voice was angry, and I thought about the wife he had betrayed and who had betrayed him and wondered what pleasure he could now find in his harlot since the price he paid at home was so heavy.

A door opened in front of me. Fanshawe staggered forth, disheveled, distraught, flapping his arms in front of him like a blind man, while from within the shrill voice of a raging woman pierced my ear. The woman—Delia, I suppose—was exhausting her store of abuse upon the man, who clearly was in retreat.

I gathered from this uproar that Fanshawe's offense was a failure to pay what he owed her, for Mistress Fanshawe had lamented their meager purse. When Fanshawe finally pierced my disguise, he stopped, his attention divided between a half-familiar face and a woman full of anger. I pulled off my hat and beard to complete the revelation.

"You . . . Shakespeare," he gasped, his speech slurred with drink. "You here?"

"To talk to you." I said. "An important matter."

"Important to you, not to me," Fanshawe snarled, and he advanced as though to shove me to the wall and thus escape me and his braying whore. But I was determined not to move from my place or let him by unless he spoke to me.

Then Delia appeared, garbed as a Moorish queen or something of the like, for her flowing robe was all colors and exposed a generous swath of snow-white flesh. Close now, I saw her lips were black, her cheeks layered with such an abundance of rouge that it seemed troweled on, her eyes made large with lashes an inch in length. Her generous breasts, exposed almost to the nipples, heaved and glistened with sweat. Then she saw me, too, studied me quickly up and down.

"Can this be *the* Will Shakespeare?" she asked.

I said yes, but had no idea what might follow upon my answer.

"I love your plays, sir," Delia said, "and I have wanted to meet you. I didn't know that Jack was your friend." She swept toward me until she stood next to me, her bosom heaving and her breath slightly sour with decaying gums. Before I was aware, she took me in her arms and kissed me long and hard.

When I escaped this noxious embrace, I said, "I must speak to Master Fanshawe. Alone. It's a matter of personal business."

"Oh," she said, "without a doubt, but come within that your conversation might be private. I myself will be your sentry."

She smiled, the paint on her face cracking with the exertion. I could not understand what Fanshawe found to heat his blood in this woman, who was without either beauty or youth but mocked both, and whose mouth might have competed with a drunken sailor's in its vile cursing. Granted, his wife was no queen of hearts, yet neither was she whore.

Fanshawe waited. Now Delia beckoned to him, smiling, her attitude apparently much changed. "Come hither, sweetheart, that Master Shakespeare may converse with you."

Fanshawe hesitated, then looked at me, glowering under his beetle brows. No love was lost between us, but he seemed relieved to have his lover soften. He nodded, and we both moved in the direction that Delia had pointed. It was not what I had intended as a place for our meeting, but Delia was right in one regard. Given the confusion below stairs, Delia's room might be the nearest thing to privacy to be found.

The room revealed a narrow bed with filthy sheets and window curtained to exclude the day and night. A solitary candle was all the light there was. I sniffed out the recent exertions of my erstwhile lawyer and his queen fantastical in rancid concoction of sour sweat and semen, the rot of wood, and stench of piss.

But all this foulness I put by. I had grave business with John Fanshawe, and although his punk seemed determined to stay and hear our conversation as rent for the use of her room, I was impatient to find out what he could tell me about his mysterious client. After that, I'd make my seeming voyage and hie home to Stratford.

So Delia stationed herself next the door, closing it firmly and bolting it behind us. Then she looked at us, her mouth firmly set, and nodded her approval.

I had decided before to speak Fanshawe fair, despite my dislike of him. By this stratagem I thought honey might do more than gall to make him honest whilst we talked. But my first efforts to persuade Fanshawe to give over the name of the person who had paid him to know of my business were futile. He flatly refused, denied that there was such a person, and renewed his claim upon my purse for his previous services.

Then I said, "Mark my bargain. I pay your fee twice over, and thus our legal dispute's resolved. You, in turn, give me what I want—the name of him who hired you to make my life your business."

Fanshawe gaped at this sudden turn, which it was clear he looked not for.

"Jack," Delia said, "it's a fair and generous offer Master Shakespeare makes. He pays you what he owes, and with the rest you pay what you owe me. What could be fairer?"

Fanshawe looked at Delia, then at me, less hostile now.

I said, "Take my money, Master Fanshawe. Who will know, but we three? I will keep it to myself, and I have no doubt this lady here will do the same."

"I will, Jack," Delia said. "I swear it."

Fanshawe thought. He said, "Do you have it with you, the money?"

"I do."

"I'll have it, then," he said.

"When you tell me what I want to know. It's a fair offer, Fanshawe. Yet tell me no lies. Let's be honest with each other."

"Oh, Jack'll be as true as a post, Master Shakespeare," Delia urged, throwing her bare plump arms around her lover's neck and burying his face until it was half hid in her flowing crimson robes.

"Very well," Fanshawe said.

Our pact concluded, he began his tale, which to his credit he did not swerve from once he embarked thereon.

"This man comes to me whilst I was walking upon the street and greets me as if I were an old friend."

"Was he?" I asked.

"He did not look unfamiliar, yet I could not give the face a name. He chided me for my bad memory. Said his name was Whorley."

"Whorley. His Christian name?"

"Didn't say. Just Master Whorley. He said he had been at Gray's when I read law there. Now, this was some years past, and much water had flowed beneath that bridge, I warrant. I asked him what he did. To this he gave no certain answer, save something about having been abroad. In the wars, I think."

"His purpose for all this?"

"Information."

"A valuable commodity?" I said.

"For him, yes. He paid me well. He heard I had represented you in certain contracts and purchases, and he assumed an intimacy thereby wherein I would know as much as anyone about your comings and goings, your income and outgo, your present and your past."

"And how were you to deliver this so-called information?"

"In writing, or so he directed. The truth was that I knew less about you than he supposed and so was put to the task of inquiring."

"Among my friends?" I said, not able to restrain my anger at this invasion of my privacy.

"Whorley urged me to keep my business to myself. If I had

gone to your friends, you would have found me out. By the way, how did you come to know about my client?"

I was tempted to give him the name but felt I owed my former prisonmate my oath of secrecy. I said, "Rumor."

"And her thousand tongues," he said, somewhat skeptically, but he did not pursue his inquiry.

Fanshawe told me what he sold to Whorley. I could not hide my astonishment. My business with the King's Men, my associate's names, my investments here in London and in Stratford, a roster of every play I writ, my wife and children's names, our house there and our friends, whom I knew at court and who knew me, what legacies I had received, whom I had cause to mourn— my father and my son, Hamnet. All of this was to this man an open book and held open to a total stranger to myself. Fanshawe might be a dubious lawyer, but he was a better ferret. What privacy remained me after Fanshawe's digging?

"What was Whorley's Christian name?" I asked again.

"He never said. Presuming upon our supposed acquaintance at the Inns of Court, he supposed I knew it, yet because he was a client I spoke to him with great respect. Master Whorley, I called him."

"Are you certain you knew him at Gray's, that his claimed acquaintance wasn't a lie?"

Fanshawe seemed not to have considered this. He thought for a moment, then said: "Whorley's money was good, although I spent it soon enough."

Fanshawe and Delia exchanged glances, and I knew where the money had gone.

"Maybe it was a lie he told," Fanshawe continued. "His knowing me. I never remembered his face even though he invoked the names of certain he said we had in common. Now that I think upon it, I cannot be sure Whorley was his true name."

"Then it all may have been a lie—his name, your supposed acquaintance, his soldiering. What did he give as a reason for this curiosity?"

"He said he had a mortgage on some property you owned and he feared he'd lose the value thereof."

"What property was this?" I asked.

"He didn't say, only that it was a debt you owed him."

"I owe nothing to anyone named Whorley," I said.

"I report only what I was told," Fanshawe said. Then he asked for the money I'd promised to give him.

"One question more," I said.

"Ask," he said. He looked impatient, as though he were as eager to resume his lascivious intercourse as he was to have the money I'd promised him.

"This Whorley, he that has no Christian name. What manner of man was he?"

"How did he look?"

"Yes."

"To tell truth, I saw him but once."

"Once!" I said. "I thought you had much commerce with him?"

"By letter after the first interview, which was brief, and he all muffled for the weather. Besides, I paid him little mind. He was a stranger to me. A passerby. Later I received a letter from him contracting for my service and saying what knowledge he lacked. I accepted his offer by the same means, as he directed. Thereupon he paid me half of what was promised. Later, my inquiry done, he paid the rest. I saw him once, Master Shakespeare, in the street. On a rainy day. Never since."

"Do you have any of these letters?" I asked, thinking the man's handwriting might provide me with a clue.

But here Fanshawe disappointed me again. "I was instructed. Destroy all, said Whorley. Letters, reports, whatever there was between us. I obeyed. Why keep 'em? My task was done, and what I did, after all, was not a matter of law but a personal service."

"What can you remember of his appearance, then?"

He paused and scratched his beard; his hairy brows furrowed in a great show of concentration. "As to his character—the height and girth of every second man in London. His age, who could tell? Neither young nor old. His eyes, gray, I think. His beard—I don't know if he had one. His hair? He wore a hat. As I say, it was a day of heavy rain, the cobbles shiny wet, and I in a rush to get me home again. He was fully cloaked, even as you are now, Master Shakespeare, not eager to expose himself to the unkindly elements."

I had no more questions for Fanshawe. The man's acquisitiveness and dishonesty disgusted me. He was a disgrace to his profession, which, despite my frequent jibes against the brethren of the law, I held in some regard.

I paid him what I'd promised, enough for him to live well for half a year, although I suspect that as soon as I departed the virtuous Delia demanded her pound of flesh.

I took my leave of these lovebirds, assumed my false beard and my old man's gait, and descended the stairs, where there was still a stir about the murdered man. I had nearly made the door from this den of iniquity when I heard my true name called behind me. "Master Shakespeare, Master Shakespeare."

I knew it was Delia before I turned to look.

"Jack didn't tell you all, sir," she said, taking my arm and pressing her body next to mine as we passed into the cold night air and I was free of the unsavory odors of the place. "Whilst he did business with this Whorley, he told me what he did, and sometimes used me as his instrument."

I thought it obscenely meant, but it was otherwise. She went on: "There are questions a woman may ask a man that no man may ask one of his own sex without jeopardy to his honor or his life. Jack knew your legal matters, but it was I who told him all your London friends, and was not surprised when more than one had pleasure of my body. You do get round, sir."

"What didn't he tell me?" I asked, eager to be gone and doubting this woman had much more information of value to me than had her debauched lover, the facts regarding Whorley being so uncertain.

"He probably thought it nothing, what Whorley said. But

when he told me the story, he said Whorley said he'd been a player. In proof whereof this Whorley quoted lines."

"From my plays?"

She laughed. "I know not, sir, which play it was. The words were very poetical and grand—what a prince or king might say. It was a son's lament for a father who is dead, murdered."

She offered then for love of me to do me service of a kind I need not relate here, since you now know the manner of woman she was and place this was. I gave her thanks, pleading a traveler's urgency. I sailed for Italy the next morning, I said. Sea voyages were wont to try my stomach. A good night's sleep was my only remedy.

I thought the more I spread the news of my travels the better. Someone to whom I passed this on might tell Whorley.

If that, indeed, was my stalker's name. If there was, indeed, such a man.

Nineteen

TRAVEL, TRAVAIL. I could soliloquize at length upon the theme, and every mother's son who's endured hardship of the road would say amen. Travel wastes time that might be better spent, and in any season the roads are rutted and mired thanks to poor maintenance by pennyscrimping burghers who give not a fart whether a London traveler can make haste through Essex or Shropshire.

But when I must take the road, I travel like the Arab, who carries all his worldly wealth within a broad sash. A man's real needs are few, at last. A little wool for warmth, even less leather for the feet, a simple hat against dirty weather. My baggage was an excrescence, lugged for show. I was bound for Italy, preparing for a sea voyage. And worst, it was winter.

The next morning, toting a leather scrip with fresh shirt and hose, I found outside my door a coach and six, with the same number of mounted men, all wearing Cecil's livery and well armed with sword and pike. Thomas Stanleigh stood by, and before we could exchange greetings he snatched my gear and flung it up to the driver of the coach as though it were a child's ball.

This coach was German made, tight and polished with brass and silver fittings and a crest upon the door. It was drawn by Bar-

bary stallions as black as night. Atop were several trunks and canvas bags. Stanleigh followed my gaze.

"Your baggage, Master Shakespeare," Stanleigh said. "To make your sea voyage the more to be believed. It was Lord Cecil's conceit, very clever, I think. The trunks, the armed guard, the coach. To make a show of your setting forth."

I looked about me in wonderment. The street was full to overflowing. Cecil's equipage and retinue had done more than trumpet and drum to draw my curious neighbors into the street to see this new thing—a grand coach calling upon a humble actor. None of my previous honors and distinctions matched this new dignity. I'd become a man who rode in coaches. I searched the faces before me; they were fifty, maybe a hundred—men, women, children, dogs. To some I could give a name, to others only a nod of recognition. The great bulk of them I did not know from Adam.

Yet there was one face I would fain lock my eyes upon—the face of the man who, learning of my departure, might forsake his stalking and give me back my life. Then, seeing him, would I look upon him with a basilisk's eye. For that night I had dreamed of Stratford and Anne and Judith and Susanna, and I had been afraid for them.

Strange it was, that in the dream no evil thing or shadow fell upon their happiness. They simply were there, in my fair new house. Going about their business. Then someone, a form, a man. I stood behind him, so I could not see his face, only his hat and shoulders. And it was that concealment that made me afraid. For the intent and silent watcher can induce more fear than the enemy with sword drawn and wrath displayed.

But now my guard gave commands. Stanleigh took my arm and hurried me into the coach. He joined me there and bade me wave to the crowd, which I did, though I felt the fool. I saw I must play my part. I waved to all, who had no thought of my real state—not a gentleman traveler but a refugee from a faceless menace.

The coach advanced, my guards and driver commanding that

the crowd disperse. They cursed and railed but made way, fearful of being trampled. For these were no ordinary horses but great and powerful stallions, horses of war, their black nostrils puffing clouds in the cold moist air.

Quickpace we proceeded through London streets, drawing much attention all along and Stanleigh ever urging me to show my face at the window, that all might see me and know of my intent.

It wasn't long before the Thames came into view, ships riding on the swelling tide.

"Well, Master Shakespeare. I wish you bon voyage," Stanleigh said, grasping my hand and shaking it warmly. "I trust it will seem but an hour that you are gone, this journey to fair Italy."

So I was destined to go avoyaging after all. A pinnace stood at hand, and I and my showy luggage were brought aboard by a swarm of sailors in their rig—big brawny whiskered men, their skin all leathered by salt and sun, their mouths full of their sailor's oaths. Before I knew, I stood on the deck of a goodly bark whose position in the stream spoke of its readiness for sea. The vessel's captain—his name I've forgot—made me welcome; my luggage but for my scrip was stowed below while I went with the captain to the raised poop, from which I could view the northward bank, the Tower of London and good St. Paul's, all begrimed with smoke from a thousand chimneys. Then this hardy captain trumpeted his commands, the anchor was pulled from its watery depth, and the sails were set in a great whirl of activity on deck.

Thus we made downriver for the sea.

I was too taken by the view to question the captain about my fate. All's one for that, for he was a laconic sort save when his lungs filled with commands. And yet it seemed that Cecil's stratagem of feigning a voyage was no feigning at all. I was indeed bound for open sea. Was I at last then going to see the place where many of my plays had been set, fair Verona, Genoa, Venice, and Rome?

The pinnace had not been brought aboard but trailed behind,

bobbing in the wake. I began to suspect the truth: The little bark that had brought me onboard would take me off again. That's what Stanleigh meant about the time, how a voyage of no more than an hour would be my lot.

The city now behind us, the river narrowed. Ashore, flat land, marsh and meadow, wintered woods all stark and sere. My ship sailed on, its crew all scrambling upon the deck and below, a nether world I had never seen. My laconic captain, his own pilot, kept eyes fixed upon the helm. Finally he spoke.

"There's where we'll put you ashore, sir," he said, somewhere below Greenwich, which I recognized.

I looked and saw a little cove, a swelling bank where in the spring the grass would grow to a madness, soft like a pillow. Not now in cruel December, yet welcoming after a voyage brief but too long for this hopeless hapless landlubber.

"Did Lord Cecil tell you who I was?" I said.

The captain, who was a tall, robust man looking a little like Sir Francis Drake, said, "I know nothing of Lord Cecil. I dealt with Master Stanleigh, his secretary. I took my orders from him."

The ship did not heave to but maintained sail and speed. Two sailors pulled the pinnace alongside, and I and my scrip were helped down a wobbly rope ladder to its uneasy deck. Untethered from the ship, we floated free, watching the ship's high stern grow smaller on the stream, the cries of sailors less distinct.

Before I'm aware, I'm set ashore. It is England still, but it might have been Illyria, and I my own Antonio set naked upon alien ground.

Then I remembered my captain had been most careful in selecting a place for me to disembark. I knew that I had not been abandoned but deposited—like a bundle set upon a doorstep for its owner's return.

I waited there forlornly for an hour or more, leather scrip the sole companion of my thoughts. Thank heaven the sky was clear, the ground dry. I was confident that in the country I was at the least free of my adversary, though he found me when he wanted me in the city. It amused me to think that, having observed my departure from London or having heard word of it, he would give up what his malice had been so careful to create.

Then, hoofbeats, whinnies, a human voice. I leapt to my feet and stared about me with alarm. A rider bore down upon where I stood, leading a horse behind him. One horse was a gelding, his rider a young man wrapped and capped, his face red and sweating and marred by pox. He led another horse, a mottled mare, its withers straight and sharp. Though this newcomer bore no weapon that I could see, I braced myself for attack, but before I could withdraw my dagger, he doffed his cap and addressed me with great courtesy, smiling broadly like an old friend.

"God save you, honored sir."

"God save yourself," I said.

"Would you be Master Stanleigh's friend?"

"I would."

"And bound to the west?"

"To the west," I said.

"Then by your leave this mare's for you, sir."

Then he told me that his name was Elijah Marsh and that he had been appointed my guide. He proceeded to name what towns we'd pass by and what streams cross. These towns and streams I knew, for I had traveled much in my own country.

The generality of his description made me think that my genial yeoman did not know my ultimate destination any more than my good captain had. Herein I saw the wisdom of my great patron's plan. No helper in my escape would know my name, or my purpose. My journey would thereby be secure.

Emboldened by this thought, I shook Marsh's hand, offering him silver for his pains, but he, honest fellow, refused, saying that he had been paid enough. To receive more from me would dishonor him.

I do not ride a horse for pleasure. I never feel I'm master of the beast but do him the honor of mounting him. This he knows of me right well, and holds me in contempt though he be dumb and made by God to serve me. It's a strange opinion, I grant you. Perchance you think the less of me for holding it. For a gentleman, as I now style myself, should ride well and proudly. But in this book I've sworn to tell the truth about myself, and so I will. Horse and I do not well agree.

Nonetheless I mounted, Elijah Marsh having fastened my scrip to my saddle, and the two of us set forth.

We rode steady through desolate fields, avoiding roads. We scattered hares and sometimes roebuck and dodged nettles and brambles where they grew but saw few persons. In the distance I could see villages and sometimes towns, but we rode clear of them. It was late in the afternoon and my bum and thighs aching when we finally stopped, even then, Marsh explained, not so much for our comfort as for our horses' care. Marsh was half my age, strong in the saddle. His pocked visage looked no more weary now than when our long day's ride had begun by the riverbank.

Our place of refuge for the night was an inn just at the fringe of a dense wood. It was a brave, welcoming house, with four chimneys smoking in the pale air and promising warmth within. Here, my guide said he would take leave of me.

"You need no rest yourself?" I asked.

"Nay, sir, I'm used to riding, and my horse is used to being ridden. I'll stay with you for supper; then I'm bound away. I have a wife and child at home, sir, and I fain would be with them this night."

"You'll ride in the dark?" I asked, wondering at the yeoman's hardihood.

"Oh, yes, sir. I know my way like the back of my hand, every hair and freckle."

We went indoors and were greeted by the innkeeper, a great whiskered man as bald as an egg, very merry. He showed me to my chamber, which was quite comfortable. Most wondrous, when I asked him the cost of my night's lodgings he disdained payment but, like young Marsh, said that he had already been paid and that he dared not ask me for more on pain of displeasing the gentleman who had arranged my stay there.

After that, we sat down to supper.

There were few other guests at mine host's table. I remember a man and wife named Stock. He was a clothier and constable, from Chelmsford, I think. A portly, good-natured fellow, he said he had seen me before somewhere and tried through most of supper to remember where. His little wife had a quick wit, and the two of them together reminded me of Anne and myself when all was well with us.

Also at dinner were two quiet gentlemen who may have been clerks or scriveners, who kept to themselves and did not join in the conversation at table, which was very sparse, since everyone seemed weary of the road. The food, though plentiful, was not what I was used to at Madame Mountjoy's table.

After eating, I said good-bye to young Marsh and went straightway to bed, drained of my strength and eager to get the rest I needed for the next day.

I slept as restlessly as a condemned man, waking it seemed every hour, and several times sitting bolt upright, wondering where I was. Then I would remember, lie back down, and it would be a while before I slept again. I kept worrying about my wife and daughters and somehow feared that, for all Cecil's precautions, my adversary would know where I went, would know that my so-called foreign travel was a mere show. I would arrive, God willing, in Stratford, but somehow he would be there, too. And perhaps my enemy was there already, waiting—to slash a throat, to set a fire.

I fear God, but I'm not a praying sort. My life cannot endure the scrutiny of the Almighty, although I suppose I'm no better or worse than the common man. Yet on this night I climbed from my bed, dropped to my knees, and for a long while prayed for deliverance from my present troubles and for protection for my family. I rose, feeling like King Claudius that my words had flown upward while my thoughts had stayed below, for there is that thing about fear, that like an actor ambitious of the main part, though fear be pushed into the corner, yet it will command the stage, drawing all attention to itself.

Before taking his leave Marsh have given me my route to Stratford and a bundle that when opened turned out to be clothing of
a plain kersey wool that made me look less citified, more humble.
I guessed its purpose and approved, for I knew that my clothes
too readily marked me as a gentleman and that while I might be
invisible in London I would arouse curiosity, even suspicion, in
the countryside, where no stranger went unmarked. Besides, I was
already planning to don a disguise somewhere along the way, and
my night of distressing fears made me even more convinced that
in Stratford I could not merely be myself.

As to my route, it was not to be the main, Marsh said, but a
covert road that would take me now north, now south. He seemed
to understand that I was a fugitive, although from whom or what
I suspect he was in doubt. Elijah Marsh had been, as he said, paid
well. He seemed content with his bargain.

I bypassed mine host's breakfast, which gave promise of being
no more delightsome than supper, and said my adieux. My night's
restless sleep had done little to ease saddle sores. I mounted my
good mare, winced with pain, and set forth by the route assigned.
If the weather held, Stratford lay four days beyond.

I was no longer riding across fields but on a rutted road that at
times dwindled to a mere path. The land about had changed, was
less flat than before. I saw herds of sheep on rolling hills, passed
an occasional herdsman, and once encountered a large cart piled
high with thatch and cut timbers, to which I had to give ground,
there being no room to pass. No one paid me mind, or seemed to,
and I was thankful for my plain garb that made it seem I traveled
from one town to the next, no cross-country rider who might
have silver in his purse or designs upon the safety of the state.

At noon I stopped to take my ease in a little copse, not far from
where a brook sweetly ran. I tied the horse to a bramble bush and
lay me down upon brown grass, my kersey cloak my blanket.
Within a blink I fell asleep. How long I slept I did not know, or
how I knew to wake, but when I came to again, I heard the sound
of horses coming. My own mare was where I'd tethered her,

standing still as though asleep herself. Her great moist eyes regarded me with care.

I propped myself on my elbow and peered through the bramble toward the road. Three riders passed by, then reined in at the stream. I thought they might stop to let themselves or their horses drink, for the water I knew was pure and sweet, but it was otherwise. They only stopped to talk. One drew from his cloak a piece of paper, which I took to be a map. They studied it together, the one pointing with his finger in the same direction that I headed.

I couldn't hear their words, but they seemed rancorous. One shook and gestured wildly with his arms. The others seemed as roused. I looked at my horse, pleading with him not to betray me, for I did not know who these men might be. Their horses were as fine as mine, well muscled and groomed. The men were outlanders, as was I. Winter travelers, as was I. Going somewhere on an unlikely road—as was I.

I had no reason to let them know my being there, and perhaps no reason to fear them, for I did not suppose they knew or cared I witnessed their wrangling. Yet some inkling told me to be circumspect, for while I saw no reason they could do me good, I did imagine they could do me harm.

Thus I waited for them to cross the stream. Instead, they stayed, and presently they dismounted to let their horses drink.

The tallest of the three men carried a leather bag by his side. This he pulled something from, handed part to his companions, and then sat down on a fallen tree. Their quarrel done, they began to eat. I myself was not provided with food. My route, Elijah Marsh had said, would bring me well before dark to another inn, where I would find everything I needed. And so I watched the men, my own belly covetous of their fare, even though I couldn't see what it was they ate.

Neither could I see them clearly, except for their size and shape.

My sleep had whiled away the afternoon. It must now have been three or four o'clock by the angle of the sun. The men lingered. Their map evinced their journey to have purpose, but that purpose evidently did not demand haste. I would have untethered my horse and stolen away, but I was afraid they'd hear me. Meanwhile my mare conspired with me to keep my presence secret. So still I waited for the men to leave.

They rose at last, and the shortest of the three moved away from the others and toward my hiding place. Now I feared discovery, wondering if I had been detected after all. Still I resolved not to move.

I contemplated my dilemma as might an old Roman philosopher, determining that I would either be discovered or not. If not, all was well. But if discovered, then I could plead ignorance of them, explaining that I fell asleep and when I awoke they were there. I did not know who the men were, but I did not want them to think I spied on them. They might think me a highwayman. Even a meddler might deserve a beating.

Or they might be highwaymen themselves.

The one man drew closer, so close now that I could almost see his face. I hid myself deeper in the bramble, waiting for him to come upon me, for that was the course he'd set, as though he knew exactly where I was concealed and had set out for it with the intent of discovering me. I could hear him stumble through the brush just beyond my hiding place.

I dared to look again.

There he was, not a dozen paces from me in a little clearing. He had removed his cloak and hung it on a limb, undone his hose and pulled them round his ankles. He was down on his haunches, relieving himself, grimacing with exertion.

I could see his face clearly.

It was Marbury, one of my jackdaws. One of the others, I thought, must be Spurgeon.

But who was the third man?

Twenty

I'D NOT SEEN my jackdaws since my arraignment before Justice Swallow when one bird lied and the other scattered, the devil knows where. Stanleigh and his master had given me to believe that both were gone—unreproved, unpunished, sought but unfound. And so I had imagined them flitting around Paul's, pecking for some new employment and finding none because their whoreson avian countenances tell all their predatory natures, pecking for maggoty bread, purse snatching, or off to sea on some rat-infested galleon where if there is a God in heaven let them drown dead the first tempest blasts them.

These imaginings were cold comfort when I remembered the humiliation of my arraignment and imprisonment, the stark, clammy cell, my disreputable cellmates with their foul mouths and fouler breath. And now the causes of my misery were here, my treasonous jackdaws, in this remote wood.

I did not fail to consider that they might have repented of their lies, been forgiven by their lord, and assigned anew as my protectors. Yet, forgive me God, I could not forgive their villainous testimony against me. After that, there could be no trust.

And so I watched while Marbury relieved himself in the hard cold dirt, wiped his filthy arse with a fistful of dried leaves, and trussed up. I watched while he made his way back to where he'd left Spurgeon and the man I did not know, and I watched while my two jackdaws mounted, talked, forded the stream, and then disappeared from my sight.

Me they never saw.

Some time passing, I crawled from my hiding place, untied my most discreet horse, and climbed aboard her. Since there was a possibility of my catching up with Spurgeon and Marbury, I decided to follow with caution. I forded the stream as they had done and proceeded round the same hill. Before me was a long sodden meadow. I strained to see, cocked ear to hear. Nothing. I rode at a steady pace, as watchful as a hawk. The light began to fail. I came to the crown of the rise. Before me I could dimly see in the far distance three men mounted. I was deep, deep in their traces. At least, they weren't in mine.

Somewhere west, my destination, lay an inn called the Fallen Man: The name did not inspire confidence given where I was and what vile and treasonous company I kept. I knew I would come upon it if I kept to this road, but I'd lost time in the wood, sleeping and spying, and so I had little hope of reaching the inn before dark, of getting supper or bed, although I woefully needed both. The cold had long ago reached deep within my woolen cloak, pressing its icy, deathlike hand on chest, limbs, and loins. Even if I were to push on through the night, my jackdaws might have reached the inn themselves. I would find them waiting.

I had spent my childhood amid stream and field. I hunted and fished there, set traps for wary hares, and several times, the day spent before I knew, I'd made a humble bed beneath the stars. The prospect of reliving my youth from necessity did not daunt me, save for the prospect of going to sleep hungry and cold.

I turned from my way and headed into open land, across raw windswept fields where little grass still grew and scattered sheep struggled for a meager livelihood. The day was gone, and I could not pierce the fastness of the gloom. In the east was a poor excuse for a moon, a cold, parsimonious crescent hardly worth the name. Then ahead I saw a shadow on the land, a mound and yet another.

Hayricks, three of them. Farmstead or manor to which the ricks belonged I couldn't see.

I left my weary horse to feed and made one of the ricks my inn. The straw retained the warmth of sun, and weary in the bones I rested, thinking about my jackdaws. I considered that their being here the same time as I could be mere chance. An Englishman was free to roam, should he choose, so why not they? Perhaps, like me, they had some business in the west. Perhaps they had determined to return to some native place, although neither spoke broad Devon, Welsh, or Cornish to suggest they hailed from those distant parts.

No, I was their quarry right enough—and I think to do me harm, either because I told their former master of their treachery or because they were employed by my adversary. Indeed, I thought, perhaps one or the other was *he*.

Whatever it be, I saw now my journey to Stratford would be no easy one. Like the fox that escapes the hounds only to run into the hunter's net, I'd left London perils only to fall prey to the greater danger of the solitary traveler.

FOR ALL MY worry, I slept more soundly buried in the good farmer's rick than I had since my worser spirit's death. When I woke and crawled forth it was already day, but such a day that made one wish for night again. The sky was bruised and blustering, and toward the west even darker clouds bellowed high like the sails of ships. I brushed the straw from me, untethered my mare, and rode her back toward the road. I thought by this time Spurgeon and Marbury would be far gone, come to the Fallen Man, inquired of me there and, finding me not, settled in to wait. I imagined them there feeding their bloated faces, then watching for me, planning my death. But then I thought, when they arrived and found me not there before them, would they not return to search me out?

While I mulled this in my poor head, weak from hunger and uncertain of my plan, I soldiered on. I could not go back. With

Cecil and Stanleigh in London, no one stood by to help me now, or to direct me in this new exigency. All I had was young Marsh's directions, and I had little doubt but that they would lead me into the ravenous maws of traitors.

Midmorning it rained. It pelted hard, a vicious squall, so that within a few minutes I was wet to bone. I had to look for shelter, and no sooner felt my need but spotted my refuge. Ahead, beyond a ditch and scraggly hedgerow, lay more hut than house, a squalid lair. It had no windows and was covered with thin, brown thatch, and from a hole—for it was too humble for a chimney—smoke streamed like a dusky thread. I slogged on, unhorsed, and ran to rap upon the door, the rain pouring off my hat.

Abruptly, the door opened a span and a small heart-shaped face looked out. A slight girl of about twelve or thirteen, I thought, her hair a rat's nest of yellow curls and her face dirty and snotty, her eyes the pale blue of a robin's egg. So baleful was her stare I thought she might be mad, but then I supposed it was fear and maybe hatred, too, although why she should feel enmity toward a forlorn traveler I couldn't understand.

"May I come in?" I said, intimidated by her glare.

She stood there looking at me as though I were the strangest creature she'd seen. Then I heard a voice behind her. It was raspy and deep, as one might speak from the depths of a cave or a well. "Let 'im come. I turn no Christian soul from my door."

I write here what I later came to understand of him. At the time, it was nothing I could comprehend, that croaking, that voice of a dying man.

The child drew the door wide. I entered. No surprises within. No reason to expect a palace. Dirt floor, a few wretched furnishings filched from some middenheap, the stink of sweat and sick. In the corner was an open fire, and it gave the squalid room its light and heat. Beside it was a crude bed, and in it lay two bodies, a man and woman, their heads above a tattered coverlet drawn up about their necks.

The man's face was all blotchy, his eyes hollow and deeply shadowed; he shook and coughed in a raging fever. Next to him a woman, skin and bones. His wife, I assumed. She was asleep, or dead, I couldn't tell. I saw that I was in a house of sickness, but of what nature? It wasn't the plague. I knew its signs. Something else, something as mortal.

On the fire, a pot, and in it something seethed that had a savory smell, mutton I thought, but more likely humbler stuff, a hapless hare caught in a trap.

The sick man asked who I was and where I went. I almost gave him my true name but then thought better. Instead, I mumbled, and this satisfied, the man too awed by a stranger's presence in his hovel to ask me to repeat.

"You are most welcome, sir," he whispered as though speaking took the last of his strength, and waved a thin arm toward the gurgling pot. "Feed you, sir. God has stricken me and mine, as you can see, yet we will not turn you away unfed or unsheltered in so great a storm."

The girl, who had somehow escaped the fate of her father and mother, went to a corner, squatted in the dirt, and watched me with an evil eye. Her father's gracious invitation had not diminished her suspicion of a bedraggled stranger. To her I might have been the angel of death, or the devil, or maybe just the bailiff demanding rents her father didn't have.

Was I concerned with this threat to my own health? I was indeed, yet thought of my empty stomach, the foul weather, and decided that if contagion were to seize upon me, it would already have done so, even with my walking in. Thus I was resigned. The daughter had been spared, and she lived in the place. Perhaps I would be as fortunate.

I dipped a wooden cup I found next to the pot into the boiling broth and raised it, cooling it with my breath and then sipping carefully, fearing what it might be but too far on the road to starvation to care. Mutton, hare, or rat, it tasted heavenly. No cook's as good as an empty stomach, and a starving man will relish toads and snakes if that's the all of his larder.

In such a state was I. Near two days had not seen me eat or drink, and I was faint with hunger and thirst.

I made the little fire my friend, drank more of the broth, and found a beweeviled crust of bread near by and gobbled it up, the weevils crunching in my teeth, tasting salty but a little bitter, too.

My belly satisfied, I looked shamefacedly at the stricken pair, guilty now that I had eaten their food. I begged their forgiveness for my gluttony and asked the man how I might help him and his wife.

At this his eyes filled with tears. "Oh, sir, I need little, and my wife, nothing at all. She's dead."

"Dead," I said, looking at the woman and then at the man who slept almost in her arms.

"She died yesterday. Whilst I slept. I didn't have the strength to bury her."

I glanced at the girl. She did not seem shaken by this. She knew.

"My daughter made the broth, but I cannot eat. When I try, it—" He did not finish. The man closed his eyes and for a moment I thought he had gone to sleep. His breathing was more a snort, short and desperate.

I looked at his sullen daughter and then back to her father and dead mother. I didn't know what to say. I badly needed a bookholder ("Pray, sir, my next line if you please"), but there was only silence, only me, the child, and this awful dying.

Outside the storm's fury had given over. I walked to the door and saw where my horse had taken refuge of her own beneath the eaves. I was prepared to mount, thinking there was nothing I could do for the poor wretches within, one dead, the other dying, and the girl who but for some miracle would die, too.

But then I heard a voice, more a whimper, and looked at the door. There standing in the light rain was she who up to now had been dumb. She whimpered again and stared at me, and I felt more rightfully accused before the bar than ever I did in Justice Swallow's court.

I gave my mare a reassuring pat and went indoors again. Ashes glowed where flames had been. I found the man's supply of wood and built up the fire until the room was full of heat. I offered some broth to the girl, who would not take it but sat making little mewling sounds in the corner, watching me as though she could look at nothing else.

I knelt by the man's bed and daubed his forehead with my damp handkerchief. It soothed him, for his raucous breathing ceased and he fell asleep. Then I took off my cloak and hung it near the fire.

Within an hour the rain had stopped. I looked out to see the sky a pale cerulean blue and all the fields dripping wet. Then I heard the girl cry out. I rushed in to find her kneeling by the bed and holding her father's limp white hand, which she kissed and kissed and wouldn't stop.

BEFORE DUSK, THE sky all ruddy like a virgin's blush, I, Will Shakespeare, player and maker of plays, turned gravedigger, my maiden voyage in that noble calling. I say noble by design, for what is more noble than to usher him who's dead into the world to come? Oh wonderful intimacy, oh most elevated vocation! Move over priest, make way king! I buried man and wife in a shallow glen behind their hovel, buried them entwined within a single winding sheet, the best they had, and in soil as moist as bread dough.

The woeful daughter showed me where her parents should be planted. There, she said, pointing, where come spring ladysmocks, marigolds, and cuckoo-buds do grow in rich confusion. Her phrases pleased me. They had poetry about them, though I doubt she'd ever read a book or even heard of such a thing as verse.

Yes, the girl spoke to me now, now that she could see I meant no harm, might even be a friend. I asked her why she was so afraid of me when first I appeared at her door, why her alarm and hate-filled eyes that marred the countenance of one as young as she.

"I thought you were one of the other men," she said, looking up at me uncertainly.

"What men?"

"Three who came riding by. They were looking for another man, a friend who they said had been lost along the road. But I knew it was no friend."

I knew of whom she spoke. Who else? My jackdaws. They had doubled back, just as I supposed, when they found me not arrived at the inn.

"When was this?" I asked.

"'Fore the storm," she said. "Last night. They woke us from our sleep with their much pounding on the door. That's why I was afraid."

"How did you know it was no friend they sought?"

"I don't know, sir, but I knew, sir. They didn't have the look of friends—not to any man."

I smiled at her youth's wisdom but didn't question it. There's more prophecy in a child's discerning eye than in fortune-teller's cards or proud bishop's sermon.

"What did you say?"

"That we'd seen nothing."

"And that was enough?"

She shook her head. "They thought I lied. A penny if I'd tell 'em, they said. But I did not because I couldn't. I had seen no one but them. And so I told truth."

"Good girl," I said, thinking now she might be older than twelve years, maybe fourteen or fifteen, though with a body so undernourished who could say?

"Then they thought to frighten me," she said. "They said a lying child might end in prison, or burn to a crisp in hell. That our house was the only one in miles, that it was near the road, and so their friend must have passed our way, must have stopped for food or drink or to ask direction."

"But you weren't afraid," I said with confidence, for I admired this strange, wild child with her precocious courage and strength of will.

"Nay, never a whit."

"You did what was right," I said.

"They said the man they followed did murder."

"I thought they called him friend?"

"So they said, but then after I would say nothing they said he was a murderer who'd killed his wife and his children. They said they were constable's men. That if I helped 'em I'd have a reward, and if I didn't I'd go to prison, or hang, because then I would be as bad as he, the man they sought, the murderer of his wife and children."

"Did you believe them?"

"Nay. They didn't look like constable's men. They looked like they were making it up, the story."

"So they were. I'm no murderer. My wife is alive in Stratford. My children, too. Did they speak to your father?"

"They came in, but when they saw folks sick to death they went back out again."

I looked at her heart-shaped face, wiped away a smudge from her pale cheek, and remembered my Judith and Susanna when her age. I needed to move on, to save my own, but I couldn't leave the girl behind. Where could she go? Even if she had a place, what perils awaited a lone child on the road from robbers and brigands in such weather as was?

"Fetch your things. Whatever you will take with you."

She understood, grinning. In a few moments, she was back, a pathetic bundle in her hands. I wasn't surprised by how little it was. This family's wealth was all each other, little that was material: their hovel full of shabby cast-off stuff; the land they worked and house itself rented from some bastard bailiff, doubtless, full of himself and his little brief authority.

Now all of worth was buried in the loamy ground, and she as naked as Mother Eve when she and Adam were cast into the lone and dreary world.

I mounted and reached down to pull her up behind me. The girl weighed nothing at all. She threw her slender arms round my waist and held me so close I could smell the sourness of her sweat, feel her warm breath at my neck.

Twenty-one

No CHRONICLER WILL memorialize my journey west for speed. The year the old queen died, Sir Robert Carey rode from Richmond where her body lay to Edinburgh. Rode at sweating, breakneck speed, commanding fresh horses as he went, disdaining sleep or rest. Thus it was the little Scots king learned his fortunes had improved. No more drafty Scottish castles or cheapskate peers of that barbarous realm for him. With his mother's murderer dead—I trust I do not sound disrespectful of our late queen—James Stuart came into his kingdom.

Carey, as I said, made the journey in three short days. Four hundred miles. That was a wonder then. Is yet. A good horseman can make thirty miles a day, with the right horse. That was true in the poet Chaucer's time; I think it may always be so. God fixes the limits of man as well as horse. If he go too fast, man's heart will fail. If he go too far, the horse will die.

So it's thirty miles a day—unless you're Sir Robert Carey—though mostly you think yourself blessed to make fifteen or twenty, far less in winter, less still if snow and ice and not just cold drab days and chill rain keep you company.

As for me, even if I had the skill, which I confess I don't, I could not have moved my horse faster. She carried now a double load with my ward riding pillion. The girl—she said her name was Jessica Childe—complained of weariness as we rode, and sometimes of fever, though not unto death as was her luckless parents' case. She was a sweet girl, and I could not leave her. There was no one to leave her with—no kind villagers or house of piteous nuns. She had no kin but what we buried, or so she said. She was alone in the rotting world. It was not the time for me to take on such a duty, but then duty comes so oft unsought and inconveniently. A man bears it as he can.

My knowledge now of my traitorous jackdaws' complicity in my misery made me ride more warily than ever so as not to run afoul of their sharp beaks. The girl sensed my worry, yet found comfort in my presence, which gave me some joy that I was not always a beggar of another's help. As we rode, I saw the two of us drew more attention from the passing stranger than I did when I rode alone, although given the month the roads and byways were little traveled.

So my ward, not foreseen by Cecil or his agent Marsh, complicated my journey. I thought hard what I should do. My circumstances had changed so swiftly. In the afternoon of that first day of our companionship I turned toward Hertford, and in that busy market town traded Marsh's mare for an ass, put off the yeoman's clothes I had of him, and donned a patched cloak and broad-brimmed hat. In sum, I became my Jew Shylock, an effect I improved by my old man's gait and by a false beard I bought from some failed actors I met in the street, disbanding and selling all their stuff and resolved to turn to honest work.

As for the Jews, London had not above several hundred, converted Christians it was said, though I doubted it. They lay low and built no synagogue to advance their sect. Several of the tribe I knew and one I counted mongst my friends, a certain actor with the Lord Chamberlain's Men. I was there when Her Majesty's physician Lopez, the Portuguese Jew, was hanged, drawn, and quartered for his plot to poison the queen, though I suspected Lord Essex framed him. Bloody business that, popular entertainment, and we Christians condemn old Romans for their circus spectacles. My Venetian Jew I wrote to trump Kit Marlowe's Jew of Malta, to make my Shylock overdo his Barabas, swallowing Machiavel whole.

Thus I knew Jews, their ways and manners, and had to more than moderate applause played Shylock on the stage. In truth, I did not despise their kind any more than I hated Indian or Moor. Let live who keeps the peace was my philosophy. If God created all, let Him weigh the merits of each race. Not my task to judge. A wise man minds his business, serves his God according to his lights.

So Shylock I became, at least in look. The girl, dressed in her single tattered shift, old moth-eaten blankets for her cloak, her hair disordered, her eyes wild and sunken, became my Jessica, as Jessica was her name indeed.

She raised no protest. She thought she owed me after what I'd done, or was relieved I didn't leave her in some Hertford alley. Or maybe she thought it a childish game, my disguise, my new name, her new identity. Besides, she loved the ass that bore our gear, called him Adam. Don't ask me why. I bought her a better cloak to replace the blankets.

Marsh's mare brought a goodly sum. My purse was full. I bought such stuff to make me seem a tinker, making my way from town to town, selling this and trading that. It was a passable disguise, aimed to draw no more attention than a glance. I was confident I could pass within a dozen feet of my jackdaws and they'd never know me.

Or so was my hope.

By dusk we Hebrew pilgrims set forth, our stomachs full, and we both well rested from the rigors of the road. We traveled an hour or more, Jessica riding upon the ass's back along with all our gear. I walked before, comfortable in my loose-flowing cloak.

I knew our Adam would not speed my journey to Stratford, but I believed he would make my getting there alive and unobserved more likely. We found a place along the road to stop at sunset, a farmer's barn well provisioned with hay and oats. We stole therein without the good man of the house knowing he had guests. I thought, why put the man's hospitality to the test? He might fail and we be the losers.

Five miles or more from Hertford. In all the day I had not seen my jackdaws.

ALL THE NEXT day and the next we walked, the weather warmer, no bone-wracking cold now, the road rutted and boggy but passable. Sometimes my Jessica walked beside me, sometimes she rode Adam. The land was flat as a board and strange to me, for while I'd gone back and forth from London to Stratford many times, never this way and never in cruel December. Yet had my eagerness to make Stratford not been so pressing, I might have enjoyed this curious interlude of my life. My long absences from home had hardly nurtured devotion to my own flesh and blood, but during these two days Jessica talked incessantly, and in her prattle I found a cause to love her and forget the notion of dropping her at some doorstep.

Upon donning my gabardine and scraggly beard, I had decided not only to play my Jew but to play the tinker along the way. It was not idle vanity to see if I could make the countryside my stage. I did it also should we be observed, either by my ravenous birds of prey or by the authorities, ever suspicious of wanderers. Although a tinker is not always a welcome sight in the countryside, at least he's a known sum. He arouses no suspicion beyond that to which already his vocation and tribe subject him. Thus twice or thrice we stopped at farms and I sold honest housewives some utensil or bobbit to amuse the children there. Since my purse was heavy from what I had brought from my lodgings and added upon in selling Marsh's mare, I gave the money to Jessica.

"What shall be done with them, Father?" she asked, her eyes wide as she looked at the pennies in her small dirty hand. Ever since I had buried her own, she had called me father. It pleased

me. It was part of our disguise. I looked the Jew, but she was so
skin and bones and rags that she might have been a daughter of
any wretched tribe.

"What you will," said I. "The money's yours. If there's more
sale, that's yours, too."

She was pleased with this, though she didn't understand the
cause of my generosity. She was a child who had less than nothing
in her life, save for the love of her parents. Possessions meant
nothing to her. If the pennies were of worth, they were so because
I had given them to her, and in so doing had forged a bond that
was very like love.

I couldn't tell her that in the world beyond, money was far different stuff—that there love, faith, and honor were bought and
sold for coin. She would learn that soon enough, I thought, and so
held my peace.

Of nights when we rested on the way, I told her tales from all my
plays, told her of kings and princes, brave knights, and treasonous
earls. Line after line I recited. I played a dozen parts, danced and
sang. She listened in a rapture to these tales and begged me to tell
her more. She laughed and cried according to the part and swore
that when she'd grown she'd write such plays herself.

I laughed at this and said she had strange notions of the
world. Women don't write plays, I said, no more than act in
them. Why not? she asked. Did not women feel and think and
see and hear, and could they not learn to write and read and put
pen to paper? Besides, she said, who plays the parts of women if
not women themselves? Boys, I said, young boys, boys no older
than yourself.

She wondered at this and said it was passing strange. Still she
could not be convinced that women were not born unto my craft,
for though woman's lot was breed and brood, was there not yet
time for crafting plays?

At that, I said some questions were so far beyond reason's pale
they could have no answer.

———

ON THE THIRD day together I learned we were halfway to Stratford, for we passed a miller and his sons on their way, and they told us where we were and how the land lay far ahead. I myself had been traveling for five full days and was much weary from my walking. My feet were sore, my legs ached. I reckoned, too, that with less than fifty miles to go we might take three days to cover such a distance. If weather held and misfortune turned its face.

But that day misfortune came our way when our sturdy ass broke its leg while we crossed a stream. The poor animal fell on its side and would not rise, and because the bone thrust through the flesh it bled full richly. I had neither means nor will to spare its misery.

My poor daughter was desolate at this ill stroke of fortune, for she loved her Adam like a brother. I comforted her as I could but grieved myself, for now my disguise was half taken from me and Jessica must walk by my side the whole way, as I had not the strength to carry her.

We left the dead animal in the stream and made our rude camp not far ahead, where the rough ground sloped downward and where trees gave some shelter from the wind and storm. That night, Jessica did not ask me for my tales of other lands and peoples beyond her imagining. She sat as pensive as a nun and would not be consoled. God knows I tried with weighty scriptural truth and philosophy. But I was neither philosopher nor priest, so, wanting words to assuage her grief, I built a fire as big as I was able and wrapped her up in my gabardine and held her close. She shuddered in my arms, and when she had no more tears to spare she fell asleep.

I lay broad waking, thinking what was next to do. Adam's loss meant trouble, exposed us to greater risk. I decided that we must find another town. I wasn't poor. I could buy another ass or horse to spare our legs. Since we had seen nothing of my pursuers, I supposed it might now be safe to make our presence in this country known.

Resolved, I gave myself to sleep.

I WOKE WITH a jolt, a hand upon my shoulder, urgent words pouring in my ear. I had been dreaming, dreaming of the theater, seeing myself with Burbage, Armin, Kempe—all of us costumed. Now I sat up. It was Jessica. She put her small hand over my mouth to silence my surprise.

"They're here. The men."

I thought she might be dreaming herself, her dream worse than mine, full of grit and iron.

"Who?"

"The men who came to our house. The men who spoke to my father and spoke then to me. They're here."

I was fully awake now. Jessica no longer masked my mouth. I said, "Where?"

"Down the hill. By the stream. Where our Adam died."

Poor Adam. He had become a telltale corpse. Yet what was I to do? Bury him? Drag him off? I had not the strength.

"But how do you know? How did you see them?" I whispered.

"I woke and walked a little farther off to do a thing. Then I heard voices, voices coming down the hill to where the stream was and where we'd left Adam. I crept down and listened. One voice I'd heard before. It was the man who came to our house."

"What did they say?"

"One said—he who had threatened me—that the carcass belonged to the old Jew, he with wench in tow. He said the man's name."

"What name?"

In the dark I could see her frowning with effort. "Shakes—"

"Shakespeare?"

"The same," she said.

I wondered how my jackdaws knew. My disguise I thought most perfect, my young companion making it more so. But there was no time to speculate.

My guess was that it was hard upon the middle of the night, the time when even owls forgo their vigil and close their eyes to sleep. If Spurgeon and his fellows traveled so late, they would only do it in hot pursuit. Finding Adam's body, they might well infer that we were close at hand. They'd continue their search throughout the night until they tracked us down.

I looked about me. Our fire turned to ash, well and good. No light, then, and our voices whispers, the distance to the stream too great for them to hear.

I told Jessica to collect her things, I gathered mine. We left the tinker's gear, no use now.

We'd stopped before dark, so I had memory of how the land lay before us. This was good. I had no lamp or torch, nor would have dared to use them if I had. We set out in the darkness, wandering Jews.

Twenty-two

DARKER THAN EREBUS was that night. I stumbling round with my arms stretched out in front of me like John-a-dreams, my eyes desperate for some little light, but there's nothing there, nothing.

Yet I was not blind in my imaginings. The night was full of hideous shapes, everything I'd ever feared or believed might be since before I became a man. We could not be choosers. We had slept; I supposed my jackdaws had not. Our hope now was that their weariness was greater than our own, for we stood no chance to outrun them, not these well-mounted men, resolved and violent in their dispositions.

I prayed now that we would come upon an inn or a town, somewhere where I could empty my purse on good horses and let my Jewish gabardine go. My old disguise was a known quantity now. Useless.

The lay of the land I knew, an easy ride to the west, but I'd not reckoned the nettles and brambles, the stones and rills that we fell upon before we were aware. We slogged onward. No clock to mark the hours of our flight. Before dawn we collapsed upon the cold ground, too weary to go on. Jessica sobbed childlike. I heard her as I fell asleep and felt a great sadness, as though I were to blame for her ordeal, yet I suppose the opposite was the case, that I had saved her from death or worse.

At dawn I woke to find the girl snuggled up against me, quivering. I could see now the cause, not merely cold and fear but a cruel gash made in her leg. Somewhere in our journey she had stumbled but never did complain. She had bled much, I could tell. I tore a piece of my shirt to make a bandage, tied it, and knew this was no casual wound but must be seen by one whose medical knowledge was greater than my own.

"Can you walk?" I said, and knew she could but shouldn't.

"I'll try," she said, looking up at me piteously. She hungered. As did I. We had had nothing to eat or drink but water all the day before, and my belly was as hollow as a drum.

I lifted her up into my arms and moved forward. With Jessica to carry I could only walk a little way before setting her down. We would rest and then struggle along. The sun rose and warmed us a little, but then the sky clouded and it looked to rain again. Around us the woods and meadows were desolate. The countryside was a world I knew, but I felt no affinity for its solitude or indifference to our suffering. Soon we came across a path that became a rutted road. By midmorning my strength was gone; I was weak-kneed and faint. I sat upon the ground, Jessica beside me.

Suddenly behind I heard the clop-clop of plodding hooves, cart's wheels squeak, and merry singing to top all. I pulled my charge into a thicket to hide us and waited, my heart pounding, my arm 'round her frail shoulders. Soon the cause of my alarm appeared—not my dreaded jackdaws but instead a lanky youth driving a heavy-laden, steaming dung-cart pulled by two plow oxen. I scrambled from my hiding place, Jessica following, and in a feeble voice cried out for help.

He stopped both song and cart not far from where we stood and looked me up and down. He was, as I've said, a youth of twenty or twenty-one, able bodied, his beardless, rawboned face plain but intelligent. "Who would you be?" he demanded, as though the land we stood upon were his own.

"Travelers," I said. "In distress."

"What distress?" he asked. His mouth was firmly set, his hands still gripping the reins of beasts.

"My daughter has a wound where she fell. We have been traveling for a week and have neither food nor drink. Money either."

I lied about the money, but prudently. It is unwise to divulge to a stranger the heft of your purse. Even if he's no highwayman, who knows but he may convert to the trade. Greed is a cannon that has broken down many a man's honesty.

This rough husbandman, for it was plain that's what he was, reached beneath his seat and withdrew a leather scrip he tossed toward me. I dropped it but picked it up again. Inside was half a loaf of black bread, a chunk of goat cheese wrapped in a cloth, and two apples. A feast. "Here," he said. "Help yourselves."

He dismounted and came round his cart to give us closer eye. I didn't stand on ceremony but ripped a piece of the black bread and gave it to Jessica, who ate it with voracious concentration. I myself ate and felt at once both a gathering strength and a hope. The rest we happily consumed.

"That looks bad," he said, peering at Jessica's wound. "You've lost blood." Then he looked up at me. "Where are you bound?"

"Stratford-upon-Avon, in Warwickshire," I said, thinking it would not hurt to let him know our destination.

"This is that county, sir," the youth said.

I could not tell from his expression that he had so much as heard of Stratford-upon-Avon, and remembering that we were probably a good day's journey if not a little more from my goal, I was not surprised. I knew plenty in Stratford who had never been more than a few miles from their birthplace and were quite content that their life should be so circumscribed.

"You have friends hereabouts, then?"

"None," I said.

"I asked because three men on horseback stopped me. They were looking for a man and a girl. Like unto her," he said, pointing to Jessica. "The man was a tinker."

"It was I."

"You!"

He looked hard upon me. I explained about the beard, that it was false and abandoned along with the tinker's gear. I told him the men were not our friends but enemies, pursuers.

This rustic youth had an honest face, or so I thought. I count myself a judge of men, an earnest scholar of the human countenance, and hold, therefore, that the immortal soul shines forth in mortal eyes. And so I satisfied myself that this youth was no more than he seemed, intended us no ill, meant nothing more in his queries than to satisfy his curiosity about strangers.

"My name is Richard Aland," he said, "Dikkon, I'm called." He thrust a hand toward me in a friendly fashion. "I take your name to be Will Shakespeare. That's what the men called you."

I took his hand; his grip was firm, his palm callused. He knelt beside Jessica and unbound the rag. "That's ugly," he said.

"She needs a physician," I said.

"Small chance hereabouts. We've no physicians here."

I sighed heavily.

"In faith, sir, I know a wise woman," Dikkon said. "She lives not far hence. She knows what can be known of herbs and simples. She cured my father in his sickness, who was near unto death."

We had such a woman in Stratford, so I was not unbelieving of these claims. "Can you take us there? This poor child cannot walk, her leg as it is. I don't have the strength to carry her farther."

Dikkon looked at Jessica and smiled kindly. "She'll fit upon the tumbrel, if she mind not the dung. She'll make no heavier load for Nut and Nan. You can walk beside, sir. It's not more than three or four leagues to the wise woman."

Nut and Nan, whom I took to be the oxen, seemed content with this arrangement, but the three leagues were daunting. Yet before I could protest, Dikkon leaned down and scooped Jessica up. Jessica did not look unpleased by this service. She smiled at Dikkon, and I found myself envying Dikkon's youth and vigor, his decisiveness as to our needs.

Dikkon made sure Jessica was firmly placed upon the cart, then turned to me and said, "Come, sir. We'll go see the wise woman. She lives in the forest. The Forest of Arden it's called."

The Forest of Arden! Familiar territory to me, then, lying to the north and east of Stratford. I felt another surge of hope.

We set out with Dikkon as our guide. My belly full, I now felt my legs full-blooded and walked without complaint, yet kept looking over my shoulder, expecting to see my jackdaws bearing down upon us. Dikkon sensed, I think, my fear.

"They'll not be coming after you this way, sir," he said.

"Why not?"

"I sent them south after you, sir."

I laughed. "Why would you do that?"

He shrugged. "I liked not their faces."

Again, I asked him why.

The hardy youth looked out across the bleak winter fields and distant patches of snow. "Because they said you were a Jew. A Jew who stole a little girl away from her mother." He glanced behind him into the cart where Jessica, rocked gently by its motion, looked half asleep upon the pile. "The girl didn't look stolen to me. Anybody can see that."

I said, "I'm not truly her father. Her parents fell sick and died. I buried them, then took her with me. She had no one in the world. No other family. No friends."

"An act of Christian charity—for a Jew." Dikkon said, with a sudden broad grin.

I started to say that I wasn't a Jew. A baptized Christian I was—not a good one, but more Christian than Jew. My protest stuck in my throat and I couldn't say it. I know why. I knew that minute right there on the road. I felt like a Jew, like my Shylock—persecuted, hated, a stranger in my own land. Shakespeare the Jew.

Then Dikkon said, "Our Lord Jesus was a Jew."

I said he was.

"It would be an odd thing if I, being a Christian, hated them. The Jews, I mean, our Lord himself being one."

"Yes," I said. "That might be a contradiction in the order of logic."

"Oh, I hardly know what logic is, sir," Dikkon said. "I've had no schoolmaster to teach me much, though my father taught me to read and write and I can do sums. Yet I know right from wrong, and a lie will stick in my throat before I tell it."

"You've learned a right good lesson," I said, and believed my own words, for this youth had a kindly heart.

"So I reckoned that if these men hated you because you were a Jew, they were no Christians. That's why I sent them south, sir, not west as we went."

WE TRAVELED FOR hours, the plodding oxen at their dull office. Fields changed to woods that thickened as we past. Jessica oft slept, and sometimes Dikkon would sing to her to ease her pain. He knew a great many songs, some of which I'd heard before, others not, and he was a fair singer with many a hey-nonny-non and wellaway. The weather held. The sun came out and warmed us.

At day's end we came at last to the Forest of Arden.

Dikkon's wise woman lived in a low cottage in a hollow shaded by an oak's bare branches, a second thatch. Dikkon told us to stay with the cart. He would soon return, he said. I watched him approach the door, knock, bend to enter. In a short time he returned to tell us that the wise woman, whose name was Mildred Hale, would grant us leave to enter.

As I've said, I have known old women who lived far from others, who extracted from flower and weed their wondrous virtues, women who were both feared and sought out under night's cover to abort a child, to inflame a passion, to bring eternal sleep to an enemy, or to prophesy of things to come. As a youth in Stratford I came to respect these powers. So I anticipated my audience with her—for audience it was—as no small matter. I did not like the look of Jessica's leg. It had swollen and discolored. I could tell it caused her great pain even when she did not complain.

Dikkon lifted Jessica from the cart and carried her toward the cottage. I followed. At the threshold stood the old woman. This Mildred Hale of whom I write was of greater age than I would have imagined possible. She was double bent and bald. Her face had wrinkles upon wrinkles within which were watery eyes without color or expression. Her lips were so thin she seemed to have no mouth at all, and at her pointed chin was a little beard that made her look less her sex than man, which I might have supposed she was had she not had withered dugs. She stood aside to let us enter.

Inside smelled stale and old, like something long unburied. The room was glum, smoky, and dark, with an earthen floor and rough-hewn beams for ceiling. Along the walls were shelves with vials and little boxes in which she kept her mysteries. Some of the vials were made of colored glass, and I could see within strange moving things or things that seemed to move.

In the middle of this vile chamber was a rickety chair; in the corner, a straw pallet, a cat asleep. Mildred called him Graymalkin. She told Jessica to sit, then bent to look upon the wound.

She began to speak, but beneath her breath in a hoarse whisper as though she were talking to some invisible presence. Her familiar? Some spirit?

She motioned to Dikkon to carry Jessica to the pallet and lay her there, urging him to take great care. A fire burned in the hearth, and within it stood a seething cauldron. Its contents I can but imagine, for no pure thing ever reeked so. Now the old woman fetched something from one of the vials and something else from another and yet another thing from a box. She moved slowly, probing the vials with bony, arthritic fingers. Then, raising eyes to heaven, she sprinkled all into a wooden bowl and stirred it with a pestle. She used a ladle to pour steaming liquid from the cauldron into the bowl.

She stood holding the vessel in her two hands like an offering. I saw her shut her eyes as though in prayer, yet from her lips came no sounds ever uttered by priest or penitent. Some words rhymed and some did not; some were soft as velvet, some harsh as the scraping of a fingernail upon stone. This she did for some time. I looked at Dikkon, but he never took his eyes from Jessica.

Then the old woman stopped, opened her eyes, and turned to where Jessica lay.

She dipped a cloth into the bowl. Baring the smooth white leg, she daubed the wound, tenderly as one might wash an infant, crooning all the while in the strange language that she spoke that was not English. Was it Welsh? Or Cornish? Or some obscure tongue long dead save to this ancient dame? I tell you truly, there are those in England who speak languages no one knows but they in their own household, and if some of these languages be the devil's tongue, I would not be astonished thereby.

Jessica made no objection to these ministrations but kept her eyes downcast or shut. Was this her maiden's modesty or fear of her strange apothecary? Whichever it was, when the woman had done I heard Jessica say "Thank you" in a voice so soft a little wind might have carried the words off into the gathering night.

Jessica lay back on the bed and shut her eyes. Dikkon said, "She'll sleep now. Mildred will take care of her. The wound will heal. In no time at all."

I nodded, believing every word.

Dikkon lifted Jessica from the pallet and signaled me with a nod. I understood, reached for my purse, pulled out the money I'd told Dikkon I didn't have, and placed it on the table where she could see it. The crooked old woman didn't look at the coins, but I didn't doubt she knew where they lay and that they were hers. I turned to go, the noxious smell so strong my soul rebelled at it and I thought if I stayed I would be sick. I needed air. I needed great mouthfuls of the sweet stuff. But the old woman gripped my arm and held it with surprising strength.

"Stay," she said. "I have a word for thee."

"For me? What word?" I said.

"Thou art he they call the Jew?"

Now this was strangest yet, how she knew of my disguise if I no more played the part. Had I been marked—transformed to another man, my tribe changed, my blood transmuted quite?

I might have answered yes to keep things simple, but I said no. I was no Jew, I said, but my denial did not deter her.

"Thou art the man," she said, speaking now in English but in a form that was old-fashioned and biblical. "Thou'rt known and well thought of. Dost keep children in thy house?"

"Two daughters," I said.

"Their names?"

"Judith, Susanna."

"Hebrew queens. No sons?"

"I had a son. He died."

"That's sad. I have a thing for thee."

"I pray you, what thing?"

"A word for thee, sir. If thou wilt hear it."

"Speak," I said. "I'm grateful for what you did for the girl."

She nodded. My head began to ache. I felt queasy in the gut. Graymalkin came to rub against her legs. She picked the cat up and looked at me.

"Thou art wived, Jew?"

"I am."

"With children in the house. Not this girl."

"Yes," I said, marveling that she knew Jessica was no child of mine.

"They suffer because of thee."

My blood went cold at this.

"They suffer," she repeated, nodding.

"Suffer what?"

"Danger."

"What danger?"

"From four men."

"Four? Not three?"

"Four men. Seeking thee out."

She had multiplied my enemies. "Do you prognosticate?" I said.

She smiled but did not answer. I thought she might not know the word. "Do you foretell?"

This word brought no more answer than the first.

I reached into my purse and gave her more money.

She began to chant, to me meaningless sounds. Meanwhile Dikkon had carried Jessica back to his cart. I was alone with the old woman, standing before her, dumbly waiting for my prophecy, my stomach churning.

I saw now that she was no mere minister of simples and herbs. She was a witch and, understanding, I wanted more than anything to flee. Yet my feet would not move. I was as a tree rooted in its place, a sword tight within its scabbard with no man of sufficient strength to draw it forth.

Then she ceased, reached out, and took my hands into hers. They were as cold as my blood, and I shuddered despite myself.

"Thou art the cause," she said. "The cause of all. And in thy sin lies the curse."

"What curse? What sin?" I asked.

"The seeds of danger are in thy deeds, for that thou hast plowed the devil's field and now must reap what thou hast sown. The sins of the father will curse the children, thy wife, and thee."

Her voice trailed off, and then she repeated her cursed prophecy, word for word.

Horrified, I could not speak but motioned her to say more, dreading at the same time that she would. Finally I found voice to urge her on.

"Pray tell, what's in store for me and mine because of this curse you speak of?"

"Why, nothing more than death," she said. "Death before thy time and death to thy seed. For thy sins will not be erased, but you must pay every farthing."

"Is there more?" I said, determined to hear the whole of my fate.

She shook her head and said, "Isn't that enough, Jew?"

It was.

I WALKED FROM the wise woman's into the night, fearing God and the devil more than ever I did. I did not answer at first when Dikkon asked where we were to go now. He had the dung to carry to his father's farmstead, and yet he would not leave us unattended, not at night and most surely not in so dismal a place.

I thanked him for his courtesy. He dismissed my thanks and regarded his passenger in the cart. I could see now how he looked upon my Jessica. He'd come to love her, and all within a day. I could see it in his tender manner, as if it were written upon his forehead. I knew it perhaps more than he recognized it himself. This pleased me well, for I knew that while I could render aid to Jessica, only a husband would mend her heart.

Dikkon said, "I'll take you to my father's house. You'll find shelter there. Then go your way. Tomorrow, if you choose."

"How far does it lie?" I asked, not eager for another march. "Travel's a dish I love not."

"Not far."

"Upon oath?" I said.

"I swear it, Master Shakespeare. Two hours will see us to food, clean sheets, peaceful sleep. Our land lies just beyond the forest."

"Agreed," I said. I took a deep breath, and we set out. The prospect of a night in the forest wasn't pleasing to me, not after the old woman's prophecy.

It was late when we came to Aland's Croft, which was the name of Dikkon's father's farm, although it was no croft but a substantial farmstead with a sturdy half-timbered house with a narrow main dwelling, low gables, and a large kitchen. Within this commodious habitation all was noise and bustle despite the hour, for Dikkon's family was large. Many children rushed at him as we came in, all clamoring for their older brother's attention.

Pilgrims in distress, we were so received. Dikkon's mother, a pleasant round woman with beaming countenance, fussed over Jessica and would not be content till she was tucked in bed and fast asleep. As for me, I was given place at a long trestle table with such a repast provided—fowl, succulent pig, and tender veal—I thought I'd gone to heaven. I ate and drank my fill while

Dikkon's father, a stalwart yeoman named Geoffrey Aland, as lithe in his years as was his son, played a gracious host. It was hospitality of simple country folk, savoring nothing of the city or the court, and it would have given me great comfort and joy had my heart not been so weighed down before.

While we ate, Geoffrey Aland questioned me about our journey, where we traveled and why. He said Stratford he knew, and my family, too, but only by reputation. He was honored to make my acquaintance and had heard of my plays but had yet to see one. He told me the way most expressly, each twist and turn of road, each stream to cross. He seemed already to know that we made our journey secretly, but he did not inquire into that mystery, satisfied, it seemed, that he whom his son trusted he could himself befriend, though he had known me not more than an hour or two.

My hunger satisfied, I was put to rest myself, given Dikkon's bed, I suspect, a small chamber under the eaves most clean and wholesome. Despite my exhaustion I lay awake, my addled brain so tortured by fears and doubts that I could do nothing more than beat my breast, send vain prayers to heaven, and curse the dark of my own ignorance.

I am not that fool who takes to heart every word of prophecy uttered for a fee at London Bridge or Whitefriars. These for the most are simple entertainments with no harm in them—if taken lightly. Nor would I seek in some hag's gloomy den, cursed with odoriferous fires and obscure mumbling, the outlines of my future. And yet I know right well our future's known before our lives are writ, by God in heaven, by His angels, and by His satanic opposite. To these great sources of knowledge may be added many mortal conduits from prophet to sorcerer and, yes, even witchcraft, which I, like any Christian, deplore and yet believe.

Therefore, I did not doubt the wise woman's prophecy. It echoed my adversary's threatening letter, sounding the same terrific theme of fathers and sons, sins and retribution.

Were my daughters then to be sacrificed?

Was my wife to suffer for my sins?

Had I fled my fate in London only to encounter it in Stratford?

Twenty-three

NOW DOES THE sky of Warwickshire glow like old pewter and, beneath, every aspect—town, heath, or wood—conspires to tell me I am home.

Well, not in Stratford yet, but floating down on Avon's chill sheen, floating under Clopton Bridge until stolid Holy Trinity comes into view. I found the boat, a sturdy shallop with ne'er a leak, upriver and freed it from its line without an if-you-please to its owner. I've added thievery to my sins.

Looking back, I see where I went wrong. Shylock. Jews aren't that common in England, and while no one saw *me* through my great beard and gabardine, my bundle of goods, my wretched ass, everyone who saw me remembered who I *appeared* to be. The Jew. A blind man might have tracked me, proceeding solely by rumor.

"Have you seen any strangers passing through?"

"Only a Jew. And his trinkets and things. Had a girl with him, as thin as string."

As a fugitive I had much to learn.

Now Jessica was safely stowed at Aland's Croft, I was alone again. My old disguise was no good, and I needed another. Something like my poor ravaged cloak to go invisible by. Something that would allow me to be both seen and unseen.

What manner of man is so invisible? Not the pauper, who

vexes the conscience of good men with implied reproach. Not the itinerant wanderer, who must be watched for fear he's a robber or thief. Certes not the gentleman traveler, whom everyone notices, envies, reports. But rather a man who provokes neither curiosity nor envy, fear nor suspicion.

That's how I became a sturdy husbandman, the backbone of English yeomanry, in loose-fitting britches, patched and smudged with good Warwickshire dirt and dung, a plain, much washed russet shirt, a buckram jerkin with ties, not buttons, and boots too large as though inherited from some elder brother. To top all, a floppy hat so misshapen by use, so sweat-stained and greasy, that I must pay to have it stolen.

To my face I did nothing. I hadn't used a razor in two weeks. I hadn't washed in one. I stank of my own sweat, and my new garments, sticking to me like a second skin, reeked with the previous owner's. My new garb I had by crude barter. My clothes for his. No questions asked, though the poor fellow I traded with must surely have had some since he had by far the best of the bargain. It was as simple as that to become another man.

My countenance was a different matter, though the countenance is not merely the face. It's a composition, framed by attitude and will. I was an actor; I knew how to make my face my mask.

And needed to. I had more than wife and daughters in Stratford. I had mother, brothers, sisters, cousins, friends who had known me since my first cry. Who in Stratford didn't know me by name, face, reputation? In Stratford I couldn't get lost in a crowd. In Stratford I couldn't be lost.

Thus, as I've said, I became a rustic like my good Dikkon, one of thousands of tillers of our good Warwickshire soil, come to market to see the sights and buy some bauble to take home to his children.

I came by river to avoid the main road, where I might be known despite my disguise and where I knew my jackdaws would be waiting. I put the shallop ashore a quarter league from the church, tucking it up among some willows that grew near the bank.

I will not speak here of what mutinous memories assailed me as

I walked toward the town, for fear of wetting these pages with my tears. It had been I know not how many months since I had been in Stratford and seen Anne and my daughters. I would see them now, perhaps for the last time if my adversary had his way. Yet I wasn't sure they would see me. So I had grief and I had fear, but I had no plan.

ON BRIDGE STREET little booths were set up on market day, which day it was. Two hundred, three hundred of God's souls in the street; some I knew, many I didn't, and that was well and good, for of strangers come to market I numbered now myself.

Such a multitude. It was hard to move there, elbow to elbow, hot breath to hot breath, and the racket of buying and selling. Animals, too. Horses, cattle, sheep, pigs, goats, all the way up the street to the Guild Hall. Did I include the dogs, without which we English seem unable to live? I kept my eyes to the cobbles, looked not about, didn't need to since I knew my way. Where was I going? To my own house, but first to buy apples from a farmer, a little salt, a bag of oatmeal, all of which I put into a scrip to give the impression I'd come shopping.

When I had the chance, I looked before and behind—looked for my jackdaws, who'd have no need to lie low. No one to recognize them in Stratford; no one to care whom they followed or why.

Then Chapel Street. New Place. My house before me, I lingered, bending to the street as though I had dropped something there and was kneeling but for a moment before continuing on my way. Pride that it was mine and the second grandest house of the town seized me for a moment before my unease returned. The door was shut, the windows shuttered. A death?

For a fearful moment I thought it might be so. Imagined the death as my own, my wife and daughters in mourning. Dear Susanna. Dear Judith. Dear Anne. My mourners. My women.

Even if Anne had been there, standing on the doorstep to watch the people pass, what might I have done? I couldn't approach her directly. I couldn't be sure my own house was not under some steely eye. I was sure it was. My flock of jackdaws was now three, four by the wise woman's count. Was my adversary not sufficiently well-heeled but he could buy a company to dog me?

I rose and continued on my way, determined to pass by again and again, until I could see her face. But that wouldn't be enough. I needed to approach her. To warn her.

I felt myself a very ghost, a voyeur of the living. Every second woman I passed I imagined was Anne, and each did indeed share some feature, some small detail, that made me think it she.

Still lost as to what I might do, I wandered down the street until the river was in view. There stood Holy Trinity and its churchyard, where my father and my son, Hamnet, lay buried.

Into the churchyard on cat's feet then. Looked all round but saw no one there and no one watching from the row of little white houses across the street where a number of my friends and their families lived, blissfully innocent of London curses. No sign of them. Everyone gone, I didn't know where. I was indeed a ghost, wandering in shadows of my past.

I found the graves, imagining myself at rest, six feet under, next to father, near to son, safe from my jackdaws and unnamed stalkers. A space beside me for when Anne should join me at last.

Then into the vaulted sanctuary. It was quiet there. For a while I stood, subdued, facing the high altar, like one come to pay respect to the Almighty, not a fugitive from law and the lawless. The figure of a tortured Christ that I remembered from my boyhood had been removed. In its place was a plain cross, more commodious to the new religion with its rampant distaste for ornament and papist idolatry.

"May I help you?"

A thick, unschooled voice, younger than mine, but not Warwickshire, some place further to the east, almost to London, but not quite so far and somehow familiar. Heard before, but I didn't know where.

I hadn't heard the familiar "sir," took offense, and then remembered how I appeared, a simple peasant, out of place even in God's house. Worthy to plow and harvest, to sweat and freeze, to serve the king in armies and navies, but not to walk upon the stones of the respectable and the righteous of Stratford.

I was relieved to see it wasn't the priest. He knew me well enough and might have penetrated my disguise by the flicker of my eye or the curve of my jaw. By his sober cloth and pious countenance, this callow gentleman was a man of God, and because he was young, say not more than twenty or twenty-one, I supposed he was the new cleric who I had heard had come to Stratford shortly after my last visit. Fortune favored me. Yet there was that about him that struck a familiar chord. Was it his voice? The expression in his eyes?

"Something you want?" he repeated, looking at me suspiciously now.

I was not prepared to answer this. I had disguised my form but not my reason for being in Stratford, much less for invading the precincts of its most sacred edifice. I thought of saying bread was what I wanted, shelter, soft words, but I knew that would only mean I'd be shunted off to the poorhouse. There was little charity to be had at Holy Trinity. I knew that well enough, so I said something that surprised even me.

"I'm looking for him who's minister here. I'm told he's a learned man, expert at solving mysteries of God and man."

"He's not here. I'm Roger Manwaring, the new curate."

"I've heard your name mentioned, too," I said. "A very learned man indeed." In truth I had not heard of him, but truth was not my business then. My lie had its intended effect, or so I thought. Manwaring's expression changed. The mask of piety fell away and was replaced with a boyish pleasure at the compliment.

"I'm he," he said. "From whom have you heard this of me?"

"It's all over the county, sir. Most especially where I'm from."

I'd altered my voice and thickened my accent to fit my new self; I spoke slightly bent as though from respect with my eyes peering upward and felt contempt for myself in doing so. I, Will Shakespeare of the Stratford Shakespeares, reduced to obsequiousness before a callow, tooth-sucking cleric, who was doubtless as great a hypocrite and poseur as he seemed.

"Indeed," he said encouragingly. "What is it that they say of me?"

"That you are wise beyond your years, sir. That you know the Scriptures from beginning to end as though you had written them yourself. That you know a dozen languages, the old Roman and the Grecian, the Russian and the Turk. They say you know everyone who is of substance in Stratford and they know you."

With this fulsome blather, invented for the nonce, I'd come to my point. Unfortunately, Manwaring was not quite there himself.

"You have a question of doctrine? A case to put to me?" he asked.

I nodded, spinning out my narrative as fast as I could and hopeful that the end would turn out right.

"As you say," I said.

"Come sit, good man. How are you called?"

I made something up. After all these years, I don't remember what it was I called myself, but something savoring of the soil, no townsman's name.

He directed me to a corner of the cold sanctuary where a stone bench was. We sat. In the light from the tall clerestory window, I could see his face clearly. His hair was light and his skin so fair as to be almost translucent. His nose was well shaped, but his mouth had a perpetual sneer.

"Your case, then," he said. "A case of conscience?"

He had helpfully provided me with my story. I am not always sound but am always quick.

"There's a well-to-do lady of the town and her two daughters. The Shakesbeers, I think."

"Shakespeares," he corrected.

"As you say, sir."

Humility is an attractive asset, yet none easier to counterfeit.

"A family well allowed in Stratford. Master Shakespeare is an actor and playwright. In London. You've heard of London?"

I pretended I hadn't, and he believed me, for it is the vanity of the learned to think that those who are not learned are not only deprived of education but fools unworthy of it. So it was with this reverend young gentleman. I played the part he expected. I could tell he delighted in it.

"London's a great city," Manwaring said pedantically. "Where the king dwells."

I wondered if he was going to ask me if I had heard there was a king now, that great Elizabeth was dead at long last, but he spared me that indignity.

"I know nothing of this man," I said, "but of his wife, his daughters."

"What have you to do with them?"

"I did the ladies a service. They were out in the countryside, picking berries. It was summer then. They became lost there and came upon me in my field whilst I worked. I helped them find their way home again."

"An act of Christian charity," Manwaring said approvingly.

"I thought nothing of charity, Christian or otherwise," I said, shrugging. "They was three women, one older and two younger, each of them weeping their hearts out for fear."

"So what is it that you want to know of me?" Manwaring said.

"A ring she gave me, the lady," I said. " 'Here, good man,' she said, and smiled upon me most sweetly. See, Master Manwaring, I've it here."

I pulled from my pocket a silver ring that indeed Anne had given me. I always kept it about me to remember her, and so in this I told no lie but God's truth.

I showed the ring to Manwaring. He examined it. "It's inscribed," he said.

"What does it say?" I asked, knowing right well what it said. A single word. *Fidelitas.*

"*Fidelitas,*" he said. "That's Latin. It means fidelity, faithfulness."

"Marry, I know nothing of Latin, sir, or any language but what my mother taught me," I said, "but I knew the ring was something worth, not for its silver, if that be what it is, but for its—" I hesitated.

"Sentimental value," Manwaring said.

I made an expression of ignorance at this vile phrase, which Manwaring no sooner uttered but I despised it.

"Do you want me to return it, for I take that's your meaning?"

"I was going to do it myself."

"And wherefore did you not?"

"Mistress Shakespeare wasn't at home. Besides, I'm a simple man. Her house is a great one, not fit for the likes of me."

Manwaring nodded.

"Pray God the lady's well?" I said, coming to my point and hoping it wasn't so sharp it would pierce the veil of my disguise and expose all.

"Well? I think she be well enough," Manwaring said. "She comes on Thursdays to the churchyard. To visit the grave of her father-in-law and a son she had, now dead. Sometimes her daughters come with her, sometimes not. Give me the ring. I'll take it to Mistress Shakespeare, and warrant that she'll thank you for its return."

"I ask too much of you, sir," I said.

"No, no," said Manwaring. "No trouble. I need to go over to Henley Street anyway. It will be no trouble, I assure you."

I handed him the ring. He examined it again greedily, but while I supposed him a hypocrite and fool I assumed him to be too stupid to be anything but honest. So I let the ring go. Anne would know whence it came, that I was in Stratford—not as myself but as a simple lout. Of that I was sure, for surely Manwaring would give her an account of me when he delivered the ring. Anne would see through the device. She was clever in that way. You couldn't fool my wife.

Later I found out I hadn't fooled Manwaring either.

Twenty-four

THIS SEEMING EARNEST cleric off on his assignment, I left the sanctuary and found a place to hide me in the churchyard. I lurked until noon, a monument among monuments, making fresh my grief at my Hamnet's death and numbering the sins for which I sometimes feared his life had been sacrificed.

Not long after, my wife appeared. I was disappointed to see her unaccompanied. My heart yearned to see my daughters, but then I supposed her solitude gave promise that she understood the meaning of the ring she'd given me, thus that Manwaring had been faithful in his errand.

Unobserved as yet, I watched her stroll among the stones until she came to my son's grave, and there she stood like a monument herself. Watching her, I felt like my own ghost, rising from my grave to watch the living mourn, desirous of embracing but unable to move beyond my tether.

It was most of a quarter of an hour before I found backbone to approach, and then maintaining my disguise, not only in my dress but in my manner. The caretaker of the dead I'd made myself, and I was upon her before she noticed me.

She gave a start, a little mewling sound, and looked me straight on, then up and down as though to verify I was indeed the husband she supposed.

My wife had aged since last I saw her face. In her older age—
she was near fifty winters—her looks had coarsened. Her jowls
were heavy, her white throat slack. Her face was webbed round
the eyes and mouth, and more gray than gold crowned her head.
She didn't speak my name, nor I hers. We stood looking at each
other as though perfect strangers—until I wanted to laugh for the
absurdity of us. I would have, too, but her face was frozen, hard,
accusing. No laughing matter that face.

Finally she said, "Good morrow, husband. You've fallen from
grace if this garb you sport is your best. How now? Player to
bumpkin? Is this the king's good servant? Must I now trade my
newly won state for worse?"

She'd penetrated my disguise, and yet I knew she would. It's a
rare woman that cannot detect her own bedmate though he wear
a dozen false beards and darken his face until it's as black as a
Moor's. I had only changed clothes.

"I'm glad to see you," I said.

"I'm sure you are," she said. "You tend these graves alone?"

"Yes."

"And traveled far to do so?"

"Through much travail," I said.

"To bring me this." She held my ring between her fingers. Still
no smiles for me.

"True," I said, "and news."

I expected her to ask what news I'd brought, but she held her
peace, looking at me, knowing who I was and yet pretending still
she knew me not.

"News of court?" she said. "News of some new love of yours?
Some Moorish wench you've pricked and prodded to my dishonor?"

I sucked in air, felt blood rush to my face. Until now I never
knew she was aware of my betrayal. She had never said anything
in the interval. Never hinted that she knew or reprimanded me for
crimes against our marriage bed, although she always knew my
nature, that while my soul could fly in verse, my feet were firmly
rooted in the clay.

"Did you think I didn't know, William?" she said, calling me not the endearing name of Will but the longer, which she was wont to use when she was angered or annoyed.

I shook my head. "No, I didn't think you did." I started to tell her how lonely I'd been, vulnerable, bewitched, but knew how little weight she'd give such excuses. ("If you were that lonely, you might well come home again. Why didn't you?") She'd make me abhor myself as just another philanderer brought to account by an outraged wife, a comic role without an ounce of dignity to save it from corruption.

"How did you know?" I said.

"Your own confession," she said simply, and for the first time her expression showed something more than indifference—but surprise, as though I'd said something she really hadn't expected.

"My confession?" I said. "Whenever did I confess this? It was ten years or more ago."

"Did you not have conversation with this black creature not this very month? Did you not prick her with your unruly awl? Conjugate her verbs?"

Anne had a salty tongue, and never so much but when by jealousy possessed. Of course, I denied the charge.

"Liar."

"I did converse with her," I allowed.

"*Converse* you call it! A new name for a naughty deed, false husband. You plowed her field. Made free with her privy parts, I warrant."

"Talk, I mean. Nothing more. She was sick. Poxed. Dying. She tried to extort money from me."

"Money. Why?"

"Need," I said. "Desperation."

"And you gave it her, money?"

"Not a penny."

"That's a lie, husband."

"It's true." We had both grown shrill, hot-eyed, indifferent to who heard, saw.

"True? And for this reason you confessed it?" she said.

"I never. It's not to my credit, Anne, but I never confessed to you. I don't know whereof you speak."

She stood there beside our son's grave, studying me as though I were some strange creature crawled up from scummy earth. I felt the contempt. But didn't I deserve it?

"I have your letter," she said. "In your hand and signed by you and making mention of things known betwixt us and by no other, whereby I knew it was no counterfeit, and a true confession that it made of all you'd done. Oh, Will, you might as well have taken a knife and cut out my heart, for so I was pained by your so-called confession. You might have kept your base adultery to yourself. It was cruel of you to be so honest in your dishonesty."

Again I denied writing such a letter, but she proceeded to tell me what it had contained, and she was right. There were things mentioned there that I thought were family matters only. She promised to show me the letter itself, written in my own hand.

"Why have you come back to torment me, left London, which you prefer before Stratford, and your theater, which you love more than wife or child or God?"

"Danger," I said, almost in a whisper. I looked round me, for during our rancorous talk I'd quite forgotten the reason I was in disguise. No one. Just husband and wife, beside the grave of a dead son. Wrangling over the soiling of the marriage bed.

"What danger? To your honor? To mine?" she said, her voice rising and shaking a little. "The danger's done, my honor's sullied. Your whore's made."

"My whore's dead," I said bitterly. "And the danger is yours as well as my own."

This stopped her. There was a long pause. "How dead?" she said. "Did you kill her, then?"

I denied it, even then wondering if it wasn't so, for I was yet to know why she died or by whose hand.

"I didn't. There was a fire. She leapt from the roof. She fell on the cobbles. She broke her neck, I think."

She looked at me strangely and shook her head—in disgust or

dismay, I couldn't tell, for I had known her body, every nook and cranny thereof, and perhaps, once, her heart, but never her mind.

"Will you come home?" she asked.

"I can't. It's too dangerous."

"You said that before. You spoke of danger. What danger?"

I took a deep breath, suddenly uncertain how to proceed. My hesitancy made her more suspicious.

"What danger, Will?" she asked again.

"Three men," I said. "Three men followed me from London. There was a boy—"

"You're for boys now, are you?" She said, sneering, which she didn't often do. It made her look like quite another woman, a false Anne Shakespeare.

"He was a baker's apprentice. He'd seen my—" I stumbled for a word. "Her," I said.

"Your swarthy drab?"

"If it please you to call her such," I said. "The boy—Edward Goode—he'd seen who killed her. I took him into the company because he said he wanted to act. He was talented."

"And so?"

"He was murdered. The blame fell on me. I spent three, four days in prison. Lord Cecil got me out—out of prison and out of London."

"In prison!"

At these words it seemed for a moment her stony expression, so full of resentment and disdain, softened, became something more gentle, compassionate. It was the Anne Hathaway I'd known at times in our married life. Anne of sweetness, Anne of wit. I took courage from this change and told her how I had been followed from London. How I had turned into a pitiful pawn in my adversary's game, running here, running there, and only ending up where my adversary had directed me to go.

I stopped speaking. She stood looking at me. Concern was written on her face, but not, as it turned out, for her endangered husband.

"You brought your trouble home, then," she said. "Brought it home to your wife and children."

I shook my head. "No," I said. "Not to bring you trouble. To save you from it."

"Save us?" She laughed a sharp, humorless laugh. "By leading these villains to the house, these murderers as you would have them? You might as well have brought the plague with you, for all the good you do coming home, my husband."

She'd made me mad with this. My face burned, my hands shook. I cried, "My intent was to warn you, to save you and the girls."

"How?"

"By getting you out of town. They were going to come to Stratford. I had the proof of it. The man who wants to kill me."

"You mean the three?"

"They're his henchmen, his toads. There's another. I don't know his name. He's their leader, their employer. I don't know why he hates me. He drags me about, makes me his puppet. I dance to his strings, and he plays me for a fool."

She took this in, and for a while said nothing. I cooled, my chest heaving, my face running with sweat despite the chill air of the churchyard. Finally she pointed to our son's grave. "Swear on your son's grave that what you've told me is true—about that woman, these men, and this conspiracy you speak of."

I swore.

"Swear your paramour is dead and that you don't dream of her."

I swore.

"Swear that you love me and no other, Will Shakespeare."

I swore that, too.

But I would forswear all these oaths at last and somehow knew it even as I uttered them.

Twenty-five

IN THAT DISTANT page of my history, my daughters were no longer children. Susanna, my firstborn, was twenty; her sister, Judith, the lone surviving twin, was two years the younger. With their mother, they were a regiment of women, inhabiting New Place in some degree of accord but as often quarrelsome and tendentious, for they were as strong willed as men and every whit as rancorous.

Susanna was her mother's looking-glass—at least as Anne was when in her flowering: fair of face, clear eyed, full and rosy lipped, big breasted and broad beamed, a strapping girl made to breed and give suck. Yes, I'd known my wife when she was twenty-one, although we did not come together until after that. Nor did we wed until she was twenty-six and swollen with child and I a callow youth of eighteen with hardly a beard and called a fool for wedding a woman so much more senior.

Daughter Judith was more like unto myself, with narrow shoulders, pin-buttocks, and long, slender arms and neck, and almost as tall as I. I'd loved them as babes; I'd held them with pleasure as they danced about me, sat upon my lap, and heard my stories, Ovid warmed over. As grown women they had changed, becoming remote and reserved, critical of me and my London life, and indifferent to my muse of fire, allies of their mother. I'd spawned homespun women with horizons no more distant than Stratford itself, which to them might have been the whole world. Both could read, but read what?

As for Anne, my intermittent bedfellow, my *fidissima conjux* (if I be not cuckold), the lover of my youth, mother of my children, and sometimes bane of my maturity, she had schooled my daughters well. That I sent money home regularly made no difference in their affections. That my much despised art allowed them to live in the second finest house in Stratford made no difference. That now I was prepared to give my life for their salvation from my enemy—and theirs—made no difference either.

I bade Anne fetch our daughters, pack nothing more than could be bundled and tucked beneath her arm, and return straightway. No trunks, no scrips, no beasts to carry them or their stuff.

She looked aghast.

"We must go now," I insisted. "And tell no one, not even the servants. Not the family either—yours or mine. Only the cleric will know we've met, and he won't know I'm your husband."

"What cleric?" she said.

"Why, Manwaring."

"Who's Manwaring?"

"He who delivered the ring to you. He who told you I was in Stratford."

"He was no cleric," she said. "I'd never seen him before in my life. He was a stranger in town. He was doing a favor for you. He said nothing about being curate or priest."

"He called me by name—Shakespeare?" I asked, astounded.

"Marry, he did. He said Master Shakespeare my husband was come to Stratford, and should I want to see him I should come to the churchyard. To confirm the same, he gave me the ring I gave to you."

SADLY, I WATCHED her leave. She did not run, but walked as she was wont, straight shouldered, hip swinging, deep in thought.

As for me, I pondered the mystery of this counterfeit cleric. Who was the man if not what he had claimed to be? Why was he in the church, full of pious sentiment and dubious charity? If he'd known who I truly was, why not say as much? Why indulge my clownish act as unlettered farmer? Could he have been the fourth man in the old woman's prophecy?

Within an hour, Anne returned with my girls in tow. Each carried a bundle and had a sour, skeptical face, full of hostility and suspicion toward me and my designs. Before she left, I thought I'd convinced Anne of the truth of my story. Despite all my solemn swearing, I read no such conviction on her face now. And I could well imagine her pouring her grievances, like poison, into the smooth porches of my daughters' ears, calling my fears delusions, my excuses for adultery pretty springs to catch woodcocks.

While she had been gone, I hid myself in the grove of willows near my shallop, emerging only when they approached and I saw the coast was clear.

"Where away, husband?" Anne said, sober faced.

"Away from here," I said.

"London?"

"Not London."

She breathed relief. London to her was the other side of the world, as far as the moon and as unwelcoming.

"Far off, then?"

"Nay, a half day's journey."

My plan was to remove them all to Aland's Croft, to pay Dikkon's father for their keep and bid him hide them well. This faithful yeoman had taken Jessica in. I was confident he would show similar charity to my wife and daughters. Besides, who else was there? I had a hundred friends in Stratford who might show similar hospitality, but I had no confidence that they could keep my family safe without danger to themselves. Everything led me to believe that, to my stalkers, my life was an open book with not a syllable unread.

"A farm!" my wife groaned.

"You're a farmer's daughter," I said. "You grew up with sheep and cattle, with their moans and stink. Your complaint, wife?"

"None, I suppose," she said doubtfully.

My daughters gave no voice to their discontent but maintained their sullen expression, as though their faces could express no other humor.

"I won't go," Anne said, apparently losing her resolve. "This is tomfoolery, Will."

"Far from it," I said.

"It's winter, Will. And coming up Christmas. For heaven's sake."

"Winter or summer, it makes no difference," I said. "What must be, must."

I looked over her shoulder, across slabs and crosses to Trinity Street. There walked four men, two and two. Spurgeon and Marbury side by side, the counterfeit cleric behind. With him was a fourth man. I had not been close enough to him before to see his face. Now I was, and in an instant felt an icy grip 'round my heart. This fourth stalker was he who had been called Clarence, my larcenous fishmonger. And then it dawned upon me where I had seen this Manwaring before. He was bearded then, clean shaven now. Rough speaking then, smooth speaking now. It was Clarence's fellow in his assault upon me. The other fishmonger. Now all events conspiring against me fit into one single pattern.

I hushed my wife, drew my family back behind the gravestones, and pointed the men out to Anne. She had not spent twenty years reading by lamplight. Her vision was sharper than my own.

"The man in dark cloth, that's your Manwaring?" she asked.

"That's he. The others are Clarence, Marbury, and Spurgeon. The latter two testified against me; all followed me from London."

Seeing, my wife believed. My daughters' sullenness turned to alarm. They all looked at me with frightened eyes, as though I were now to do something, to protect them, or at least cry for help. I was husband. I was father. But I was also a weary, confused, and frightened man. Besides, what help was there? We four were alone in the churchyard, a man and three women. We had no weapons for our defense; I had nothing I could allege against the men that would not want more proof than I could offer. I motioned my family to follow me.

I led them to where I'd hid the shallop. With four of us we fit uncomfortably, especially Anne, yet she did not complain, so fearful she was of the men.

Shoving off, I rowed us down the river, uncertain if we'd been seen, wanting, if we had, for them to think we'd floated south and west.

ABOUT A MILE downriver I beached the shallop on the opposite bank, then we doubled back on foot, none in the mood to speak for fear and misery, for it had begun to rain, the way was rough, and the air turned colder each step we took. Through meadow and wood we traveled. From time to time I looked back to see if we were followed but never saw a soul and so concluded that we were safe—at least for now. By late afternoon the rain had stopped, and we came at last, exhausted and soaked to the skin, to the Aland farm.

There, my family and I were welcomed as though we were personages of some importance in the county, with Dikkon's father making a great to-do about having the Shakespeares beneath his roof, of which roof he spoke disparagingly although it was to my mind a very fine house he lived in, well maintained and prosperous. Jessica was there, standing next to Dikkon. Her hair combed and lustrous and her old garb replaced by new, she looked healthy and radiant. Quite transformed. She ran into my arms and held me for a long time, whilst my wife looked on this embrace with obvious mistrust.

"Pray tell, husband, is this skinny wench a child by you?" Anne asked when we were alone.

"Not of my loins," I said, falling into the biblical phrase and wishing at once that I had not.

She snorted but evidently decided not to pursue the charge.

Indeed, later Anne herself seemed to be won over by Jessica's lively disposition and sweetness of temper.

At the farmstead we were well fed and then bedded the same, with Judith and Susanna tucked away with the servants and Anne and I given Dikkon's parents' best bed, for we were well-honored guests.

There, as private as we pleased, my wife undammed another flood of scorn for me and my plan for her salvation.

"A fine state, this," she said. "Drag us from our house. Terrify us with this London trash of yours. Half kill us with walking. Pray, what have I done to deserve such abuse?"

"Married me," I said, deep in melancholy.

"Humph," she said. It was a word of hers.

"I only wanted you safe."

"We could have found protection in Stratford, where we were known. Our neighbors would have come to our defense. There's the law, Will, the constable."

I was about to remind her how little good the law had done for me, how it might have got her husband imprisoned, disgraced, hanged, but I thought the better of it. "We have good neighbors," I said. "Yet none would have been able to protect us. You don't know these men. You don't know what they can do."

"There's but four of them," she said.

"No, there's another. He who's in charge."

"Who?"

"I don't know."

"How then do you know there is such a fellow? How do you know he's no more than an unsettled stomach, a bad dream—or one of the characters in these plays of yours, one that never was?"

"Upon my honor, I know."

She made her obstreperous noise again. It vexed me, the slur upon my honor, but I let my protest go. What purpose now? My aim had not been to convince her of my danger but to save her from it.

"Are we to live with this farmer forever, then?" She said. "Shall

I herd sheep and milk cows, who was but yesterday on the verge of gentry?"

"Not forever," I said.

"Until when, pray? Our daughters want husbands. Shall they find them here? And what of our house in Stratford, our friends, our family? What will they think to find us gone, without a word? We told no one. No one saw us leave."

"They'll think what they will."

We lay side by side in the narrow bed. I could hear her breathing heavily in the shadows, almost hear her thinking, but thinking what? More retribution? More curses? Then, after a time during which neither of us spoke, she said, "Will?"

"Yes," I said.

"What's to happen now?"

"In the morning I'll back to Stratford."

"Back to Stratford. Why? Those men are there. They'll be seeking you out. They'll kill you."

"Maybe," I said. "And maybe not. Maybe they only want to frighten me, to pull my strings."

"Then why can't we return?"

"Because," I said, exasperated by her slowness, "the risk is too much—for you and the girls. You see, they—Spurgeon, Marbury, the others—know all about me, about us, but they don't know about this farm. I met Dikkon on the road. He was our good Samaritan, and the girl and I but innocent travelers set upon by brigands. None will know you're here. You'll be safe. Meanwhile, I'll go back to Stratford, let them sniff my traces, and then to London."

"But you left London to escape them," she protested, alarmed.

"To come to you."

She thought about this. My eyes searched the ceiling of our room; my ears were attuned to the regularity of her breathing. Finally she spoke, telling me to put out the light. I did. Warm darkness.

I was about to say good night when I felt her hand touch mine, squeeze it softly, and then move to my upper thigh and rest there as lightly as a feather.

"Your dalliance with this woman—"

"What of it?"

"Did you love her?"

"Yes. Once."

"Hotly?"

"Insanely."

Silence.

"Do you love her still?"

"No."

"Swear, Will."

"I have already sworn, sworn more than once. How many times must I swear? Seventy times seven?"

"Swear again."

"I swear. I hate her."

"Swear you hate her."

"I swear. My oath upon it."

My oath? I knew she was thinking about my oaths and their deficiencies but knew she wouldn't say. Most women I'd known had spoken their minds, even as their thoughts were minted. They held nothing back. Not so with my wife. Always a brooder, she. So now.

I said, "Sweet are the uses of adversity, which, like a toad, ugly and venomous, wears yet a precious jewel in his head."

"What's this of toads?" she said.

"Something I wrote once."

"Jewels and toads—at a time like this, Will? In faith, you poets are truly mad."

"It means that even adversity can be a blessing, after its fashion."

She said, "I see no blessings in this adversity, husband. Do you really believe this thing you wrote?"

"I did when I wrote it."

We made love then, and it was good.

———

THE MORNING SKY was limpid; the sun graced us with its wan winter face, and despite my ordeal my spirits lifted. I offered Dikkon's father money to keep my wife and daughters for a month or more, but he would take none. I bid my wife farewell and received kisses and embraces from her and my daughters, which pleased me well. The pall that had hung over us had somehow in this crisis been removed and we were one in our resolve, although in no less danger from my enemies than before.

Dikkon offered to be my guide, but I said no. I knew the way to Stratford, I said, and from there to London again. Then Jessica appeared, all disarrayed from sleep, and threw her arms about my neck, sobbing and begging me to stay.

I told her why I had to go. Still she clung to me, while my wife and daughters looked on in wonder, and I think scowled a little, too. Who was this interloper, their glances seemed to say, and who was I that I should so regard a stranger's child and make her equal to those I'd sired?

I bent and kissed her on the cheek. It was cool and smooth upon my lips. Then I commended her to God and so set forth without more ado, not glancing back for fear I'd dissolve in tears.

THOMAS ALAND, THAT goodly yeoman, had lent me a piebald nag for my journey, which made it the briefer and saved much shoe leather. By noon I was in Bridge Street, drinking at the Swan, where I was joined by a dozen or so friends, including my brother Gilbert, all of whom were right glad to toss a pint or two in honor of my homecoming.

After, I went openly to my house, astonished our serving wench with my appearance, and explained that my wife and daughters had gone to Warwick to visit a dying cousin. This was invention pure and undefiled by truth, but the wench knew little of our family affairs and accepted the story without question. I had supper, read some twenty lines of Ovid, then gave over, and so to bed and a tormented sleep.

In the morning I dressed as I was wont in Stratford: a sober doublet over fresh shirt and white collar, shoes with pewter buckles, and a hat of the kind I was used to wear. No need now for disguise. What I wanted, rather, was to be seen—and my family's false whereabouts to be known, for which I encouraged the wench to gossip freely. I had no doubt but that by nightfall everyone in Stratford would know where Anne and the girls had gone and where I was now.

Down Chapel Street I went, making my return fresh news, and spent much of the middle part of the day stopping at one tavern and inn after another—the Bear, the Falcon, the Swan. Name tavern, inn, or alehouse and I darkened its door. The Prodigal Son was not welcomed with as much joy as was I, or hosted so royally as was I, who was well known in Stratford for having made my fortune in London. Yet in all my mixing with my friends, I kept an eye out for my jackdaws, for I imagined they were still in Stratford, watching for me.

I was not disappointed. By evening as I headed home I saw Marbury loitering at the street corner, his grim face showing no surprise at my appearance. With him was Clarence. For a moment we exchanged glances, then he turned away, as though satisfied I was again safely within their purview.

Straightway I went into my house and armed myself with a strong staff that was my father's. I inspected every door and window, secured all and retired to my bedchamber. Too unnerved to read or sleep, I kept watch till well past midnight, when sheer exhaustion had the better of me.

That night I dreamed again, wherein I saw myself in a spacious field all wintered over with snow. I traveled alone but soon felt my mount sink beneath me. I looked down and saw I'd wandered into a fen where cold black water was all foul and stinking. Down and down I went, my horse struggling beneath me. I cried out in my sleep and woke myself, sweating.

I woke not in fear but in a seething rage. My stalkers had defiled my birthplace, polluted its well, spoiled the triumph of my homecoming. I could never walk Stratford streets again without thought of their lurking and stalking, their threats and their murders. I would never be safe again in my own house, in my own bed.

My enemy had done this, and still I had no knowledge of why.

COME MORNING I rode north from Stratford on Aland's nag toward Wilmcote whence my mother's people had come, making sure that my departure was viewed by twenty or more persons and that I returned salutations as though I were on the stage projecting to the highest and most distant gallery. I had not seen Spurgeon or his companions in the crowd, but that meant nothing. I was sure they had seen me, and I was sure they would follow. When I was not beyond a mile from town, I turned from the road and concealed myself and the nag in the woods and waited. It wasn't long before I saw behind me four horsemen. I could not see their faces, but I supposed by their number it was likely to be my stalkers. This I presently confirmed as they passed by.

I watched. Their faces were hard and full of evil purpose. Spurgeon and Marbury were armed with pistols; Clarence and the man who'd called himself Manwaring followed after. I waited until they were far beyond me on what road there was, then headed out across the meadows. For once I had advantage of my stalkers. I knew the land here, which they did not, and knew how to get ahead of them again without their having been aware. Soon I was upon the road and caught a glimpse of them far behind. Well and good. I was the fox, they the hounds.

By midafternoon I was in the Forest of Arden, or what remained of it. It had deserved its name in times past, but in more recent years its ancient trees had fallen to the ravishments of greedy lords and their enclosures, and now its great oaks were scattered and the shrubs and bushes grew thick on its slopes and in its fennish bottoms. I knew I now rode within a few miles of the wise woman's hut. I racked memory for the way and found it. A wonder. I rode forward at a pace, mindful always of my trackers, whom I occasionally glimpsed, then turned at a burned oak onto the path I remembered, and in no time I came upon her cottage. I leaped from the nag and ran to her door, beating upon it furiously.

Straightway she opened her door, recognized my visage, and motioned me to enter.

For the old woman's prophetic powers I now had more respect. She had been right about the number of men who sought me, and she touched upon the same dismal theme of sinful fathers that my enemy had sounded. If such foresight could put fear into me, I thought it might do likewise to my pursuers.

I gave her a Portuguese cruzado, a coin I'd carried with me for months, and said, "Men will come here asking for me."

"Friends or enemies?"

"Enemies," I said. "I want you to tell *their* fortunes."

"The four men?" she said.

"Just so. But I want you to tell them a fortune as I set down for you."

My request surprised her. I dug into my purse and withdrew more coins. They were each of less value than the cruzado, but I thought the quantity would impress her.

"What fortune wouldst thou?" she said, seeming satisfied with our bargain.

"What you will, mistress, but include therein certain words and phrases that I will set down for you."

I WATCHED MILDRED Hale's cottage from a rise, ensconced in branches to which enough dry leaves still clung to mask me. I knew Spurgeon would stop there. He might have guessed what sort of place it was—forlorn, gloomy, a witch's den. He may even have heard of Mildred Hale and her cures, her spells. I watched as Spurgeon dismounted and advanced upon the cottage. Before he could reach it, the old woman came out to meet him.

The two conversed. I was too far away to hear; I read lips, parsed gestures. Spurgeon reached into his belt and handed her something, I presumed payment. The old woman was talking—

my script, I thought—after which Spurgeon laughed and Mildred let out a loud cackle, both of them nodding and smiling as though they'd come to some meeting of the minds or settled a wager.

I could understand Spurgeon's merriment if my paltry device had failed, but why Mildred's? What had moved her to laugh? Then I knew. The old woman was cunning. My cruzado hadn't been enough. She had my money; now she had Spurgeon's. She had sold her knowledge to the highest bidder. Spurgeon was still laughing. He turned to his fellows, and they began to laugh, too. I was steaming at this betrayal when without warning, and to my wonder and shock, Spurgeon struck the old woman with such force I heard her bones crack.

For a while Spurgeon stood appraising his work. He was no longer laughing but regarded Mildred's supine form as though waiting for her to rise. His attack must have surprised his friends; they watched coldly, curiously. Then Spurgeon reached down and snatched something from Mildred's bosom. Going for his money, I assumed. After that, he dragged her into the cottage. She might have been a sack of corn or a dead dog.

He came out again some minutes later, went to where his confederates waited, divided spoils, and then rode off, his men after him.

Through all this I dared not move but held my breath for fear my pounding heart would betray me. Later I saw the fire. First it consumed the thatch, then the walls, then all.

Twenty-six

I HAD BEGUN to give the ancient crone her lines, but she'd bristled under my tutelage. Dire prognostication was her business, she said in sum. I was to leave all to her. The prophecy? He who followed the man called Shakespeare would fall afoul of bugs and goblins, misfortunes manifold, disease, despair, death. His only recourse was to abandon any thought of pursuit.

To her wit I left details of this corrosive fiction. She knew my mind. She knew my enemies. I did not fully conceive then of her duplicity, nor for all her powers of the dark had she herself imagined Spurgeon's treachery. He who sups with the devil must needs use a long spoon.

And so all was lost, bringing much evil to the old woman, more than she deserved from him or from me.

When the men were well out of sight, I went to where I had left Aland's nag and rode on. There was no path, but the undergrowth was sparse here, and I could make a trail where none had been before. I rode with a heavy heart, fearing that just beyond my sight Spurgeon lay in wait. In about an hour I heard a rider behind me. I stopped and listened, continued, then stopped again.

I caught a glimpse of movement through the trees. A deer? A fox? I prayed as much, but then I saw it was a man, a single rider, coming on fast.

I took my dagger from its sheath and prepared to defend myself. What relief I felt when I saw it wasn't Spurgeon or his men but Dikkon.

"God in heaven!" I exclaimed, homing my dagger to its sheath. "You put me in a great fear."

"I've been following you for a league or more," Dikkon said, breathless. "They told me in Stratford you'd been seen leaving town and heading north."

"Who told you?"

"Any number of your neighbors. You must have made quite a show of your leave-taking."

"But why? Why follow me?"

"Your good wife entreated me, and I could not deny. She was afraid for you, being alone. Good thing, too. I saw the smoke from the old woman's cottage. It's finished, the cottage. Not a stick standing. The old woman and her cat are dead. Do you know who did it?"

"Spurgeon and his men," I said. "Spurgeon robbed her, then killed her and set the fire. I saw him do it."

"Then God damn him for his murder," Dikkon said. "She wasn't a bad woman and did much good."

I didn't tell Dikkon about my plan to frighten my pursuers off with prophecies of their destruction. My scheme had failed miserably, and I feared he'd think me a dangerous fool for concocting it. Spurgeon had murdered the old woman, yet but for me it wouldn't have happened. She'd still be mixing her medicines and cures, casting her spells, fondling her cat.

"I came upon your friends," he said.

"No friends of mine," I said.

"Riding hard, single file for the most part, but sometimes they fanned out. They're coming for you, Master Shakespeare."

"How far behind me?"

"An hour, I think."

"God help me." I sighed deeply, confused and uncertain of what I should do. I had believed that my stalkers meant only to harass, that while some darker misfortune might await me in London, at present I should look only to be threatened from afar, menaced as though through a window. The brutal murder of the old woman told me Spurgeon had broken from his leash. I could no longer assume that he would treat me or mine with any more delicacy than he had her.

"I can't go back to Aland's Croft. It's too dangerous."

Dikkon agreed.

"It's London, then. A long ride, but I have no other choice."

"I'll go with you," he said, resolved. He had with him a cudgel, and he parted his cloak to show me the long knife he had affixed to his belt. It was no dagger like mine or a mere poniard. It was some awful blade forged for farmer's use, broad and stumpy like an old Roman sword. Its edge looked all hacked but deadly nonetheless.

I protested. "You can't leave your farm. Besides, you'll help me most by seeing that no harm comes to my wife and children."

I wanted to say that Jessica, too, needed protection from the men, but I knew there was no need. I knew Dikkon was thinking about Jessica, about protecting her.

"But Master Shakespeare, you've just said. They'll dog your steps. That may be to your advantage."

"My advantage!" I exclaimed. "How so?"

"You'll see," Dikkon said. "Come, sir. Follow me. You're in my country now. I know every wood, heath, and bottom within these ten leagues. They don't. We'll make our own road."

WE RODE UNTIL dark, stopped briefly to rest the horses, and then went on, ever mindful of what might follow. What distance we traveled cross heath and wood I know not. Dikkon never faltered. He was indeed a forester. When darkness was full upon us, we dismounted and walked. There was no moon, and a soft rain had begun to fall.

Soon we came upon a flat, damp ground. It was all fenlike and rank and covered with an impenetrable mist and a few wretched trees whose dead limbs thrust upward and made ghostly shapes. I called to Dikkon to stop, for I was afraid we'd slip into a pit or hole and sink beneath or be seized by some damned spirit of the desolate place, some drowned man thirsting for the blood of the living.

"Come, sir. Take heart," Dikkon said, his voice muffled by the mist, his form ahead of me as ghostly as my fears. "Just a little farther."

He spoke truly, for it was but a little while before we climbed onto higher and firmer ground where thick shrubs grew. In a little clearing, we stopped. It was very cold, and the rain had turned to snow.

"Will they follow us here?" I asked.

"Oh, they'll follow right enough," he said.

"What shall we do when they come?"

"In faith, we shall be men, sir, and do what men must."

WE WAITED, SHIVERING with cold and damp, for an hour or more. Then I could see lights whence we'd come, and I knew it was Spurgeon and his crew. They had a torch to show their way, for they had no fear of me, that I should see them. It was the very thing they wanted, that I should know they followed always, vigilant and dangerous, without ever offering me the danger, torturing me with possibilities. Yet they had littered my way with the dead. First my old lover. Then young Edward. Then the ancient crone, defenseless against Spurgeon's strong right arm.

"What shall we do?" I whispered to Dikkon.

"Why, be rid of them." He did not look at me when he said this but spoke in a low growl.

"How?"

"Peace, sir. You shall see."

For me this was no satisfactory answer. I've already admitted that while no coward, neither am I given to discord, much less to brawling. Age had tempered me, invested me with a more reflective disposition. In mind and body, I am more philosopher than soldier, a man of many words and many thoughts who'd rather wield the pen than draw the sword. Dikkon was of a different breed. He was full of youth as I was not, seriously armed as I was not, resolved as I was not. My dagger, a mere bauble to enhance a gentleman's suit, was of dubious value in my hands, for I had never threatened a man—at least not when I was not strutting costumed upon the stage. There, indeed, I had wielded many a dagger and rapier, but all in play, well rehearsed, and careful not to cut or wound. My soul was now in an uproar. I smelled the stink of my own fear and wondered by what misalignment of the planets I had come to this pass who not a month before was merely melancholy and bemused in London but slept well of nights thinking no evil.

"Have you your knife?" This from Dikkon, huskily.

I withdrew it from its sheath and held it out against the misty darkness and the advancing lights, feeling helpless and wanting ever so much to mount Aland's piebald nag and return to Stratford, say my prayers and so to bed.

But I could hear them now. Their voices were muffled, like actors whispering behind thick curtains. I couldn't tell who spoke or what. I turned to where Dikkon crouched. He was barely visible in the murk although he was not much beyond my reach. So thick a snowy mist I'd rarely seen. He held the cudgel in one hand, his long knife in the other. He wasn't looking at me but at them.

I looked back to where they came, Spurgeon and the others, and saw now that two of the men held torches and that they rode not in a file but had spread out before us at intervals of a dozen yards or more as though they knew where we hid. The thickness of the air did not permit me to know what man was which.

"Will you be ruled by me, sir?" Dikkon asked.

"They are armed—with pistols," I said, trying to keep my voice as low as his.

"Count to a hundred, sir. Then stand and hail them."

"What?" I whispered, astonished at this counsel.

Dikkon repeated his advice, yet still I had no idea of what he meant or how my doing what he asked would do much more than hasten our discovery and destruction.

"Trust me, sir," Dikkon said more urgently. "Stand you up and call out. Let them see and hear you. But give me time to circle behind them. While they concern themselves with you, I'll give them what they deserve for killing the old woman."

Without waiting to see whether I now understood or agreed, Dikkon moved off. I couldn't see him anymore. It was as if he had never been there at all. I was alone.

The four men were closer now. As I counted, I could hear their converse clearly. One—I think it was Spurgeon who spoke—was berating another for his fear, yet sounding timorous himself, for surely these men, too, as brave as they thought themselves, were not unmoved by the stark solitude of this place and the dismal murk. I reached me to a hundred as Dikkon said I should, then stood as he bade me do.

Surprise and confusion were what was needed, that I understood. My pursuers thought me an isolated traveler and themselves invulnerable to an ambuscade of one. Dikkon, moving round behind them, would prove them wrong—or so I hoped—but first they must be distracted from their purpose.

When I stood up I knew that I must speak. But what? Then the circumstances of the place—the dismal night, the ghastly mist, the thoughts of treason and murder foul, my discovery that my pursuers, too, were afraid, not of me, but of what might exist in the dismal fen—all this combined, bringing in an instant to my lips a speech I'd spoken a dozen times or more as King Hamlet's ghost.

I stood, revealing myself. "I am thy father's spirit," I cried at the top of my lungs, "doomed for a certain term to walk the night, and for the day confined to fast in fires, till the foul crimes done in my days of nature are burnt and purged away."

I spare you the rest, reader, although I may flatter myself to think you recognize the lines. I tell you I did not spare the four men who reigned in their horses in apparent confusion and dismay at this most unlooked-for spectacle. I went on, and when I finished the dozen or so lines of that speech I started over again. Did Spurgeon and the others know it was I who so declaimed, or did they suppose themselves challenged by a real ghost of the fen, horrid and threatening in the gloom? Perhaps they recognized the lines after all. It was all one. My acting, though undermined by my terror, achieved its end. Their confusion, their amazement, had given Dikkon opportunity. Even their mounts seemed unnerved, for they stomped and whinnied as if they wished nothing more than to be gone from this cursed place and would not be schooled by their riders.

Then above my own declaiming I heard a shriek of surprise and pain. From the left of me, one of the riders—I think it was Spurgeon—yelled, "What is't, Clarence?"

In quick succession came more angry shouts, cries of pain, and warnings, all in a confusion of shadows. I stopped my declaiming and hid myself to watch the outcome.

Spurgeon galloped toward me, while the man on the right—I could not see who it was—now moved toward his friend. The torch fell away. I saw another rider fall without seeing what had struck him. Manwaring, I think.

But our advantage couldn't last. It was one thing to strike down one rider and perhaps two, both taken by surprise and from behind. Now Spurgeon knew the game we played. He turned and charged Dikkon, who, mounted on one of their horses, came swinging his cudgel as though it were a mace and he a knight on horseback and not a simple yeoman's son. I heard a pistol shot. Then another.

All this time I had concealed myself a second time, frozen in fear. Yes, I confess it. My voice was raw from declaiming. My dagger trembled in my hand as I heard the cries of anger and the sound of Dikkon's cudgel crashing down upon one of his assailants, the only one I could now see.

Then I saw Spurgeon swing his torch at Dikkon, who leaned aside to avoid it and tumbled from his horse. Spurgeon leaped from his, and the two men disappeared in the snowy mist. I listened a while to the sounds of the struggle, the grunts and groans of violent men. To my shame I did not rush to help but held me back a coward.

Then my self-loathing rose to its full. I could stand myself no more if I did nothing. Finding some little courage, I dashed forward, dagger in hand.

Spurgeon, the larger and stronger, had Dikkon half submerged in black icy water, drowning him. I cried out, ordering him to let Dikkon go, thinking I might possibly have still some authority with the man who had once served me, even though traitorously, but Spurgeon, absorbed in murder, ignored my cry and pressed Dikkon deeper in the water.

I did what must be done. I raised the dagger high and then brought it down on Spurgeon's broad back. The blade entered as though his body were a piece of cheese.

Spurgeon howled, released his hold on Dikkon, and for a moment tried to withdraw the dagger, but I'd stuck it high betwixt his shoulders and he couldn't grasp it. He twisted toward me, his face so distorted he seemed a different man entirely. He seized me round the neck, digging his thumbs into my vulnerable flesh.

I hadn't strength to match his youth and vigor. I struggled for breath, reeling like a drunken man. Then did I know what death was like, or at least know what dying was, for an even deeper darkness descended upon me. My knees buckled and I fell hard upon the frigid ground with Spurgeon astride me. I felt a loosening of all my parts, sinews and bowels. Death is not pretty, reader, but the dying is the worst.

Then it was over. I heard a sickening thud and a groan from my assailant and felt a release of my poor throat as sudden as its seizure. Above, Dikkon peered down at me, his chest heaving. He was filthy with mud. It covered him entirely; he looked not like a man but like some strange creature foreign travelers write of.

Spurgeon sprawled facedown beside me, a grotesque bedfellow. Dark blood ran from his scalp and ears. He wasn't dead—I knew that—for he gasped for air and babbled incomprehensibly.

I heard Dikkon curse. He'd lifted his cudgel above his head to strike Spurgeon one last time, but I raised a hand to stay him. "No," I cried hoarsely. "Let him live."

"In God's name, I shall not," Dikkon cried. And he raised the cudgel again.

I threw my body across Spurgeon's to save him. I hated him as much as Dikkon did and blamed him for all the deaths charged against my soul, yet I needed what he knew, and I was determined that he should tell before he died.

All this I tried to make Dikkon understand. It wasn't easy. Dikkon had risked his life for me, putting himself in harm's way when he had no more duty than what he'd taken on himself. Like a young Hercules he had felled four of my enemies as though they had been his, for I did not believe his reprisal was aimed at mere revenge for the old woman's murder. He stood now bloody and dirty, inflamed with unspent anger.

One of the torches still burned. I struggled to my feet, limped toward it, and returned with it to show the scene.

Spurgeon lived still. His eyes were open, but his stare was vacant as though he were blind. His face was bloody. Dikkon reached down, pulled my dagger from Spurgeon's back, then turned Spurgeon over with his boot. I knelt down beside him.

I told Spurgeon he was dying, a hard thing to tell a man, even one you hate, but I thought it might loosen his tongue. The worst of villains might seize his last moments to repent, to save his soul from hell with a benign truth. He seemed not to hear. I repeated myself.

His eyes cleared for a moment, and he regarded me with a glance full of hatred. As I have said, his face was a mask of dark blood that gave his countenance the horrid expression of the devil he was. When he spoke, he did not so much speak as hiss.

"Curse you, Shakespeare. Curse you and all you mincing players."

I asked him what I ever did to him so to offend. "Why did you stalk me? Threaten my family? Murder my friends? The plot wasn't yours. Say who employed you."

This last question was for me the important one. I did not know Spurgeon's motives, but I did know his nature. He was one who took orders rather than gave them. Who had given the orders? Who had conceived the plan?

He was gagging, bleeding from nose and ears. He said, "To hell with you, Shakespeare. Go you to the devil. Ask him your questions."

"I shall," I said, "in due time, but you, Master Spurgeon, your time is now, so speak the truth, shame the devil. Ease your conscience, if you have one."

He made a noise, part laugh, part cough, hardly human now. Then he said, "I'll tell you this, player, and let it be my epitaph. Not the king, not mighty Cecil, not your ragtag band of players. None of these will protect you—"

His voice dissolved to a whisper. I leaned to hear him, leaned so close I could smell putrid death on his breath beneath the stronger smells of sweat and blood. Then he spoke again, in a weaker voice but clearly.

"You speak of heaven, Shakespeare. I'll quote Scripture for your comfort."

I told him he might quote what pleased him. He was dying.

He shut his eyes, and I thought he might be praying or maybe might be dead, but then his eyes opened again and fixed upon me.

"The sins of the fathers," he began, then paused.

I waited. The torch trembled in my hand and cast so pale and spectral a light on Spurgeon's face that I was half afraid to look upon him.

"Shall be visited upon the children—"

Then he departed from his text, saying, "And what then shall the children do?"

"What shall they do?" I asked, numb with cold and horror.

"Why, kill their fathers."

Silence for a space, then he continued.

"Shakespeare?"

"What?" I said, hopeful he had changed his mind about confessing, hoping he was done quoting Scripture.

"That was a most ridiculous, absurd speech you made."

"What speech?"

"About your being your father's ghost."

"You believed none of it?"

"Not a word."

"I DID NOT think him so religious as to quote Scripture," Dikkon said. He'd found a rock to sit on and was wiping mud from his face with my handkerchief.

"He wasn't religious. He filched the words."

"From whom, sir?"

"His employer. Whoever he may be."

"Shall we bury the bodies, Master Shakespeare?"

"Only if they're dead," I said.

"If not, yet they shall be presently," Dikkon said.

"Let nature take its course," I said. "Should God spare any we'll let Him have His way. We have no duty to see them underground."

I limped over to where we'd left our horses, strangely excited by the violence in which I had part. The mounts of Spurgeon and his band had wandered off into the forest. I cared not. They weren't my horses. Some farmer or cottager would discover them and thank his stars for an undeserved benefit. The law said you must keep and feed a stray a year and a day before it was yours. Any time during, the owner might return and claim it. I doubted these horses would ever be claimed.

"What was that you were speaking so loudly there while I was getting round behind them?" Dikkon asked.

"My speech?"

"It gave me the shivers, sir, whatever it was. Did you make it up, just for the nonce?"

"It's from a play I wrote called *Hamlet*. Hamlet is prince of Denmark, whose father's murdered. The speaker is his father's ghost, who reveals facts of his murder to the prince so the prince can avenge his death."

"Who did the murder?"

"Claudius, the dead king's brother. He did it so he could have the kingdom and marry his brother's wife."

"Does the prince have his revenge?"

"Yes, but he dies in the end."

"A fine sort of folks these kings and princes," Dikkon snorted. "It must be a fearful thing, that play, if it has such spirits in it. The words almost undid me in the dark."

"Thank you," I said, still stung a little by Spurgeon's harsh judgment of my speech, although what did he know of my craft, since his skill was all menace, robbery, and murder?

"Oh, sir. You forgot this."

I saw by the torch that Dikkon held out my dagger, held it to me like an offering or trophy. He had not wiped off the blade. Blood dripped from its edge like black tears.

WE BURIED THE dead after all. The sodden winter woods were full of pools, some, Dikkon said, without bottom. I helped him drag the bodies to one broader and deeper than the others. Manwaring and Clarence were so hacked up their mothers wouldn't have known them. I think Spurgeon might have been alive still when we dragged him in. It matters not. We weighted them all with stones—weighted them all so they wouldn't come up again but sink down to the profundity of that bottomless pit.

Christmas day it was.

Twenty-seven

AT ALAND'S FARM, Anne fell into my arms, all tears and laughter, kissing me full upon the mouth and making such a fuss as to my condition that one would have thought me Lazarus risen from the dead. Which I suppose I was, for I had been near enough to death to resign myself to its embrace, and that is near enough for any man.

At her heels came Susanna and Judith, they crying, too, for I had sent Dikkon before me to wake his father's house. I was covered with mud, gore, and worse, and by torchlight—it was now well past midnight—I must have seemed wounded myself, whereas the only hurt of my person was my raw throat, which was still tender from Spurgeon's viselike grip.

I assured my women that I was unhurt but gave no particulars about the four dead men we'd left behind. Dikkon and I had agreed that the fewer who knew what had happened that night the better. I write it now freely, my conscience devoid of offense and firm in the conviction that after a dozen years not even the bones of the men would be left to tell tales.

"Come, husband," Anne said, making a face at my state. "Rid yourself of this filth, then to bed. Let us come all to bed betimes."

I surrendered myself most willingly to my wife's charge, thanked Dikkon with what words I might, and made for the chamber we had been allotted. There I shed muddy boots and bloody shirt, taking off all until I stood as Adam on the day of his creation. A basin with warm water had been provided; I washed, dried; then naked, I crawled into as soft and welcoming a bed as I ever lay upon.

I was dimly aware of Anne slipping in beside me and of feeling her warm breast upon my cheek, her warm, moist kisses on my cold, chapped lips. Once her fingers touched my neck where Spurgeon's grip had left his mark. I flinched, for it was still tender there. She begged pardon and caressed me all the more.

I might have used the occasion to my body's advantage had not sheer weariness unmanned me. That and the lively images of death, which contrary to common belief are more likely to deter passion than stimulate. For a while I relived my terror. I couldn't clear my head.

Her hand slipped down to my soft belly, my hips, and lower still.

Next, not pleasure but oblivion.

COME MORNING I told Anne to make ready to return to Stratford. Since the prospect of a month or two of farm life had never pleased her, she was not unhappy at this turn. Anne asked me how I could be sure they were safe.

"Trust me. There'll be no more trouble from my jackdaws."

"Jackdaws?" she said.

"A euphemistical phrase," I said. "To spare myself the recalling of the vile names of those men who hunted us."

She nodded and said, "Whatsoever you say, husband."

Dikkon insisted on accompanying us on our way, as did Jessica, and we invited both of them to stay with us in Stratford. After all, the house was big enough with its three stories and thrice that many rooms—more than my little family could fill.

Despite the night's violence, Dikkon seemed his old self. Bright-eyed and fresh, eager to be of use, the lanky young yeoman of our first meeting. I wondered he could so readily expunge the memory of his slaughter, which haunted me even by daylight. I saw now in all his dealings with Jessica—youth and maid seemed inseparable—that he was a thriving wooer for her love. This gladdened my heart, for given all the blood in my wake, it pleased me well to see from such evil come some little good.

AT NEW PLACE my wife sat me down and said we'd talk. Her words were more command than entreaty. I reckoned I owed her the explanation she wanted.

The grip of cold had passed for the moment, and while no spring or summer, the air was temperate. We went into the south garden behind the hedgerow where we could talk privily, for the parlor was occupied by Dikkon and the girls. Jessica, younger, fit in with my daughters, and all seemed enchanted by Dikkon, though Susanna and Judith were perhaps a little envious that Jessica had found love at so tender an age while they still waited their husbands.

In that same garden—for we were blessed with two at New Place—was a little orchard. There I had set out a table and some chairs, and on summer evenings we would enjoy the mild air and the sweet scent of Flora's bounty. Here, in a less hospitable season, my wife and I found refuge and I began my story, this time not in shreds and patches as before but in whole cloth. I told her not only about my dusky mistress but also about Cecil, Edward Goode, and the wise woman whom Spurgeon had murdered. Anne listened well, and when I was done she expressed great sorrow for all I had seen and suffered. I might have been my Othello telling of wounds and wars and she Desdemona, such sympathy my tales evoked from her. Then she said, "You're sure we're safe, Will?"

"I have said."

"I know. But I think you're still holding something behind your back."

I looked at her. Why not tell her? My secret was safe enough with her. She was my wife.

"Spurgeon, Marbury, Clarence, Manwaring—these men you saw at the churchyard. All are dead. Dikkon did me yeoman's service in the forest. He saved my life."

"He killed all four?"

"All but one," I said.

"But four are dead."

"And buried where they'll never be found."

"You killed the fourth man?"

I nodded.

She regarded me strangely. I was relieved when she did not press me for more on this grim subject.

"God bless Dikkon," Anne said. "Then you're free. We're free."

"Not yet," I said.

She looked at me questioningly.

"They were lackeys, these men. They have a master who directed them, who spun their web that they might crawl upon it and entangle me. Someone in London. Before Spurgeon died, he confirmed as much."

"And told you who it was?"

"He did not so much fear hell as to do that," I said. "Worse luck. He died with the secret, hating me. God knows why."

"He said nothing."

"He quoted Scripture."

"The devil he did," Anne said, making a face of disapproval. "What Scripture quoted he—and by what right, being the devil he is?"

"That about the sins of the fathers being visited upon the sons. And then he said wherefore the sons might in justice slay their fathers for the curse."

"What has that to do with aught?"

I shrugged, pretending that I was as mystified as she, but this, of course, was only partly true. My enemy was then my son. But what son? Hamnet, who was dead and buried in the churchyard? Some other child? I had no other.

At least none that I knew of.

And even if I did, who was this person who sought vengeance for my sin?

All I knew was that he was in London, that his purpose was not to kill but to torment—to be the audience for my confusion and my misery.

I told this to Anne.

She searched my face. Then she said, "What is it you did, Will? These things don't happen to the innocent. Heaven wouldn't permit it. It was your whore, this ill-favored slut. That's why the letter came, false though it might be. She wasn't just the victim of your enemy. She *was* the enemy, or at least his bedfellow. She tried to get money from you. Did she try the same with other lovers?"

"I don't know."

"But what do you think?"

Again I pleaded ignorance of this mystery.

"And what of him who set the fire? Was he her enemy or her friend—a conspirator?"

Her questions were making my head pound.

"Think, Will. Think hard. I'm not learned, but I know this. Conspirators fall out. There's no trust betwixt them. Not every victim is innocent, but is sometimes himself at fault. The connection is there. Were it otherwise, why should someone have sent me such a letter? On such a matter, your supposed confession?"

"I told you I hadn't sent it."

"Oh, I know, I know," she said. "My argument is otherwise, Will. Whoever sent it knew of your adultery. He wanted me to know, too. Dividing us, stealing our peace. This thing is not about money or honor or land but about lust and betrayal, shame, and a sullied marriage bed. Think hard, Will. Search those years you've spent in the city. It must have happened there. It must be about that woman. I can think of no other explanation."

I did think, and knew she was right, yet still was reluctant to admit it. I should have seen it myself. I hadn't because I did not wish to dwell on my shame.

"She knew who it was, I warrant."

"What?"

"Your lover, your mistress, the woman you despise as do I."

"How do you know?"

"I just know," she said, opening her hands as though no other explanation would serve. "All ties together. Mark my words, Will. Mark me on this."

"I don't know, Anne, I—"

"Mayhaps it's her husband that's behind it all."

"She had a husband. She was married to him whilst I had her. He's dead."

"A new husband—or a lover?"

"But she was killed by him—or as good as killed. He set the fire, endangering her. Why would he do that?"

"Then her son," Anne said.

"She had none."

"None that you know of. Such a woman hops from one bed to the next. If she be not barren, then she will breed. All nature speaks for it."

I could not counter her. I did have reason to believe my mistress had no children when we were hot and passionate. A son born since would be, unless a prodigy of nature, too young to contrive and execute so complicated a plot. Besides, why would he endanger his mother, even assuming such a child existed and claimed to be mine as well as hers? My devil mistress had always shrouded her history. Even in death she was mysterious—a name and a form without a past.

THAT NIGHT I presided at my own table, free of my enemies, not in disguise but bathed and barbered, resplendent in my green satin doublet, silver buttons, and a collar of fine needlework I kept at home for special occasions. Anne and our two daughters had prepared a veritable feast and looked very comely though tired from our excursion. The table filled to overflowing with a great haunch of roasted beef, brawn, which we do ever eat round Christmas, fish from our pond—roach or dace if memory serve—and I do not recall what complements at table, sallets and sweets. For drink we had beer of Anne's own making, and I would swear there's none better, not even in London.

We sat and drank and made merry and no one spoke of what had happened. This went on until eleven of the clock and then good night to all, prayers, and bed.

Ensconced in our chamber, Anne wanted to know what I proposed to do next.

"To London," I said. "Tomorrow morning."

"I like not that," she said, with a fierce and sudden anger. "I like not that one whit, Will. You've escaped the frying pan. Are you now to leap into the fire? Why not stay at home? We have enough. Give up the stage, forsake London and all its works. It was your plan in due course anyway."

"Too early for that," I said. "I've not enough, not yet. There are still things I want to do, plays to write, stories to tell. Besides, we are the King's Men. He commands us."

"He is the king. Let him find entertainment elsewhere."

"Anne, he *is* the king. I'm his servant."

"Can't Cecil do something?" she wailed.

"He expects me to resolve this for myself. He said as much. I have no choice."

She started to weep, so softly it was a while before I aware.

Then she said, "If you're to go, don't go alone. Take Dikkon with you."

"He's a farmer—a country boy," I said. "He'd be lost in London."

"So were you once. A country boy. Yet you found your way to, around, and from that city."

I thought about this. At times my wife could be annoyingly logical.

"Take him with you. Speak him fair, he'll go."

"I don't expect trouble."

From her, then, a burst of sharp laughter, mirthless, derisive.

"Tell me another, Will. Though I be unlearned, yet I'm no simpleton. There have been enough lies between us. Now's the time for truth. Lackies you called them, those men. You said he that paid them is still in London. Do you really suppose he's finished with you? Do you really suppose this is all there is after what's done? Are you fool enough to think there won't be more?"

I buried my head in my hands. I did not want to listen to this. What she said was true. "I'm weary of running, Anne. I'm weary of being his puppet."

"Then don't be. Be you master of him!"

I turned to look at her face. "What do you mean?" I said.

"Good husband, you're an actor. You've played the hare. Now play the hound. If you must go to London—and if you say you will, then heaven knows I cannot stay you—pursue your enemy. Trap him. Run him to ground."

"Easy enough to say, Anne."

She grabbed me by the forearms and stuck her face into mine, close enough that I could see the small flecks of black in her eyes.

"Easy is sometime right. That's what my father used to say."

"What trap could I set?" I said. "With what bait?"

I blew out the candle. The fire died slowly. I fell asleep watching it and thinking about hounds and hares and the question to which my wife had made no answer.

Twenty-eight

SPURGEON AND HIS fellows were dead, rotting in the Forest of
Arden, yet I was not so mad as to think I could broadcast my salvation by openly returning to my London lodgings, much less to
my theater or to my life as I had once lived it.

My happiness seemed a piece of history, as dusty as
Herodotus.

The dead men, I knew, were the dogs of some master, his
enmity, if anything, more swollen and rabid than ever. More so
were he to discover how his men had been served. Was he aware
of my escape? Would he interpret his henchmen's delay as death,
desertion, or sure evidence of my survival?

And so, come to London again—Dikkon being my fellow traveler—I found a fleabag inn on the outskirts of the city, where I
took a room. Again I assumed a false name and a different guise. I
forsook my wonted clothing to adopt a different style, dressing
myself like unto some country merchant come to London for
commerce or the sights. I had acted the country burgher myself
more than once. I knew the plodding walk and the burred speech
of Yorkshiremen. I had played York more than once and might, I
thought, have passed for a native of the place.

To this I added a false beard, bushy and black.

Safely ensconced, I dispatched Dikkon with a message to Dick

Burbage, for while during my travels to and from Stratford my actors had been far from my thoughts, now I was anxious to assure my friends that I was alive and well. I don't remember the exact words of the message I fashioned, but in a nutshell this: that I was returned from Italy safe and sound and would appear at a certain time and place, none to know of this but Burbage. The others were not to know until the event when I should, like Jove, suddenly show myself.

For this meeting I chose a Shoreditch tavern not often patronized by us, but one I knew had a private upper room. Dikkon returned to say he'd found Burbage and delivered the message, and, reassured by certain tokens and passwords provided by me, Burbage promised that if I were to appear at the stated place, I would not find myself alone or unwelcomed.

"How does my friend Burbage?" I asked.

"Cupshotten when I met him, sir."

"Cupshotten? What's that?"

"Marry, sir, it means potted, splayed, soused—moving arms, legs, mouth, able to sit upright."

"Drunk or sober, he'll be as good as his word," I said. "Let's be about it."

THE TAVERN LAY in a narrow street of cheap tenements that looked ready to collapse upon each other. It was the sort of neighborhood I avoided in London, filthy and dangerous, the haunt of the new poor and foreigners fleeing the greater misery abroad. We entered not by the public door but by the postern, finding ourselves in a dark, stinking passage and slipping up the narrow stairs like thieves in the night, avoiding the taproom, from which came an uproar of boisterous laughter and singing. I had set the meeting for eight o'clock but had deliberately waited until half past to be sure that all my friends would be present.

I left Dikkon to watch at the top of the stairs and to warn us if anyone came up. I knew Burbage would have told the host that we wanted strictest privacy and paid the man well to see to it.

I paused before opening the door to listen. I heard voices, none but familiar to me. I felt my heart draw out to them. I was in disguise. Would they see me for who I was? My pride said no; my love for them hoped otherwise.

Taking a deep breath, I knocked softly and entered without waiting for a response.

Inside, there was no face to which I could not put a name and no name that did not have a history in my mind. A history, personal and theatrical. The faces turned toward me, the talking ceased, slowly at first, then completely. The room was heavy with tobacco weed, which more than one smoked. Through the haze I could see they had been well supplied with food and drink. Burbage had planned well. It was clear my secret homecoming was to be no solemn occasion but a kind of revel—not the Last Supper but the Marriage at Cana. In that moment, though, standing at the door, I was a stranger to them, an intruder. Then I spotted Burbage at the end of the long trestle table round which all were sitting. He was grinning ear to ear, wide-eyed, his mouth chomping some delicacy from the table, his beard unkempt and wine-stained. He had seen through my disguise and bellowed out my name like a war cry.

"Shakespeare, you devil! God damn me, if Italy hasn't made a different man of you. I hardly recognized you."

Next, everyone was on his feet, pressing toward me, shaking my hand, patting my back, plucking my false beard, which I removed for it itched monstrously and did me no service now that I was known. Questions flew like archer's arrows. They had thought me in Italy and had despaired of my return. Having no word of my travels, they had concluded the worst, that I had been abducted by brigands, seduced by some Roman beauty, or had my throat cut in Verona. I couldn't answer their questions. I could only smile and laugh with them, inwardly joyous that I had been so missed and saddened that my concealment could not end here but must go on until all danger was past. At that moment I confess I wanted peace more than I wanted knowledge or justice.

The uproar subsided. A place was made for me at table. I was furnished with a bowl of wine and a full plate, endured the good-natured ridicule of my plain clothes, then told them so much of the truth as I thought they deserved.

"I haven't been in Italy," I said. "I went to Stratford."

This revelation led to another round of questions and some disappointment that I would have no Italian adventures to relate, no Italian mischief to expose. Over this I raised my voice almost to a scream. "It was a device," I said. "A trick to keep me safe."

I briefly explained that I had been stalked by a band of ruffians, that my life had been threatened, but that the same rogues were now dispatched, and that I hoped my life might go on as before—but not yet.

Robert Armin, sitting beside Burbage, shouted, "We'll kill them for you, Will. Only tell us who these villains are."

Other of my friends added their voices to my support.

I thanked them for their loyalty and their trust. "What I need now," I said, "is not your weapons but your discretion. No one but you must know that I've returned. None but you must know that I even live. Hence this disguise you so much mock."

A dozen voices reassured me that my clothes weren't that bad and that they could be trusted to keep lips sealed. I looked at them, remembering the last time I had suggested I might be stalked and how they'd mocked me. There was no mockery now. I was relieved, for they might ridicule my clothes, my beard, my rustic gait, but not my fear.

I bade the men continue their eating and drinking, which they did with great zest, and drew Burbage aside for private conference.

Burbage said, "What's all this, Will? There's more here than meets the eye. You were supposed to have fled the country to avoid the law. You were seen boarding a ship. Now we hear of Stratford."

"You saw me board. You didn't see me disembark," I said. "We sailed but a mile beyond Greenwich before I was set ashore. From there I traveled by horse to Stratford."

I had decided earlier that, whatever I revealed about my disappearance from London, I would not reveal the murderous events on the road or in the Forest of Arden. Those enormities I would keep to myself, buried in memory even as the four dead men lay hidden in the ooze.

"It was all a trick of the eye, concocted by Lord Cecil," I said.

"Cecil? God's blood, watch yourself, Will," Burbage said. "The man's tricky, a damned politician."

"He's shown me much kindness," I said.

"I say he's tricky. A man doesn't climb to that altitude by being virtuous. A politician, I say. So his father, old Lord Burghley, so the son. The apple doesn't fall far from the tree, so say I."

I didn't argue with Burbage or his proverbs, even though I trusted Cecil and knew nothing evil of him. Burbage was a political man, as I wasn't. He followed court gossip and had opinions about everyone. It had been Cecil's idea that I leave London and rescue my family. I didn't hold him answerable for the treachery of Spurgeon and Marbury, although I knew Burbage would have had I told him about them. Cecil had bailed me out of prison, had promised to protect me from further legal action.

Their feast continued, the roar of talk. It was time to go. We could not all leave together.

I bid them all good night, aware that nothing guaranteed that I would see them again. I shook each hand, called each by name, embraced my favorites, and practically wept upon his hairy cheeks when I said good-bye to Dick Burbage, for I've never loved a man so much as he.

Dikkon was at the landing, maintaining his vigil. He looked relieved to see me. I handed him a leg of chicken wrapped in my handkerchief and a slice of cheese. He'd missed his supper, but his plain, guileless face showed no resentment.

I might die, but I would die among friends.

And that's no small thing.

ON THE WAY to London, I had meditated a thousand times the bedeviled course of my recent life. I was sure that somewhere amid the warp and woof of my experience there was meaning that escaped me, a thread to unravel all, something that explained my old lover's murder, the stalking of Spurgeon, the sins of the father. What was the reason for such enmity? I had asked myself time and time again. Cecil had tried to help, but from him I got only treason and perjury. Indeed, I had got more help from my wife. It was she who had started me thinking about my mistress's futile effort to extort money and what it might mean. If she begged money from me, why not from someone else, someone with more to lose? Someone who might have supposed that in being found with her I was her accomplice rather than a victim?

I had not considered it. But Anne had. And with this realization I had, for the first time, a theory of my case.

Dikkon and I returned to our Shoreditch inn, locked up, and went to bed, Dikkon sharing the modest four-poster with me. His soft snoring told me he had fallen asleep almost at once, for Dikkon was among the innocent despite his manslaughter, and so such men sleep, untroubled by dreams or guilt while angels smile upon them.

Twenty-nine

THE NEXT DAY, oblivious to voices in distant rooms, barking dogs, intrusive light, I slept late. When I awoke, Dikkon was gone, but I had not time to become worried before he was back again, his sanguine self, bringing with him fresh bread and salted herring he'd bought in the street. Of this we made our breakfast.

"What now, Master Shakespeare?" he said, eating the bread happily.

"There's someone I must see," I said. "Someone who may know more about my enemy than I."

"You aren't going alone?"

"There's no danger. The man knows me. He's a great gentleman. Someone I knew when I was your age. He's a nobleman—an earl."

"An earl! Marry, you keep great company, sir. Still you shouldn't go alone."

"I must," I said. I could see the injury in his honest face, which hid so little of his emotions. I didn't beg pardon for my words. It would have done no good.

So I went alone to the London house of Henry Wriothesley, the third earl of Southampton and baron of Titchfield, for both titles were his—he whom I had once called the true begetter of my sonnets. I had once great affection for him, which I believed then he returned, but had not spoken to him in years. For a while he had been as besotted with my dusky mistress as was I. Our friendship did not survive our rivalry. Yet if the woman could extort money from me, she might have done likewise to him.

Southampton House was on the Strand, not far from Cecil's house, for Henry Wriothesley had once been ward of Lord Burghley, Cecil's father. The house was spacious, princely, surrounded by an iron gate within which was a cobbled courtyard the size of a tennis court. A liveried porter came to attention at my approach and, regarding me with contempt because of my modest dress, demanded to know what I wanted. To him I gave not my true name, nor the one I had used to disguise myself at the inn, but a special name his master and I had used for one another when we were close. It had begun as a joke between us; later it had become a kind of password. I was confident its use would guarantee my admission.

I assured the porter that my purpose touched upon the king's business—which in some far-fetched sense I believed it did since I was His Majesty's servant—and that his master would be most displeased were I turned away at the gate. To reinforce my plea, I paid him well for his tolerance. He took the money, regarded me with some doubtfulness still, and bade me wait.

I did not mind this minor indignity. It gave me time to write my script, to block my scene. Besides, I was grateful that he was home at all. I had heard he traveled much since the Essex affair, when he barely escaped my lord Essex's fate, and had sought and found honors with the king. Once or twice I had seen his face in the Globe's audience. He was there when I played Sejanus for my friend Ben Jonson. Presently a servant, an arthritic old man with a fox face I think I remembered from the old days, appeared and said that his master was with another gentleman at the moment but he thought he would leave soon and prayed for his master's love of me that I be patient a while.

Finally, when I had grown weary of my status as a petitioner, the old servant returned and beckoned me to follow him, smiling as though he knew me.

I entered the main part of the house, a richly paneled vestibule with a fortune of hangings and tapestries depicting various lewd and lascivious scenes from antiquity, and then was shown through the great hall into a withdrawing room where my old friend sat.

As a young man, Wriothesley had been slender and clear-eyed, with smooth white hands and the longest fingers I'd ever seen. His was an almost feminine beauty, and because our mutual love was swarthy, his golden fair and her blackness complemented each other in a way my looks and hers did not. Perhaps that's why, at last, she chose him—because of his beauty, for I do not flatter myself: I am not ugly, but neither am I Adonis reborn. Wriothesley at eighteen might have been thought to be just that—a young Greek god.

Or maybe it was only his money and his station that advanced him in her affections. After all, in those days I was only a poor player. That Wriothesley bounced between women and boys only enhanced his favor in her sight. My dark mistress liked novelty.

Wriothesley's rumored wealth and the splendor of his furnishings suggested he need not worry about the cost of candles. Yet there were only two tapers in the room alight, and so he sat bathed in shadows like a creature that preferred the night. He stood to greet me, an uncommon courtesy his rank did not require, and seemed shorter than I remembered him. Indeed, he was much changed. His once burnished cheeks were pale and jowly; his wasp waist had thickened, and there was in his countenance the satyr's lecherous smirk. He had been married once, I'd heard, but his wife had died in childbirth. He had been contracted to several women since, one I knew distantly; nothing had come of these engagements. Some men are not fit for marriage. I had sometimes wondered about myself in that regard, yet was always sure that Wriothesley was of that misogynistic breed despite my fawning sonnets in which I urged that he marry and beget, largely for my fee and his avoiding the ire of Lord Burghley, his guardian.

"Will Shakespeare, God in heaven! Where have you come from and what's happened to you?"

"In the flesh, my good lord," I answered, with a courteous bow of a sort I had perfected.

I ignored the indirect mention of my modest clothing. In London, a man wears what he's worth and never less, save he's a madman or a fool. Relaxed in his own house, still royally velveted and silk slippered as though at any moment he would entertain the king, my lord of Southampton said, "Not 'my good lord,' Will, but plain Harry, as in the old days betwixt us. We have a history together, don't we? And a good one."

He pumped my hand most warmly, all smiles, which did not flatter him, for I noticed he had lost several teeth. Then he directed me to sit beside him, which I did. A new servant, younger and with golden looks, emerged from the shadows with a princely flagon and filled his master's goblet, then mine without inquiring whether I would drink or no. I knew the wine would be good. Spanish or French, maybe even Italian. And very expensive. Harry Wriothesley did not drink water.

He immediately began to talk of a new play he'd seen some months earlier, not one of mine, and to bewail the closing of the playhouses. I listened, nodding my agreement, impatient to come to my own business. At last, I found a slit in his discourse and inserted my own question like a thin blade.

"I saw our mutual friend a few weeks hence."

"Our friend?" he said, not comprehending. He drank from his goblet, wiped his mouth on the sleeve of his velvet gown, and placed the goblet carefully on the little round table between us. He looked at me curiously.

I said her name, and he was at once like a man who starts from a dream, shakes off sleep with a curse, and glares at him who's waked him. He scowled and swore, not like a lord but a commoner.

"A bitch, a very Medusa!" he cried. "What did the harlot say to you?"

"She begged for money."

He leaned forward in his chair, his eyes widening with comprehension. "Why, so did she of me. Did you give her any?"

"Nay, my lord. Not a penny. But when I refused her flatly, she said she'd tell my wife what we'd done, she and I, tell the king, bring me to ruin."

He laughed bitterly and shook his head. "Great gods, what ballocks this woman has. She summoned me by letter, pleading some desperate need. I ignored it. For Christ's sake, I have my place, my position. What does she think of me? I was not about to venture forth to pay respects to a slattern. Then she sends me a second letter, more insolent than the first. She claims I'd fathered a bastard upon her and the need was his. In sum, she assumed too much about my credulity—and my capacity for pity."

"Was it true, about the bastard?"

He shrugged. "I'd heard she had a child. Later. After she and I had gone our separate ways. You were always right, Will. She was a slut, a novelty, for me, a diversion. Your own ardor for her pricked me on. I confess it."

"Her proof, then? About this bastard, I mean."

"Only her earnest affirmation. To speak true, Will, I don't know whether this child she claims was mine or no. I couldn't care less. If the bastard's mine, he may well then join a legion of them and be damned. But I'll not be bled dry by a base extortionist."

"Did she write a third time?"

"No."

"Then nothing came of her entreaties?"

"Nothing."

"When did she write these letters?"

"Last summer. July, I think. It was a foolish effort. You say she's dead?"

"Her house was set afire. She tried to escape, fell, broke her neck."

"God's will, then," he said, turning a little pale, I thought.

"There's more, my lord."

"More? Well and good—so it work her ill."

"She was rotten with pox."

This news brought him up quickly enough. He sat pensive, staring into the darkness, yet I could read his mind.

"You saw her?" he asked.

"I did, my lord."

"How'd she appear?"

"Her face covered for shame. I caught but a glimpse. She was changed, looked sick, what you'd expect with the pox."

I paused. He stared at me intently, hooding his eyes with his hand as though massaging a headache.

"There's more?" he asked, probably knowing that there was, that I had only begun my tale.

"She was murdered. The fire was set."

"Set?"

"An arsonist."

He sucked in air, but no astonishment showed on his face. I saw only the hint of it in his flat, expressionless stare.

I went on. "I was at her house. I barely escaped with my life. Whoever set the fire knew I was with her. Afterward, I was followed, stalked. I think by the same person and certain of his men. They followed me all over London, killed a baker's apprentice who had witnessed the deed, then contrived to have me accused and imprisoned. From that fate I escaped with the help of certain high-placed persons who knew me to be innocent. Whereupon I fled to Stratford under the guise of going abroad. There I was also pursued but managed to lose my pursuers."

"That's quite a story, a better plot than half the plays I've seen this year."

"It's God's truth," I said solemnly as though I were taking an oath.

He made a gesture of dismissal. "That goes without saying. I know you to be honest, Will. But what think you? She tried to mine both our pockets. She must have had other lovers after us, for certain it is she had them before. She was a married woman, for God's sake. We gave the hapless husband the cuckold's horns right royally. Her body saw more traffic than Paul's at noon."

"That occurred to me," I said. "The extortionist always puts himself at risk. The greater his threat, the greater his victim's desperation. Murder must seem a natural remedy in such a case.

That might explain her death, but what of mine? What of my tormentor?"

Wriothesley thought about this, then he said. "Were I in your shoes, friend Will, I might suppose this: that this other person or persons she threatened, seeing you with her, might have thought you to be confederates, joined in a common enterprise to extort money from him."

"Possibly," I said. "The same thought struck me, too. But if that were so, his failure to kill me would have only prompted him to try harder next time. Yet when next time came, he was content to torment. To play cat and mouse with me. No, I wish it were as simple as you say, my lord, but it can't be. There's malice in my enemy. His motive is deep rooted. Death isn't enough for him. The plot was never about money."

I heard myself echoing my wife's phrase and was surprised.

"What then?" he asked.

"I don't know," I said. I drained my goblet. My lord's servant appeared to refill it.

I spent another hour with this man, during which time we did not talk of our old lover again. He talked of court, of his lovers, both female and male, of the prospect of travel, and, again, of plays, of which he was very fond although he did not have such intense interest when I knew him. To all this I half listened, my mind traveling back to the dark woman's upper chamber, my last conversation with her, and, now, brought vividly back, my enemy Spurgeon's last words about the sins of fathers.

If the child was not Wriothesley's as he claimed, could it have been mine? What else explained this harping on generational vengeance in my enemy's intermittent messages? The sins of the fathers visited upon the children? Did I have a son who wanted to kill me because he thought himself a victim of my sins? Which sin? Playing the beast with two backs with his whore of a mother? Infecting her with the pox?

My lordly host grew drowsy in his cups, stopped talking, and slumped in his chair, his chin rested on his chest. I, frenzied with thought and mad speculation, rose to go, but as I reached my feet he awoke suddenly and looked up, startled as though he had forgotten my presence and I now seemed to him to be an intruder.

"Oh, Will. Still here?"

"And it please your lordship, I'll leave you."

He nodded, as though he understood, not just that I must go, but that the perils I had spoken of must be seen to. It was no business of his. We were no longer what we were, and no attempt had been made on his life, nor were his friends slaughtered in some mad sacrifice for his guilt.

Then he looked at me pitifully.

"What can I do for you, Will?"

He no sooner asked the question but I had an unlooked-for answer. Men talk of sudden inspiration, of bypassing the faculties of cold reason. This I did in my resolve. Past reason, past prudence. I said, "You can tell your friends in the city and court that Will Shakespeare has returned from Italy. That he can be found in his customary lodgings, that he rehearses when weather permits at the Globe, and that he plays before the king on his royal command."

"I thought you were afraid for your life?" he said.

"I was. I am. But I grow weary of waiting. If I'm to be killed I'd rather it were done quickly."

He nodded and rose to shake my hand again. "Fare you well," he said. "I congratulate you. You have more courage than I thought. Commend me to Sir Robert."

I was dumbfounded. I was sure I hadn't mentioned Cecil's name. I had deliberately avoided doing so. "But how did you know it was he I spoke of before?"

"Lord Cecil was here before you. We supped together. The chair you sat in was still warm from him when you came in. We spoke of you, most favorably I might add."

I was about to ask what of me was discussed when the young servant with the golden looks returned and waited by his master's chair while we said our farewells. I could see that they were intimates, master and servant. Wriothesley had physically decayed, but in all he was the same Harry Wriothesley I had known years before, a lover for all seasons.

The old manservant came to show me out. I walked through the vestibule, listening to my heels click on polished marble. What o'clock was it? Eleven or twelve. I knew it was late, I could feel how late it was, and yet, for all my weariness and confusion, I felt free. Tomorrow I would rid myself of this false sartorial front and be Will Shakespeare again, son of John Shakespeare, and father of Hamnet Shakespeare who is dead.

Outside the gate, I was startled when a form emerged from the shadows—then relieved; it was Dikkon. He said he had followed me to the house and waited. He asked if all was well with me. Even in the darkness, I could see the concern in his eyes.

"I'm well," I said, deciding not to upbraid him for his disobedience. "I'm very well."

"You saw my lord the earl?"

"I did."

"Marry, sir. It's a very great house he lives in. He must be a rich man indeed, learned and virtuous."

"He's but a man like other men," I said, and then added, "maybe not exactly like other men."

"Did you learn what you wanted?"

"Just so," I said.

"And what might that be, sir, if I may be bold to ask?"

"A simple thing, Dikkon. That I am the bait I sought."

"Bait, Master Shakespeare! Will you be going afishing, then?"

"In a manner of speaking," I said.

Thirty

COME MORNING, I sent Dikkon with two messages, the first to
my friends, releasing them from their oath of silence. I offered no
excuse, trusting they would not need one, and indeed encouraged
them now to tell all and sundry that Will Shakespeare had
returned, was well, and could be found at home on Silver Street
and at the Globe.

The second missive I sent to Cecil, wherein I announced my
return to London, begged him to do what he could to relieve me
of my troubles with the law, said I would presently have more
news of my situation, and assured him that my company and I
would perform for the king as he might command.

I knew, of course, that Cecil was well aware of my return, he
having been told by Wriothesley that I had come to Southampton
House, but it seemed politic to inform my great patron directly,
that he be not offended that I had come to the earl before him. In
such matters as these one cannot be too careful.

That done and it being the Sabbath and dry, I went for a walk
in the city, making my way toward Paul's Cross, where despite the
bracing air a large group of onlookers listened to a sermon of a
learned divine whose name escapes me. The sermon was more
witty than pious, I thought, yet since God made man, I doubt He
objects to so elegant a demonstration of wit. There I made a suf-

ficient spectacle of myself in my lavish greetings of acquaintances and bowing and scraping at what lords and ladies might be abroad.

After the sermon I joined a group of friends and walked along the Strand with them, looking at the great houses. I passed Cecil's house and considered inquiring for him, but then thought the better of it. My letter must serve.

Suddenly I heard my name; I turned and saw it was Fanshawe, my scapegrace lawyer. When I had last seen him in Lucy Negro's brothel he was a disheveled and dissipated wretch; he seemed to have come into some money since. He wore a handsome cloak, had a clean collar, and sported a ridiculously tall hat of the kind then in fashion. With him were two women, dressed very finely but with coarse complexions and worse manners. One hung on each of Fanshawe's arms, and I could tell that although the lawyer's state had improved he kept the same base company as before. Neither of the women was Delia, but I suspected they were of the same sisterhood.

I returned his greeting, for although I detested the man, it occurred to me that I might inquire again about the Whorley that Fanshawe had said paid him to stick his nose into my affairs.

I invited Fanshawe to walk with me, letting him think I had lawyer's work for him, although I would sooner have hired the devil to plead my cause. He agreed, sending his doxies off ahead—with some complaining on their part, for evidently he had secured their services, and they were not taking his abandonment of them lightly.

I bid my friends go on without me and lingered with Fanshawe. Nearby was a little church I knew of. I led him there under the guise of confiding in him. Inside, we sat upon a bench. He asked what legal matter I had and smiled broadly, doubtless in anticipation of his fees, for he had no reason to love me or otherwise desire my company.

"Information," I said. "Only information."

Disappointment, then annoyance, crossed his face. I took my purse and gave him two crowns. "A retainer, I said—for information."

He took the money and grinned obsequiously. I assumed he had little memory of our last conversation; he had been too drunk. I reminded him of what he had told me, about the man named Whorley.

He said what he had said before, that he seen Whorley but once, in foul weather, all muffled.

"This Whorley said he had once been an actor?"

"He did."

"His very words?"

Fanshawe couldn't remember the man's very words. He stroked his beard and looked thoughtful. I said, "How did he describe what he wanted you to do?"

"He said whatever suits, contracts, affairs, litigations—"

"His exact words?"

"More or less."

"He might then have been a lawyer, someone familiar with legal matters?"

Fanshawe laughed. "Not likely," he said.

"Why say you that?"

"Because he vilified the profession."

"Lawyers, he vilified them?"

"Yes, I didn't mention it to you before. I didn't think it was important. He called lawyers vermin."

"This slander didn't offend you?" I asked.

"Marry, he was my client," Fanshawe said, shrugging. "A man may call me what he chooses, so he pays my fee."

I said, "So this Whorley, as he called himself, wasn't a lawyer, but he knew a smattering of law, enough to give things their right names? A university man, a scholar?"

"He was particular in his words."

"He may have studied law at the Inns of Court," I said, "but be no practitioner. Were he that, he might have done your business himself and saved his money."

"Perhaps," Fanshawe said.

"But he had also been an actor."

"He said this. There was something else."

"What?"

"Nothing important. I would have told you earlier, but I didn't want to give offense."

"Offense to whom?"

"Why, you, sir."

"Me? What insult?" I was amused, but interested.

"He said you were—" He hesitated, screwing up his face as though trying to wrench by violence the phrase from his memory. "He said you were—"

"He said what of me?"

"With all due respect, sir, he said you were a piss-poor player, prince of plagiarists, a wretched judge of talent, and a whoreson dog."

In the theater, one gets used to invective and random insult. Yet Whorley's reported slander shocked me. I sat silent for a moment, then regained my composure. "In faith, elegant language," I said. "This Whorley has a fine wit to put a dog last in the order of excellence. Were he no better a player, he was well advised to pursue another trade."

Fanshawe's grin had turned to a broad, derisive smile full of impudence and self-satisfaction. Could I trust this account or had this scurrilous pettifogger turned fictionalist? If he was right and neither he nor Whorley was lying, Whorley had been a student of law and a would-be thespian, perhaps one who had read for me and I had rejected. Was that, then, what this was about? The sour grapes of a failed actor?

DIKKON HAD BEEN my constant companion on these forays, but at a discreet distance, watching me and watching those around me. When I had told him my plan of publishing my return, he shook his head and said I was a fool and threatened to return to Warwickshire, where he would most happily look after his cows and sheep. "For they have more brain than you, with all due respect for your authorship," Dikkon stormed.

I protested that I was neither fool nor mad, explaining that while I was coming out of hiding I would not do so save he were by my side. This calmed him, and he begged pardon for his outburst, which he said was only for concern for my safety. His words I freely forgave. Dikkon was not my servant although I paid for his expenses; he was fast becoming my friend. Nothing signaled his emerging state more clearly than his indignant outburst. It was the act of a friend, an equal, not a servant.

Despite Dikkon's admonishments, for the next three days I made myself a public man, spending little time at my lodgings, but never alone, always in a company where Dikkon was never far distant and I walked in a cloud of witnesses. Each day I expected a message or a sign, a letter slipped beneath my door or delivered by some boy who could not say just who asked him to deliver it. This message, I supposed, would be filled with dire prophecies of my death, harp upon fathers and sons, or threaten someone near to me.

But no letter came, and in that appalling silence I gained not so much peace of mind as more profound worry. I could not believe that what the mysterious Master Whorley had commenced he had finished. It was not in the scheme of things for life to be so simple or for me to be so fortunate.

Thirty-one

SO ENDED ONE fateful year and began the next. I resumed my life as I had lived it before my dusky mistress's tragedy. All winter I kept me warm, passed time with friends, plied my craft, tried to forget. We did not perform *Measure* before the king, a disappointment to me. The play would wait for another and better Christmas. But Lord Cecil freed me from Justice Swallow's unrighteous dominion, the bill of murder against me quite erased. For that I was profoundly grateful. Sometimes I dreamed of bloody Arden Forest and, more frequently, of that nameless being (Was it really Whorley?) who had engineered my downfall. But in my waking hours these sad events seemed ever more alien to my true history, ever more an interlude of some other's life.

April came. It was my birth month and the month of spring when England woke from its gray, dreary winter and life seemed worth the trouble. Then two evils blighted my joy. One a resurgence of the plague, which closed the theaters again for much of the month. Worse, the nightmare of my stalking returned—and in a way I did not expect and for which I was little prepared.

Mark you this: I was abroad in the city, Dikkon with me. In Bread Street, I think, or perhaps the Strand and on some errand time has blotted out. The day was fair with a light sweet wind. He and I were talking about some matter when suddenly I saw ahead of us a familiar figure. I say figure, for it was only that I spied, an impression blurred. The person's face was turned away and I saw but a backside, cloaked and but a few strands of black hair. Yet I did note the carriage of this person, the sloping of the shoulders, most particularly the stride, which I would argue is peculiar to each soul. In sum, I knew her as I might recognize myself were I to see my double.

"That woman," I said to Dikkon, without really intending to say anything at all.

"Which?" Dikkon asked.

I pointed. "She, there."

Dikkon searched the street ahead.

"I think I see a ghost," I said, hardly believing my own words. For if it was not my false mistress walking ahead of me as alive as I, then it was her twin. My conviction based upon this view of her backside was no sooner uttered but confirmed when she stopped to stare into a window and I saw her profile.

Upon my oath 'twas she; unthinkable for it to be otherwise. The sweep of her brow, her swollen nether lip, and the deep-burnished skin that separated her from English beauties and spoke so eloquently of her exotic birth—all this was proof 'gainst reason and experience both, for I had seen her sick and dead, and while I believed in the Resurrection I had no reason to suppose that great day had come.

Her ghost, then?

She did not see me, or so I believed, and when she resumed her course I could do nothing else but follow. She walked briskly, made toward the great bridge of London, and started across.

Dikkon hurried to keep up. "Who's the woman? She's lively for a ghost."

"Someone I used to know, or so I think."

I could see that nothing I had said had eased my young friend's bewilderment as to why we should follow this woman, what urgency there was, or why whatever we had set out to do that morning was no longer important, but only this. Besides the which, I swear I did not know myself what I should do were I to catch her, what to say. I wasn't even sure the woman I saw was substantial. Perhaps when I came to her and reached out to touch her hand or cheek she would prove as immaterial as a dream, as thin as a shadow. But what amazed me was this: It wasn't hatred I felt for her now, nor disdain or fear, but a reawakening of that passion that had undone me years before. I disgusted myself. I abhorred myself. I was as vile a traitor to my better self as she.

Turning a corner in Bankside, we came upon two men violently engaged with fists and clubs; they had attracted a crowd of onlookers who were choosing sides and crying out in support of their favorites. My mistress moved through them without looking to the right or the left, but when I attempted to do so, everywhere I encountered rude jostling and curses. The crowd thickened. I lost sight of her but kept advancing against the tide. Behind me Dikkon called my name. I didn't stop, didn't look back. I feared I'd lose her now and, having lost, never find her again, always wondering if I had seen a true ghost or had finally descended into a world of madness where my love and hate for this woman would remain at eternal war.

I emerged from the broiling crowd, and she came into view. She had maintained her course, turning down a street I knew well. Ahead was the rotund shape of the Globe.

She walked toward the theater as though she had business there. I think I could have up caught up with her if I'd run, or even quickened my step, but seeing now where she was headed I held back, my heart beating. I suppose in the back of my head still lingered the possibility that it was not she at all but some other dusky woman who, by accident of fortune, happened to be in the vicinity of the Globe.

It was not beyond reason—and certainly more likely than a ghost.

Then there she was again. By the theater, walking around to where the locked door was. I started after her, then turned to make sure Dikkon followed, but when I looked behind me he, too, had vanished. The street was empty. Where had he gone?

Had he been lost in the unruly crowd? Or had he grown disgusted with my mad pursuit of a whimsical spirit?

I determined I would not go back to look for him, no matter how dangerous continuing my pursuit alone might be.

She was not to be seen on the other side of the building, but the back door of the theater was slightly ajar. We always kept it locked when the theater was not in use. I had the lock made especially, of strong brass and a clasp an inch thick. The lock hung open. She had somehow gotten in. Was this an apparition, then, or a corporal spirit who must open locked doors to enter? And if she was the mortal she seemed, where and how did she obtain a key? I had one. Each sharer in the company had one. Who or what else?

I stepped into the great cockpit of the theater and felt the chill both of my apprehension and of the desolation of the empty space, which at some later and happier time would be so filled with spectators that one could hardly move. I walked toward the stage and searched the galleries. They were as devoid of life as I might have expected them to be.

Then I heard a noise above me and turned again to the stage. And there she stood.

Her features, her complexion, told me it was she. She pulled the hood of her light cloak back and unleashed the long sable hairs that I remembered although had not seen at our last interview when I supposed her killed. She said nothing at first but glared, striking terror to my soul. My knees shook. Had I been called upon to speak at that moment I would have been as wretchedly mute as Titus's disarmed and tongueless daughter, helpless to declare her assailant's identity.

In my muddled state I silently prayed for deliverance, for this was indeed a ghost. No two humans could be so alike as this. Her mute, accusing stare was more terrible than any voluble ghost I'd ever conceived and given life in my plays. Hamlet's murdered father, a talky and expansive spirit full of resounding sentences and metaphors, was not so stark and dreadful. Nor Banquo's horrid ghost, who stalked the bloody Macbeth, which tragedy I'd begun to work upon in idle hours.

It wasn't dreary midnight but shy of noon, not in a deserted place of clouds and gloom but amidst habitations. And yet her awful presence transformed the theater into a scene more fearful than the murk of Arden's forest.

Then she spoke my name, yet not she, not her voice, but a strange unearthly summons. Her mouth moved and the strange voice came forth. Once, twice, three times before I could find within me power to respond.

I almost mouthed Prince Hamlet's lines when confronted by his father's shade. *Whither wilt thou lead me? Speak. I'll go no further.*

"Mark me now," she said.

"I will," I answered, my voice quavering and dry as dust.

"You know me?"

I nodded dumbly.

"When I lived, you swore to me your love."

Her lips moved, yet as I've said, the voice seemed to come from some other place, from the cellarage or from above. Or it was a trick of sound, the echo in the empty theater? Or maybe it was all my battered brain, bruised by shock and confusion.

I knew then only that I was as firmly fixed where I stood as if my feet were roots and I a tree of great pith and altitude, unmoved by wind or earthquake. I was as helpless before the mystery of this apparition as a babe who looks up wonderingly at the workings of his mother's mouth and comprehends nothing.

She repeated her words about my love for her. I nodded. She uttered them another time, and then I understood she desired that I voice my thoughts, not merely gesture.

"I remember. It's true," I said.

She nodded and raised an admonitory hand, her palm toward me. "Then I give you good counsel," she said.

I waited.

"Give over your performances, your foolish plays, your idle fancies. Go back to Stratford. Do this or die."

"What?" I gasped.

She repeated the curse and my soul withered under it.

Then silence. She made no motion but stood like a statue, fixing me with cool disdain.

She said, "Play no more. You'll die if you do, and your company of players with you."

I wanted to ask why and how but didn't dare. Men couldn't see the future, but a spirit, free from this mortal coil, could.

"Do you hear me, Will Shakespeare?"

I nodded dumbly, and when she demanded it of me again, I managed to utter a small affirmation, which left me feeling defeated, cowardly.

Then the spirit said, "Go and remember. Don't forget me."

Not likely, I thought.

My attention was drawn to a rustle or footfall somewhere in the upper gallery. I turned to look. Nothing. When I looked again at the stage where she had stood she was gone.

Astounded, I rubbed my eyes. What had I seen? What heard? Had I been dreaming in the daytime? The yard and stage and backparts of the theater, the galleries that circled round, all seemed as empty of life—or death—as they had been when I first entered. What was I to do now? I had received a curse, my mandate was clear, my fate sealed by the heavens, or perhaps by hell. Leave over my plays, my work, my London life, or face death. Did this ghost believe that my company was completely within my control? I was a shareholder, a principal, but the company wasn't just I alone. I might do what I would, but yet the King's Men would perform and perform my plays. After all, they had the playbooks.

I turned to go, but where? Then my reason, usurped by horror and dread, returned. I had been discoursing with the dead. Nothing could convince me otherwise, for my eyes and ears could not be deceived. Yet something stuck. Her ghostly form when she stood upon the stage like one of my actors, her stark stare—these might be expected of a spirit. But when she had moved through the streets, hesitating before the shop window, and then later striding across the bridge and moving through the crowd—when she knew not that I followed her—all that bespoke a hard corporeality that said she was very much alive.

I climbed up onto the stage and walked into the backparts where her spirit had been. No sign of her there. Was I beginning to doubt the testimony of my eyes? Was this all a dream from which I would presently awake?

Do not call me an atheist who denies the reality of the eternal world, spirits, ghosts, and angels. You would be wrong to think so. For am I not a Christian? Yes, I do believe. What man does not, though he disputes it, rejecting the testimony of all Scripture and antiquity? And even he who denies it is afraid to walk among the gravestones at midnight or to sit alone beside a corpse.

Nonetheless I was beginning to doubt. To that end I looked behind curtains, probed boxes in the tiring house, tread lightly on the bloodstains that marked where young Edward Goode met his end.

Slowly, timorously, I made my way up to the storage where once I had come within arm's reach of Whorley. Yet not his faceless form but my dark lady's quickened flesh mastered my thought. At any moment, at any step or threshold, I might see her again, in what new grim-visaged guise I feared to imagine. My obsession drove me on, not fearlessly but in the desperation of the soldier, who so fears death he rushes to it, his arms open, his mouth agape in a brutal scream.

I reached the door, found it locked. Went to where I hid the key. Found it there and opened. Did all this mindlessly, thinking but one thing. I went in.

Before me now the ranks of costumes, wardrobes, and shelves. No ghost, no Whorley. Nothing to fear. My brain said this. My heart thumped with a fury and my shirt was soaked with my sweat.

I didn't go farther into the storeroom but stood at the threshold staring, and then I gave it up, locked the door behind me, and went downstairs again.

I had almost descended to the stage when I heard my name called. No female spirit this time. It was Dikkon. He was coming across the yard, holding a bloody handkerchief to his forehead. I could see blood in his hair and on his hand and hurt in his eyes as he approached.

"What happened to you?" I said.

Dikkon removed his hand. A long finger of blood ran from his forehead to his right eye. He spoke haltingly, pain in his face.

"I was trying to keep up, Will, shouldering through that crowd of brawlers. Of a sudden I took a skull-cracking from some fellow. Next I knew I was on the ground. They were stamping and kicking me. Some damned hellion was going through my shirt and jerkin looking for money. Damned thieves. Your London is full of them."

I did not defend London from this largely accurate charge but led Dikkon to the benches in the lower gallery and sat him down. I examined his forehead. The cut looked worse than it was, but his head would ache for a week and he'd be lucky tomorrow if he could see out of his right eye.

"What happened here?" Dikkon asked, looking 'round at the empty theater. "Did you find her, this woman you were running after? This spirit?"

"I found her—or she found me," I said.

Dikkon regarded at me in a puzzled way.

"She *was* here," I said.

He looked round to see whom I meant.

"She's gone now," I said. "She was on the stage. She spoke to me. She cursed me."

Dikkon's eyes grew round. I could read his mind. He was unnerved by this story of a ghost, uncomfortable with one he supposed might be mad, intimidated by the chaos of London, and yearning for the familiar landscape of Warwickshire, and probably for the thin white arms of Jessica, a wench of flesh and blood, no ghost. Would he abandon me now, run in contempt or fear?

None of this he did. He said, "How did she curse you?"

I told Dikkon all but felt foolish in doing so, for now with this young man with me, so rooted as he was in this world, the threatenings of the dead seemed madness, even to me who had experienced them.

Dikkon said, "And will you give over the making of plays, this life you live in London? Warwickshire's a pretty place, you know. The air's fresh there, summer or winter. A man can breathe."

"I know that well enough," I said. "Warwickshire is a very good place. And the air is sweeter."

"But will you go? Will you save yourself?"

"Not on your life," I said.

Thirty-two

IT IS AN awful thing to face a spirit of the sheeted dead. Even to suppose in a moment of swine-drunkenness or moon-madness that the dead live, walk, and threaten us is enough to bleach cheeks, to still the heart, to silence the articulate man and make the dumb innocent babble. So I kept my counsel, not sharing my tormented thoughts even with Dikkon, or my growing suspicion about the event, of which I could make no sense myself.

Within the week, I sent Dikkon into Warwickshire with letters for my wife and daughters, telling them what I did, how I lived, and what hopes I had for their health and welfare. But not one word of my old mistress's appearance.

Dikkon returned within the month with letters for me, which I read with eagerness. Despite his complaints about London turmoil and bad air, his appetite had been whetted for the theater. He wanted to become an actor, and having seen that he lacked not the ear, voice, or agility (for an actor acts with his body whole, not merely his tongue) I persuaded my fellows to take him on as an apprentice rather than as occasional spear-carrier, even though he was too much man to play female parts.

So might my tale have ended with naught to do but doff my cap and say "and so it was" or "that was that"—an inexplicable episode in the otherwise busy and profitable life of a man fortunate in his friends and vocation.

But it wasn't to be. An even greater storm lay in the offing. My dream, if it was that, was not done, and my enemy's vengeance was still to come.

ENGLISH SPRING IS a treasure after winter's dearth. When the coffer opens, who does not seize upon its gold and bounty is a fool, for the lid will close and lock again before he's aware. No treasure then. So when the sun came forth I went walking though my city. One day, it was early morning, the weather dry, sunny, the air sweetly redolent of moist earth and flower. I had left my lodgings early in excellent humor. I was working on a new play; it went well, skipping faster than my pen could write, words tumbling forth from my fervid brain like rambunctious children. Yet the best news was this: We had received permission to reopen the Globe. Easter Monday was the day. In the tedious interim in which the Globe stood empty, we had enjoyed the bounty of our royal patron, but the King's bounty was but a tithe of our wonted income. With spring had come the promise of renewed prosperity, and our hearts were glad.

On my way I passed by the street on which my former mistress lived. I had not visited there since her death and my near escape, fearing the sight of it would provoke such dark thoughts that my melancholy dreams and visions might return. Where her house had stood, a new had been framed, sturdier than the first and now occupied by a mercer and his family, or so his sign proclaimed. Opposite, the baker's shop had also been rebuilt, its new timber and plaster all freshly daubed and painted black and white as was the fashion in those years.

And there I beheld the baker himself—Edward Goode's old master, he who had testified against me before Justice Swallow. Now that I was free from the grip of law, I thought I'd rub my freedom in his face, since he had been so busy about my hanging and must surely be disappointed at my acquittal.

The baker stood in the doorway of his shop, his cheeks flushed from the heat of his oven, his lantern jaw as I remembered it. He was dressed in a white apron and wiped his hands upon a towel. I set upon him, hailing him by name, and wishing him good morrow most graciously. He turned toward me, expecting someone else, I think, by my voice. Then dawned upon him who I was. First, he looked alarmed and took a stance as if I'd strike, despite my greeting. Then, seeing I offered him no violence, he smiled sheepishly.

"Master Shakespeare!" He returned my good morrow as though we were old friends. He bid me enter. I did, in too good spirits that day to deny him. I didn't hate the baker, only despised him as an abuser of boys and a false witness. He pressed upon me a tray of warm rolls sprinkled with sugar and cinnamon, insisting that it was free, an offering. No hard feelings, he said, about what had happened. He said he had heard about my exoneration, and mumbled something about it all being a misunderstanding, his testimony 'gainst me, and prayed I held no grudge.

I did not refuse the pastry. I have a sweet tooth that will not be appeased by moderate consumption. The baker might be a liar and cruel, too, but he was a good baker. "You were most vocal at my arraignment," I said, prodding him a little.

He said again his testimony was a mistake. He had confused me with someone else.

"A most regrettable confusion," I said. I looked out his window. From within his shop I could see the mercer's house. I praised its workmanship.

"Ah, yes," he said. "A mercer occupies it. A fine fellow. 'Twill improve the neighborhood. The last occupant was no better than a harlot."

He said this in such manner as to invite me to join in her condemnation, apparently forgetting that at our first meeting I told him the dead woman was my sister.

"She's dead," I said, offended by his words, although they were true enough.

"So I thought myself," the baker said absently, replacing the pastries in a cabinet and then returning to where I stood.

I asked him what he meant.

"In faith, sir, I saw the woman walking about Paul's this very week. Still peddling her tricks, if her gown and gesture did not deceive me. Imagine, in the very house of God! What's the country coming to?"

"You have a practiced eye for such women?" I asked.

His flushed face registered his denial. "I protest I'm faithful to my wife, sir. Yet I can smell a polecat in a bush. I couldn't have been mistaken. Was she not my neighbor?"

"But I saw her dead," I said. "Her neck broken."

"Oh, it wasn't she, sir, but some other. My oath on it."

I wasn't sure I understood. Was my swarthy mistress dead, or might she indeed be alive as I had increasingly suspected? I said, "What did this woman look like—this whore of yours?"

His brow wrinkled as he sought words to describe her. But before he could try his skill, comes his wife. Unlike her fleshy husband, she was small and thin, her face a scowl. She had been listening to us in the next room, she said, hearing all. "I'll tell you about her," she said without being asked. "Of middle height for a woman she is. Of years, maybe twenty-five or twenty-six. Of figure, bones. Of face, fair and freckled. Of hair, like unto a carrot. Of speech, vulgar, full of oaths and naughty jokes. She is a disgrace, and if she be alive, then it's a shame, for far better have died this year, I warrant."

"Fair skin and freckled!" I exclaimed. "Not dark complexioned, black eyed and browed, slender of waist but full bosomed, hair as black as coal. And older, nearer to thirty or thirty-two?"

"I saw her every day when she lived across the street," insisted the woman. "She had no more bosom than I, and as for dark, there was nothing of that about her and not so much flesh as enough to cover her ribs. What men see in such meatless baggage, I cannot fathom."

"We aren't talking about the same woman," I said.

"Marry, I think not," said the baker's wife, "if the woman you seek is such as you give account of."

"Have you seen this woman you speak of since the fire?" I asked her.

"Nay, sir, for which I have no regrets. But I've heard from others that she minds her store, if you get my drift. She haunts the bookstalls at Paul's, where I wot she looks out for scholars weary of their books. Scholars who would gladly peruse her library and turn over her leaves and worm their way into her binding."

"Where would I find her at home?" I asked.

"Within a quarter of an hour from here," she said, "or so I've heard."

She directed me. I knew the neighborhood. It wasn't where you'd want to live unless you were dirt poor, a kind of slum at the far end of Southwark.

"But I saw her dead," I protested.

"Marry, sir, it was another woman you saw, not she. I'll take the sacrament on't."

I HAD TO see this scrawny pullet for myself, if only to resolve nagging doubts. I took my leave of the baker and his wife and went to find the wench. It was still morning, too early in the day for her to ply her trade. With luck she'd be at home, probably asleep after a night of unsanctified coupling.

It took me a while to find the street, which was no street at all but a muddy rut into the fields where there was a little settlement of mean shelters passing as houses, although I've seen fitter habitations for hogs. I went from door to door, yard to yard, learned her name and where she dwelt, came upon the squalid place at last.

The baker's wife had described her well. The wench was young but looked worse for wear, her complexion pallid and hair carroty as the baker's wife had said. She peered out at me from behind her door, which was nothing more than two rough planks hobbled by old leather straps for hinges. She looked me up and down, scowling with as much disdain as curiosity, and, half asleep, complained about the hour.

"I beg pardon," I said. "About the time."

I told her I was looking for the occupant of her former house, wanted to find the woman who'd lived there. I named the street and described the place.

"I had quarters there. The house burned," she said without regret.

"You weren't there when it burned?" I asked.

"God's wounds, sir, I'd be cinders if I had."

"Was there anyone else—another woman, sick, she covered herself, someone who dwelt with you?"

"No one lived with me. I lived alone."

I reached into my purse and offered her a shilling. It was a princely sum, more than I would have paid for her stick of a body, but I knew she was lying.

She looked at the money in my hand, took it, then looked at me. "What would you have, sir?" she said.

"Plain truth," I said. "If you're of a mind to sell it."

My words startled her. She eyed me suspiciously and looked as if she might shut the door upon me. I gave her another shilling, more than I thought she'd need to open her mouth. She snatched it from my palm and opened the door to let me in, and I entered a place that was hardly bigger than a jakes and every bit as filthy.

For the wretchedness of her sty she made no excuse, but sat down upon a straw pallet, motioning me to join her. The gesture was too familiar for my comfort. I remembered my last encounter with my mistress—not her ghost, but in her poor diseased flesh. This was not she but was another tormented soul into whose house I'd come, and there was little here to inflame my lust.

"A woman died in the fire that burned your old house," I said.

"So I have heard," she said, and stared at her hands. They were red and raw, as though she had been holding them in water.

"Did you know her?"

"She gave me no name, sir."

"Or how she came to be in your house?"

"That I know," she said.

"Go on."

"A woman paid me for two hours' use."

"What manner of woman?"

"Why, brown, sir. The brownest woman I've seen. Like unto a Moor or a Spaniard."

"To use your house, how?"

"She said she wanted to meet a friend there. I thought it strange, her need, but she told me it was an appointment with her lover. Her money, it was as good as anyone's. What was it to me if she used my room? It wasn't my house. It belonged to someone else, and she and I had the same trade when all's said and done."

She shrugged. She explained she paid a pittance rent. Someone came by to collect. She didn't know his name, but she didn't think he owned the house either. The house was owned by a gentleman in the city, an absent landlord with whom she had nothing to do and whom she had never seen.

Then she said, "The woman didn't die in the fire." She concluded this revelation with a little burst of dry laughter followed by a consumptive cough.

"Not die?" I said.

"False seeming every whit, all trickery." More coughing.

"Trickery?"

"She wasn't killed, though it seemed like it was so."

"How know you that?"

"God's wounds, sir, I encountered her in Milk Street not a week after the fire. She paid me to keep mum about what happened, and somewhat more to make up for the loss of my lodgings and possessions of mine burned. She had a lover she would be rid of for his pestering—some ranting bloody fellow who pursued her. She wanted him to think she was dead. Then he'd leave her alone, she said. It was like a play, she said."

"A play?" I said.

"All pretend, all feigning. Her lover thought it was real, her death. He must have been a fool to think so."

I did not answer this, too astonished to speak. When I found my voice, I said, "Yes, I think he was a fool, a great fool to think so."

The wench pulled a worn shawl round her razor-thin shoulders and looked at me curiously, waiting for my next question. She seemed friendlier than before. She must have seen now how matters lay between us. Money had changed hands, but there would be no sweating and straining upon her pallet, no tangle of limbs, no melding mouths. Just talk, just questions, just answers, and, pray heaven, plain truth at last. I supposed that pleased her well enough. Even whores must grow weary of their work and sometimes prefer only polite conversation.

"If this woman paid you not to tell," I said, "why tell me?"

"Marry, you were the more generous, sir."

Money isn't all of life, but it is much. I should have known she'd answer so, but then what she'd said was plain truth without knowing it was I of whom she spoke. I was a fool, a wretched fool. My dark lady's tragedy had been a play, and I a most diligent player within, missing neither cue nor line.

Thirty-three

As I left the bony cotquean, one part of me was relieved, for I had no need now to feel regret or pain at my old lover's death, only indignation that I had been so deceived. I saw now that the fire had been set for me, not for her, her own escape provided for, her supposed death a trick of the eye, a magician's stunt, a most excellent performance.

As for her supposed wasting, what had it been but paint? Which if it can give false color to a face can dissolve that color in a sickly white. Ceruse, white fucus, what hadn't been used by our ladies of fashion—and some gentlemen—to cure plain brown or olive? I was an actor, but so was she with her endless variety in lovemaking, her gay impostures that enchanted once and then repelled. Why hadn't I seen it? How could I have been such a fool—fool when I loved her, fool later when I believed her pathetic condition, her dismal tale of desperation and need and false repentance.

The blood on the cobbles—false. The misshapen creature who swore her neck was broke—paid to lie like the young whore whom I paid to tell plain truth.

Her spectral presence at the Globe and curse another imposture, a palpable fraud. How she must have delighted in seeing me agape, a pale and quaking wretch, she playing her own ghost. Beating me at my own game.

More fool, I.

BY NOON I was at the theater, where I discovered my fellows already rehearsing and exhilarated at the prospect of reopening. Dikkon asked where I'd been. Everyone expected me earlier, he said, looking worried. I told him I would tell him all later, that I had news. I could tell he wanted the news now, but he didn't press me.

I joined the others on the stage and assumed the role I was to play, some piddling part, which was good, for it gave me time to think through all I'd learned. The woman wasn't dead after all. But who was this Whorley? And what did he and my mistress want with me? It was the same question I had been asking from the beginning, and therein lay my vexation and my pain. For I had somehow come full circle with her alive again, she being the center of my fears, the locus of my guilt, the instigator of a blind and burning lust.

It was four o'clock or closer to five when we completed our work. I resolved a conflict with Henry Farrar, one of the boy actors, over his costume and had a fruitless quarrel with Dick Burbage about the second scene of the first act, which he thought too full of aimless discourse. "The audience will sleep through it," he insisted.

I made cuts, although each blotting wounded my heart. Such is an author's love for his darlings. When my business was done, Dikkon waited by the door. I hailed him.

"Sup with me, Dikkon."

"Are you paying, Will?"

"I'm paying," I said. "Fish?"

"I'm your man," he said.

Since coming to London, Dikkon had learned the pleasures of pike, salmon, haddock, and conger-eels and always ate ravenously, as befitted a young man with a strong body. There was a cook-shop not far from the theater that served such delicacies. That was the port for which we set our sails.

WE SEIZED UPON a corner table, away from the talky crowd, for this shop was well known in the city. I ordered a bottle of dry Spanish wine, and we shared a trencher of shrimps and oysters, which were quite excellent.

After we had eaten our fill and talked of the play, I grew melancholy with thinking about my dark lady. Dikkon, sensitive now to all my moods and humors, said, "What is it, Will? The shrimp couldn't have been that bad. Another ranting letter, or is it your ghost come round?"

"Not she, but news of her," I said.

"Old news or new?"

"New," I said.

I rehearsed the events of the morning—my converse with the baker, his wife, and the bony slattern in her sty to whom I'd given two shillings to learn me what a fool I was. Dikkon was a sober listener and was most amazed at my tale.

"Then the woman didn't die, and it was no ghost you saw in the theater?"

"No ghost."

"The plot thickens."

"It curdles," I said.

"What does it all mean?"

"It means," I said, "that I have been a character in a play quite without knowing it. Manipulated by enemies—my old lover and her accomplice, playing with my affections, my fears."

Dikkon shook his head. "I can understand a man—or woman—wanting to kill another, out of love or sheer meanness. Or maybe to defend himself, or another." He paused, and I knew he was thinking of the four men we'd buried in the forest. He went on, "But this . . . I can't understand this. She's done you a terrible wrong. How will you answer it?"

Answer it? I didn't know. I am not above revenge but oft perplexed as to how to proceed in it. While I mulled over my answer, Dikkon drank deep, refilled and drank again, licked lips, and put down the cup in fluid motion. He was about to speak again on the subject of my gulling when he looked up sharply.

"Now here's fine company for you, Will."

I turned in the direction of his gaze. It was Thomas Stanleigh. I had not seen Cecil's secretary since my leave-taking for Italy. He was well appointed for the evening, above his station I thought, and wore a genial expression and several jeweled rings on his fingers I don't remember having seen before. The youth was coming up in the world, probably as much by slippery dealings as by merit.

"God save you, Master Shakespeare."

"And you, Master Stanleigh," I said. "And how does my lord Cecil?"

"Passing well," Stanleigh said, "and is most pleased at the opening of your theater. I was eating here myself with some friends." He paused and turned to indicate a table on the other side of the room where a cluster of foppish young gentlemen were stuffing their faces and playing at cards. "We're well met," he said. "Just this day I encountered my former employer, my lord of Pembroke. He told me to come to the theater where you were rehearsing. He invites you to supper with him and some other noble lords following your performance tomorrow."

"Commend me to my lord the earl," I said, wondering who these unnamed noble lords might be. "Tell him I'm honored that he should remember me."

"Oh, sir, he remembers you well. He has a proposal for you."

"A proposal?"

"It goes beyond my commission to say," Stanleigh said, looking very solemn and self-important.

"Where will this supper be?"

"At his London house, or perhaps at Wilton. It's as it may please him. He'll be at the play. Afterward, you can accompany him."

"A thousand thanks to His Lordship," I said.

He bowed toward me most respectfully, turned to go, and then stopped. "I wonder," he said, glancing at Dikkon, "if I might have a further word—"

"My pleasure," I said.

"A private word?"

I signaled Dikkon with a nod. He stood, fixed Stanleigh in a blank stare, and excused himself to go to the jakes.

"Sit down, sir," I said.

Stanleigh obliged me. "The earl wanted me to ask about you." He searched for a word. "He heard about your troubles. He wonders how things stand with you since you've come to London again."

"They stand well," I said, not in a self-revelatory mood and annoyed that my difficulties seemed to be the talk of court when I had confessed them only to Cecil and Wriothesley. As for Stanleigh, I did not dislike him. He had done me service in my dealings with Cecil, and for that I was grateful, but in general I disdained his type—unctuous grooms and secretaries, flatterers, eager to be of use to their employers and ever scrambling for higher place. It was not a life I coveted. It was not a kind of man I could trust.

"I'm pleased to hear it," Stanleigh said, his eyes full of what seemed genuine satisfaction. "You know the earl does ever hold you in his heart of hearts, far beyond Jonson or Marlowe."

"Marlowe's dead," I said. "He was murdered in Deptford."

Stanleigh ignored this correction. He continued, "His Lordship would gladly do you and your company good. I am of the same mind, sir. Only tell me what you need. I'll convey the same to my lord the earl."

"So will I at supper," I said, trying my courtesy, for, having been most direct with my friend Dikkon, I felt no need to confide in another who was a stranger to my heart.

Stanleigh went on, "Say, for instance, if you were still plagued by these enemies, a guard might be provided you."

"I had guards once. Masters Spurgeon and Marbury," I said dryly, hoping he appreciated the irony of my mentioning the traitors.

"Ah, a very sad thing," Stanleigh said, wagging his head. "They betrayed Lord Cecil as well as you. He's most displeased by them. When he finds them, he'll make them pay for their treachery."

"Does he look for them?" I asked.

"My oath upon't, sir. He does not take treacherous servants lightly."

It was all I could do to avoid telling Stanleigh that my two jackdaws—and their roguish accomplices—had already paid the price of their treachery and violence, and without his noble master's intervention.

Stanleigh rose. Dikkon had returned from the jakes. He stopped at a distance, watching and waiting for Stanleigh to take his leave.

"Then I'll say goodnight, Master Shakespeare. If my duties permit, I, too, will be accompanying the earl to your theater."

"You do me too much honor," I said, wearying of this courtly exchange.

Stanleigh returned to his companions of the evening, who showed no sign they were aware he'd left, for they still played at cards and ate and talked and swore and laughed as if he'd neither come nor gone. I was not surprised. Stanleigh seemed a fatuous, lackluster fellow, deferential and predictable, his silver buttons and jeweled rings notwithstanding. His friends at yonder table were no better. I didn't know them particularly, but they were all of the same slippery tribe. I preferred Dikkon's directness and unaffected sincerity. With Dikkon, like my friend Dick Burbage, you knew where you stood, and around such men I was always the more at ease. I suppose that for all my years in the city, I remain a country man at heart, more thrilled by bird's call and a pretty prospect of stream or heath than by the siren voices and vices of the court.

Yet I did appreciate the earl's invitation to supper and wondered what it meant.

Thirty-four

EASTER MONDAY AND, like the Phoenix, our Globe rises majestically from the ashes of a fortnight's sad disuse. The day is glorious; pennants fly; our hearts are glad. God in heaven has spared us. Life goes on, and it is sweet. For some, that is, not for me.

Hark how it was then: By two o'clock, all galleries are filled—with merchants, tradesmen, gentlemen of the Inns and of the court and their ladies, various lords, knights, and their punks; everyone but their dogs, which we try to keep out of the theater for their yelping, howling, and mess. The sky above the open yard, cloudless, perfection. The groundlings—tradesmen, artisans, apprentices, housewives—are a restless sea of faces, a noisy rout that will not be still for a prologue but call to their friends or cry out for hazelnuts or beer from the sellers who ply both the yard and the galleries. I detest the constant eating, the card playing, the assignations, the rough stuff in the gallery, the rude inattention of the groundlings, the hauteur in the Lords' Rooms, the wanton pissing in the corner by those who can't hold their water for two hours' traffic on the stage. A pox upon 'em all, say I. Yet all this was so.

Upon the cusp of the stage are chairs to afford more seating for those of distinction and heavy purses. Waiting for the play to begin, they smoke and play cards. The gallery above the tiring house is also filled to overflowing; only the better sort of patrons here, those willing to pay through the nose. Meanwhile, at the doors, a press of masterless men, whores, soldiers, lesser merchants, finding no room, proclaim their envy and frustration, beat upon the now closed doors with fists and staffs, demanding to be allowed in though there's not an inch of standing space and in the galleries they're sitting upon each other's laps.

We delay the first act while my old friend the constable of Southwark and a dozen of his henchmen wade into the rowdy assembly outside and threaten to jail all if they do not disperse. This threat the crowd dismisses since they know the constable, that he is a fool and a knave. I try to avoid him. My wounds have not healed and I know that if I confront him, I will strike him, maybe kill him.

Without the riot subsides. Within the crowd has grown even more truculent. I signal to Burbage we must begin.

I leap upon the stage, raise my arms to command attention, and doff my cap with a flourish. I plead with the audience to be still. The uproar grows worse. We try drums and bugle; we fire the cannon thrice. But after so long an absence from this rounded O, this wooden wonder, their joy is overflowing, and though they will not let us begin the play, neither will they endure our delay for all we can do.

Finally, they quiet enough so we actors can hear ourselves speak; and so the play, *The Most Excellent Tragedy of Julius Caesar*, begins.

FOR ALL THE hurly-burly at our commencement, we players soldiered on. I, Julius Caesar; Dick Burbage, Mark Antony; John Heminge, Brutus. Burbage was magnificent, his voice like a trumpet, his gestures Ciceronian. As for me, I delivered my lines indifferently, improvised twice, mangled a metaphor until a logician could not have unraveled it, and completely forgot ten lines or more to no detriment to the play that I could see.

So I was not at my best, but what of that? An actor's life is ups and downs, feast and famine. The crowd roared at Caesar's murder, wept and cheered at Mark Antony's funeral speech. In sum: They liked the play—even the groundlings, who grow impatient with long speeches and appreciate only dumbshows, cannon blasts, and farting clowns. Dikkon played the cobbler in the exposition—credibly, I think, given he was still so new to our craft.

Three hours later, all was confusion as the crowd flowed from the two doors and our friends and well-wishers scrambled onto the stage and poured into the tiring house like an invading army. Remembering my invitation from the earl, I looked round for Thomas Stanleigh and could see neither him nor my noble host. Soon the theater was almost empty. Our actors started to leave. All hearts were high after the success of the performance; we had raised the prices for admission with few complaints. The play was well done for our part, and we had filled the house to overflowing.

Dikkon bore down on me, still in his cobbler's costume; his face was flushed with excitement, and he was breathing heavily as though he had been running. I knew what heated him. I remembered well my first year on the boards, the knee-knocking, that surge of blood, the sweet soft satisfaction when the play was over and my fellow players told me well-done-thou-good-and-faithful. I remembered my own relief that I had not failed myself or them.

"You were a most excellent cobbler," I said. "A cobbler to the very life. Had we cobblers in the crowd, they would have recognized you as one of their own and admitted you to their company."

He laughed and shook my hand, grasping it with both of his, his eyes filling with tears of gratitude. For a moment he couldn't speak. Then we embraced.

"I have a fearsome raw throat," he said, grinning broadly, releasing me to wipe the tears from his eyes. "Malt's the cure. Come drink a tankard with me, Will."

I reminded him of my supper with the earl. "I'm waiting for Master Stanleigh. Have you seen him?"

"I've seen everyone in London, and no one. A thousand faces, but not one I could give a name."

I knew what he meant about that, too.

"Forget the earl," Dikkon said. "Come with me. This time I'll pay."

"I'd like not to offend the earl," I said. "He's a virtuous gentlemen of excellent breeding and admirable discourse. Besides, Stanleigh told me His Lordship has something to propose. That may mean money, my friend."

Dikkon shrugged and smiled sadly. "I would fain have your company tonight. No celebration is the same without you, and I've a mind to celebrate."

"Pray, do it," I said. "But without me. Think about your cobbler. Think about what may come next to you. If you don't find some of us in whatever tavern please you, I'm not Will Shakespeare. I warrant you won't want for company."

AFTER DIKKON LEFT, I walked from the tiring house to the stage and looked out over the now empty yard. It was littered with hazelnut and oyster shells, half-eaten pastries, and forgotten handkerchiefs and forsaken caps. The galleries were empty. No Thomas Stanleigh, no my lord the earl.

I sat down on the lip of the stage to wait. I didn't know what else to do. I had told Burbage and the others that I would secure all doors behind me. I fingered the keys at my side, decided I would wait another half hour. I thought back earlier to my conversation with Stanleigh. Had I misunderstood the invitation? Was tonight the night? I decided that I could not have been mistaken.

Minutes slipped into an hour or more. Enough was enough. I was hungry and thirsty, weary from the long day, and annoyed at a broken promise. I regretted now that I had not gone with Dikkon. I would not have drunk myself blind, but a tankard flavored with mace, nutmeg, or sage struck me as a most delightsome commodity at that moment. I bolted the main door from within and was making for the side door when I saw Stanleigh. He'd somehow come in without my seeing him.

"God save you, Master Shakespeare!"

"How now, Master Stanleigh. What news?"

"Only that the wicked outnumber the righteous." Stanleigh grinned amicably.

"Stale news," I said. "What of your old master?"

"I beg your pardon. The earl called me away with him for a space. He needed to speak to another gentleman he saw here—about the proposal I mentioned."

"My lord of Pembroke was here?"

"On my honor, sir. He found your *Caesar* most edifying. As did I."

I thanked him for his words, although I liked not "edifying," which made my play smell too much of the scholar's lamp. Then I said, "My lord of Pembroke's invitation—"

"Still good," Stanleigh said. "Why, you shall be the guest of honor."

I flushed with pleasure. The closing of our theater had been a heavy blow to us. The interval, though brief, had been painful. Now it was past, our prospects were bright, and I felt the earl's proposal, whatever it might be, boded well for me and for the troupe.

I started to make for the door, but Stanleigh grasped my shoulder. "Nay, sir. His Lordship prays you be patient. He'll be here straightway. Then we all shall go."

"I'll fetch candles, then," I said, for the light was fading and the theater filling with shadows.

Stanleigh followed me up the short stairs into the tiring house, where I knew there were candles. I equipped myself with a brace of three long tapers, which left us in a little circle of light. I saw then that another person had come into the theater in the meantime. At first I took him to be the earl, for he was slender and acted as though he had some business with us. I made a leg as manners required, then saw that the newcomer was not he who I supposed.

She wore a long black cloak, which she flung from her narrow shoulders and let fall to the ground in an insolent movement that seemed to say, "Mark you, sir. I need not disguise myself before the likes of you." Beneath, she wore a kind of minstrel's costume:

a loose-fitting blouse with long, flowing sleeves that quite hid her slender wrists; below, tight-fitting black hose that shaped thigh and calf most excellently; while upon her head she wore a peaked cap with a single white feather in the crown. The flowing blouse, bleached to a sepulchral whiteness, made much of her smooth dark skin, her dark eyes, and her long black hair that lay along her shoulders like a shawl and was more splendid than jewels. She needed but a lute in hand to complete the effect.

In the old days my moody mistress would often dress as a boy; she'd wear a codpiece festooned with roses and Cupid's bow. She loved the codpiece and in her amorous moments would play with it teasingly until I thought I would go mad. Now, in her hand she held no lute but instead a pistol. I recognized the same. It was an ugly instrument she once threatened me with during the stormy days of our love. The pistol was heavy and German made, difficult to load, awkward to shoot, and yet I knew she could load, fire, and likely hit what she aimed at.

She pointed that mortal tool at me and glared with eyes like hot coals.

My astonishment passed; I found my voice. "*You,*" I said.

"Not dead, no ghost," she said.

"I know. I found out for myself that you were alive, that you were no more dead than I."

I felt little apprehension at her proffered violence, understanding fully now her love of the theatrical. Besides, there was a witness to whatever injury she might contemplate. I felt strangely secure and justified, filled with righteous indignation, hot to accuse her of her perfidy, her fraudulent death, her fraudulent life.

Then I heard a chuckle. I turned suddenly to Stanleigh.

I couldn't imagine what Stanleigh might think of this intruder, whose female essence was only barely concealed in her male attire, much less what he might make of the threatening pistol. But I read no surprise in Stanleigh's face. Rather, there was a smirk of pleasure, as one coming upon his enemy's favorite hound strangled. His attention was fixed on me, not on her.

"I see you know this woman," I said, looking back and forth between them, the truth dawning slowly.

"Our acquaintance does not have so long a history as yours, Master Shakespeare," he said. "We've known each other but a year."

"And been lovers for most of it," said my quondam mistress.

Stanleigh took the brace of candles from my hand and said, "Follow me."

I thought of dashing for the street, but the woman leveled the pistol at me most expertly, and my confidence dissolved with each step.

In silent procession, we climbed the stairs behind the tiring house to the middle gallery, then to the third, then to the storage. I thought we would stop there, the scene of an older and lesser crime.

Whorley! Had Whorley been Stanleigh after all, and my treacherous lover his accomplice all along? Was my mystification over, even though my greatest danger might be ahead? Or was there yet a third person in the conspiracy?

I would have fain asked Stanleigh these burning questions, but he would not suffer me to talk. He told me to shut my mouth and say nothing or I would presently be shot dead.

The storage was not our destination. A ladder ascended to the hut above the "heavens," in the center of which stood the winch used to hoist the throne of Zeus, raising it up and down as pleased us through the trapdoor. There, too, our flying machine—a network of leather straps, harnesses, and ropes whereby, when needed, we made men fly—the contrivance we called the thunder run with its several cannonballs to make the welkin growl, barrelheads full of fireworks, the gold-painted throne of Zeus itself, and such other mechanisms to create wonders and miracles.

The hut was so small and so tightly stowed with these devices, we three filled it. Crowded against one wall as I was, with my lady's cocked pistol pressed against my chest, I did what I was told. Who can blame me?

"What follows now?" I asked at last. First to the woman, then to Stanleigh. To him, I further said, "And why, sir, have you disregarded your master's good wishes toward me and joined this woman? What's she to you or you to her that you conspire against me?"

Stanleigh regarded me stonily. "I think you don't remember me, Master Shakespeare."

It was an absurd statement, I thought, and I was uncertain how to answer it. "Yes" seemed self-evident; "no," contrary and senseless. Was Stanleigh truly mad, or was this some perverse wordplay whose point I'd missed?

I said, "You're Cecil's man, formerly my lord the earl's secretary. You're a a hanger-on, a base greasy-tongued utensil, a toady, if you will. There are Latin words and Greek for what you are, but I content myself with plain English, which I trust you understand."

I had become more venomous in my abuse of him than I intended or was prudent given where I was and with whom, but Stanleigh took these insults lightly. I might as well have been talking about someone else. He laughed, that strange derisive explosion that was neither male nor female but both. "It pleases you to abuse me, Master Shakespeare. You are very merry, it would seem, despite these circumstances."

Stanleigh's obsequiousness was gone. Before me was another Stanleigh, one who had been there all along, but I had failed to see it. He had been true to his breed, both in his foppish dress and in his manner. An innocuous disguise for villainy. Why had I not seen it?

"The world is full of actors; don't expect to see all of them in the theaters," Stanleigh said as though he read my thoughts.

"Who *are* you?" I said. "Master Whorley?"

"Whorley? Yes, sir. I have used that name, among others. An actor plays many parts, answers to many names. Isn't that so? But let that pass. I'm not here to talk about players and their roles."

Stanleigh placed the candles on a shelf next to the winch. It was warm in the closed hut, stifling. Or maybe it was just my blood racing. Stanleigh said, "When I was younger I aspired to be an actor."

He looked at me as if I should care about his youthful aspirations, but I didn't. I would not give him satisfaction by showing interest. I took revenge by seeming bored, stifling a yawn. It was a reckless gesture. If Stanleigh was Whorley as he claimed, I knew he'd been an actor. Very likely a lawyer, too. At least he knew enough dog Latin to pass as one.

"I ran away from home to that end—to be an actor. I came to London. To find *you.*"

"To find me?" I said. "Should I be flattered?"

"I read lines for you. There were fifteen or sixteen of us, all boys from the country. Some were farmers' sons, others orphans or runaway apprentices. I was a runaway, too. But no apprentice."

I searched Stanleigh's round ruddy face with its blond brows and his thick lips, trying to remember him. I saw how his story tipped. One of fifteen or sixteen. How many raw youth ambitious for the stage did I audition and discourage during a year? If it were less than a hundred I would have been surprised. Being an actor wasn't what it used to be—an outcast's existence, a vagabond's life, next door to criminality. A boy with talent could make money and live handsomely in London these days. He could grow rich and buy a coat of arms and drink with lords and their ladies. Besides, it was a life more interesting than most; there was that to be said for it.

Stanleigh said, "You laughed at my performance."

"When? What did you read for me? What part had you?"

"Eight years or so agone, this Michaelmas. *Merchant of Venice,* Portia's hypocritical blather about the quality of mercy. How it isn't strained. How it falls from the heavens. Ha, little mercy you showed me, Shakespeare."

"Your audition wasn't about mercy. It was about talent, about ability, about our need, not yours."

My facile answer did not please him. In the faint light his eyes flashed and grew darker and rounder. "Damn you, Shakespeare. I had both talent, as you call it, and ability. You ignored both."

"And all this to-do is mere grudge, a rancorous disgruntlement? I've said thank you and good day to hundreds of youth whose talent I could not find gleaming in a single phrase, yet they don't lie in wait for me, hire murderers, threaten my life and my family's."

"They weren't your son, Shakespeare!" Stanleigh said in yet another voice I had never heard from him, a voice low and without emotion. "They weren't your son!"

THE FOUR SHORT words of his declaration imprinted themselves like a blacksmith's brand upon my brain, both in their repetition and in the strength of their conviction. My astonishment must have been fully manifest to Stanleigh. He smiled triumphantly. His eyes blazed. He clinched his fists as though the next moment he would throw himself at me and beat me into admission of my guilt.

"How my son?" I demanded, furious at this outrageous claim and more bewildered than frightened of the woman's pistol or what the two of them intended. "I have no son," I said. "Not now. My son is dead, buried in the churchyard in Stratford. Hamnet was his name. But I tell you nothing you do not already know. You paid Fanshawe to search out my life, here and in Stratford. You know who my children are."

"I do. I'm one."

"I have no bastards," I shouted.

At least not that I know of. This I did not say but thought. I made myself look outraged by this impudent insinuation, looking from Stanleigh to my lady of the pistol.

All this while, she had said nothing but held her pistol steady, pointed at my head, sometimes at my heart, sometimes at my groin. Her face had been stony, showing neither pity nor hate, only an intense interest in my reaction. The truth was I did not know her mind, her black heart. She had had opportunity to kill me a dozen times and had declined. Would she kill me now upon her new lover's orders because he claimed that I was his father?

Stanleigh said, "Before I read my lines for you, you asked my name. I gave it. Thomas Bott."

I must have looked confused. He said, "My mother's name, my birth name. Not Stanleigh."

Still I could not remember him. So many young boys there were with their thin, piping voices, their Portias and their Ophelias. They fused in my memory, indistinguishable save for those few I selected, groomed, and spurred to manhood with the company. Those, I called my friends, my brethren in our craft. The others, faceless, nameless. Better that way, so I had no regrets. The memory can hold just so much and then all's blank. There was, after all, nothing personal in the rejection. It was always about craft, about what the company needed. The company and its craft always came first.

"Mercy Bott was my mother," he said. "You knew her."

"I never did," I said, although the blunt and single syllable of his true name rang some bell in my memory. Which bell? Where and when? I couldn't place it. Mercy Bott. Mercy? Bott?

"Think Stratford, not London," Stanleigh said.

I sighed. A cruel and futile game it was. I was a hostage to lunatics.

"My grandfather was William Bott," Stanleigh said, as if I should care who his grandfather was. I hardly knew my own.

Then, of a sudden, the bell of memory deafened me.

Thirty-five

THE STORY CAME to me as stories will. They're always entrenched somewhere, down 'mongst the weeds of memory, usurped by what's now, what's immediate. They must be dredged up. And when you're my age the layers run deep and the dredging is hard.

I said, "Bott? He who was alderman in Stratford forty years ago or more? The Bott who murdered—"

Stanleigh cut me off, his face twisted in anger, his voice hoarse and peremptory. "He who was falsely accused of murdering his daughter, Isabella."

"Murdered his daughter," I went on, undaunted, "by putting ratsbane in her drink. He did it to inherit land of his neighbor, some simpleton named Harper who'd married Isabella. Bott contrived to make himself the heir of Harper's lands if she died without issue, which she did. Your grandfather forged deeds, lied, poisoned."

"A tissue of lies," Stanleigh said hotly. "He never poisoned her, though it pleased the sanctimonious gentry of Stratford to think so—among whom was your father, John Shakespeare. The law never charged my grandfather for his so-called crime. There was no evidence. If there had been, he would have been charged, but he was not."

"Who was this Mercy Bott to Isabella?" I asked.

"Her sister. Isabella was my aunt."

Despite Stanleigh's denial of his grandfather's guilt, I knew the truth—or at least what I thought was truth. During the first years of the reign of the last queen, William Bott had purchased New Place, the house in Stratford I now called mine. The murder may have happened in the house. Bott had sold it to a man named Underhill, who, dying, passed it to one William Underhill, a shady lawyer, from whom I made purchase. New Place was a fine house, but its history was clouded. Most of the time I just didn't think about it.

Then I remembered more—the image of a thin, whey-faced girl with stringy mouse-brown hair, living at Wilmcote whence my mother's people came, not two miles from Stratford. Her reputation hadn't been good; her marriage prospects were dismal. How could I have forgotten? Had I been away from Stratford that long? Had my history there become someone else's history?

Yet why should I have remembered? Mercy Bott was nothing to me. We were of the same age or thereabouts, but then I was already horn-mad for Richard Hathaway's juicy, nubile daughter. Eight years my senior she was, but what of that? The difference honed my edge, don't ask me why.

"My mother was seventeen," Stanleigh said, "when she was got with child. A boy of the town, who would make a butt of her, and then got her to himself and planted seed in her. Big-bellied, she left Stratford. She went to live with her brother's family. I was that child."

"But you're a gentleman," I protested, nodding in the direction of his clothes, which were very fine. His speech was also that of the city, which mine was not. I still spoke with the strong Warwickshire accent of my youth and did so without shame.

"Master Shakespeare," he said. "Do you think you're the only one who can come to London and make himself new? I ran away to London, as you did, tried to be an actor, as did you. You succeeded, I failed. I failed because of you, damn you, even though I told you who I was."

"My son, you mean?" I scoffed. "I never lay with your mother. I knew her, not well, but as God is my judge, I never knew more of her than her name, and hardly that. It's been years since I've thought of her."

"Oh, have you not?" Bott said. "Tell me, then, Shakespeare. Was your wife, Anne, your first conquest in Stratford? We know she was not your last."

"No, she was not."

"There were other girls, farmers' daughters, perhaps even burghers' wives, weary of tedious old husbands?"

"This is none of your business, sir," I said fiercely.

"Quite true, it's not. And yet I made it so. Fanshawe was quite thorough in that regard. He's a good detector, when he's sober."

"Fanshawe says I raped Mercy Bott?"

"Let us say your mischief of this sort at so young an age was remarked upon. You were prodigious, sir. Your feats the stuff of legend. Your escape to London allowed many a father and mother of the town to rest easier of nights, knowing their daughters were safe from you. So again I ask: Was Mercy Bott among your conquests? Did you plunder the Indies of her body?"

"I would have sooner sailed into the mouth of hell," I said angrily.

This answer did not please him. His eyes narrowed; his thick lips pressed together. "She said you did. She said it was you who had her. She said you took her out in the fields and—"

"You are much deceived," I said. "Look how unlike we are. See how the color of skin, hair, our size, your greater height and heavier bone argue no relation betwixt us."

"I take after my mother," he said. "When I was twelve, I asked her about my father, who he was. No answer. Then she got sick, very sick. Before she died, she told me. The eldest boy of the Shakespeares. That's you, isn't it? William Shakespeare?

"I'm my father's eldest son."

"And I am *your* eldest, sir, for before Anne Hathaway was your wife, you made my mother your whore. Before your son Hamnet saw light, I was."

"That's a damnable lie," I said, glaring at him.

"Not so," Stanleigh insisted. "You knew that well enough eight years ago when I did Portia for you. You played then at the Swan. I remember you flinched when I mentioned my name, looked me up and down as though to see how you had minted me. Yet for all that you rejected me. You offered no help, gave no encouragement, allowed no recognition. A father's part was yours to play, but you disdained it, denying that you knew me. Nor did you recognize me when we met again at my lord of Pembroke's place in Wilton this past summer."

I was breathless with anger, confusion, and fear. My collar was strangling me. My shirt clung to my skin, which felt feverish. Denial was futile. I knew this. It would only inflame Stanleigh's passion more if I were to give his mother's deathbed confession the lie. But as I have hope in Christ, I was not guilty. What had possessed his wretched mother to name me as her child's father? Was it because my family was well allowed in Stratford, my father once an alderman, that she blamed me? Or was it one of my brothers who had done it and she been mistaken in the order of our births?

I made bold to suggest this.

"My mother said it was Will Shakespeare, son of John, sometime bailiff, alderman, glover. He who turned to drink. She could not have been more plain. She said it was the same Will Shakespeare who's gone to London and become an actor. Writes plays, she said. Who else might it be but you? Are there two Shakespeares? An evil twin?"

"Then why not declare yourself at the Swan, or at Wilton, but let me think you a stranger?"

"Think of it as a test," Stanleigh said. "Which you failed."

"You don't bear your mother's name," I said. "How was I to know?"

"Stanleigh's my uncle's name. He stood father to me in your absence. I've therefore a right to his name since I am not permitted to be a Shakespeare. After you put the quietus to my acting career, I made friends. Not hard in London, as you know. Not when you're young, smooth faced, straight limbed, and, morally pliant. My friends helped me to higher things."

"What higher things?" I asked.

"I didn't have the benefit of an education at the King's New School on Church Street as did you, but my schoolmasters were not unlearned, nor did they spare the rod. So after failing as actor, I persuaded a certain London gentleman of my acquaintance and of curious disposition and taste to underwrite my year at Gray's Inn, where I determined to speak like a lawyer, think like a lawyer, love like a lawyer, and, indeed, sir, piss like a lawyer if it pleased me."

The knowledge of the law he'd shown. I had guessed right.

"I stayed a year at Gray's," Stanleigh continued. "A year was enough. All a palpable fraud. Study law? Carouse rather, pick up a few Latin phrases to mystify the laity and justify exorbitant fees. Waste time at theaters, leaping houses, taverns, bear-baiting, cockfights, whatever delights. I can't say it improved my morals, but it did wonders for my prospects."

"And your acting?" I said.

"My acting? You ask about that?" he said, his voice becoming more shrill. "I used what acting skill I had to mimic the speech I liked best, to put on the manner of the gentleman, which I do swear, sir, is manner, not blood. For whatever our nobility claims, he is gentleman who appears so. Performance is all. Then I became my lord of Pembroke's secretary and step by step wormed my way into great Cecil's household, as you know."

We stood silent for a while. I sweat mightily.

"Say you are my son," I said, doubtfully, but wanting to get on with this. "What do you want of me—acknowledgment that I'm your father? A part in a play? Money, like your confederate here?"

I turned to look at my former lover. Her black eyes were as hard as flint. I expected her to say something, to attack me, to shoot me, but for the moment she seemed content to let Stanleigh hold forth, which he did as though every word he'd rehearsed, only waiting for the occasion to deliver it.

Stanleigh said, "I want *you,* Shakespeare. Your friends think well of you; you're beloved of my lord of Pembroke, esteemed by great Cecil; the king showers his favors upon you. You walk in sunshine always, enjoy more praise than any man should earn or deserve. You have all that, and you have the house I might have inherited in Stratford had not the malicious gossip and slander of his neighbors forced my grandfather to sell."

"I bought the house in good faith," I said.

"In good faith," he answered, mocking my tone. "A fine word, 'faith.' The world needs more of it. But I know you, Shakespeare. Your sins are manifest: pride, arrogance, vanity, duplicity, and unrestrained lust, wherein you violated my mother and disowned your son. I have had nothing of you, sir, but grief and rejection in my life, but the sins of the fathers will be avenged by the sons."

"You wrest Scripture for your own purposes," I said.

"My Scripture," he said. "The Gospel According to Thomas Stanleigh, born Bott, by rights, Shakespeare."

"You had your revenge," I said. "You drove me to distraction, caused me to be imprisoned, killed a sweet innocent boy who'd done nothing more than seen what he shouldn't have. You sent four men to follow me into the countryside, to kill me. But your henchmen are dead. They rot in black pools in the Forest of Arden."

"I care nothing for them," he said, with a bitter laugh. "I had done them favors, they did favors for me. It was all business with us. Spurgeon was my incendiary in London. The house he burned I owned. The mercer who now occupies it pays me better rent."

"How did you get into the theater, into the storage?"

"I found out who made your locks. It wasn't hard. He made you keys; he made me keys. It was as simple as that."

"You paid the locksmith?"

Stanleigh shook his head. "I used Lord Cecil's name. It does more than money can to make men cooperate. Mention Cecil's name and watch men sweat. And then they keep quiet about it. That's the best of it."

"And what of *her?*" I asked, nodding toward my former lover, and then looking hard at her as though my scrutiny would extract a modicum of truth and shame where none was before. "What was that all about in Bankside, the false fire, your false death, your performance as a ghost?"

"Mea culpa," Stanleigh said. "You see, I met this honorable lady through some gentleman friends. She gets round, you know. Soon we found common ground."

"I'm sure you did." I well imagined the ground they found, having wallowed there myself to my great shame.

"We both played parts in your secret history. We both came off the worse for it," she said.

"If so, it wasn't my intent," I said, looking at her, wishing her to remember that all those years earlier it had been she who'd dumped me in favor of Harry Wriothesley, not I her.

I turned to Stanleigh again. "What about Edward Goode? Why kill him?"

"One stone, two birds," Stanleigh said airily. "I eavesdropped on your intimate disclosures to Lord Cecil. That's what secretaries do, you know, out of idleness or boredom—but also enlightened self-interest, for they can never tell when their employer's conversation will touch upon their legitimate concerns. I realized Edward Goode had seen Spurgeon, witnessed the fire. That revelation would have been premature, given that I had contrived to have Spurgeon as one of your bodyguards. At the same time, resolving that little matter seemed an opportunity to change course, to carry the plot into a new direction, shift you into a new role as accused murderer and pederast. Spurgeon and Marbury recounted your interview with Justice Swallow. Spurgeon was a muscular brawler and dullard, but Marbury had a most excellent memory, I assure you. He recited to me practically every word you said, every fear, every apprehension, every jot and tittle. I found the scene vastly entertaining. So did your former mistress, here."

Her smile confirmed this. I felt a loathing for them both for which I had no words left.

"And Cecil. Did he know?"

"Master Secretary concerns himself with affairs of state. He's preoccupied with civil order and the king's business. I assure you I'm perfectly capable of the kind of stage management the plot required. Think of my design as a play I wrote so that you might play the flawed hero," Stanleigh continued. "Your virtue is your art. Your fatal flaw, your arrogant conviction that you can always make a sow's ear into a silk purse and, principally, that you are always in control. I sat in the wings while you slunk around town fearful of every shadow, whined pathetically to Cecil, languished in prison, fled, under my management, toward Stratford. Oh, how I had you running. All my doing, Shakespeare. You see how I have inherited your skill. Perhaps I cannot act. But, sir, I can plot well enough."

"It gave me equal pleasure to conspire, Will," my dark lady said. "And to perform. I was always interested in your stories about the theater. I would have liked to be a player myself, perhaps even playing the men's parts if there were no woman's role I savored. But like Master Stanleigh, I was forbidden, although on different grounds. I was a woman. No women allowed in your theater, Will."

"It's the custom in England," I said. "It's not a practice I invented, nor defended. You know that."

"Well, now, thanks to Master Stanleigh, I've had my chance," she said, "and, I think, enjoyed some success. I convinced you that I'd fallen and died. I heard your tears and anguished cries. And I do wish to heaven you could have seen your face when I first appeared to you in this place after my supposed death. I knew you had seen me and were following, thinking no doubt I was a spirit. Not right away, but presently I discovered you in my traces. My appearance in the theater came to me thereafter. I didn't know how else to lose you—and at the same time to terrify. Tell me, Will, did I terrify you? Did my prophecy and warning fill you full of dread?"

"Obviously I didn't heed it," I said.

"No, you didn't," she said. "Perhaps you should have. It would have been better for you."

I studied her face for a moment; her expression was hard and implacable. I needed to ask. "Wherefore did you do all this?"

"Wherefore?" she answered, although I knew perfectly she understood my meaning.

"Was it because I would not let you take the stage? Because I did not show you the respect you deserved?"

She smiled thinly. "You ruined my life."

"How ruined?"

"Your sonnets."

"My sonnets?" I forced a laugh. "You never read but one or two."

"I read enough. He showed them to me."

"He?"

"My lord the earl."

She meant my rival, Henry Wriothesley, but I still didn't understand her point.

She began to quote lines from my sonnets. Not those I had shown her—the ones speaking of the nobility and eternity of true love—but the ones I had sent privily to Wriothesley, the ones that had scorned her, that had expressed my self-loathing, that had warned him off. I had never meant them for her eyes, though they were about her, because they revealed my innermost self, the part of me I would not have her own. It was enough that she had owned my body. My soul would remain free of her, then and now.

"Marry, these are pretty sonnets indeed," she said. "You have more than mocked me, Will. You make me a polluted thing. A thing of naught. No wonder Henry would have none of me after that, after such defamation."

"He was well rid of you," I said full bitterly. "The earl has no regrets. I spoke to him. He holds you in contempt. When I spoke of your death he was overjoyed."

My cruel but truthful words—like a sword pointed at her heart—did not seem to move her to greater anger, although surely they might have done so. She continued to look coldly at me. She said, "I'm not surprised. You could not have me, and therefore you would not that I should have him."

"It's not as if the earl would, or could, have married you," I said.

"I didn't aspire to such station. It was enough that I was his sole mistress. I was a made woman when he loved me."

"He would have understood your nature, sooner or later, even without my sonnets."

"So say you, sirrah. You were a conniving, jealous bastard yourself. All your pious moralizing sonnets are a thin guise for a jealous, vindictive nature, which you set forth in pretty verse about shame and lust and heart's treason. Hypocrite. Liar. Base villain."

She vomited forth such epithets as these and then rested, breathless. All the while her black eyes killed me with their look. I felt the full brunt of her hatred. And hearing her weighty arguments against me, I saw myself as not altogether falsely accused. Her indictment was a true bill. I had ruined her prospects. I had painted her black even blacker. And I had freed Wriothesley from the bondage I'd escaped only because she rejected me. Had it been otherwise, I should have sung her praise until the end of time, so sick in love was I.

Now my first reunion with her in the Southwark shop made sense to me. Now I understood her pleas that I quote my high-minded sonnet about true love. My own words had been my condemnation, for my once vaunted love for her had indeed played the fickle fool.

"So what's to do now?" I asked them both, looking from one of my enemies to another.

"Why, your present death, sir—and disgrace. And the destruction of this palace of art."

"You mean the Globe?"

"You get my meaning, sir," Stanleigh said. "Now I've grown weary of the play. We must hasten to its climax and epilogue."

BY CANDLELIGHT THEIR countenances were as devilish as their conspiracy—cruel, merciless, violent. I looked at the pistol pointed at me, as deadly as ever. Stanleigh wore a dagger at his side but had not brandished it, although I did not doubt him capable of doing so and using it, too. Was I to die by blade, ball, or fire? Perhaps all three? I assessed my chances. They seemed slim, but when slim is all, then slim must serve. With nothing to lose, I bolted for the door, hoping to surprise them both and so escape.

The woman didn't shoot, but Stanleigh was upon me before I could reach the latch. I used all my strength to break free of his grip, but he was young and stronger than he appeared. Pummeled and throttled, I was dizzily aware of the woman pushing her face into mine and crying something—whether encouraging Stanleigh in his murder or protesting it, I couldn't tell, but I had puny hope that her hatred for me might not extend to murder, that her heart at last was not so dark as her face.

Then night, blackness, silence.

Thirty-six

I DID NOT die, only slept, and when I came round again, my first thought was of wife and children, my wife, Anne, shaking me from sleep, going on about how Hamnet was sick unto death, how the fault was mine, and how I should fetch the doctor straightaway.

My delirium passed. I remembered where I was, in the hut still, my hands and feet now bound, I in great pain, my bones and neck sore from blows and buffets, strangulation, and the hard fall on my backside to the rough-hewn planks of the floor when Stanleigh finally overmastered me.

Beyond the door came urgent whispers, which I no sooner heard than recognized as Stanleigh and my ungracious lady, and so concluded there was no purpose in my crying out, for help or mercy. My sole consolation, given my circumstance, was that at last I knew my enemies and the motive for their evil, how false son and false lover had conspired to my hurt, how my alleged wrongs to both had fueled their malice.

I tried to move my wrists, back and forth, until my flesh was raw and bleeding. The obdurate knot would not yield. I knew the lay of the room and, having spent much time there, rolled to where the winch was. This device I knew well, too, for although I rarely used it in my own plays, other playwrights did, and I had toyed with it more than once and knew its operation.

This was a great wooden spool upon which the ropes as thick as horses' tails were wound, all this set within a sturdy frame and turned by an iron handle. The shank of the handle had a sharp edge. I remembered well because one of the boys cut himself on it one day and bled until he was white faced. I rubbed the rope that bound my wrists on that same edge, rubbed harder and harder until I was winded and sweat poured down my face.

Finally, the rope gave way. Handed now, I quickly unbound my legs, and I was free, although to what fate God only knew, for still I could hear voices beyond, angry, accusing. I pressed my ear to the door and listened.

The quarrel wasn't about me, about whether I should live or die. I had flattered myself to think my treacherous mistress would pity me and confound her newfound ally. The quarrel was about money, debts, promises. She upon whom I once doted was shrill as a fishwife. I could hear her berating her new lover and then threatening him. Threatening to go to Cecil or Pembroke, or even to the king. She'd always had a temper, always a filthy mouth. Once I'd found it alluring, like the darkness of her flesh, her exotic speech, her outlandish lovemaking, her provocative costumes. But no more. Ah, lust, what pits it digs, and how happily we leap into that foul darkness.

I made out the substance of their controversy: It was quid pro quo. She had delivered me into Stanleigh's hands. She had set me up right royally. Payment was due.

Then the railing ended. Stanleigh was growling, but I couldn't make out the words. He sounded calm, and for a long time he talked suasively and she didn't answer. Then I heard a noise of things being shuffled and stacked. What were they doing? I realized my danger. I had to act or accept my death. My dark lover was armed and dangerous. They would finish me off and then make a funeral pyre of the Globe.

IN SO DESPERATE a situation a man becomes reckless. Reason is shoved into the corner and emotion seizes the throne. The throne of Reason. The throne. The throne not of Reason but of Zeus, gold painted, solid.

It was the metaphor itself that rescued me. I groped round my prison, found the throne where it sat, and shoved it toward the door as a barricade. To this I added what boxes and barrels were at hand to block my enemies' return.

When Stanleigh tried to enter, he could not. He must have understood what I'd done. He began to scream at me and curse. This he kept up for some time until his voice became hoarse and his curses more and more vile.

Then all was quiet for a space, after which I heard him speak in a seducer's voice, soft and subtle. He said he'd decided to let me go, I having suffered enough for my sins, for my rape of his mother, and he wanted to untie me and deliver me to my friends.

None of this I believed and told him so.

Then his manner became as before. He swore if I didn't open the door to him he'd kill me, shoot through the wood, set the building afire.

I looked at the wall that separated me from him, solid boards. Were they thick enough to stop a pistol ball? I thought they were, but I moved away, cautious, and crouched in the corner, desperate, wanting to live.

I waited, my heart drumming.

No gunfire.

No more threats.

Then I smelled smoke. I knew the fuel. Stanleigh had ravaged the wardrobe, as he had done before. But this time he wasn't just burning a single garment. It would be a mountain of stuff, flammable as coal dust, its foul strangling smoke more deadly than ratsbane.

I called out to them both, to Stanleigh and to the woman, telling them I was coming out. I knew it might well mean my death, but what chance had I where I was? If Stanleigh didn't kill me, the fire would, and the Globe would die, too.

My appeals received no answer, but there was more smoke now. It came curling beneath the door, seeping up through the rough planks of the floor. It was happening again, just as it had happened before, when my old lover leaped to her false death. My fate had come full circle.

I felt along the floor until I came to the trapdoor, the one that opened on the underside of our "heavens." The door swung up and back with ease. I looked down.

Below me was dark but for a dancing light I took to be the fire, burning in the wardrobe beyond me. It was a good thirty feet or more to the stage below, but I couldn't see that far. I might have been looking into a bottomless well, or into the mouth of hell.

I remembered the powder, the squibs, the encroaching flames. Desperately, I scrambled back, dragged the powder barrel to the trap, and pushed it over.

I HEARD THE distant crash, the splintering wood. I had to imagine the powder spread over the stage like pepper, away from the flame. At least for now. To whatever else I found that could ignite I did the same, dumping all, like a mariner desperate to keep his ship from foundering.

Next, the throne. I would have gladly ridden Zeus's chair down to the stage had there been someone there to lower it, but there was not. No dignified descent for me. I grasped the harness the actors used to fly. I buckled it on shoulder, waist, and thigh, then secured the thin leather thongs that sustained it to the cleats in the floor. I shoved off into space.

First I fell free a quarter distance to the floor, then pulled up hard and started swinging. My body hung suspended like a pendulum, swinging side to side in an ever widening arc. Finally I freed myself from the harness and dropped like a stone.

I landed on my feet, but my knees buckled and I fell upon my hands, my heart in my throat.

Let no one believe I'm incapable of the feat I describe. Though young no longer and badly bruised from Stanleigh's fists, I am an actor. I play parts but also dance and sing and leap and run, and while it had been some time since I pulled such a stunt, I have swung upon many a rope and done such tricks as caused the crowd to clap their hands and gasp in wonder.

I had hoped my escape from the hut would go unmarked. My plan, upon setting foot on ground again, was to race for the door and raise a cry in the street, for I feared Stanleigh's pursuit and frustrated rage. But as I, descending, looked to see how the fire progressed, I saw in the upper gallery two human shapes against the flames, and I saw, too, Stanleigh's miscalculation. In trying to smoke me out he'd started a fire he could not control, a fire that cut off his own escape.

Then I looked up to see Stanleigh, his cloak afire, scrambling over the balustrade, dropping to the next tier, missing his hold, and falling onto his knees in the yard. My dark lady lacked her lover's courage or desperation. She looked after Stanleigh, dumbstruck, I think, that he had abandoned her. Then, horrible to see as to remember, one of her loose sleeves caught fire. She twisted in a kind of feverish dance, trying to beat the flames with her hands. This only made matters worse. She tripped and fell, and the fire consumed her—clothing, hair, all alight.

I turned away, unable to watch her immolation. Stanleigh, recovered from his fall, stripped from his smoldering cloak, was standing in the yard. Seeing me onstage, he roared my name and advanced upon me wild-eyed, blocking my intended exit. He had her pistol. He raised his arm and fired.

I heard the explosion, saw the puff of smoke, and a ball whistled by my ear, embedding itself in the stage post. I fell to my knees, as though I'd been struck. Stanleigh stood fast, his face enraged, his chest heaving, but made no move to reload. Suddenly he turned and limped off toward the side door.

It was then I saw the men, the torches, heard voices raised in alarm. Some cried "Fire," others my name.

"It's Stanleigh, Stanleigh who's to blame," I cried. I wasn't sure to whom.

WHAT REMAINS I'LL tell with dispatch. The fire was expunged. There was God's plenty of water from the river, and Dikkon and others formed a chain, passing buckets hand over hand until all that was left was the acrid scent of smoke and the stench of burned flesh.

The injury to the theater was much less than I feared. The costumes that Stanleigh had used to start the fire were all destroyed. A portion of the ceiling in the upper gallery was blackened. In the middle gallery stage left, some benches would need to be rebuilt, and part of the stairs leading from the middle gallery to the third. Strange to tell, the hut in which I was imprisoned was spared any damage at all. Two good carpenters and a week's work would see the Globe whole again. In the meantime, the shows would go on.

And then there was *she*.

My friends tried to hold me back from her, but I needed to see it for myself, the body, the remains. You understand why. I couldn't take another's word this time that she was dead. She lay in a heap, hardly recognizable as a human form. Her face was all black. Now was she the dark lady indeed, blistered almost beyond recognition. Dikkon stood behind me, his hand upon my shoulder. "That was the woman, wasn't it?" he said.

"Yes," I said. I told him what happened, how I'd escaped.

"I beg your pardon for not being here," Dikkon said shamefacedly. "I knew you were having supper with the earl, then I saw him with some of his noble friends. You weren't among them. Strange, I thought, for I remembered the invitation. I dared approach him. He remembered me, both from being in your company and from my part in the play. I told him you were looking forward to supping with him. He didn't know whereof I spoke. He said no such supper had been arranged, nor invitation extended. He came back with me, he and his friends and some of their servants. We knew something was wrong."

I'd told my lord the earl that his former secretary had tried to kill me. He marveled at this, then gave orders that the neighborhood should be searched.

"He's armed, dangerous, clever," I said.

"So are we," said the earl.

But I didn't think they would find him, not ever.

Epilogue

I BORE THE cost of her burial in holy ground, in a little church-yard in Moorfields. The sexton there knew nothing of her history or her faith, and I told him nothing. It was fitting that I who had made her immortal in verse must see her mortal form deposited thus. She had no kin that I knew of, being as she was an orphan of the world—or, if naught else, a child of the devil.

The church was named after an obscure saint, whose name has long since faded from my memory, but that's all one. I won't go there again. Besides, a God who marks the sparrow's fall knows where each of us molders. That's enough.

As for Thomas Stanleigh, or Whorley, or Bott, however he call himself, I heard nothing of him for months after the theater fire, although I believe Cecil pursued him hotly in every corner of the kingdom. Then I heard Stanleigh was in Chelmsford, Essex, that he'd been taken there for some offense that left a worthy farmer of the town with his throat cut and his barn burned. The bitter fruit of a tavern brawl, I heard, or some such graceless episode. What does it matter?

And so I journeyed there to see my false "son" hanged. Waited through a dozen executions, each more grisly than the one before, for country folk do not lag behind Londoners in the craftsman-ship of their public executions or in their enjoyment thereof.

Finally, Stanleigh came forth amid the taunts, jeers, and laughter of the townsmen. Chelmsford's a placid place—like Stratford—but give them license to see a good hanging and they turn wolfish.

My point of vantage was excellent. I could see clearly faces of the officers, condemned men, and the headsman, who like all his trade was hooded so his cruel visage might be made the worse by our imagining of it.

My enemy had forsaken the name of Stanleigh and had resumed the pernicious monosyllable with which he was born. Strange, his face, thinner than I remembered, looked surprisingly in accord with the proceedings, as though he had no objection, or perhaps he was gratified that, at last, he was upon a stage of sorts and all eyes upon him.

Like all condemned men, he was bidden to speak before his death, and a good speech it was, as such solemn and sententious oratory goes. It was full of repentance and regret, how sincerely meant God only knows. I listened to hear if he would speak of me, if he would use this last occasion of his miserable life to lay claim to the Shakespeare name or assault my reputation or declare his undying hatred of me, the father who denied him.

He did not. He never spoke my name. It was as though his stalking were all for nothing, had no meaning in his life or mine. But his performance as a condemned man was commendable. He held his head high, gestured well, and spoke clearly and with confidence as though he'd written out his speech before, which for all I know he'd done, then memorized it as we players do. Perhaps I'd underestimated his talents in my craft, but that question was moot.

His penance done, he handed the headsman a few coins and whispered something in his ear. He refused the hood, stepped up to the rope most manfully, and in a few seconds was swinging, his body dancing in its futile struggle to forestall eternity.

The congregation, which by all signs had appreciated the spectacle, cried out with satisfaction as he swayed.

I felt nothing, neither regret, nor justification, nor remorse.

W AS HE MY son?

Strange how memory works—or doesn't. In the Globe that day when he tried to kill me and first accused me of forcing his mother, I spoke truly when I denied my guilt, protested to heaven, and swore he was deceived. But later, after Stanleigh was dead, I remembered a night in Shottery years ago, before I came to London, before I was a man.

I and some friends (ask not their names) had been drinking at the tavern until dawn, the petty sins of youth, hardly enough to repent of, hardly enough to remember. There was a girl whose face I can no longer see. I was blind drunk and delirious with youth, full of life and contemptuous of death. I do not know what I did or did not do that night but woke at dawn in a field of golden cuckoo-buds, my head vised and woozy. All unbraced was I, my breeches down round my white thighs. Next to me, an imprint in the dewy grass. A body, long and slender. Whose? Was that imprint Mercy Bott? Had she been my unknown paramour, my hapless copesmate?

Stanleigh's dead. His mother likewise. Some things are best lost in oblivion.

N OT LONG AFTER Stanleigh's death a more salubrious event occurred. I traveled back to Warwickshire for Dikkon's wedding to Jessica. They were too young to marry, I thought, although I was not so hypocritical as to advise them against it. I had married young myself, and despite time and tempests my wife and I have stayed the course. I wanted to warn Jessica, too, of the perils of marrying a player, but I did not. I think she already knew and had made peace with it. Later, I was godfather to their first son, whom they named after me. Shakespeare Aland.

It rings grandly, does it not?

And so all's well that ends so. My enemies were dead; my ordeal was done, its mystery dissolved in the stark light of truth.

Still, I have dreams, and in those dreams I see my mistress's face of burnished gold. I hear her low melodious voice and, for all my tears and prayers, feel the heavy burden of my guilt, for like an earnest mason I laid the groundwork of her treachery, built it stone by stone, little thinking of what mischief time might work.

The dreams all end the same: She whirls and howls like a maniacal dervish, enveloped in quenchless flame.

I watch, helpless, dumb.

And then she's gone.

Until I dream again.

Time's fool.